BODY
COUNT

BODY COUNT

E. Howard Hunt

St. Martin's Press

NEW YORK

Production Editor: David Stanford Burr

Design by Glen M. Edelstein

CIP DATA TK

Library of Congress Cataloging-in-Publication Data

Hunt, E. Howard (Everette Howard).
       Body count / E. Howard Hunt.
           p. cm.
       "A Thomas Dunne book."
       ISBN 0-312-06911-1
       I. Title.
    PS3515.U5425B63   1992
    813'.54—dc20
                                                  91-34609
                                                           CIP

First Edition: January 1992

10 9 8 7 6 5 4 3 2 1

This book is for Edward J. Dunn, Jr.
Semper Fi!

He felt he had come upon a great truth: that reciprocal responsibility between an individual and an organization is a one-sided hoax . . . they are not ethically equivalent because one has a sense of personal responsibility while the other has only a collective purpose. Any mutual promise between the two is therefore illusory and meretricious.

—Thomas Taylor, *Born of War*

The man in the wilderness said to me,
"How many strawberries grow in the sea?"
I answered him as I thought good—
"As many red herrings as grow in the wood."

—Anonymous

Cardiff I

One

ON THE DAY the Supreme Court refused to consider his brother's appeal, Thomas Enfield Burke shot off the face of the sentencing judge.

The Court's action—or nonaction—was not a surprise, and Burke had had long months to consider what he would do. He had been working at the computer terminal in his home near Leesburg, Virginia, when the TV announcement was made. The time, he noted, was 10:34 and the June morning no longer seemed bright. For a few moments he sat in the comfortable leather chair, then turned off the TV and crossed the polished random-width flooring of the old farmhouse to his file cabinet. He took out a life-size photograph of Judge Grogan's stern face and stared at it. Then Burke unlocked his gun cabinet and selected one of four long guns, a custom-made Weatherby .300, and eight rounds of Hornady 180-grain ammunition. From a cylindrical leather case he slid out an eight-power Leupold scope and mounted it on the rifle.

Leaving by the rear door, he walked down past the barn and the spring-fed pond, passing target stands at fifty, one hundred, and two hundred yards. At the farthest stand he thumbtacked the photograph to a target outlining a human body. Burke stepped back and surveyed the personalized target with a sardonic smile. A head and no entrails, a hollow man duplicating, in every important respect, he thought, Federal District Judge Roland Parsifal Grogan, who had sentenced Terry to serve five to ten years in Lewisburg Penitentiary.

3

Rifle cradled in his arm, Burke walked back to the open-sided shed, whose bench rest table held sandbags and a long, twelve-power Zeiss spotting scope. He sat on the bench behind the table and drew back the well-lubricated bolt, then slid five rounds into the magazine.

After homing the bolt Burke removed the scope's protective lens caps, nestled the fore-barrel on a cylindrical sandbag, and sighted on the target two hundred yards away. Foot-high field grass was motionless; there was no crosswind to factor in. He closed his left eye and sighted through the Leupold, letting the reticle slide down until the cross hair centered on the figure's left kneecap. He adjusted the scope two clicks up and resighted. He thumbed off the safety and pressed his cheek against the waxed black walnut stock. It felt good. A crested cardinal swooped down and rested on the judge's head. Burke smiled, held his breath, and applied trigger pressure in a slow, smooth pull. The rifle bucked and the cardinal skittered away in terror. Looking through the sighting scope, Burke noted that the bullet hole was not quite centered on the kneecap. He adjusted the Leupold with one left click, sighted on the right knee, and fired. Hardly pausing, Burke shot belly and heart; his fifth round opened the judge's mouth. He reloaded, sending bullets into each eye and the coup de grace into the judge's forehead.

As he sat back, Burke savored the gunsmoke drifting into his nostrils. Then he scanned the target through the spotting scope and his mouth drew into a grim smile of satisfaction.

But the knowledge that this was only a simulation of vengeance made him feel empty and hopeless. The tattered target would weather and disintegrate long before Terry's sentence was served, he knew, and he wondered how long his brother could survive in the hard-time, maximum-security prison that was Lewisburg.

Automatically Burke gathered up expended brass for eventual reloading and walked back to his house. On the kitchen table he cleaned the rifle's bore and chamber, oiled the blued finish lightly, and replaced the Weatherby in his gun cabinet. Then he telephoned the Sixteenth Street law offices of Porter Kenly, and when his brother's lawyer came on the line Burke asked "Does Terry know?"

"Not from me, Thomas—I thought you might want to tell him. But it's public knowledge, press and radio, so I imagine he's got word by now." He paused. "I'm sorry, but it was never more than a long chance. You knew that; so did my client."

Burke looked around the room he had paneled with so much care in the early months of his marriage. "He'll never make it," he said. "What can I do?"

The lawyer said nothing for a few moments. When he spoke he said, "If you have any political friends, politicians, use them. Try for mitigation, sentence reduction—it's the only road I know."

"I've never been political," Burke said thinly. "I don't have that kind of friends."

"Then develop them. You have money."

"Some," he admitted, "and that's an idea." He was silent for a while. "The reality's always worse, isn't it? I can't live a reasonable, even partly endurable life while my kid brother's cooped up in that hell-hole, Porter, I have to do something for him, I don't care what it is."

"I can fax you Judge Grogan's CV, maybe you'll find a bridge to him, friends in common. And there's Senator Newsome—lives out past Leesburg, not far from you—know him?"

"I've seen him, that's all."

"Well, he's big on the Judiciary Committee, and Grogan has to get past Newsome if he's to make the court of appeals, so—"

"I get the picture. Now, one final favor: Call the Lewisburg warden for me—I know it isn't visiting day—and tell him I'm flying up to see my brother. Half an hour is all I ask, a nonrenewable favor."

"Well, I'll try. Ah, is Terry's wife likely to be there?"

"Kirby?" He laughed bitterly. "If you hadn't heard, she's gone her own way—very resentful, feels abused by fate."

"A lot of wives do—it's . . . what? Human nature, I guess."

"I guess," Burke echoed. "While you work on the warden I'll be airborne."

"Good luck, Thomas. Not every man has a brother like you."

"Send the fax." Burke rang off. He opened the fax circuit, then went to his terminal and notified his office that he would be away for twenty-four hours on personal business.

He packed an overnight bag, locked the farmhouse, activated the security system, and got into his twelve-year-old Porsche convertible. Burke steered it over the rain-rutted access road toward the private airport.

As the blue Porsche disappeared, two men got up from a ridge that ran parallel to Burke's shooting range, brushed twigs from their clothing, and took off high-powered binoculars.

Short, dark-skinned, and stocky, one man wore a small, well-trimmed mustache. The other man's hair and eyebrows were albino white. He was tall and bulky, with a shambling gait. "The son of a bitch certainly hasn't forgotten how to shoot," he conceded in tones of grudging admiration.

"Unbelievable," the shorter man agreed. "Wonder where he's headed, Enno?"

"My guess is Lewisburg, Harry," the albino said with the trace of a sneer, "to hold his brother's hand. But the tap will tell us."

They walked down the far side of the rise and along a grassy lane to where a black Ford sedan was parked. Harry said, "As far as I'm concerned, Burke's our man."

Enno slid behind the steering wheel. "Premature to brace him," he pointed out, starting the engine. "He's got the skills, you saw that. He needs motivation."

The shorter man looked out at the pleasant, rolling countryside, glimpsed the creek that ran through the meadow. "I'd do a lot for my brother," he said in a remote voice. "Wouldn't you?"

"Me? Hell, I'd let the son of a bitch rot. 'Course we never got along when we were kids, and he worked it so I'd take his whippings."

As the albino turned onto the pike, he said, "From what I've heard, this whole thing has been as tough on Thomas as on his brother, maybe tougher. Of course, the kid was a dodger and big brother went to Nam."

"Terry was young," Harry said mildly. "Five years is a hell of a lot when you're young. He didn't see the issues the way his brother did."

As they were passing Langley, Harry said, "Too bad Burke left the Agency."

Enno shook his head. "If he was still there, we couldn't use him.

There'd be no plausible denial." He smiled as though at some secret memory. "Fifteen years since Burke killed for the government."

"And he came out with a DSC, two Purple Hearts, and a plate in his leg." He turned to face the driver. "Saved your ass, too, as you tell it."

Enno nodded. "There were twelve of us on long range reconnaissance. Captain Burke was our sniper, our leader, our Ranger substitute for God. Charlie ambushed us, must have been fifty of them, they threw everything they had at us—automatic weapons, mortars, grenades . . ." His face twitched. "Most of us were too shocked, too scared to fire back, but that fuckin' Burke got behind a tree and with nothin' but that sniper rifle picked off the leaders and the mortar crews, got the whole scene organized so we could pull back where the Hueys could come in. Eight of us got airlifted, two died on the chopper, and six of us got back to camp. Burke's leg took a shrapnel hit—looked like it was torn off—an' when he got off the Huey he used that damn rifle like a crutch until he got to the aid tent. Then he passed out."

There were light patches on the other man's cheeks. "Why only the DSC? Why not the Congressional?"

"The colonel wanted that for himself. He figured Burke'd be satisfied with the DSC."

"Was he?"

"He never talked about it."

"I get the feeling you don't like Captain Burke."

"Major—he made major out of that. Respect, yes, but right away I saw he wasn't the kind of soldier you'd get drunk and go whorin' with. Burke was reserved, kept to himself except when we were in the field. Then he was gung ho eager. He scared us if you want the truth of it, because he never showed any personal concern for safety. It was like he wanted to kill the entire NVN army so he could get out of Nam and get on with his life."

"Sounds professional."

"Maybe. But not every Ranger he led saw things his way."

"Like you," Harry suggested.

"That's right. I valued my life and I'm not ashamed to say it."

He thought it over, shrugged. "So what'd you get out of Nam, the Rangers?"

"Me? A PH, jungle rot, a stay at Letterman, and four years on the GI Bill."

"Better than a body bag."

"By one hell of a lot."

The Ford came down into Crystal City and entered the guarded parking basement under a glistening office building. The two men left the car at the motor pool. Harry said, "One thing we don't have to worry about now is medals. It's a different kind of war."

Enno nodded. "If your widow gets burial expenses, they figure they been generous."

He pressed numbers in a shielded sequential lock and an elevator door opened. The two men rode in silence to the eighteenth floor, where they nodded to a uniformed GSA guard, who released the lock of a heavy wooden door. Both men went in and closed the door behind them. In gold leaf its upper panel was lettered:

BUREAU OF LAND RECLAMATION

OFFICE OF ENVIRONMENTAL IMPROVEMENT

TECHNICAL STAFF

CHIEF AUDITOR

The guard waited until he heard the lock click before turning back to his sports page. All kinds of people went in and out of that door, he reflected, but he had yet to spot one that looked like he knew as much about red clay and bottomland as your average yaller dog.

Two

THOMAS BURKE'S APACHE droned smoothly along at eight thousand feet over Hagerstown and Chambersburg to Carlisle. There he turned on the frequency of the Harrisburg tower, gave his call sign, and requested landing instructions. When the airport was in view, he banked gently to line up with the southwest runway, throttled back to lose altitude gradually, and lowered flaps. As he settled into final approach, he compensated for a predicted ten-knot wind from 030° and touched down easily, full flaps and enough power to keep the aircraft stable.

A field hand directed Burke to a tie-down patch, and after paying the landing fee at General Aviation, Burke rented a two-door Chrysler and took the familiar road north along the glinting Susquehanna for Lewisburg, sixty miles away.

The prison hadn't changed in a hundred years, remaining the squat, thick-walled Victorian horror its builders had intended. Burke left his car in the visitors' lot and walked to the arched entrance. He gave his name to the guard and said he thought the warden might be expecting him. From his booth the guard dialed a number, then nodded. "There'll be a convoy along." He gestured at a bench.

Burke sat down and lighted a thin, dark cigarillo from Haiti. He took off his sunglasses and tucked them in his breast pocket. He could hear the distant hum of machinery. The stone blocks of the arched ceiling were painted green—Bureau of Prisons green, Terry once remarked. Even the entranceway had a medieval aspect to it. Low archways led deeper into the dungeons, the metal doors behind which his brother lived—existed—and waited.

Beside the guard booth a door opened and a middle-aged woman appeared. She wore thick glasses, a fuzzy sweater, and a beehive hairdo dating back to 1954. "Mr. Burke?" she chirped. "Warden Evers will see you now."

He let the guard pat him down and followed the woman along the corridor to a veneer-faced door. Opening it, she announced, "Mr. Burke, Warden."

Burke went in and closed the door. The office was carpeted in what looked like gray AstroTurf and paneled with mock-maple sheathing. The walls were hung with photographs of several presidents, two governors, and an assortment of community service appreciation certificates. One of the older photographs was labeled: Philadelphia Police Academy and showed eight ranks of uniformed policemen crowded together. Another was a hand-tinted photo of a young GI wearing a dress hat and a hard grin. It resembled the man behind the desk, who wore a short-sleeved white shirt with shoulder straps. A black plastic nameplate pinned to the shirt identified the wearer as Warden S. G. Evers. He was a short man with freckled skin, thick coppery hair on his forearms, and much less on his head. What there was, was trimmed short, military- or prison-style, Burke thought. The warden's face was squarish; its lines could have been cut by cold chisels. If he had any academic achievements, they were not evident on the walls. To Burke, the warden didn't look like a graduate sociologist, psychologist, or even a criminologist—he looked like a hard-ass LeJeune DI. His first words were, "Your lawyer called, and under the circumstances I'll make an exception. You know visiting rules, you know the regs."

Burke nodded. "I appreciate the accommodation and I won't trouble you again."

"Upsets the other inmates," Evers noted sourly. "Figure your brother's getting special treatment."

Burke said nothing.

The warden signed a letter and looked up. This time he appraised his visitor, seeing a man slightly over six feet tall with broad, muscular shoulders. The man's unsmiling face was set with deep unblinking eyes and a nose that looked to have been smashed and indifferently repaired. The close-cut hair was reddish-brown and curly. The teeth were regular and too white to be natural. The son of a bitch looks like an Eagles running back, the warden thought; maybe ten years ago he had been. "Inmate Burke is in the adjoining room. It's not bugged, you can talk freely." He gestured at a door to one side of his desk. "Half an hour."

"Thank you, sir," Burke said, and opened the door.

The carpeted room was unfurnished except for a plain table with an ashtray and two chairs. Terry got up and came woodenly toward him. He was wearing pressed prison denims, inmate number stenciled on white tape over his left breast. He was clean-shaven and his hair was neatly combed. The pallor of his face accented the redness of his eyes. At thirty-five he was as handsome as ever, but his mouth was slack and his eyes vacant.

Wordlessly they hugged each other until Terry murmured, "I knew you'd come, Tom, just as soon as I heard. I've been hoping all day."

He released Terry's hand. "Who told you?"

"Prison grapevine." He shrugged. "It's over, isn't it? Nothing left but the years ahead." His shoulders slumped, and he eased himself into the molded plastic chair. "That what you came to tell me?"

Burke sat down and lighted another cigarillo, using the match to light Terry's cigarette. Terry stretched out, closed his eyes, and inhaled deeply. "I can't do the time," he said brokenly. "It's too hard, too much. It's living death."

Burke sat forward. "I understand, but this is not the time to give up. You've done nineteen months now, proving you adjusted to the system."

"There's killings here, rapes—I hear the screaming at night," he said dully. "Every morning I ask myself what I've got to live for. I'm broke, my wife doesn't write or visit, and if I ever get out of here, I'll never have a decent job again." He drew on his cigarette, let smoke trickle from his nostrils. "Kenly's been carrying me for months and I owe him plenty."

"How much?"

"This Supreme Court fiasco runs between eighty and a hundred thousand." He shook his head. "If my appeal hadn't been turned down flat, I'd have owed Kenly even more for arguing it." He smiled bleakly. "A little economy."

Burke flicked ash from his cigarillo. "Kenly made some recommendations I'll follow up. I'm not going to tell you what they are, Terry, because the chances are small. But while I'm working on the outside you have to stay in control of yourself. It's *not* all over. Right now the most important thing for you, for both of us, is not to lose hope. If you do, everything will be wasted, understand?"

"I could be shanked here, killed . . . you understand *that?* The Skinheads and the Blue Jaguars . . . animals. Worse than animals." He shivered.

Levelly Burke said, "Terry, take it easy. There's nothing in this world more important to me than seeing you free. Believe that."

Terry nodded.

"And one thing that'll help you get through this is to accept it. You may not feel you did anything wrong, but a jury believed you did, and that's the objective situation. You *were* part of an inside-trading scheme, you *did* courier twelve million dollars from Manhattan to the Caymans."

"My boss, my partners involved me," he said sullenly. "It wasn't my idea, you know that."

"So they were a little smarter than you. They got to the SEC and the Justice Department first, made their deals and left you on the burning deck." He shifted forward. "Nothing you learned at Wharton prepared you for what really goes on in the Street and you were slow to catch on. You took chances like so many others, but you weren't able to walk away from it. They made an example of you, Terry, and wrong and vengeful as Judge Grogan was, his sentence stands until I can get it altered." He glanced at his watch, amazed at how quickly the time was passing. "At the very least I'll get you transferred to a better place, a minimum security camp like Allenwood."

"Just up the road," Terry said, "and a world away."

"Focus on that."

His brother looked away. "Maybe if I hadn't gone to Canada, done army time like you, I'd be better able to take this regimentation, the discipline. But I wasn't put together that way, Tom. Every night when the cell door slides shut I want to scream and never stop."

Burke drew on his cigarillo and stubbed it out. "Don't even think about it," he said harshly. "The others would think you're soft and go for you."

"I *am* soft," Terry whispered, "I can't deny it."

"Appearances are what count. Tough it out. And trust me."

For a while neither said anything. Finally Terry sat up. "Will you see Kirby for me? Ask her what she plans to do?"

"If you want me to, of course. But she hasn't stood by you the way other wives have. I can't force her to love you, Terry. It's in her or it isn't."

"I know, I know . . . but thinking about her, wondering. . . . It's driving me crazy." He clutched his brother's hand. "You'll see her?"

"If she'll see me."

Behind Terry a door opened. A uniformed guard said, "Time's up." Burke said, "Anything you need?"

"A few dollars in my commissary account—for cigs and candy. You know. It's a frugal life."

They rose together and embraced, hugging each other tightly, as though this were a final parting. "Chin up," Burke said quietly, and watched his brother walk away. The door closed and locked, and Burke got out his handkerchief to dry his eyes.

He left through the warden's office—now empty—and walked down the corridor to the guard booth. The guard let him out and Burke crossed to the commissary window where he deposited a hundred dollars to Terry's account. Millionaire or pauper, an inmate could spend thirty a month.

Throat painfully tight, Burke drove back to Harrisburg, gassed his Apache, and filed a flight plan to La Guardia. The weatherman said rain clouds were forming over eastern Long Island and Burke would be well advised to set down before dark. "I'll make it," Burke said, and walked out to his plane.

As he flew through the darkening sky, Burke thought of his

brother. Younger, better-looking, Terry from childhood had always turned to Burke for protection from the consequences of his actions. The pattern was being repeated, and this time, Burke conceded, Terry had reason to fear for his life. Prison gangs raped and killed, he knew that. And it agonized him that his younger brother was in danger and defenseless. What could he do? The question gnawed his vitals until the LAG controller reported him on radar and Burke got busy with the details of safe landing.

Light rain flicked La Guardia as Burke guided the Apache toward General Aviation parking. From an office pay phone he dialed his sister-in-law's number and heard Kirby answer. "It's Tom. I'm at La Guardia. Can you see me? I've just come from Terry."

There was a prolonged silence. "It's not awfully convenient, Tom, but if you can get here in an hour, I'll have time for a drink. Just."

"I'll be there," he said, and took a taxi through rain-slowed traffic to upper Park Avenue.

He gave his name to the lobby security guard, who phoned ahead and told Burke he could go up. "Eleven fourteen."

"I know."

Kirby Burke admitted him, then stood aside while Burke entered and closed the door. Lanky and model-thin, she wore a metallic-green cocktail dress, evening makeup, and a rather cloying perfume. They neither embraced nor shook hands, and her gaze was hostile. "Well, well, Big Brother. Still shootin' em' up down on the farm?"

"Just' russlers an' low-down varmints, ma'am," he replied steadily. "Them as deserves it."

Her gaze broke off and she turned away. "Keeping you plenty busy, I'll wager. Spare me, Tom. If you're having Scotch, pour one for me."

At the wet bar he measured out Glenlivet and added ice; he saw that the rain was slanting inward, spattering the floor-to-ceiling windows that overlooked Park Avenue. He thought the weather was appropriately dreary for a conversation he had been dreading since Harrisburg.

He carried their drinks across a thick beige rug to the chrome-and-leather chair where his sister-in-law sat waiting. "Dismal weather," she said, taking her glass. "I suppose Terry is pretty damn depressed."

"He counted too much on the Supreme Court." Burke sat across from her in a low sofa covered with nubby fabric. "The letdown hit pretty hard."

"And he asked you to come here. To spy on me?"

"Hardly. Otherwise I wouldn't have called first."

She sipped and swallowed, and her lips twisted. She had a beautiful face, Burke thought, but he had noted the latent hardness the first time Terry'd introduced them. It hadn't softened any.

"Well," she said, "for your information—and Terry's, if you care to tell him—I'm dating." She held up her left hand showing ringless fingers. "I assumed so," Burke said, sipping the heavy single-malt liquor. "Anyone special?"

"Not yet—but then, I'm a rather notorious personality, wouldn't you say? Wife of a convicted felon."

"You can say that," Burke said mildly, "or you can say Terry took the fall for others." He sat forward. "He did, you know."

She shrugged. "Bottom line: five to ten." She looked at Burke curiously. "Will he make it?"

"He won't do that much," Burke said firmly. "We'll get a mitigation, reduced sentence."

"How?"

"Too soon to say."

She drank deeply, glanced at her sparkling Piaget wristwatch. Starting as a high-fashion mannequin, Kirby had become a designer for large houses. Then Terry had backed her own boutique on Madison and she had made it successful. The apartment she and Terry had shared had been confiscated by the government. This one was her own and it showed no masculine hand. Not even a picture of Terry on the wall. She said, "I suppose you want to know what I'm going to do about my marriage."

"I think it's time to talk about it."

A cigarette appeared in her fingers. She lighted it before Burke could offer, inhaled deeply, and looked up at the ceiling. "He's been away nearly twenty long months. I'll wait two years before I file, Tom. If he's out before then, there's a slight chance for us—very slight. If not, I'll deserve freedom and another chance. I'll have paid my dues."

"Paid how? By not writing or visiting?" he snapped. "How about the for-better-or-for-worse clause?"

"That's romantic bullshit," she said sharply. "I didn't tell Terry to take up inside-trading, or make that bag flight to the Caymans. That was his mistake and he's paying for it. I don't know why either of you feel I should pay, too."

He felt too tired to argue the point. Instead, he drank and eyed his sister-in-law. "So the message I take back—the one you haven't guts enough to deliver—is that you'll stay his wife in name for another four or five months." He put down his drink and got up. "Since it bothers you so much, Kirby, don't wait. File tomorrow. Your husband's a five-year felon; divorce is automatic in this state."

She looked up at him. "I know that, and you're probably right. This clears the air, Tom; I don't think you need stop by again."

"Agreed." He turned to walk out of the apartment and heard her voice thin, high, and quavering. "Anyway, what do you know about marriage, macho man? Yours was a disaster, so lighten up on me. I've stayed by Terry longer than Joyce stuck with you."

"You're an angel." He heard her glass smash against the inside of the door as he pulled it closed behind him.

The doorman whistled down a cab for him. Burke rode back to La Guardia and checked in at the airport Holiday Inn. It was too dark, too rainy, and too late to fly back to Virginia. In his room he took a shower, thought about eating, and instead had room service send up five drinks. While he lay on the bed watching pay TV, he drank Scotch and water until he passed out and slept without dreaming through the rainy night.

In the morning, through clear weather, Burke flew back to the Leesburg airport, checked in with his office by computer link, and made an appointment to see his neighbor, Senator Claude Newsome, later in the day.

Three

AFTER PEELING KENLEY'S FAX off the machine, Burke studied the Federal Register's bio of Judge Grogan. Fifty-eight years old, Grogan had been born near Scranton, Pennsylvania, gone to Muhlenberg College and Catholic University Law. Married to Rita Zawacki, two daughters and a son. Appointed to the Federal Court by President Carter. Member Lawyers Club and D.C. Bar Association. No home address given. Burke put aside the sheet and decided it would be a long and unrewarding search for social friends of Roland Grogan, aside from those he'd left behind in the Pennsylvania coalfields.

He left the workroom he loved and went out on the porch where he lighted a cigarillo and watched smoke drift away on a vagrant breeze. A vee of mallards came up over the rise, braked with wings and webbed feet, and dropped onto the pond. Without pause they began paddling and tipping for food. Above, a wide-bodied jet banked and started its long approach to Dulles. Burke owned the thirty-four acres on which the old farmhouse stood. At today's prices he could sell it in a week for five to six hundred thousand dollars. And selling was part of his plan.

Before their parents died, Burke had promised that he would be responsible for Terry, and he had managed their small inheritance well enough to send Terry through Penn and Wharton after he'd gotten through Cornell on a combined Regents and athletic scholarship, plus ROTC. Burke had never resented all he'd done for his brother, nor

Terry's easier path. He had been designed for burdens heavier than Terry, and he carried them without complaint. In time he had even come to understand Terry's flight to Canada, though at the time his brother's desertion had sickened and disgusted him. Later Burke realized that because of Terry's defection, he had tried harder in Vietnam, volunteered for the hairy patrols, stayed to fight while others dropped back . . . doing Terry's share too.

After the operations on his leg, after the months of physical therapy, he'd taken his discharge at Walter Reed Hospital along with accumulated pay and walked down the steps wondering what he was going to do with his life. As he reached the sidewalk a well-dressed man had gotten out of a black government car and approached him. "Major Burke," the man said courteously, "unless you have a pressing engagement, I have a proposition you might be interested in listening to."

"What kind of proposition?"

"Let's talk while we ride," the man said, opening the car door for him. And that was how Burke began five years with the CIA. He'd liked the training, he remembered, the night exercises down at the Farm, redoing familiar things without the jungle danger. The office stuff—the paper shuffling and power gossip—was what he'd tried to avoid, but he'd soon learned that all of it was part of the Headquarters scene. So when the chance came he was eager to go to Taiwan and launch Chinese agents against the mainland, later infiltrating South Koreans north of the Demarcation line.

At Tokyo Station he'd met Joyce Masters working in the counterintelligence shop, saw her again at Headquarters, and married her before he'd gone to Peru to train *altiplano* peasants in the ways of protecting their villages against Maoist guerrillas who called their movement *Sendero Luminoso.* To Burke it was the Nam Hamlet program all over again—at fourteen thousand feet—with part of the old Phoenix program adapted to thin out Sendero leadership.

And while he was advising, tracking, and fighting in the Peruvian highlands, Joyce left the Agency and entered Georgetown Law, so that when he returned discouraged from his mission, he found his wife a full-time student he seldom saw.

He bought the farmhouse then, as a focus for their lives, a place they could share, but Joyce made it plain that her studies came first and that children were out of the question until after she had connected with a good law firm. Long after, Burke inferred.

Soon afterward Burke had agreed, over Joyce's bitter opposition, to go on a combined operations mission into Beirut. The Mossad claimed they'd located twelve prisoners, including six Americans of whom two were TV journalists. The night scheme involved launching two fast boats from an offshore carrier, isolating the target building, and lifting off prisoners and combat personnel with Blackhawk choppers from the carrier.

For a month the team trained at Bragg, in the Arizona desert, and Baja California before being flown to the Mediterranean. This time—to avoid another Desert One disaster—a pathfinder infiltrated Beirut to contact the Mossad agent and verify that the prisoners were still in the target building. But at H-Hour minus one the pathfinder radioed that the building was empty and the prisoners were said to have been moved into the Bekaa Valley surrounded by sixty thousand Syrian troops. The fortunes of war, Burke had told himself, flying back to Fort Bragg, but he regretted and resented the wasted time. When he finally got back to the farmhouse, he found that Joyce had cleared out, leaving only a note taped to the refrigerator door.

By then Burke had come to realize that he was not cut out for an Agency career with its months of comparative idleness then an occasional hurry-up operation that yielded small results, if any. So he resigned "to pursue personal interests" and began sending out résumés that stressed his Cornell degree in communications. The only significant response came from Eddie Deems, a Cornell classmate and lacrosse teammate. Eddie was half-owner of Deems & Abernathy, a midsize Washington advertising and public relations agency, and Burke had joined the firm as a trainee, learning the trade quickly while taking night courses in computer science and graphics at George Washington University. For the past two years Burke had been the agency's creative director, working mostly from his home PC linked to the downtown office on Pennsylvania Avenue, half an hour's drive away. Every Friday he lunched with associates in what extended into a staff meeting to evaluate accounts status and discuss prospective new business. Burke liked the tangible nature of his work; he could actually *see* results: printed texts and colored graphics of his own creation. Moreover, there was durability to his work product and a satisfaction he had never found in the CIA. Unlike the variable, often transient goals of CIA projects, the policy of Deems & Abernathy was fixed and understandable: to produce high-quality work for reputable clients and make money in the process. For Thomas Burke that was enough.

He tossed away his cigarillo butt and went back into the farmhouse. The modernized kitchen had been wasted on Joyce, so Burke had learned to prepare simple, satisfying dishes: oriental stir-fry in a wok, casseroles in the microwave oven. Wherever he relocated he'd have a kitchen, but he'd miss other amenities he'd installed at the farmhouse, especially the shooting range. Well, he could join the Manassas gun club, and perhaps shoot competitively as he once had on Cornell's rifle team.

As he sat behind his desk, looking at the blank computer screen, he realized that he had decided to sell the place and use the money to gain Terry's freedom. One way or another.

Senator Newsome's residence was set back from Leesburg Pike on a knoll overlooking white-fenced paddocks and horse runs. The house was three-story red brick trimmed with white-painted window frames and dormers, the gingerbread of a hundred years ago having been removed to yield cleaner lines.

Burke had driven past the place many times but had never noticed signs of habitation beyond a few horses grazing off the Pike. Now, as he drove up the asphalt access road, he saw a young woman cantering a thoroughbred toward a three-bar jump. She wore a pink shirt, white breeches, and black boots. A blond ponytail trailed from her velvet hard hat, and as she guided the thoroughbred toward the barrier she rose slightly in the stirrups, crouched forward, and took the jump cleanly. Then she reached over and stroked the chestnut's neck, turned him, and readied for a second approach.

Burke drove up to the gravel turnaround and left his Porsche in the shade of a huge oak tree. He took the steps to the porch and a manservant opened the screen door. "Mr. Burke?" he asked.

"Yes. Is the senator in?"

"Expecting you. This way, sir."

Burke followed him through a cool, handsomely furnished parlor, then a large living room, and past a dining room that held a polished walnut table ample for twelve. The day was pleasantly warm, and Burke found the senator seated on a screened porch that overlooked a grape arbor and cultivated fields beyond. The senator was wearing an open-collar lemon sport shirt and tan linen slacks. His face was tanned but drawn. Newsome put aside a thick classified document, rose, and extended his hand. "Mr. Burke? Good of you to visit me. You're one neighbor I haven't gotten to know, but I certainly know *of* you." He gestured at a cane chair.

Seating himself, Burke said, "That good or bad, Senator?"

"If you're referring to your brother, his problem has no bearing on you. I had my office prepare a rundown on your achievements and I must say I'm impressed by your military record. As far as I know, you're the only DSC winner around." His face sobered. "My son, Wayne, didn't get back from Hue—his body was never found."

"I'm sorry, sir."

"You may have noticed my daughter, Claire, exercising in the front paddock."

"She rides extremely well."

He nodded. "She should. She attended a school for young ladies that specialized in equestrian skills. But she married early and un-wisely—against my advice—divorced two years ago, and when she's not concentrating on her mounts she serves as my hostess." He looked away, his gaze settling over the distant fields. "I've been widowed almost seven years." For a few moments he seemed lost in reverie, then he turned to Burke. "Some refreshment? What's your pleasure, sir?"

"Whatever you're having."

"There's fresh-made lemonade—or something stronger."

"Lemonade will be fine."

The servant, lingering just off the porch, nodded and went away.

"Inasmuch as you are one of my constituents," Newsome continued, "I assume there's a reason for your visit. Does it concern you—or your brother? I read about his appeal."

Burke tensed, taken aback by the senator's directness. He looked at the silver-haired solon's regular, almost handsome features, considered the man's immense power, and felt an impulse to bolt. Then he thought of Terry's anguished face, the hopelessness in his brother's eyes, and he steeled himself.

"I was considerably less optimistic than Terry over what the Court might do. Yesterday I was with him at Lewisburg, and he was shattered. I promised to do everything in my power to get his sentence reduced—at the very least have him transferred to better conditions of servitude."

The senator's eyes narrowed. "I was startled at the time. Five to ten years for a first offense?"

Burke nodded. "What money was left him after government confiscation went to legal fees. His wife is divorcing him, and his prospects are devastating." He accepted a glass of lemonade from the servant, waiting until the senator was served before sipping. The pause, and Newsome's attention, encouraged Burke to go on. "Guilt is not an issue Senator. What seems unconscionable is the sentence."

The senator sipped from his glass before saying, "Sentence reduction is up to Judge Grogan, as I assume you know. And Grogan is a rather peculiar fellow from what I know of him. Came from a hardscrabble background, worked his way through college and law school washing dishes, waiting tables, shining shoes—anything to bring in a dime or two. Made a name for himself as prosecuting attorney in his home state, Pennsylvania, and reached the federal bench through merit." He grunted. "Certainly not through political influence or social graces, which he never had."

"Do you know Judge Grogan?"

"Not socially—I don't think he socializes with anyone—just from his brief appearances before the Judiciary Committee when we confirmed his appointment." He sipped from his glass. "As a Carter appointee, Grogan probably realizes his chances for elevation to the appeals bench are slim to nonexistent in a Republican administration."

He eyed Burke. "I assume the customary motions for sentence reduction have been made."

"And turned down flat."

Newsome nodded. "As I said, the judge is a curious fellow. Unfortunately he's carried early economic resentments to the bench and loathes any defendant who ever made a buck. Those who accumulate dollars dishonestly he considers especially reprehensible. Grogan probably thinks white-collar crime is worse than street crime, so he hands out maximum sentences." He set down his glass. "Doubtless I'm only repeating your own conclusions."

"I entertained a slim hope that the judge might be approachable, that someone he respects might persuade him to be reasonable."

"Someone—such as myself?"

Dry-mouthed, Burke nodded.

"Even if I were willing to make such an overture, Mr. Burke, my reading tells me it would only make matters worse. Grogan's not a man inclined to honor special pleading."

"Even from you—the chairman of the Senate Judiciary Committee? You were a judge yourself, Senator, with a reputation for tempering justice with mercy. It wouldn't be like you to be comfortable with anything else."

Newsome sighed. "One sees many injustices in life—I think of my son's needless death—and those things we can avert or ameliorate we do, if it's within our powers. Grogan, I'm afraid, is a block of stone, cold and deaf to reason." He shook his head. "With almost any other judge there could be a chance, but Grogan. . . ."

The porch door opened and Newsome's daughter came in. Burke hadn't seen her face before, but it was lovely in a fragile, delicate way. She pulled off her gloves, tilted back her hard hat, and wiped perspiration from her glowing cheeks. Newsome said, "My dear, this is our neighbor, Thomas Burke. My daughter Claire."

She gave Burke a strong hand. "Delighted to meet you. I was admiring that handsome Porsche when you drove up."

"While I was admiring your horsemanship."

"Thank you." Her cheeks reddened slightly. "I'm just getting back into it, really. Lots of work to do."

"Not from what I saw," Burke said as she sat in a facing chair.

"If I'm not interrupting anything terribly serious, I'll have a lemonade with you." She dropped her hat on the floor and shook out her hair.

"Please do," Burke said, glad her arrival had interrupted a conversation that seemed to be going nowhere.

When her glass arrived Claire sipped lengthily and turned to Burke. "So, what do you do? Gentleman farming?"

He managed a laugh. "I wouldn't know how to begin. No, I work for an ad agency out of my place."

"Which is—where?"

"About a mile down the pike. You may have noticed a pair of fieldstone posterns in bad repair, clumps of ivy hiding part of the ruin. Mailbox lettered Burke."

"Of course. But your house—farmhouse, I guess—looks quite attractive. That hasn't fallen to disrepair."

"I manage most of the maintenance myself. Not hard when you live alone."

Her father said, "Mr. Burke holds a distinguished war record, Claire. Extracted most of his unit under heavy fire, killed at least twenty enemy, and won the Distinguished Service Cross." He paused. "And promotion to major."

"You're well informed, Senator," Burke commented.

"What a staff's for," he said with a wave of his hand.

Claire said, "After all that action, Major, you must find sedentary life boring."

"On the contrary, it's restful and rewarding. And please don't call me Major. I'm Thomas or Tom."

"Tom," she said with a slight smile.

Newsome said, "Mr. Burke was with the CIA for five years before becoming an adman."

"What a curious transformation," she remarked, "but then adaptability is supposed to measure intelligence. I'm glad to have met you." Rising, she gave him her hand again. "Hope I'll see you around. Do you ride?"

"Badly. Do you shoot?"

"Poorly." She kissed her father's forehead. "Back to the ring, Dad. Hold all calls."

Newsome finished his lemonade, "Well, what do you think of my daughter?"

"Beautiful," Burke said, "with a forthright personality."

"Since the divorce she's sort of shut herself in, apparently blaming herself."

"I'm familiar with the syndrome," Burke said, "having experienced it myself."

"But you're over it."

"Work is a great curative."

"What kind of work does your brother do at Lewisburg?"

"Makes mattress covers. Hot, dusty, demeaning work. At minimum I'm hoping to see him transferred to a work camp—like Allenwood, which isn't far from Lewisburg."

"Minimum security prisons are usually for inmates with less than five years to serve."

"I know. But isn't 'usually' the operative word?"

"In some cases." He nodded thoughtfully. "The director of the Bureau of Prisons can make transfers of that sort."

"Without reference to the sentencing judge?"

"I'm not sure about that. As a matter of courtesy he would probably clear it with the judge. In your brother's case he would be sure to, since the trial engendered so much publicity."

"And Grogan would veto the transfer."

"I'm afraid so. Grogan would consider it an infringement of his sentencing prerogative."

Burke sat back, thinking it was now or never. "My farm may be worth as much as six hundred thousand dollars, Senator. Speaking hypothetically, I wonder if such a sum would be attractive to a civil servant making less than a hundred thousand dollars a year?"

Newsome considered before replying. "Since we're speaking hypothetically I would assume a sum on that order of magnitude would tempt almost anyone to do whatever was requested to be done. My Senate salary is less than a hundred thousand dollars a year, Tom, but I would never consider accepting money to act on a constituent's behalf. Those Abscam convictions settled a pall of ethical conduct over the Senate from which I hope it will never recover. Now a federal judge makes less than a hundred thousand annually, and you may be aware of several judges convicted for accepting bribes. Another faces impeachment by the Senate, and as chairman of the relevant committee, I'm required to see that process through. So it would be a very avaricious, injudicious judge who could be swayed by the prospect of personal and illegal enrichment. Judge Grogan is—to put it bluntly—a hard-ass character who gets satisfaction from exercising his considerable power. As far as I know, Grogan enjoys neither friends nor confidants, and anyone interested in tendering him money in return for a judicial favor would have to find a confidential bridge to make the offer." He sat back and stretched his shoulders. "Since we're speaking hypothetically, I would evaluate Grogan as probably the least approachable judge on the federal bench."

Burke absorbed it all, feeling progressively more despairing as the senator spoke. They had observed the line between philosophy and subornation, yet Newsome's message was perfectly clear. "Mind if I smoke?" Burke asked.

"Not at all—though I'm a four-year abstainer."

Burke lighted a cigarillo, careful not to exhale in the senator's direction. "My brother's life, his future, are more important to me than anything else, Senator. I'd willingly sacrifice myself and anything I possess in order to free him. After listening to your review of the overall situation I realize I don't have anywhere to turn."

"Has Terry applied for a presidential pardon?"

"I don't think so."

"It's fairly routine, Tom, and he can fill out the papers himself. Might help his morale."

"Would you support his application?"

Newsome nodded. "That, too, is standard for an elected representative, and in view of what you've done for our country I will be more than willing." He drained the last of his melted ice. "It's a long road, though. The FBI conducts a postsentencing investigation, the warden is required to levy a value judgment, and it takes at least a year before the full dossier reaches the pardon attorney's desk at the Department of Justice. He doesn't make the decision, of course. The pardon attorney is a mere focal point for paperwork, which he eventually forwards to the White House staff. The staff's recommendation usually decides whether the president will grant the pardon—unless there are, let us say atmospheric factors that persuade the president in one direction or the other."

"Jimmy Hoffa and Tokyo Rose were pardoned."

"Hoffa had the Teamsters behind him in an election year. And Tokyo Rose had half the Philippines backing her, that half being those who collaborated with the Japanese and shared her guilt to some extent."

Burke got up. "I'm more than grateful for your counsel, Senator. I'll communicate your advice to my brother and hope he'll follow through."

Newsome rose and extended his hand. "Now that we've met I hope it won't be the only occasion, Tom. In fact, Claire and I are having roast lamb this evening—just the two of us. I'm sure my daughter would be as pleased as I if you'd join us for dinner. Can you?"

He hesitated. "I'd be happy to, Senator. What time?"

"Oh, we usually have a cocktail around six, dinner at seven or so. Look forward to it."

"Thank you again." Burke left the house, started the Porsche, and idled down along the fencing, beyond which Claire was watering her horse. They waved at each other and Burke continued on until he reached the Pike. As he turned toward home, he was impressed by the senator's subtlety and discretion; much had been conveyed both overtly and covertly, sparing each of them embarrassment. He could interpret the dinner invitation as the senator's means of letting him know that the episode was behind them, no offense taken. Or was the senator parentally interested in bringing together a potential suitor and his marriageable daughter?

He hadn't really wanted to dine with the Newsomes, but in view of Terry's pardon application, he felt a clear obligation to accept.

*   *   *

Senator Newsome watched Burke's car disappear down Leesburg Pike before going into his study. He closed the door and went to a secure phone, selecting a number from a short list carried in his wallet. He dialed the number and heard a voice respond, "Land Reclamation— Environmental Improvement."

"William?" Senator Newsome said, recognizing the voice. "Claude here. Your candidate just left. He began a tactful attempt to bribe me or the judge, but I detoured the conversation before it could get indictable. He said he'd do anything to get his brother out of of prison and I believe him." He listened briefly before saying, "I have to tell you I feel lousy about manipulating him because Burke is a fine man—I see him in some ways as the man my son could have been. So I don't want him treated badly, and I insist all commitments be honored by you people. The last thing you want is publicity, and most of the correspondents in Washington are friends of mine."

He listened again, said, "Yes, he's ripe for approach," and broke the connection.

He left the office and walked through the house to the front porch where he stood watching Claire rub down her jumper. Maybe if her mother had lived, he thought, she would have avoided the disorientation she was still going through. A steady, dependable man like Thomas Burke could make all the difference in her life, but unfortunately for them both Burke wasn't going to be around for long.

Four

ON HIS WORD PROCESSOR Burke wrote a long letter to his brother, summarizing his visit with Kirby and his talk with Senator Newsome. He urged Terry to start the pardon application without delay. After signing the letter and addressing the envelope—all inmate mail went to a P.O. box—Burke acknowledged relief at not having to sell his property immediately, although he had mentally converted it into a half-million-dollar bribe that he hadn't yet found anyone willing to accept. That time might come in months ahead, so it was premature to abandon the idea.

He mailed the letter in the Leesburg post office, then returned to his work area and got on line with the downtown office.

An informal message from Eddie Deems welcomed him back, said he understood the downtime, and reminded Burke of the printing deadline for an institutional ad. Burke replied that he'd fax the text by mid-morning, and assumed that the accompanying color graphics were in hand. Shutting down the console, he checked the WP printout of the text as far as he'd gone. While considering the final paragraph, Burke made instant coffee in the kitchen and lighted a cigarillo. Back at his desk he heard a car driving up his access road. He knew it wasn't the mailman—delivery was roadside rural—and wondered if it might be Claire Newsome—in fact he found himself hoping it was—but as the car pulled into view Burke saw that it was a government-issue black Ford, a model he'd come to know all too well. Uncomfortable, he walked out to the front porch. A uniformed driver stayed behind the wheel while two men got out of the rear. Burke recognized them both.

They waved, and General William Arness called, "Hi, Major!"

"General! What brings you here?"

The man with him, a tall albino wearing dark shades, eyed Burke as he neared. "Afternoon, Major."

"Hello, Enno," he replied. Enno Poliakoff had been his master sergeant in the Ranger team ambushed at An Phuac. Always correct despite an undercurrent of insolence, Enno fought well and courageously against reasonable odds. But when the odds were overwhelming, as at An Phuac, Enno took cover to save his own life, and the memory set Burke's teeth on edge.

General Arness, then a brigadier, had overall command of the Ranger batallion, and it was his recommendation that brought Burke his Distinguished Service Cross. Arness gave him a strong handshake, while Burke and Poliakoff merely nodded at each other.

"Want to come in?" Burke inquired. "Or just passing by?"

Enno said, "You've got a table and bench in that gun shed—that's a good place to talk."

"Okay." Burke led the way. Beside him, Arness said, "Sorry about your brother's latest defeat. I imagine he's taking it pretty hard."

"He is, but he'll survive." As they reached the opensided shed, Burke turned to the albino. "How come you know about this place, Enno? Moonlight reconnaissance? If so, stay away, hear me?"

"Yes, *sir*," Poliakoff said with sardonic emphasis. "You still shoot pretty good."

General Arness sat down on the bench, Poliakoff beside him, and said, "Pretty good isn't adequate," From under his coat he drew out the photograph Burke's bullets had shredded yesterday morning. "Not even Rita would recognize her husband's face, Tom. While we're at it, let's dispense with military titles, eh? You're out; so's Enno; and I've been retired nearly four years." He laid the tattered photo under a sock-sized sandbag. "Can't blame you for disliking the judge—but I'm glad you took it out on his photo. Otherwise, I wouldn't be here."

"Well," said Burke bluntly, "why not tell me why you're here?"

Arness took a deep breath. "It concerns a trade, Tom. Your brother's facing a long stretch of hard time. He wants out, you want him out."

Burke glanced at Poliakoff. "Does he have to be part of this?"

"Enno's my executive assistant, handles a number of things that require discretion in our business."

"I must have missed something," Burke said slowly. "What's 'our business'?"

"If you're thinking I've stacked arms over at Langley, forget it. I work for our government—and I don't—but in a way that's never been tried before."

"Explain."

"No one needs CIA background to know that the British intelligence service—SIS—has no official existence. No budget is presented to Parliament and it's a crime to print the director's name. Yet SIS functions, and has for more than four hundred years. Hell, some scholars say Chaucer himself was a British spy, and it's known that Daniel Defoe was a onetime head of the king's intelligence service. Such successes as SIS has had over the years have been partly due to its anonymity. Members of Parliament can't interrogate SIS personnel, only a few people high up in government even know who they are. So they don't have press and Congress hounding them, second-guessing everything they do." He paused. "Leaking secrets of state."

"I'm familiar with their setup.

"Things came to a head here—converged, a bureaucrat might say—about two years ago when the new administration took office. The director of Central Intelligence told the president frankly that he was unable to carry out his statutory mission because of Congressional kibitzing and the leaking of classified information by congressmen, their staffers, and the media. He offered to resign and came close to insisting on it. At the same time, the Drug Enforcement Administration chief told the president he faced insurmountable problems trying to curtail the flow of addictive drugs into the United States. He explained that one-crop countries in Central and South America were nearly powerless to prevent the cultivation of opium and coca leaf.

Drugs also come from Turkey, Iran, Syria, Pakistan, and Southeast Asia—as you well know if you'll recall our zonked-out grunts."

Burke nodded. "Those glazed eyes . . . too far gone to grab a rifle when Charlie started coming in. Yeah, I remember." He looked down at the remains of Grogan's photograph. "What's the narcotics traffic got to do with me? And what's this trade you mentioned?"

"Bear with me, Tom. Some of these producing countries are our defense allies—Turkey, Pakistan, and Thailand, for example—and our leverage there is limited by political considerations. But when the Mexicans alone can discover and confiscate four tons—*four tons*—of 85 percent pure cocaine in less than a month, you get an idea how much shit *hasn't* been interdicted."

Burke nodded silently. General Arness continued. "The DEA chief's further complaint concerned our judicial system. We catch a major dealer, he posts a million dollars bail, and he's on the next plane back to Panama, Colombia, or Guayaquil. Those few denied bail hire lawyers to roadblock trial, or they're given wrist-slap sentences that see them back in business a year or so later. Then the cycle starts over again with drug traffic basically unaffected."

"Is there a solution?"

"We hope so. As a first step, the president authorized the establishment of a covert organization funded by a special allotment about which he doesn't have to report to Congress. I'm the head. I report to one man on the president's staff, and he reports to the president. The men I've recruited have come from Special Forces, CIA, DIA, Customs, Immigration, and of course, DEA. Every presidential candidate has been promising to eradicate the scourge, but until now it's been all talk, forgotten when the campaigns are over." He paused, "This administration is the exception."

"So what's going to make the big change?" asked Burke. "Sounds like just another alphabet agency to me. The laws aren't going to be changed, General, not in time to do any good. And courts and prisons deal out revolving-door justice." He glanced away. "Think of it. If my brother had been dealing drugs, he'd be on the street now. Too bad he dealt in currency." He shook out a cigarillo and moistened the tip.

Arness's lips formed a grim smile. "The difference, Tom, is that we're authorized to kill." He got up from the bench and stretched his back and arms. "This is war, Tom, a new kind of war, unacknowledged, invisible, deadly. The concept is to cut off the snake's head. Eliminate the keystone of the structure and the rest falls apart in pieces we or the locals can better destroy."

"You mean the president has actually authorized assassination as an instrument of national policy? I thought Jerry Ford disavowed it—permanently."

"Ford was referring to heads of state, Tom. We're talking about individuals who hold no public office but can be even more powerful than presidents or prime ministers. Drug barons, chiefs of underground empires that dispose of unlimited funds that corrupt armies and governments. Those men are the targets, Tom, and my unit is authorized to go after them until they're eliminated."

Enno Poliakoff spoke for the first time. "Around the world, twelve men were identified as wielding that kind of power. Eleven now, because our man knocked off the Chiang Mai boss in Thailand."

"He controlled the Golden Triangle network," Arness elaborated, "and with his death the tribes, sects, and private armies began fighting among themselves for control, destroying each other's poppy fields in a kind of feeding frenzy." He paused. "Unfortunately, our man made the mistake of putting on his boot without first shaking it out—a krait killed him in five minutes."

"Otherwise," said Poliakoff, "it was a successful operation. Untraceable, disavowable, plausibly deniable."

"But the surgeon died."

Arness nodded. "A good man, too, one of the very best. You'd know his name, Tom, because he did your kind of work in Nam. And good men are still very hard to find. We can offer money as an inducement, of course, but some aspects of mercenaries' characters leave something to be desired. In Nam you didn't fight for soldiers' pay, neither did I—or Enno here. There was Ranger spirit, a Green Beret spirit.

Burke blew smoke toward the duck pond, where six downy ducklings trailed the mallard hen. An overnight miracle, he thought, in an infinitely renewable cycle. "What's your outfit called?" he asked.

"At this point you have no need to know. We exist because private groups and some congressmen were calling for military involvement—*posse comitatus*—that neither this nor the previous administration wanted. Detractors felt it would turn our armed forces into a police force—a huge Gestapo or KGB."

"Works in Russia. I don't hear of drug shipments reaching the USSR."

"We're a democracy," Arness said a bit testily, "where civil liberties count."

"You called it war. In war the first thing disappearing is civil liberties."

Arness sighed. "Granted, but this is also highly political. So the administration's compromise was to establish a quasi-military organization—mine—and keep it completely covert and deniable. Now, let's get back to business: Tell me what you want most in the world."

"Easy—my brother's freedom."

General Arness nodded. "I can offer you a presidential pardon for your brother. He'll walk out of prison a free man, his record totally expunged. That's what you want, isn't it?"

Silently, Burke nodded. He tossed away his cigarillo and his eyes narrowed. "What do I have to do?"

Enno Poliakoff grunted and looked down. General Arness leaned forward. "What you were trained to do, what you do so very damned well, Tom. Kill."

Burke moved away from the table, stood for a moment looking down the target range and walked back. "Drug kings, right? How many?"

"Three." Before Burke could say anything, Arness gestured at the albino. "Bring the briefcase, Enno." Poliakoff walked quickly away.

"In principle," Burke said, "I agree. And though I don't doubt your personal word, General, I've seen a number of fellows who thought they were carrying out presidential intention and bidding take the fall. I must insist on the president's verification—face to face."

Arness nodded. "I can arrange that. What else?"

"How much support can I expect?"

"As much as you need. Of course, you'll do the job as a singleton. I'd say that enhances your odds of survival."

Burke nodded. "One last stipulation, General. As a show of good faith I want my brother moved from Lewisburg and transferred to Allenwood up the road."

Arness nodded. "That can be done, even if it means giving Terry another identity for a while. Give me a few days for that."

"And the president?"

"Sooner."

Poliakoff placed a leather briefcase on the table. Arness opened it and took out three numbered dossiers. "These contain everything known and usable about your three targets. You'll be given one, and when that job's completed, the second, then the third. That way—"

"—if I'm caught, I can't name the next target. Okay. I need weapons refresher, General, physical conditioning to get back in shape."

"We have facilities."

"And I'll have to ask my firm for a leave of absence. If I get back, I'd like the same job."

"I have reason to believe," said Arness, "that Deems and Abernathy will cooperate in a matter of national security, Tom. I wouldn't ask you to go on a suicide mission." He replaced the dossiers in his briefcase. "I hate the feeling I'm taking advantage of your family tragedy, but it happened. I need you, and now you know the full story."

Burke smiled thinly. "I doubt anyone knows the full story on anything that goes on in our government." He gazed at the general. "Suppose the president gets fainthearted and rules out assassination. Do I get the pardon anyway?"

"That's a stipulation." He stood up and returned the briefcase to Poliakoff. "You could start putting your personal affairs in order, Tom, give yourself a bit of lead time. And under no circumstances discuss this project with your brother or anyone else." He smiled. "Not even your priest."

"I lost God in Vietnam," Burke said levelly, "or maybe he lost me."

They shook hands and Burke watched the two ex-soldiers walk away.

When their car vanished in a trail of summer dust, he went into the house, thinking how remarkably and unexpectedly their visit was going to change his life. He hadn't asked Arness the obvious question: What happens to my brother if I get zapped before I can deliver? Because he knew the answer.

The clock showed five-thirty. He had just time enough to shower, shave and change.

Five

THE CROWN ROAST of lamb was charred on the outside, deliciously pink within. Pommes de terre rissolée done to perfection, frenched beans crisp and tasty under a dab of hollandaise. The wine was a light Bordeaux, better than anything Burke had tasted in a long time. He sat across the table from Claire Newsome, her father at the near end, and he realized that she had gone to some pains. Her blond hair appeared professionally coiffed, her makeup subdued, and the low-cut bodice of her blue dress revealed an enticing slope. A single strand of baroque pearls circled her neck, and the only ring was a gold signet on her little finger.

She was, he thought, twenty-five or twenty-six, younger than his sister-in-law, Kirby, much younger than Joyce, still in the first flush of maturity. He couldn't decide if her face was oval or triangular; it seemed to alter in the soft lighting when she turned to address her father. But she was a beautiful young woman, self-possessed, voice low without being kittenish, her accents those of a fashionable boarding school. Without wanting it, he knew that he was attracted to the senator's daughter and tried not to show it.

For his part the senator steered the conversation away from politics, saying a politician's day was a long one and home should be home, not an extension of the office. From Burke the senator drew a description of his work for Deems & Abernathy. "I enjoy it," Burke acknowledged, "particularly being able to work at home. I never liked fighting downtown Washington traffic or business luncheons with too many drinks."

Senator Newsome said, "I take it you prefer it to the CIA."

"It's a vast improvement, sir."

"You don't miss the . . . excitement? Being in on national secrets?"

"Not at all. I'd expected more field duty, but there wasn't enough of that. So—"

Claire said, "I have friends at the Agency. Perhaps you knew Tubby Cushing?"

"Afraid not."

"Jake Withrow? Sally Carmelis?"

He shook his head. "It's a big place. Know their sections?"

She smiled. "They never told me, and Dad cautioned me never to ask."

"It's not easy to fend off questions from friends," Burke said, sipping his wine, "but you have to maintain security."

"I suppose even now you can't talk about the things you did," she said.

"And risk prosecution?" The senator snorted. "Of course not. Tom, what plans have you for the summer?"

"Uncertain, Senator, they haven't jelled, but I expect to be doing some traveling."

"Aboard?" Claire asked.

"Possibly."

"Your firm has foreign accounts?"

"Not as many as we'd like."

The senator said, "Let's have coffee on the terrace. Brandy, Tom?"

"Please."

A servant drew back Claire's chair and she rose gracefully, following her father to the screened porch, where a table was set with silver coffee service on a large gadroon tray. Burke found the cool night air refreshing.

Hardly had coffee been poured when the senator was called to the telephone. He left reluctantly, and Claire leaned forward to murmur, "I applied to CIA."

"And?"

"They were very polite, but said with only two years of college and French my only language, they couldn't offer me a place. Now please don't ever tell my father. He'd be upset that I applied and furious at the Agency for turning me down. But after my divorce I didn't know what I wanted to do with my life. The idea of two more undergraduate years was daunting, too." Burke declined her offer of sugar, saying "Your secret's safe with me."

"Thank you." Holding her cup, she sat back. "I'm very sorry about your brother, Tom. He got a bum deal, didn't he?"

"Compared to others."

"Has his wife been supportive?"

He shook his head. "She's divorcing him. At least that ends the uncertainty."

"Then Terry has only you."

"And a mountain of legal bills. Can we change the subject? It's with me all the time."

"Of course—Tom—and I apologize for bringing it up."

The senator appeared. "One day," he groaned, "I'll leave the Senate, become a private citizen not obligated to take calls from so many people." He sipped his coffee.

"It's been a thoroughly enjoyable evening, Senator, Claire, and I'm much in your debt," said Burke, meaning it.

Claire said, "Not at all, Tom, it was good of you to accept on such short notice. As neighbors, perhaps we'll see you more often."

"I'll make sure of it," he said.

He rose as she got up saying, "I'll leave you gentlemen—I have an early date with a horse."

Senator Newsome said, "So you do—Warrenton?"

"I'll be taking the pickup with Comet in the trailer." To Burke she said, "It's my first competition in a long time—a local meeting, insignificant to everyone but me."

"She feels she has to prove herself again," her father explained.

"I'm sure she'll wow them," Burke said. "Good night and good luck."

After she was gone, Newsome said, "Tom, that call was from the White House. You're to be at Leesburg airport for chopper pickup at eight-thirty in the morning. I assume you'll be seeing the president."

Burke stared at him. "I won't ask your source. However, I assume you know General Arness. Are you part of his setup?"

"We were in Korea together, and stayed in touch. Occasionally he favors me with bits of information he thinks I might find useful. As for his present work, I was one of a very few the president consulted before authorizing it."

"I see," Burke said slowly. "So you knew my travel plans before you asked."

"No specifics. I don't want them."

"I understand," Burke said. "Where will the chopper be taking me?"

"Camp David, I assume, since that's where the president is."

Burke got up. "I'd planned on finishing some work in the morning, but I'd better get back and do it now."

Senator Newsome rose and they shook hands. "I appreciate your joining us this evening, and my sentiments were expressed by Claire. Hope we'll see more of you—when that becomes possible."

When Terry's free, Burke thought. "I'll look forward to it."

Going out through the darkness to his car, he saw Claire coming toward him from the stables. She was wearing slippers and a tweed hacking coat over her pajamas. Moonlight made an aureole around her hair. "Checking on your horse?" he asked.

"Saying good night to Comet—he expects it, so I usually do." She sighed. "Actually I'm very tense about tomorrow, so I thought a few minutes with Comet might reassure me."

"Has it?"

"I think so." She was close enough that he could scent perfume he hadn't noticed before. Burke was drawn to her, at the same time realizing the absurdity of following it up. Awkwardly he said, "It was a most pleasant evening, Claire. Perhaps you'll have dinner with me before I leave on my travels?"

"Sounds delightful." She drew the coat more closely around her shoulders. "Especially since you're working for my father."

"Am I?"

"Why else would you be here twice in one day, talking confidentially out of earshot? What are you doing for the senator?"

Her assumption irritated him. "Ask your father."

"Need-to-know, I suppose? All right, since you won't tell me anything, I have a request to make. Whatever you're doing for my father, please do it well and quietly—I can't have any unpleasantness affecting him just now."

"Just now?"

She looked away and he saw her perfectly molded profile. The moonlight softened her face, making her seem very young—and vulnerable. "Dad has only a few months to live. Cancer is spreading from his liver to his kidneys, invading his body like wildfire." She choked and he saw that she was fighting back tears. "Inoperable. The doctor told me—Father doesn't know I know."

"So that is why you're home."

Fiercely she said, "It's not because I love the stench of the stables. So you must guard the secret and not do anything that would degrade him if it became public knowledge."

"I can promise that," he told her, "and I'm very sorry to know he's . . ."—Burke searched for the right word—"unwell. I admire the senator and the truth is I'm doing nothing for him, he's doing something for me."

"Oh," she said in a quick exhalation, "and you let me go on and blurt it all out." She shook her head angrily. "You could have spared me that, you know."

"I'm sorry—we were working on different assumptions." He got behind the wheel. Claire turned and walked quickly away.

Burke started the engine and steered down the drive, followed the pike back to his house. There was a lot of pent-up grief in Claire, he mused, and she was handling the situation as well as she could. They shared something, too; each had a loved one in peril.

In his kitchen he made coffee, turned on his word processor, and finished the ad text by midnight. He put it on the fax machine and transmitted it to his downtown office.

As he got into bed he wondered why he felt no thrill of anticipation over meeting the president of the United States. Perhaps, he thought, because it's nothing more than a business confirmation of a bloody bargain. Making the president no less an outlaw than himself.

Six

BURKE REACHED THE AIRSTRIP a few minutes before the chopper arrived. Unlike other helicopters from the White House squadron based at Anacostia, the Blackhawk bore no military markings. Pilot and copilot, however, were uniformed marine officers. The passenger in civilian clothing was from the White House Secret Service detail. Burke's escort.

Burke was wearing a seersucker suit, white button-down shirt, and a Cornell tie that was beginning to fray. After he'd strapped himself into a seat next to the Secret Service agent, the chopper rose, circled, and headed for the Catoctin Mountains. Often Burke had driven past the unmarked road near Thurmont that provided land access to Camp David. The presidential retreat had been built for Roosevelt by CCC labor and was whimsically named Shangri-la by FDR. Eisenhower officially named it Camp David in honor of his grandson. Burke knew little else about the place, by air about forty miles from Leesburg.

They were flying only a few thousand feet over rolling hills covered thickly with pines and aspen. Above them the air seemed smoky, but it was only morning haze lifting and dissipating in the sun-warmed air. The effect was surreal, and the chuffing throb of the rotors was lulling, hypnotic. Burke glanced at the SS detail man, face half-disguised under dark lenses. There was a colored button in his lapel—the day's identification symbol—and a bulge under his left arm located the holstered MAC-10 machine pistol.

He'd often wondered why the presidential protection detail scored so poorly in protecting presidents. After JFK, when the boobs didn't even know where the shots were coming from, they'd let a couple of nuts within lethal range of Jerry Ford, and then the Reagan fiasco when Hinckley had fired more shots than Burt Lancaster at the O.K. Corral. Still, he reflected, what we don't know is how many assassinations they've prevented.

None of his three targets could possibly have the kind of close-in protection the SS detail gave U.S. presidents or the computerized all-source information that flowed to the Secret Service. Burke had no doubt that he could get within killing range of his yet-unknown targets. The trick would be in getting out alive.

He saw the swimming pool first, glinting through the haze, then the presidential compound with its lodge and cabins connected by carefully laid-out walks. The SS man was using his walkie-talkie now, and the pilot was cutting power, spiraling down toward the helipad where two men stood waiting.

After touchdown Burke followed his escort from the chopper. One of the reception committee went over Burke with a metal detector loop, said "Okay," and stepped back. The other man said, "Follow me."

The graveled walk was bordered with creosoted timber. Patches of flowers interrupted well-tended lawns surrounding the rustic cabins. Burke noticed gardeners at work, Secret Service men strolling apparently casually, and he realized that he was being led toward the swimming pool.

Well before he reached it, a man came out of the cabaña and strode toward Burke, who recognized him as one of the president's chief aides. Burke had seen him occasionally on Sunday morning talk shows and had always been surprised at how Tor Daggitt managed to say nothing of substance while taking considerable time to do so. This morning the aide was wearing powder blue shorts, black socks, and street shoes. A yellow, short-sleeved Lauren sport shirt showed thick reddish hair on his arms. His face was pale and his lips were thin, as though contracted by alum, Burke thought.

Without preliminaries Daggitt said, "The president has instructed me to say that he will abide by the agreement made with General Arness."

"Not good enough," Burke said. "The agreement included presidential verification, not yours."

"I speak in the president's name," he snapped.

"In which case the president shouldn't mind telling me in person." He paused and saw the aide's face redden. "I didn't go to your people, they came to me," Burke pointed out bluntly.

Daggitt took a deep breath. "You're being difficult, Mr. Burke."

"And you're being obstructive. Now either the president confirms the deal face-to-face or there's no deal." He shrugged. "I'll ask Senator Newsome to clarify matters."

Daggitt glanced at the pool. The president was climbing out of it. An attendant draped a large blue terry-cloth robe around him. "Very well, I'll check with the president." He walked away from Burke, who waited while the president arranged himself comfortably on a poolside lounge and put on glasses. Daggitt bent over and Burke saw their lips move. Daggitt gestured at Burke, the president grimaced, then nodded, and Daggitt beckoned Burke to come over.

Without on-camera makeup the president's face looked older. The famous jaw was there, of course, but facial skin was stippled with age spots and there were wrinkles around the mouth. No trace of the customary presidential grin. This was the Man Himself, Burke reflected, not the packaged figure so often seen by the nation. He stopped near the president, who peered up at him. "You're Burke? What's the problem?"

"Second best isn't good enough, Mr. President."

The president glanced at his aide, who moved away. "Very well, I'll confirm that your understanding with General Arness has my approval."

"Specifically," said Burke, "I assassinate three drug barons and you pardon my brother, Terence."

"That's the deal. Satisfied?"

"Yes, Mr. President."

He smiled thinly. "They say you're a pretty tough hombre. I tend to believe it. Anything else?"

"No, sir."

"Have a good flight back." He took a sheaf of papers from his aide and began to read. Burke stepped back and returned to the helipad. His SS escort fell in beside him. The rotors began turning before they reached the chopper, and in a few minutes Burke saw the glittering pool recede until it was screened by tall pines.

He hadn't expected any witnesses because the whole transaction had to be disavowable. He could *claim* to have spoken privately with the president, but he could never prove it. Still, he'd had the satisfaction of forcing the president to deal with him directly, indicating how seriously his services were desired.

Twenty-eight minutes later the chopper left Burke at the Leesburg airstrip and whirred off in the clear morning sky. Burke was back in his workroom in time to answer the first text query from the typesetter.

After that he took off his shirt and removed a miniature wire recorder from his left armpit. It was an East German model he'd "forgotten" to return to the supply office before leaving the Agency, and in the privacy of his office he played back the recording. The quality was good; his voice, the aides', and the president's were easily identifiable. Burke rewound the recording and placed the plastic-housed recorder inside his stereo tuner, figuring the cache was as safe as any.

He began making coffee, reflecting that beginning with FDR every president had surreptitiously recorded important conversations, for self-protection or as a source for future memoirs or both. Do unto others before they do it unto you, Burke muttered, hoping he would never have to use it. Still, it was available.

The coffee was strong. He added more sugar and tasted again as the telephone began to ring.

Seven

BURKE EXPECTED HIS BOSS, Eddie Deems, but the voice was Enno Poliakoff's. "How did it go?"

"Satisfactory. What's next?"

"You're scheduled to start conditioning in three days. That time enough to get a leave of absence?"

"It'll have to be. Got a number where I can reach you or the general?"

"Yeah. Use a public phone and call yourself Cardiff." He gave Burke a number and repeated it. Burke wrote it down reversed and tucked the slip in his wallet. Then he punched it into the personal section of his computer's memory bank along with the day's date and his operational alias: Cardiff.

Just in case.

He finished his coffee and used the computer link to advise Deems that he was coming in for a personal meeting. Then he locked the farmhouse and drove to the Pennsylvania Avenue office three blocks from the White House in downtown Washington.

Eddie Deems's office was carpeted in navy blue and decorated with Oriental objets acquired during the Vietnam War. His large, black-lacquered desk came from Hong Kong and held a small jadeite bowl and several figures carved from rosewood. A three-section sofa was covered in eggshell linen. In front of it stretched a long Peruvian coffee table of dark leather whose surface was impressed with Inca designs. To Burke it had always seemed out of place, jarring.

From behind his desk Deems looked up and frowned. He was a light-skinned, balding man with Ben Franklin lenses. "Two months, Tom? You're a key man here. How can I spare you that long?" He pulled at his lower lip. "Can you give me a reason?"

"National service."

"Classified?"

Burke nodded. "Suddenly I seem to be indispensable."

"You're sure as hell indispensable here. Recall to active duty?"

"Not exactly."

"Spook stuff?"

"Look, Eddie, I can't say more."

"Okay, okay. I understand, but Stan Abernathy—how do we square it with him?"

"Will General Arness do?"

"Arness—hell yes."

Burke phoned Poliakoff's number, got an answering machine, and explained that Cardiff was having a leave-of-absence problem. He suggested that the general meet with Deems and Abernathy to resolve it.

Eddie drummed a pencil on a pad. "I'll have to hire a temporary replacement, you know. Not asking for paid leave, are you?"

Burke shook his head.

Deems pulled off his glasses and massaged his eyes. "This concern your brother?"

"Arness will tell you what he can, okay?"

Deems looked away. "I don't want to lose you, Tom. My room-mate, Jack Bryan, got himself killed in some ridiculous way. Remember Jack?"

Burke nodded. "A good guy. Took his wife to Pamplona for the running of the bulls, remembered all that Hemingway stuff and joined the crowd ahead of the bulls stampeding toward the ring. He got hooked and gored, trampled, skull smashed. With Joanie looking on." Burke paused. "Too much wine, too much bravado."

Deems looked at him with a surprised expression. "I only heard he was killed, not the details."

"Joan told me," Burke said, remembering running into her in New York's Barberry Lounge a year later. He'd bought her drinks for old times' sake, and she'd insisted on taking him to her apartment for the night. It hadn't been a successful encounter, Burke remembered; in bed Joanie had been tentative, nostalgic, then maudlin, confusing him with Jack as he tried manfully to make love while she sobbed and went into near hysteria. It chilled Burke beyond recovery, and he'd left Joan before she broke down completely.

So, yes, he'd learned details of Jack Bryan's avoidable death, in a way he preferred to forget.

To Deems he said, "I don't run unnecessary risks, Eddie. Hold the job for me." They shook hands, and Burke went over to the University Club for a mixed grill, endive salad, and a bottle of Beck's. Then he drove back to his farm.

In midafternoon Burke took a call from Eddie Deems, who told him his leave of absence was okayed. "Stan was pretty impressed by the presentation. Matter of fact, so was I. Just call me when the job's done, okay?"

"Okay."

"Have luck."

He disconnected his PC and word processor from the power line and phoned a security service that did occasional external work for the Agency to ask for a protective installation that connected with their office and the local police switchboard. The computer complex, his car, and the guns were his most valuable possessions, and he didn't want thieves or vandals getting into them while he was away.

Poliakoff called to ask if everything was straightened out at his office. "So they say," Burke replied, and thanked Enno for prompt action. "Next contact?"

"This is Wednesday. Friday morning a call will come for you. All you'll need is an overnight bag, shaving gear . . . everything else supplied."

"Just like the army."

"Yeah, everything real GI—you'll feel at home."

Burke took the taunt without comment. He hung up and eased back in his chair. What else to accomplish before he left for the unknown? His will was in order—Terry sole beneficiary. The security service would be installing a protective system later in the day, tomorrow at the latest. His plane was hangared—oh, yes, disconnect the Porsche's battery terminals and lock it in the garage.

Though his mind was relaxed he felt a sense of uneasiness that an officer of General Arness's experience and discernment would have selected Enno as his aide. Or was Poliakoff only a gofer? Well, the less he and Enno had to do with each other the better. They knew each other far too well. Fortunately Arness was his principal.

What else to be done? Disconnect telephone. Suspend newspaper delivery. Let mail collect at the P.O. Burke made reminder notes and posted them on the refrigerator door. All perishable food to be frozen or discarded.

Aside from the Newsomes, he had no acquaintances in the Leesburg area who would look in from time to time, and he could hardly ask the ailing senator or his flaky daughter. Since leaving the Agency his associates were, like himself, involved in advertising or PR, and they lived either in metropolitan Washington or suburban Maryland. None were what he could consider friends except for Eddie Deems, and Burke realized that since his divorce he had become isolated, physically and psychologically. Many bachelors frequented singles bars, but he was a little old for that, and the superficial gaiety of those places turned him off. Besides, the thought of endless drinking repelled him. For occasional sex, the price was too high.

As Burke contemplated his present and future, he realized he probably ought to have some sort of legal advice and protection. He knew only three attorneys; one had drawn his will, one had handled his purchase of the farm, and the third, his divorce from Joyce. None had the kind of background he needed.

Peter Ward came to mind, a legendary figure around the Agency. Multilingual, combat-skilled Ward had been a highly ranked protégé of Director Avery Thorne until Thorne was replaced by the disastrous Admiral Turner. In those down days the emphasis had been on technology *vice* human intelligence sources, a changeover old hands like Ward had found so uncongenial that they'd resigned or retired. Burke had become acquainted with Ward through a series of covert operations lectures Ward had delivered at Camp Peary, the Agency's training area widely know as the Farm. Ward, he remembered, had played hockey at Brown and gone to Yale Law School before military and Agency service. No longer Agency-connected except for occasional guest lectures, Ward practiced international law in the District.

He looked up Ward's office number and reached for the phone, then drew back his hand. It would be like that bastard Poliakoff to tap his phone, and Burke wanted his relationship with Ward to remain their secret alone.

From a public phone near the Leesburg courthouse, Burke identified himself as ex-Agency, said they'd met at the Farm some years ago, and asked Ward for an appointment.

"How urgent is it?" Ward asked.

"I have only today and tomorrow."

"I see. Well, I'm free after five, that agreeable?"

"Perfect," Burke told him. "I'll be there."

He drove back to his farmhouse and recovered the East German wire recorder. A truck from the security service arrived and Burke took the foreman through house and grounds explaining that he'd be vacating the place for an indefinite period.

"We'll start now, finish up tomorrow."

"Have the bill ready so I can pay before leaving."

"Welcome words," the foreman said. "We'll do a good job, Mr. Burke. By the way, we like to know how a client heard of us. Yellow pages?"

"Agency," Burke replied. "Before I resigned."

"Then you know we're dependable."

"That's why you're here."

He left them to install their hair-fine wires and silver conducting tapes for windowpanes, their magnetic interface gadgets for door and window frames, and other exotic items of their craft designed to protect honest homeowners from burglary and vandalism. Burke had a basic understanding of alarm systems and how to defeat them, but he had not been a surreptitious entry practitioner and so he'd left entry ops to specialists.

His phone rang and he heard the operator asking if he would accept a collect call from Jim McNally in Allenwood, Pennsylvania. Used to taking collect calls from Terry—the only way inmates were allowed to make long distance calls—Burke agreed and almost at once heard Terry's voice. "Tom—thank God you took the call—I'm only allowed one before going into isolation. Yes, I've been transferred—before dawn this morning—and whatever you had to do to arrange it, I'm forever grateful. I'd forgotten what sun and sky looked like. You'll see for yourself when you come up."

"It'll be a while—Jim," Burke said. "Meanwhile I'm relieved you're better situated. If they let you write from iso, send your mailing address and I'll get back to you as soon as I can."

"You said it'll be a while. Going away?"

"Don't know how long. But by the time I get back you'll be in population, have a camp job, and—"

"Hell, I've been assigned to the cattle detail. They run a dairy farm up here—it's a real camp. Guess I'll finally learn how to milk a cow." He laughed uneasily. "A new skill."

"Just don't forget your pardon application."

"I'll be working on it." His voice lowered. "Thanks again, Tom. I can handle it now. And, wherever you go, take care, will you? You're the only family I've got."

"You're my family, too," Burke said emotionally. "See you as soon as I can."

As he hung up he felt a surge of satisfaction. He, Tom Burke, had managed it by not underestimating the value of his special skills and his willingness to kill—for a cause. Burke was impressed by the general's clout. Arness had probably not had to reach higher than the attorney general, who controlled the Bureau of Prisons. The day was passing fast and much had been accomplished in the hours since he'd dressed to meet the president of the United States and confirm their Faustian agreement.

A silver gray Ram Charger pickup rumbled up his access road and braked near the security-service truck. A girl in jodhpurs and blue button-down shirt jumped out of it, and after glancing at the truck, walked rapidly toward the farmhouse. Claire Newsome gained the porch and was stamping dust from her jodhpur boots when Burke opened the screen door and said, "Hi, come on in."

She looked over her shoulder. "What is it with the security boys? Are you being threatened?"

"Work that should have been done long ago," he said dismissively. "How did Warrenton go?"

"Oh, they gave me a compassionate third—based on past performance, I'm sure. Got anything to drink?"

"Almost everything. Lemonade?"

"Beer?"

"Couldn't be easier. Bottle or glass?"

"Bottle's fine."

She followed him into the living room, stayed there looking around while Burke got two bottles of Beck's from the fridge and opened them. "Here's to Warrenton," he said, "and the meets to follow."

"Nice toast." She touched her bottle to his.

"Well, I like girls who drink beer. Even in college I did, especially then when money was tight."

She sat on the sofa and Burke sat facing her. Claire wiped forehead perspiration on her sleeve. "You're a hard man to reach. Either you haven't been answering your phone, or it's been busy every time I called. So I thought I'd check in person."

"Senator have a message for me?"

"Expecting one? No, I shouldn't have said that, scratch the question." She looked down at her hands. "I'm not usually feisty, Tom. But at the moment I'm uncertain, a bit off balance. We parted on a false note—I didn't intend that."

"I understood your concern for your father. Perfectly natural, Claire."

"That's a generous judgment." She sighed and sipped her beer.

"I'd like us to be friends."

"I'd like that, too." He studied her face until her eyelashes lowered. She said, "Do you have a—a lady friend?" Her cheeks colored. "I mean, are you seeing someone? Tom, I don't know how else to ask what's probably an impertinent question."

He smiled. "As they say at press conferences, I'm glad you asked that. Anyway, the answer is no, Claire. That clear the air?"

"It does," she said with a frank nod, "and allows me to make up for last night's bad behavior by inviting you to dinner."

"It's not the least necessary, but let's do it. I'd suggest we have dinner here, only there's not much to offer." He looked at his watch. "I have a Washington meeting at five, but I should be back by six-thirty. Your place?"

"We've dined with my father—I didn't invite him."

He nodded. Good. She preferred dinner for two—as he did. "Have a place in mind?"

"Like seafood? We could meet at Herreshoff's."

"I do, and it's not far. Seven? Seven-thirty? Eight?"

"Seven-thirty's good." She finished her beer and stood up. "Mustn't keep you from your appointment, Tom. See you at Herreshoff's."

He saw her off the porch, watched her jog to her pickup, in which, he thought, she used to tow horse trailers around the riding circuit.

In Burke's experience not many girls or women had shown the guts or grace to acknowledge they'd been out of line. That Claire Newsome had joined their select company pleased him, and he realized that he was revising his earlier opinion of her.

Dinner was a pleasant prospect. Burke put on tie and jacket and drove into Washington for the second time that day.

Eight

"YOU WERE WITH the Agency how long, Mr. Burke?" asked the lawyer.

"Five years, give or take a few months." He sat in a comfortable leather-upholstered chair in an office whose paneling and furnishings suggested a London club. Peter Ward was a handsome man with deep-set eyes, broad shoulders, and an easy smile. His brown hair was silvering at the sides, and Burke estimated his age as forty-five or so. Not much older than himself.

"Mind telling me why you resigned?"

"Same reason you did—lack of opportunity."

"Opportunities for action, you mean." Ward's smile was smoothly confident. As Burke nodded, Ward continued. "Since then you've been in advertising. Quite a contrast to our sealed-lips profession. Now, to avoid any possible conflict of interest, does your situation have anything to do with Hong Kong?"

"Nothing I know of."

"My brother-in-law is active there, and I represent his business interests."

"I see. If it turns out that I'm unexpectedly involved in Hong Kong, I'll let you know."

Ward nodded. "Fair enough. Now, I assume you're consulting me on a confidential matter."

"Highly confidential—it involves the president of the United States."

Ward's eyebrows raised. "The president, eh? Well, let's have the background."

Burke got out the minirecorder and placed it on the polished desk. After a glance at it Ward said, "East German model."

"You've used it?"

"I brought in the first exemplar from a GDR agent who had no further use for it. Gave the TSD office plenty to think about."

Burke smiled. He could visualize Ward taking the recorder from a body. "A few days ago," he began, "my brother's appeal was turned down by the Supreme Court."

"I'm aware of that."

"And within hours I was approached by General William Arness, who made me a proposition." Burke recounted the full story. He mentioned Senator Newsome's peripheral role and touched the recorder. "Listen to the conversation if you want. But I think you might prefer to be in a position of saying your client left it with you for safekeeping."

"If the conversation confirms a conspiracy to commit certain crimes—such as you've mentioned to me—I'd have an obligation to call in the FBI. As things stand you've told me a tale that may or may not be true—and I don't want to know. So I'll accept this item as is and keep it securely until such time as you may request its return. That what you have in mind?"

"Exactly. Know General Arness?"

"We had dealings years ago when he was a colonel. Do I trust him? I did and I do."

"Judge Grogan?"

"I've appeared before him in a couple of pleadings. Not the most congenial fellow on the bench. Another judge might have been more lenient."

"We know that, Mr. Ward, and to prevent Terry from being lost in the prison system—if anything happens to me—he's been transferred to Allenwood as Jim McNally." He saw the attorney note name and place.

"So. What," asked Ward, "do you want me to do—beyond taking custody of the recorder?"

"For now, nothing. But I view my agreement as binding on this administration. If the president dies or is incapacitated, the VP takes over, and as far as I know he's not witting to any of this. The recorder could convince him not to renege."

Ward pursed his lips, said, "A wise precaution, Mr. Burke. Like you, I've grown weary of seeing the Oval Office hang good men out to dry." He smiled wryly. "Around town there's a parody of the old Chicago song that started back with the Watergate and later the Iran-Contra convictions: *I used to work in the White House—I don't work there any more.*"

"Hadn't heard it," Burke said, "but I sure understand it." He got up. "I pay your secretary?"

"No charge," Ward said. "Consider it a professional favor. Also, it's encouraging to learn that finally, after all the talk—just talk—about a war on narcotics, that war is actually being waged. If you should become a casualty, I'll see that your brother is pardoned."

They shook hands, and Burke took the elevator down to the underground parking garage. He drove up on Sixteenth Street and joined slow-moving traffic into Georgetown and over Key Bridge toward Leesburg.

Dusk was falling over his fields when he pulled in at the farmhouse. He shaved, changed, and drove through Leesburg to Herreshoff's where he had gone a few times for fried oysters, hush puppies, and draft beer. Rafters and walls were hung with fishnets, cork buoys, and replicas of fish likely to be found on the menu. There were patinated diving helmets, and a couple of ancient harpoons. A mural behind the bar displayed King Neptune and a bevy of bare-breasted mermaids. Nothing unusual about the place. The dim lighting was enhanced by candle lamps on stressed-wood tables, and he found Claire Newsome at one, sipping a Kir.

She was wearing an off-the-shoulder blouse of light blue silk, a three-strand pearl choker, and a minuscule platinum wristwatch. "Hi," she greeted him, as he sat down across from her, "you're right on time."

"Aim to please, ma'am," he smiled. The candlelight gave her skin a golden glow and made her look about eighteen. He was glad he'd come.

"Look," she said, "this is my treat, but I'd like you to order the wine, okay?"

He asked the waiter for a bottle of Pouilly-Fuisée, well chilled, and turned to Claire. "One of the nice things about this place is that the waiters don't say, 'Hi, I'm Paul or Jeffrey or Stephen and it's my pleasure to serve you.' "

Claire laughed. "Easy there. Tom, do you have anyone to look in on your place while you're gone? Sort of check on things?"

He shook his head. "That's one reason I'm having an alarm system installed."

"Would you accept me as a checker-upper?"

"Gladly."

"I have an ulterior motive," she admitted frankly. "I need pasture for my horses. I'm buying three more for steeplechasing—and as you probably saw, our land is mostly under cultivation. I'd be glad to pay for grazing privileges."

"Don't think of it. Goose Creek borders my property, and unless there's an exceptional dry spell, there'll be plenty of water for your horses. There are a few trees for shade, and you could keep your trailers in the barn."

"Terrific! You'll be there tomorrow?"

He nodded as the waiter showed them the blackboard menu. Burke said, "We're in no hurry."

"The wine, then?"

"When chilled."

"I love this, Tom," Claire said softly. "It's been ages since I had a real dinner date away from home." Her hand touched his.

"Same with me," he admitted, "and when I get back, we'll pick up where we leave off. Unless you're otherwise engaged."

"Not likely. I need to stay close to my father, do whatever I can for him. And train and jump my horses, so my summer's cut out for me. I gather yours is, too."

"To some extent." The wine arrived in an ice bucket, and Burke sniffed the cork, approved, and touched his glass to Claire's. "To a good summer."

She echoed his words, adding, "Think you'll be back by Labor Day weekend?"

"I'm hoping so."

"We have a place over on the Eastern Shore near Bethany Beach. I'll open it up so we can spend the long weekend there." She looked down at her wineglass, shyly. "If you'd like to."

"Of course I would, It'll give me a date to aim for. Back by Labor Day is the slogan."

"From—wherever you go." She sipped wine and set down her glass. "It must be something classified—for the Agency."

"Not a bad assumption," he conceded, "and we'll leave it at that."

Light background music came on at an unobtrusive level and Burke recognized the piano of Oscar Peterson, one of his favorite musicians. Presently they ordered dinner: chowder and bouillabaisse, trout for Claire, salmon steak for Burke, a Caesar salad to share, and for dessert lemon ice and coffee.

The other diners were well-dressed couples, one family group with three children in a far corner. Burke studied Claire's face and thought how ironic it was that after years of loneliness he had met this attractive young woman just as he was leaving for a mission from which he might well not return. Her summer's-end invitation had surprised him, for it was implicit that they would become lovers. Until now he had refrained from letting himself desire Claire Newsome, but in response to her move he lowered the barrier and thought of her lips and breasts, the texture of her body. . . .

His thoughts were interrupted when Claire spoke up. "It won't be long before my father will be in Walter Reed or Bethesda. But he won't vacate his Senate seat until he and the governor agree on a replacement." She shook her head. "It was one thing for father to be a judge—we lived quietly then, the four of us—but the life of a senator is far different."

"I can imagine."

"So I loathe politics, Tom. You're not political, are you?"

"Not in the least."

"That's a relief. It's so demanding and so phony."

He nodded. "They say truth is the first casualty in war; I guess the same holds true for politics." He looked at her. "Starting with the Congressional Record."

"I know. The 'corrections' and 'emendations' that bear no resemblance to what was actually said on the floor." She sighed. "Well, it's a sad subject, since Dad won't be playing any part in it much longer." Her voice trailed away.

His hand reached over and covered hers. "There's always remission, you know. . . ."

Her eyes were moist, glistening in the soft light. "My glass is empty."

After dinner Burke took cognac with his coffee, Claire Kahlúa with hers. After tasting it, she said, "We've both had disappointing marriages, so we're veterans in a sense, aren't we? Walking wounded."

"Everyone's entitled to one marital mistake. It's only afterward we can sort out the reasons things went wrong."

"Or should never have happened in the first place."

"Exactly. But I've never dwelt on it, and you shouldn't either."

"I think it's different with a woman, Tom. So much of her identity is tied to a successful marriage. If it fails, we assume the guilt, wherever the fault lies."

"Isn't that pretty old-fashioned? I don't know anyone who's burdened by it."

Her gaze lifted to his. "Me."

"Well, unload it. Your father's well-being is a legitimate concern, your former marriage isn't. Why not talk it out with a counselor?"

She looked away. "It's been a hang-up. I never had the courage to make an appointment—nor anyone to encourage me."

"Until now."

She nodded. "So I'll probably get into that while you're away." She beckoned to their waiter and handed him a platinum AmEx card.

In the parking lot Burke followed Claire to her silver Mercedes roadster. As she took out car keys he said, "Thanks for a special evening, Claire. It's been a long time since I enjoyed anything even remotely comparable."

"I enjoyed it, too—very much, Tom." She looked at her wrist-watch. It was an awkward moment and Burke bridged it saying, "Unless you're pressed for time, we can stop at my place and I'll begin showing you around. And a nightcap might be in order."

"I have all the time in the world," she said. "My father will be in bed watching TV, probably asleep by now. And I'd like to see your house." She unlocked the car door. "Is the alarm system installed?"

"Not quite. They're supposed to finish up tomorrow. Incidentally, use the house whenever you like—everyone needs a pied-à-terre."

"Especially me. It's very hard to hold back tears when I'm with my father." Her lips trembling, she ducked down and got behind the wheel. "I'll follow you, Tom," she said tightly.

Ten minutes later they pulled up in front of his dark house—he'd neglected to leave a light on—and Claire followed Burke to the front porch. He opened the screen door and was about to slide key into door lock when he saw splintered wood around the jamb.

"Get in your car and lock the door," he told her quietly, "while I have a look around."

Nine

BURKE WAITED UNTIL Claire was in her car, then slammed the door open and raced around to the rear of the house.

The kitchen door burst open and a dark figure emerged. As the man began running, Burke tackled him and brought him down. Burke was on his knees ready to apply an armlock when his opponent rolled away, sprang to his feet, and kicked at Burke's face. Instinctively Burke snapped his head aside, and the toe caught his collarbone. He grabbed at the ankle and twisted. With a grunt the man pivoted free and raised his arm. Moonlight glinted on metal in his hand as it slashed downward. Burke lifted his left arm to protect his face, but the blow landed on his skull.

Briefly his mind registered an explosion of light, then darkness. When he came to, he was on his back, Claire kneeling beside him, inchoate whimpering coming from her throat.

He touched his head, felt an icy towel, and reached for her hand. "I'm okay," he said hoarsely. "Did you see him?"

"I—I saw him run away, that's all. Oh, God, I was afraid he'd killed you!"

His head throbbed abominably, his collarbone ached. "Could have," he managed, and he tried sitting up, but a lance of pain pinned him back. "Did you see his face?"

"It was masked. A big man, but he ran fast." She gestured at the woods. "As I was coming here I heard a car start. He's gone."

"I feel like a fool," he said, forcing his body to sit upright despite shooting pain. There was light in the kitchen. Bravely Claire had gone for the icy towel. He draped it around his neck and stood up. She rose to steady him, and they went into the house.

He rested in a kitchen chair while she brought the cognac bottle and poured a glass for him. "I could use one myself," she said, and she poured a second glass and drank.

"There's aspirin in the bathroom cabinet," he said, "or should be."

When she returned with the pills, he said wryly, "This isn't my idea of showing you the house."

"Strangest ending for a date I can remember."

He swallowed four aspirin with cognac and took her hand. "Thanks, Claire."

"I couldn't leave you lying in the moonlight, could I?" She removed his towel, soaked it in ice water, wrung it out, and replaced it around his neck. "Want me to phone the police?"

"What can they do?"

"I didn't see the burglar carrying anything, so maybe nothing's been stolen. Let's hope."

He sipped more cognac, held out his glass. After drinking again he got up slowly and trudged to his gun cabinet. Intact. He turned on lights around his work area and saw that the computer's power line had been connected with the mains. The disk slot was open, the storage disk he'd been using for ad texts was gone. His operational alias, Cardiff, and the contact phone number were secure on another disk.

Claire said, "Anything missing?"

"No." He leaned down to disconnect the power line.

"You must have interrupted the burglar."

"Guess so." Suddenly feeling faint, he sat heavily on the nearby sofa. Claire hurried to him, pressed the cold towel to his forehead. "Shouldn't you be x-rayed?"

"I'll be good as new by morning." Who the hell wanted that disk. Someone from the White House destroying any possible record of his presidential meeting?

The aspirin-cognac combination was beginning to dull the edge of pain. He went into the bathroom and stared at a drawn and haggard face. The middle of his collarbone was bruised blue but his face hadn't been smashed by the kick. His scalp was moist; blood stained his fingertips. Well, far worse injuries had always healed. Scalp bleeding would stop in a little while, and he had tomorrow to recover before he was taken away by Arness's people.

Claire was standing in the living room finishing her cognac. "You've made such a nice place of this," she commented. "Rustic furniture, hooked rugs, Grandma Moses on the walls . . ." She smiled.

"Not exactly Grandma," he admitted, "but plenty primitive. Anyway, I'm glad you came to see the place—and help me out of my stupor."

"Are you feeling better?"

"Reasonably functional, I'd say." But he felt ashamed that even with the advantage of surprise he'd let the intruder get away. Lost your edge, Burke, he told himself, as he went to the kitchen for a glass of cold water. Claire watched him silently—uncertain what to do, he thought. She said, "I guess we'll never know who the burglar was."

"No, but his timing couldn't be better. Tomorrow the protective system will be in working order."

"At least nothing was stolen—you have some very nice silver."

"My mother's," he said.

Claire sighed. "The best thing for you, Tom, is to get to bed."

He glanced at the staircase to the second floor, then at the guest-room door off the living room. "The stairs look formidable. I'll bunk down here tonight."

He walked unsteadily to the guest bedroom and said, "Another drink will help me sleep." He pulled down the quilt and sat on the bed. Bending over to untie his laces was a mistake; the rush of blood to his head made him feel giddy. Bringing his refilled glass, Claire grasped his condition and knelt to take off his shoes. "Pajamas?"

"Only in cold weather."

She left the room while he pulled off his clothing and got between the sheets, returned with her own glass. "I'll wait a while," she offered, "to make sure you'll be all right." She turned off the light.

Burke managed a smile. "I can imagine what kind of impression I've made on you."

"Why would you think that? The man had a weapon and you didn't. Tom, you were damn brave." As she sat on the edge of the bed and sipped her drink, Burke held her free hand and watched her face in the almost-dark. After a while he said, "I have no right to ask it, but I'd like you to stay."

Bending over, she kissed his forehead. "I *want* to be with you. . . ." She set her glass on the night table. "It's forever until Labor Day weekend."

He heard her shoes drop to the floor. "Months," Burke said tightly. "And—"

"—you don't know if you'll make it back," she completed the thought. "Right?"

"Right," he echoed. Her fingertips pressed his lips and she murmured, "All the more reason to be together now." Standing, she deftly pulled off her dress, undid her bra, and peeled down her panty hose.

In the moment before she slid between the sheets, he saw that her breasts were small and conical—girlish, he thought—her waist narrow, hips nicely rounded and modulating into firm, tapered thighs. Her right side touched his left and her flesh was warm, life-infusing against his cooler body.

For what seemed like a long time they lay passively, as though each was waiting for the other to move first. Hesitantly, almost fearfully, Burke clasped her hand, drew it above the covers and kissed it. Breath caught in her throat.

She turned against him then, pressing her body to his until he could feel the soft curls of her pelt. Almost inaudibly she whispered, "We don't have to do anything, you know—you're in pain, and for me it's wonderful just to hold you like this."

Hands, small-boned and strong, stroked his shoulder, his back, trailed along his hip. Quietly he said, "No pain at all," and pressed his lips to hers.

They were warm and soft, her open mouth even warmer. Her tongue was velvet against his. She pressed into the curve of his body, her nipples like rubies against his chest as she molded herself to him. Desire pulsed through his blood. She sensed it and held him tightly as her thighs parted. Gently she pressed him on his back, straddled his hips lightly, and shuddered as she lowered herself onto his maleness. Then she lay forward on his chest and framed his face with her hands. Her mouth covered his, and as their hips began to move in rhythm Burke felt the magnetic exchange of life forces begin.

After their climax she stayed where she was, breathing subsiding, eyes closed as though in a secret impenetrable reverie. After a few minutes he decided she was sleeping and whispered, "Claire," very softly. Her head lifted and her eyes opened. "I don't want it to end," she sighed. "It was too wonderful." She kissed his lips. "Are you in pain?"

"Ecstasy is a better word."

"Ah, Tom . . . me, too." She shivered and her shoulders hunched. "It's disloyal of me, but if it hadn't been for the burglar, I wouldn't be here. With you. Like this."

"Don't be too sure of that." His fingers moved down her spine, making her shiver again.

"You had plans?"

"Vaguely."

"So did I." She pried herself upright and gazed down at him. "I can always blame it on the brandy."

"What's to blame?" He nuzzled her breasts, kissed her nipples. "Champagne's the standard excuse."

"Words of experience?"

"Uh-huh."

"Do I have to go now, master?"

"Only if you insist, sweetheart."

"Then I'll stay. Is the cat out, dear?"

"Mousing in the fields, pumpkin."

"TV turned off, precious?"

"Dead for hours, pet."

"Phone off the hook, dearest?"

"Won't ring till we let it, darling."

She sighed. "I suppose you'll want scrambled eggs in the morning, honey?"

"Medium dry with bacon, baby. Did you bank the fire?"

"Tried, but it's burning hot." She wiggled her hips and fitted her pelvis to him. "You talk too much." She closed his mouth with hers and slowly, tenderly, they made love again.

Later as she lay beside him she whispered, "That proves it."

"Proves what?" he asked drowsily.

"That you were made for me."

"Hmmm. Tell me that in the morning and maybe I'll believe it."

"I'm a believer. Oh, am I *ever* a believer!"

Over the breakfast table Burke said, "The eggs were perfect."

"Sorry there wasn't any bacon."

"Well, I told you there wasn't much of anything left." He sipped coffee and put down his cup. "How do I square things with Dad?"

"Suppose you leave that to me. It's hardly as though I were a maiden at boarding school. Besides, the senator likes you."

"That was yesterday."

"He's too much the politician to express an opinion. C'mon, let's go tramp the fields. I'll bring over a couple of trail horses today—if that's okay."

As they left the house the security system crew arrived and Burke asked the foreman to repair the broken door.

"Sure," the foreman said, "and no charge. If we'd finished yesterday, Mr. Burke, the burglar would have been in real trouble."

"I called you a day late," Burke said. "My fault, not yours." He rejoined Claire and they walked past the pond with its fast-paddling ducklings, and down to his shooting shed. She looked through the sighting scope at the two-hundred-yard target and gave a low whistle. "Doesn't seem possible you could hit anything accurately at that range." She looked up at him. "But I'm sure you do."

He made a mental note to bring in the Zeiss scope when they came back. Then they went down to the edge of the creek and watched nearly colorless crayfish foraging on the sand-slate bottom. From there they walked arm in arm to the far end of his fields marked by barbed-wire fencing, then back to the shed, where Burke collected the scope.

Outside, men on ladders were securing second-floor windows and setting floodlights under the eaves. "Looks very thorough, Tom," she commented. "If I stay here from time to time I won't worry about break-ins."

"I don't think there'll be another try." He circled her with his arms. She faced him, face tight. "You know something I don't?"

"The burglar got something he came for—a memory disk."

"Was it—is it terribly important?"

"Could have been—if he'd taken the right one. But the break-in tells me what the competition is capable of doing. Anyway, my computer wasn't damaged, so we'll forget about it."

"Look, if you still think of me as a starry-eyed child, you're very wrong. To prove it, I'm going to take handgun instruction while you're away. Does that please you?"

"It does. Then I won't worry about you driving alone at night."

"Ah, so you possibly care for me—a little?"

"More than I should," he told her, "but we have to keep our heads about this. For now I'm dedicated to straightening out my brother's life."

"I understand," she said quietly, "and I can wait, Tom. Last night I realized I'd been waiting for you a long time. Of course you must do everything you can for Terry—but after him there's me."

Silently he kissed her. Claire glanced at her watch. "I should go home and calm my father—and you have things to do."

"Very little," he said, "so bring over your horses and we'll spend time together."

"Terrific, and I'll bring food for a couple of meals."

He walked her to her car and watched her drive away. As he returned to the house he tried to sort out his feelings and realized he was on the verge of falling in love.

Only this was no time for it. His mind had to be able to focus completely on the tasks ahead. Last night fate had brought them together and in the morning he would be gone. Distance and detailed preparations inevitably would edge Claire Newsome from his mind.

If he got back, after Terry was free, then they'd see both how their mutual attraction had fared.

Leaving the workmen to complete the wiring, Burke drove into Leesburg and called his contact number from a public phone. To the answering machine he gave his alias, Cardiff, and the number of the phone from which he was calling. Then he hung up, lighted a cigarillo, and waited on a nearby bench.

When the pay phone rang, Burke heard Poliakoff's voice.

"I want the general, Enno."

"He's not available—out of town."

"Then tell him my place was burglarized last night. No valuables taken, only a floppy disk."

"Strange kind of robbery, Cardiff. Was the disk worth anything?"

"Only to me."

"Then—there's no security breach?"

"None. I don't have classified material there or anywhere."

Poliakoff laughed unpleasantly. *"You're* classified. Keep that in mind."

"What time's pickup tomorrow?"

"Be ready at six-thirty."

"Will I be able to come back here before the first project?"

"That's not up to me."

"I didn't notify the police about the break-in. I figured the general wouldn't want that."

"He wouldn't."

"Swell talking with you, Enno. Carry on." Back at the farmhouse, the work crew were loading their gear in the truck. The foreman came over. "We'd better go over it now, Mr. Burke." An electronic sequential lock had been installed on the front doorjamb. Last night's damage had been repaired and painted over. "You won't need keys any more, just the release number to memorize." He handed Burke a slip of paper: 14-79-38-21. "If you make a mistake, you've got ten seconds to punch in the right sequence before bells ring, sirens blare, and lights flash all over the house and grounds. At the same time our main office is alerted and so's the police switchboard." He showed Burke how to disarm the system. "If you're having a party, for instance."

"What if the thief cuts wires or destroys this electronic box?"

"Same hellacious racket breaks out. If the main power line is cut, there's a battery fallback system, in the attic. All cables are shielded from water and humidity." He paused. "You have to disarm the system if you want to open a window. I left a pamphlet on your desk. Any questions, call me." He handed Burke the bill.

Burke whistled, but wrote out a check for more than four thousand dollars. Pocketing it, the foreman noted, "Since you use your home as an office, the cost should be tax deductible. And thanks for choosing our service."

Burke put clean sheets on the bed he'd used last night, washed breakfast dishes, chilled a bottle of rosé, and tidied his upstairs bedroom. Unless the senator prevented it, Claire would share it with him tonight, their last night together.

At one o'clock he heard her pickup rumble up the road, and saw she was towing a two-horse trailer. He went out to greet her, helped lower the trailer ramp, and together they walked the horses, both Appaloosas, down to the duck pond. After the horses had drunk their fill, Burke and Claire left them grazing on rye grass. From the pickup Claire brought a lunch basket to the kitchen and served deli cold cuts, potato salad, and assorted breads.

She was wearing faded denim breeches, scuffed Top-Siders, and a Hot Springs T-shirt. Beneath it her breasts moved invitingly. Burke watched until she said, "Lecher!" and tucked the shirt into her her waistband, tightening the thin fabric even more.

Burke described the security system to Claire and gave her the electronic lock combination. She said, "I won't come in often, maybe once a week to look things over. And when I buy the other horses I'll have them delivered here. By the time you return there'll be quite a stable on your land."

"Much better than having it unused." He took her hand. "Claire, listen to me: It's very hard not to say I love you, but I'm not going to because of life's uncertainties."

"Your life, you mean."

"Well, you could meet someone you prefer, and I don't want you under any sense of obligation."

"In my twenty-six years I haven't met your equal, Tom. It's not likely I'll meet him now."

"Still, I want you to feel free to live your own life as you choose. Knowing you're here gives me even more reason to survive and come back." He released her hand. "Was your father troubled about last night?"

"He asked no questions—he's a pretty wise man. Actually I think he's relieved it's you instead of some unknown character met at a bar. Not that I've ever done that," she added quickly. "By the way, how's the head?"

"The pain's mostly gone. Headaches when I bend over or do lifting, but a big improvement over last night."

She unbuttoned his shirt and looked at the collarbone bruise, then kissed it. He refilled their wineglasses and led her to his upstairs bedroom where they undressed and made love through the afternoon.

As evening fell they strolled down through the fields, where they gave sugar and carrots to the Appaloosas who munched gratefully. "Rye grass isn't optimum forage," she said, "so I'll be bringing hay to supplement their diet. Oats, too." She kissed his cheek. "You *will* ride with me, won't you?"

"Unless training an amateur will be too painful."

"A day should do it." They walked back to the farmhouse, where a small larded tenderloin was roasting in the oven.

Burke's wristwatch alarm woke him at five-thirty. He left the bed carefully to avoid waking Claire, whose head was buried in the pillow. As he shaved, Burke remembered how exciting their lovemaking had been; her body scents still filled his nostrils. He showered, dressed in casual clothing, and packed shaving gear in a small athletic bag.

"Were you leaving without saying good-bye?" Claire's voice came from behind him.

"Of course not." He turned and saw her sitting up, silent tears streaming down her cheeks. He went over, held and kissed her. "Don't make me feel worse than I do. Try to understand."

"That's the trouble—I do. You're going off to risk your life somewhere doing God knows what. It isn't fair, Tom, not when we've only met." She began drying her eyes. "Will you be able to call me?"

"No, but I'll try getting messages to you."

Her arms circled his neck and they kissed for a long time. Finally she released him, silently mouthing *I love you.*

Throat tight, he kissed her a final time and left the farmhouse. Looking back, he saw one of her horses at the pond, the ducklings swimming unconcernedly behind their mother. It was a scene whose serenity he wanted to remember. He closed the gate and smoked a cigarillo until a black Ford sedan stopped for him and drove him to Dulles airport. The driver entered the tarmac by a side gate and drove directly to a twin-engine Learjet whose white fuselage was lettered: UNITED STATES CUSTOMS SERVICE. "There's your ride." Burke left the car with his bag.

Pilot and copilot wore white shirts with shoulder loops, black ties, black trousers, and shoes. "Sit anyplace," the copilot said as Burke entered the cabin. Burke chose a window seat and buckled himself in. The folding staircase rose and joined the cabin. "We'll be airborne about three hours, sir. No liquor aboard, but there's coffee and sandwiches."

"I'll be fine," Burke said as the engines began whining. "Can you tell me where we're going?"

"New Mexico. Ever hear of Artesia?"

"No."

"It's maybe thirty miles north of Carlsbad. Nearest town to where we're landing." The pilot went forward, buckled in, and completed preflight checkoff. The Learjet moved toward a runway, and they were wheels-up at 0715.

Burke pulled a dog-eared copy of *Time* from the seat holder and began reading. The jet climbed steeply, entering cloud cover at fifteen thousand feet, breaking clear at twenty thousand, where the sun was blinding. He pulled down the window shade, adjusted his seat, and closed his eyes. Sleep was a good idea, he thought, having no idea when he'd have the chance again.

Puma

Ten

THE LANDING STRIP, lined by rusted flare pots, had been scraped from sunbaked soil. A tin-topped open shed sheltered a few drums of aviation fuel and a table with a transceiver. Above it a striped wind sock hung limply in the sun.

The jet touched down smoothly, reversed thrust immediately, and braked, wheels skidding on the loose surface. For a moment Burke thought they'd overshoot the strip, but the Learjet slowed before reaching spiky cactus, turned, and taxied slowly back toward the radio shed.

A man wearing a black baseball cap, dark sunglasses, and a red jogging suit left the radio and came out to meet the jet, waiting while the stairs unfolded. The copilot called, "This is your destination, sir," and Burke unbuckled. He took his bag and went down the steps. The man came forward. "Good flight?"

"Slept most of the way." Burke blinked at the glare. Behind him he heard the whirring sound of the staircase rising into the fuselage and wished he'd thought to bring dark glasses. The man said, "My name's McIntyre—naturally I'm known as Mac. You're Cardiff, right?" Burke nodded. The man was a couple of inches shorter than Burke, his stride was springy, his face deeply tanned.

The jet was moving toward the end of the strip. Mac said, "I thought you might be bringing mail. No such luck, eh?" He stopped and peered at the jet while Burke kept walking.

Suddenly Burke felt iron against his spine. Mac barked, "Disarm me!"

Burke slammed his right elbow backward into Mac's ribs, whirled, and slammed his bag against Mac's face, knocking off cap and goggles. He tripped Mac's left foot and kicked him backward. Mac fell on his back, but before Burke could go for the pistol in his hand it fired. Burke felt gunpowder strike his face and arm. Mac sat up grinning. "You're dead," he said and blew smoke from the pistol muzzle. "Still, you were pretty good. What you forgot was this baby." He held up the pistol. "Go for the weapon, Cardiff, forget everything else. Now, let's do it right." He sprang up like a gymnast and handed the pistol to Burke, placed himself slightly in front. Burke jabbed the muzzle in Mac's spine, saw Mac's right arm come back and lever the pistol aside. Mac's left hand gripped Burke's pistol wrist and his knee came up from under. Suddenly Burke's grip on the pistol was broken. The weapon would have fallen had Mac not caught it. He tucked it into his trouser top and slapped Burke's shoulder. "I've read your file," he said as they walked toward a jeep parked behind the shed. "Sterilized, of course, and I see that you're a qualified sniper, highly qualified. How well do you do with handguns and knives?"

"Average," Burke said, rubbing his wrist. "Probably *C minus* or *D.* Not much use for them in Nam."

"I know, I know. Well, that's a gap that needs filling. How about unarmed—karate, judo, kung fu?"

"Some judo," Burke said, "but not for a lot of years."

"Will your leg take rough-and-tumble?"

"Depends. The plate's held for fifteen years." He got onto the jeep seat and Mac started the engine.

"You're probably wondering about this place. A lot of drugs passed through here, tons and tons of white cargo. Then DEA moved in and confiscated it from the traffickers who ran it." His arm swept the horizon, flat but for distant mountains. "All this is government property now—'forfeited' is the term of choice. The original owner was a crackpot neo-Nazi with enough money to raise a private army that was going to take over Artesia, recruit sympathizers, and move on to Washington."

"Obviously he wasn't successful."

"Not hardly. He had about thirty sorry types here, Tex-Mexes, wetbacks, and hillbillies, when the FBI cracked down. Colombians bought the place, bulldozed the strip, and used it for drop-off and refueling." Whatever else he said was drowned out by the Learjet screaming off the strip. Burke watched its wheels folding inward, thick dust swirling in its wake.

"How long will I be here?" Burke asked.

"That's pretty much up to you, sir. You're here for physical conditioning, weapons refresher, and targeting. When you feel you're ready, you go."

The jeep bucked down into an arroyo and ground up the far side, and in the distance Burke could see a building that resembled a Spanish-style hacienda. As they neared it he made out a rifle range. To one side of the hacienda stood two long, low buildings. "Barracks?"

"That's where the Nazi nut housed his recruits. We use the buildings for supply storage—the one farthest from the house holds ammo and weapons. There's you, me, Leroy, and Sid. Leroy's the weapons and demolitions specialist, Sid's physical trainer. And there's a Mex cook. I don't know where DEA found her—probably some border whorehouse—but she can wash dishes and laundry and doesn't ask questions." He paused. "You like Mex food?"

"Not much," Burke admitted, "but anything's better than what I got in Peru."

"Up there, were you? Working against the *cocaineros?*"

"Only incidentally. They supplied the Shining Path guerrillas with coca and the guerrillas sold it for arms. They're still doing it."

"So you've had some background in the drug trade."

"I can recognize cocaine by sight, texture, and taste. Also gum opium."

"We've got samples of all that shit, for the neophytes."

They were nearing the white stucco building with the red-tiled roof. "Welcome to El Quiote," Mac said, "and in case you don't know what a *quiote* is, it's a sharp spine along the edge of a maguey leaf. There was a sign here once—like Bonanza's—but the *narcos* took it down for anonymity." He parked the jeep in the shade, and with the engine dead Burke could hear the chuffing of an unseen generator. Burke followed Mac into the air-conditioned house. Mac led the way to the dining room, where two men were drinking coffee, and made brief introductions.

Sid was a tall, well-muscled black, and Leroy a smaller white version. The cook, a plump Mexican woman, waddled in with a cup and saucer for Burke. "You got hunger, señor?"

"*No tengo hambre, gracias,*" Burke said, and was rewarded with a smile.

Sid said, "You'll get a high-protein diet with lots of fluid. What's your weight?"

"One eighty-eight," Burke said, stirring his black coffee.

"You need to lose five or six pounds," Sid said, eyeing him critically. "Been on a regular exercise program?"

Burke shook his head.

Sid smiled. "That'll change. They want you in and out of here fast."

Mac stretched and laid back his head, revealing a long row of stitch-scars where his throat met his chin. A repaired knife slash, Burke recognized. An inch lower would have severed the windpipe, and Mac wouldn't be alive to bark *Disarm me!* and fire his blanks.

Burke scanned his instructors. They looked as hard and combat-ready, as he was not. But he excused himself on the grounds that after Nam he hadn't expected to return to the business of killing. These men, whatever their service origins, were professionals, hired or detailed to prepare him for his mission.

Just what that mission was, they had no need to know—much less his presidential bargain. They were here to do a job, and so was he. It was apparent that Mac, at least, knew something of his background; if they knew he'd been an officer, they'd make it harder for him, so he had to be ready for tough times.

Coffee finished, Burke followed Mac to the second floor, where he was shown a bare corner room. "Presidential suite," Mac cracked. "We're billeted downstairs, near the chow and liquor. Sid's waiting for you."

The corner windows gave Burke a broad view of the outbuildings and surrounding desert. Endless spiky agave and stands of bizarrely twisted Joshua trees poked at the clear sky. A ridge of purple mountains bordered the far distance. The Nazi and the *Colombianos* had chosen the site well, Burke reflected. No casual drop-ins or inquiring reporters.

He unpacked his bag in the bathroom, washed dust from face and hands, and went downstairs. Sid led him outside to the barracks that served as a supply room. There Burke was outfitted with lightweight desert camo, jump boots, and running shoes.

Sid said, "No laundry service here, so dump dirty stuff in a corner—plenty of fresh BDUs to draw from. Everything's expendable."

Including me, Burke thought, and changed into issue battle dress. Sid handed him a canteen and a musette bag, and they moved to the farthest barracks—the armory—where Leroy was waiting.

It had been a long time since Burke had seen so much firepower in one place. M-16s, FALs, Heyms, Uzis, H&Ks, MAC-10s, and Thompsons lined the walls. A long cloth-covered table held a large variety of handguns: Colt Army .45s; Berettas; S&W revolvers; Brownings; Walthers; derringers; Astras; Llamas; sawed-off shotguns, repeating and slide-action. It was a dazzling assortment of weaponry. Ammo crates were stacked along the end of the building.

"Anything you want and don't see," Leroy told him, "we can get."

"Like phoning the corner liquor store."

"Radio contact only." He ran his hand caressingly over several guns on the table. "I see you're rifle-qualified and then some, so we'll concentrate on handguns, okay?"

"Whatever you say," Burke nodded. "In Nam we didn't use pistols."

Leroy reached under the table and brought up an aluminum case. Burke saw four black pistols on the foam lining. Leroy tossed him one and Burke was surprised at its lightness. Leroy picked up another and twirled it by the trigger guard. "A strictly illegal weapon," he said. "Molded from polymer plastic and fiberglass. Eight nine-millimeter shots in the magazine, which is sealed. Use it and throw it away. These are Brazilian versions of the Austrian Glock-seventeen—ever hear of it?"

"I read that a plastic pistol undetectable by airport scanners had been outlawed."

"Right. But there's a demand for them in, let's say, the less law-abiding areas of the world." He twirled the pistol again. "Lacking a metal barrel with lands and grooves, the bullet tumbles, which is short-range okay since it makes for greater shock impact. At twenty feet this baby will put eight rounds in the A zone. At fifty yards, slow fire, you'll still get a minimum of five rounds in the A zone."

Burke handled the light weapon. "Bullet weight?"

"A hundred fifteen grains. Eight rounds fired and the barrel burns out. But if you can't do the job with eight bullets, you've got a problem." He took a plastic holster from the container and thrust the pistol into it." "Concealed carry," he said, "clips *inside* your belt." He reached for Burke's pistol and replaced it in the case. "We'll burn a bunch of these before we're finished." He moved down the table and picked up a small pistol with flat black finish. "Compact Smith and Wesson nine-millimeter," he said, "a real combat piece. Six magazine rounds plus one in the chamber. Weighs four ounces more than the throwaway and it's concealed carry. Great accuracy if you need it." He looked questioningly at Burke, who said, "The drug thugs seem to favor Ingrams and MAC-tens."

"Sure, for close-up work. Like, you pull up alongside another car and spray it with a MAC-ten. Those steel-jacketed rounds tear through the car—both sides—and anything in between." He paused. "Like bodies."

Moving down the table, Leroy opened a thin aluminum case and took out what looked, at first glance, like a toy model of a Buck Rogers ray gun. Its flat-sided barrel was holed with vents its entire length. No point in asking, Burke figured, Leroy would tell him—in detail.

"Space-age technology," Leroy said, gripping and sighting the pistol away from Burke. "The Gyrojet. This is the fifty-one caliber version banned by the nineteen sixty-eight Gun Control Act. No gunpowder in the casing—the projectile is fired by solid rocket propellant, which accounts for the vented barrel." He handed Burke a round. "The steel-jacketed projectile contains an explosive that detonates on impact. Let's step outside."

They went into the sunlight, and Burke followed his instructor to a stand mounting a steel slab two feet square. "Three-eighths thick," Leroy said, "which is the max on armored limousines." He walked back to the ten-yard line and motioned Burke to stand behind him. Then, taking the Weaver stance, both hands gripping the pistol, Leroy fired.

The detonation was deafening. The impact explosion echoed and a thin line of white smoke momentarily connected weapon and target. "Hell of a bang," Burke remarked, checking out the two-inch crater. "Think of the Gyrojet as a pocket bazooka," Leroy suggested. "Take out the driver, and the vehicle either stops or smashes. The explosive projectile is especially effective against choppers, when they're in range."

He handed the rocket pistol to Burke, who saw that it was formed of die-stamped metal. "What's effective range?"

"Around twenty-five yards. As I say, it's a special-purpose weapon. The projectile passes through a side of beef without exploding, so it's not ideal for human targets." He took back the pistol. "Unless you want to scare them to death," he added with a grim smile.

"What'll they think of next?" Burke asked rhetorically as they walked back into the armory.

At the near end Leroy lifted a trapdoor and turned on an overhead light. In the cool concrete-lined bunker were crates of explosive: dynamite; gelignite; 4-X; plastique; and several cartons labeled SEMTEX. Tapping one, Leroy said, "This is a Czech-made explosive they used to export to the Middle East. It's a terrorist favorite because airport sniffer dogs can't detect it. The stuff is malleable, so it's modeled into toys and souvenirs, dries hard in the sun. Goes off with a detonator, or you can fire a round into it and it'll explode. Lots of nasty uses." He opened a dynamite crate's lid and drew out an orange stick, scraped the side with one finger. "Guess you know nitroglycerin seeps out of this stuff when the temperature's too high." He grunted. "Castro's people stored a couple of tons of dynamite in an old Spanish bunker between La Cabaña and El Morro, but those assholes forgot about temperature control. Nitro pooled and damn near took out East Havana." He chuckled. "Naturally CIA got credit for that one—the glorious revolutionaries couldn't admit incompetence. So Soviet advisers showed them how to build an air-conditioned ammo storage, and there hasn't been a major explosion in Old Havana in a long, long time." He spat on the duckboard flooring. "Too bad."

"Yeah."

Leroy replaced the stick and checked a thermometer. "So this is what you'll be working with, Cardiff. Sid wants you now, so you and I'll start on the range tomorrow, okay?"

A section of the hacienda basement was an exercise room, carpeted, and featuring weight stands, rowing machines, a big Nautilus rig and a bubbling Jacuzzi. Burke stripped to his shorts and Sid gave him a strength test: legs, back, and arms. "So we know where to start," he explained. "I don't favor jogging in the desert—dehydration and heat exhaustion can come on before you know it—so there's a cycle. Pedal a mile now, relax in the Jacuzzi, and we'll have dinner."

Pedaling a measured mile at low resistance winded Burke, whose leg pained from the unaccustomed strain. The warm Jacuzzi restored him, and he was hungry by the time he reached the mess table. Mac, Sid, and Leroy indulged in Mexican food, but Burke was given a charbroiled steak trimmed of fat, a salad with lemon-juice dressing, and sugar-free Kool-Aid.

After dinner he walked around the hacienda's outbuildings, heeding his instructors' warning about rattlesnakes, and when the sun set behind indigo mountains, Burke went to his room, opened the screened windows, and got into bed. As night blanketed the desert he could hear owls and coyotes, the whisper of a jet far overhead. He was physically and mentally tired. The new environment was a strange one, and he wondered when his first human target would be presented.

He thought of Claire Newsome, remembering the smooth warmth of her body against his. It seemed unlikely that she was on the pill. Were she pregnant, the responsibility was equally his, but he hoped that she was not. They needed time to probe and discover, laugh and do foolish things, explore the range of their common interests, their compatibility.

For all he knew, Claire, thwarted, could turn into a shrew. For all she knew, liquor made him coarse and brutal. So there was an entire human landscape to survey. God willing, they would do it together.

His thoughts turned to the reason for his being in this desert stronghold—his brother Terry. Slowly, as often before, his mind examined aspects of his brother's crime.

Usually people did funny things with money out of greed. That was part of Terry's motivation, but it also involved Terry's willingness to please. Although Terry's income had been enviably high, his overhead—including Kirby—was enormous, and as a junior partner Terry was not included in the year-end bonus, when full partners divided the golden melon among themselves. Terry aspired to full partnership, of course; it was the corporate way. And distinguishing himself from his peers had seduced him into chicanery the law termed felonious.

The night air was turning cool. Burke heard lizards cheeping and croaking in the roof tiles, calling mates, exchanging nocturnal information among their tribe. Clouds parted, the gilded moon appeared. Burke slept.

Eleven

HIS DAY BEGAN at sunup with cereal, juice, and a plate of sliced melon and papaya. While breakfast was settling, Mac showed Burke the communications room at the rear of the first floor. It contained VHF/VO radio equipment patched to a scrambler; tape recorders; teleprinter; and dissimilar black boxes stored on shelves. "As a quasi-government outfit, we don't communicate much," Mac told him, "which is a blessing. Some of this we inherited from the *narco-traficantes*, saving us a few bucks when this place was set up."

And how long ago was that? Burke wondered, but said only, "And another set at the airstrip."

Mac nodded. "For ground-air messages. When we need supplies or equipment we transmit on this setup. Usually it's flown in a day later." He yawned. "Too much poker last night—lost eighty bucks—but I'll win it back tonight. Our TV's on the blink and no repairmen around, so they'll fetch us a new one. Nights can get pretty boring around here." They left the room, Mac locking the door behind him. From there they went down to the gym, where Mac outfitted Burke in a white karate uniform and cup jock. He produced an unloaded pistol, a rubber imitation hunting knife, and a nightstick. "Okay," he said, "you may have had all or part of this at Bragg or Benning, but the point I want to impress on you is that the aim of close combat is to kill or seriously disable your opponent. It's not fancy-dancy karate with ballet moves and shouting—that's show-time shit, right?"

Burke nodded, flexing his muscles.

"Eyes, balls, throat, neck, spinal cord—all targets. We'll go through disarming an opponent using each of these weapons. Then, unarmed hand-to-hand, okay?"

"Okay," Burke said as Mac's foot rammed at his throat in a swift sideways kick. Burke moved aside, grabbed the ankle, twisted, and as Mac went down he jammed his foot in Mac's crotch, hitting the protective cup hard.

From the padded mat Mac looked up in surprise. "Okay, fine." He picked up the pistol and tossed it to Burke, then did a spring flip to his feet. "You've got the piece—what do you do?"

The pistol was pointed at Mac. Burke pulled the trigger three times.

"Right! Don't fuck around like in the movies."

Together they went through a series of attacks and fend-offs with each weapon, exchanging roles after Mac's initial demonstrations. When the hour buzzer rang, Burke was perspiring heavily, and his body ached from kicks and punches he hadn't been able to dodge. Mac tossed him a towel and showed him where to hang his sweat-stained uniform. "Leroy gets you next," he said, "and for a first session this went pretty well. Leg hurt bad?"

"Always hurts some," Burke told him. "Always will." He changed into fatigues and went out to the pistol range where Leroy was waiting beside a bench. Morning sunlight glinted from a spread of handguns on the table. An insulated drink cooler held boxes of ammunition and extra magazines. Profile targets were staggered down along the range. Burke picked up a visored cap and put it on. Leroy grasped an S&W nine-millimeter Model 639, put on foam ear protectors, and handed Burke a set. "We're not here to match-shoot Olympic trials," he said in his Southwestern drawl. "We're learning quick-draw, quick-fire, combat crouch, aiming stance, stuff like that, which'll help you kill fast and walk away. Put on your earmuffs."

Leroy spun around, dropped, and fired five times—so rapidly the individual pops blended. Peering down-range, Burke saw a well-placed hole in each of the five targets. After blowing smoke from the muzzle, Leroy said, "You notice I didn't aim and squeeze off—I pointed—the way you point your finger. One hand. Because there were five mothers down there comin' at me. Choose your weapon."

From the table, Burke took up the compact S&W he'd handled yesterday. "This one." He ejected the magazine, seated it, and chambered a round.

"Okay, back to the targets. One . . . two . . . *Go!*"

Burke whirled, dropped into a crouch, and began firing at the targets in order of distance. He stood up and saw that none of his bullets had hit. Patiently Leroy demonstrated the principles of point-firing until Burke could hit three targets—the closest—in under three seconds. "Keep at it," Leroy ordered and refilled Burke's magazines.

Burke noticed a hawk at ten o'clock. Its wings folded in a whistling dive, and from between targets four and five a jackrabbit bounded away from them. Leroy's arm shot out and he fired once. The jack lifted a yard and dropped dead. The hawk's wings braked; it orbited a few moments, then glided down and snatched up the motionless jack. "Life and death in the desert," Leroy observed, "and meat for the nest. Okay, Cardiff, stay with it."

Using yesterday's strength-test tables, Sid adjusted the bars, pulls, and levers, and told Burke how many sets he was to accomplish. "The point here is conditioning, muscle tone." He fitted Burke into the Nautilus frame and had him grip the pull bars. "Deep breath before exertion, let it out as you pull, okay?"

It felt as though he were trying to pull down a building, yet Sid had lowered the bar with one hand. Burke strained until the bar was chest-low, then let it up slowly. Sid took off a ten-pound weight. "Smoothly, rhythmically, don't grunt and strain. Easy does it."

This time the pull was slightly easier, but Burke's back and shoulder muscles were groaning. Set completed, he moved to the next machine, then the next, and so on until sweat salted his eyes and his heart beat like timpani.

The Jacuzzi, then a walk around the hacienda and lunch: meat, vegetables, and Kool-Aid. Everyone took an hour's siesta before resuming work. Afternoon repeated the morning's drills until sundown. Dinner and bed.

He was wakened by the sound of a plane coming in. He looked out and saw flare pots outlining the landing strip, heard the jeep engine, and returned stiffly into bed. In the morning there was a new TV in the living room, orange juice at breakfast, and lamb chops for lunch.

After five days of workouts and instruction Burke felt well satisfied with his instructors. Although he had no way of knowing how long they had worked together, he sensed an easy camaraderie among them and an acceptance of their roles. They seemed, he thought, like lodge brothers. He decided that Leroy was—or had been—army, a rated handgun expert on a competition team. Sid used the word *gear* and the phrase *standing watch,* suggesting navy background. Mac, he extrapolated, had served in the marines, then joined the Seals, for at one meal Mac mentioned the difficulty of getting through heavy surf in an inflatable boat, then struggling ashore under heavy equipment. Whatever their background, Burke realized that if his missions failed, it would not be for inadequate preparation.

On the sixth night, after dinner, Mac took Burke into the commo room and opened a safe set into the floor, concealed under a serape. He withdrew a brown package closed with plastic bands and red wax seals. "For you and only you," he said, handing it to Burke. "Read it here and put it back in the safe, okay?"

He left the room and Burke cut the heavy bands, then tore off the waxed wrapper, exposing a red-covered loose-leaf notebook. Across its top was a single hand-lettered word: PUMA.

Puma? Burke opened the notebook and saw an 8 × 10 glossy of a man's face. He stared at it, absorbing details: broad, Indian nose, swarthy skin, heavy dark hair that looked like an unkempt wig. Scraggly hairs covered his upper cheeks, thickening into a full beard that joined scalp hair at the ears. Lips were mostly hidden by a flowing mustache, but the lower one was thick and sensual. Eyes narrow, heavy-lidded. From the left eye's corner a thin scar—souvenir of a knife fight in his youth, Burke thought; he guessed Puma's age at thirty-five or thirty-six.

He turned the sheet and saw color prints taken with telephoto lens. Puma getting out of a long limousine. Puma exiting a building. Puma entering a discotheque. Puma's head and shoulders in a parked car on a shady street. In each the subject wore tailored leisure clothes. Light reflected from wrist jewelry and heavy gold necklaces. He wore pointed boots or shoes. The fifth shot showed a pistol grip protruding from his belt. The sixth showed Puma standing at the doorway of a Beech 400 jet, whose silhouette had all the grace that Puma's lacked.

So this is Puma, he said to himself. Nasty-looking bastard. Target Number One. *Numero Uno.* Read on, Thomas, and learn why the president wants him down.

The following page, top and bottom, was stamped:

SENSITIVE

LIMDIS/NOFORN

meaning the material was sensitive, required limited distribution, and was not to be seen by foreigners. The issuing-classifying agency was not identified, unsurprisingly.

Puma's name was given as Luís Quintana Rios, the third name being the matronymic, and it was vaguely familiar to Burke in connection with newspaper and magazine stories of the narcotics trade. Puma's underworld aliases were listed as *"El Ciclón"* (the cyclone), *"El Rey"* (the king), and *"El Varón"* (the kid). Only a partial listing, according to a notation.

Luís Quintana had been born to peasant parents in the mountain village of Tecotitlán, Sinaloa, some eighty miles from the state capital of Culiacán. Birth date uncertain. His parents were probably not married, not unusual in rural Mexico, and his present age was believed to be thirty-six—from passport and related civil documentation.

Quintana had attended the village's one-room school long enough to learn numbers and the alphabet. He was able to sign his name but was otherwise said to be illiterate. As a child he helped his father plant corn, raise chickens, and forage the hills for firewood they sold in the village. He stole rice from the *tienda* and toys from his playmates, quickly becoming a clever thief.

When a truck slid off a mountain road, killing the driver, Quintana pillaged it, stole the driver's wallet and revolver, and killed a soldier guarding the scene. Quintana was fifteen at the time. Leaving Tecotitlán ahead of the rural police, Quintana emerged in Culiacán as one of a gutter gang—*rateros*—who snatched purses and broke into automobiles. Arrested, he served eight months in a brutal prison which became his college and graduate schools in crime. Quintana developed his body, first to withstand prison violence, then to apply his own. The scope of his crimes increased: house burglary, armed robbery, two banks, a travel agency. Again arrested, he found that bribes would spare him another prison term, a lesson Quintana never forgot.

The mayor of Culiacán had enemies political and commercial, among them *campesino* leaders opposed to his appropriation of peasants' lands. Quintana was hired as one of the mayor's enforcers, and was believed to have murdered the head of the chamber of commerce, a political rival, and two *campesinos* who had threatened the mayor's life.

By then Mexico had become the principal exporter of marijuana, and a few farsighted entrepreneurs had begun growing poppies for the heroin refiners. Quintana returned to his home village and induced former playmates and neighbors to cultivate marijuana in place of corn—poppies where *frijoles* had grown. In short, Quintana formed an agricultural collective, whose harvest he marketed to middlemen in Culiacán. Cement block houses rose where adobe huts had been for generations. Quintana brought electricity, telephones, and running water to the village, became a local hero protected by the villagers whenever army or police came around, as they occasionally did. Quintana organized other mountain villages as he had organized Tecotitlán, finding the *campesinos* eager.

Quintana was believed to have murdered a powerful middleman and taken over his distribution network into Texas, California, and New Mexico. To protect his burgeoning business, Quintana gave a share of his proceeds to the mayor of Culiacán, the governor of Sinaloa, and the military commander of the region. Now he could expand with impunity.

Well aware that marijuana was a big-volume, high-risk product to transport, Quintana developed relationships with cocaine producers in Medellín, Cali, and Bogotá, flew bulk cocaine into Sinaloa and arranged its onward shipment by trucks, mules, and low-flying aircraft. Cuban exile *narcotraficantes* in Miami bought cocaine and heroin from Quintana, filtered it into the Florida Keys aboard high-speed racing boats. Invited to view their operation firsthand, Quintana boarded a rusty freighter—the mother ship—in Veracruz for the voyage to the Keys. Offshore the mother ship heaved to and unloaded three tons of cocaine and heroin into Cigarette speedboats. Never having been outside Mexico before, Quintana decided to touch U.S. soil, and started ashore on a speedboat. It was intercepted by the Coast Guard, Quintana was arrested and arraigned in Miami. Without a U.S. criminal record, Quintana was granted bail of a hundred thousand dollars. On leaving the federal courthouse, after less than forty hours in the United States, Quintana caught a taxi to the airport and a plane to Mexico City.

Back in Sinaloa, Quintana developed a private army and air force to safeguard his supplies and ensure their transportation. He invested in real estate in Guadalajara, Mexico City, Mazatlán, and Acapulco, in restaurants, condominiums, and travel agencies. He bought a bank to launder his money, developed fraternal ties with banks in Miami, Switzerland, Nassau, and Panama. In Culiacán, Quintana constructed a thirty-room pleasure dome with ballroom, concealed behind a twelve-foot wall, with the latest electronic protective system and a cohort of armed guards. His wealth was such that Quintana built a duplicate palace near the outskirts of Guadalajara, whose mayor was said to be in his pay.

Arrested by the attorney general of Jalisco for "crimes against the national health," Quintana was imprisoned. After bribing the warden, Quintana was allowed to have a spacious suite constructed in his cell block. Decorators brought in fabrics and expensive furniture; a modern kitchen was installed. Prison guards kept his freezers stocked with delicacies, and prostitutes came to entertain Quintana when TV movies bored him. Two reliable informants stated that Quintana's carpeted "cell" contained a wardrobe of thirty tailored suits and at least twenty pairs of custom-made reptile-skin boots. He also had three telephones, a shortwave radio, four handguns, two shotguns, stun grenades, cases of champagne, whiskey, gin, and vodka. On occasion Quintana had shown other inmates as much as three hundred thousand U.S. dollars in his suite.

Quintana's lawyers suborned a judge who, for a half-million-dollar bribe, dismissed charges and freed Quintana before the minister of foreign affairs could rule on a pending U.S. request for his extradition.

Repeated efforts to persuade Mexican authorities either to extradite Quintana to the United States or to suppress his massive trafficking were met with diplomatic smiles and promises—and no action. Upon Quintana's release from prison he resumed shipping narcotics to the United States in amounts estimated at no less than two hundred tons annually, making him the largest narcotics distributor in the western hemisphere.

Witnesses against Quintana for the torture-murder of two DEA officers near Guadalajara were either murdered or "disappeared." Before the two officers died, they were hung by their feet and skinned. Allegedly Quintana gave the order and was present, drinking brandy and enjoying the barbaric scene. Recently a DEA officer, his wife and four children had to be emergency air-evacuated from Guadalajara when it was discovered that they were being followed by thugs from Quintana's organization. The officer—since reassigned to ZI—had developed a successful penetration of Quintana's organization. The informant was detected and under torture revealed the officer's name, whereupon Quintana ordered his family kidnapped, tortured, and killed along with the DEA officer.

Quintana had proved immune to prosecution on either side of the Rio Grande. That he had enemies and narcotics rivals, however, was evidenced by numerous attempts on his life, so far frustrated by bodyguards. A personal aircraft Quintana was about to board blew up on the ground because of a faulty timer-detonating device. Journalists in Quintana's pay blamed the attempt on the DEA; however, informants stated that a member of the Cali Cartel was responsible.

Quintana has used marijuana and cocaine, and had been observed injecting heroin, but was not believed to be addicted.

Mexican informants indicated that Quintana was most vulnerable in Guadalajara, where he relaxed in restaurants, and at five-star hotels, cockfights, and nightclubs. On these R&R trips from Culiacán Quintana brought five or six trusted lieutenants with him, leaving bodyguards at his base.

Quintana was always armed, as were his aides. Customarily Quintana traveled around Guadalajara by night, in either a black Mercedes limousine, a black Grand Marquis, or a Rolls Silver Cloud.

Quintana was believed to be unmarried, having remarked publicly that he would be foolish to have a wife and children vulnerable to enemies. His most visible mistress was a Mexican TV soap actress, Luana Villaverde, whom he visited on trips to Mexico City. Quintana had supplied Villaverde with a luxury condominium in the Zona Rosa, servants, a chauffeured Mercedes-Benz sedan, expensive jewelry, and costumes from Paris couturiers. Her personal bodyguard was in Quintana's employ; he was said to be a former member of the judicial police dismissed for brutality, and a firearms and close-combat expert.

The entrance to Villaverde's condo building was guarded and equipped with video scanners. Her condominium, on the top floor, was protected with security devices. No successful burglary of the building had ever been accomplished. A color photo from a Mexican magazine showed Luana Villaverde seated at a table, drink in hand. Her hair was long, the color of red gold; her face boasted high cheek bones, cool dark eyes, sensual lips, and a challenging expression. Other faces at her table had been airbrushed out, Quintana's presumably among them.

Closing the briefing book, Burke massaged eyes tired from the burning sun of the pistol range. After a while he opened his eyes and speed-read the last four pages of text. He reflected on Quintana's trips to Guadalajara, away from his guarded compound and protecting army. The "trusted lieutenants", of course, would be trained killers, but if they were all having dope . . .

He recalled the smoky, boisterous atmosphere of a cockfight ring, the shouting of bettors; two hundred men pressed close together around the sand-centered circle. Everyone concentrating on the jumping, hacking birds . . . opportunities for close-in knife work or a pistol shot muffled by the roaring crowd. A dead man would be held upright by the pressure of bodies around him, until the fight was over and the crowd broke up to gulp tequila and collect winning bets. . . .

But except for infrequent licensed occasions, cockfighting was illegal in Mexico. Even so, he reminded himself, illegal cockfighting was commonplace in Mexico as in Puerto Rico, Los Angeles, Miami, and the Dominican Republic, so there had to be clandestine sites all over Mexico.

He couldn't track Puma night after night without being noticed. Local ground support would be needed, along with a current list of Puma's haunts.

He returned the red binder to the safe, closed the door, and spun the dial, then covered it with the bright serape.

His trainers were watching TV, Burke noticed. Mac turned his head, "Finished?"

Burke nodded and went up to his room. He felt almost too tired to shower, but the pummeling hot water would relax his muscles and help him sleep.

In bed Burke wondered what they thought of him, his trainers, the specialists. They knew he'd been military, done Nam, knew he was rifle-qualified, sniper-rated, knew he was preparing for some special deal. SENSITIVE LIMDIS/NOFORN.

Too bad the president didn't demand I shoot three perfect range scores. Hard enough under ideal conditions, but easy as breathing compared to filling three body bags with human targets to buy my brother's freedom.

I know about Puma now; who are the other two?

Fatigue fogged his mind. He slept.

Twelve

TWO WEEKS INTO CONDITIONING, Burke was pedaling five miles against strong tension, pressing two hundred, and curling one-fifty. Diet and exercise had flattened his belly and toned his muscles, and he was handgunning with a speed and precision that surprised both Leroy and himself. And Burke's defensive combat sessions with Mac were finding Mac pinned as often as Burke. Burke calculated that another ten days would see him as skilled and fit as he was likely to get.

Late that afternoon Leroy had taken Burke to a position near a series of gopher holes. As the sun dropped, gophers emerged on the rim of their holes, and cautiously began to search for food. Leroy fired into the air and as six gophers spurted for their holes Burke dropped three with five rapid shots. "Hurrah," Leroy said laconically. "You hit behind those last two—point *ahead* of a fast-moving target."

Burke nodded sheepishly, mentally excusing himself on the grounds that his reflexes weren't as sharp as the younger man's. But against Quintana and his thugs, excuses didn't count. He'd have to do better.

Walking back to the armory, Burke refilled his pistol's magazine, homed it, and pocketed the pistol. "Good idea to get used to its weight," Leroy said. "A concealable like that should be as much part of you as your belly button. Tomorrow, for a change, you might want to spend a couple hours on the long-gun range. There's a factory-fresh Mannlicher and a twelve-power scope. I figure you'll want to polish the bolt and trigger sear before firing."

Cosmoline had been stripped from the weapon's metal, and the gun lay in its wooden case, burled walnut stock gleaming in the light of the overhead bulb. "Beautiful," Burke said admiringly, lifting it. The fore-end and pistol grip were checkered, the barrel and action were finished in deep matte. It was tapped for scope mounts that hadn't been emplaced. Conventional hunting sights—rear leaf and front ramp—were factory set.

Leroy took sheets of jeweler-fine emery cloth from a drawer and handed them to Burke along with a box of .375 H&H cartridges. "Jungle Jim," he said, "you're set for safari."

"I guess. But I don't usually shoot heavier than thirty-aught-six."

"Then this'll give your shoulder a thrill—if it doesn't fracture it." He turned off lights and they left through the open door. As they walked toward the house Burke said, "I've noticed things are pretty free and easy around here. Doors never locked, no guard dogs. . . ."

Leroy smiled. "Who's gonna drop in? The Nazi nut's in Leavenworth and the druggies are either jailed or back in Colombia. No one knows about this place, Cardiff, which is why we use it. If we had to hire perimeter guards and get sensors installed, too many people would know." He glanced around. "The desert's our best protection."

After a dinner of sirloin steak, bean sprouts, salad, and Kool-Aid, Burke watched TV for a while with his trainers. The program was a replay of last winter's Super Bowl, and because Burke remembered the final score he lost interest after the first quarter.

In his room he took down the Mannlicher's action and felt carefully for metal burrs. The trigger pull was heavy, so he sanded the sear and the action before reassembling it. He slid six heavy-caliber cartridges into the magazine and checked spring feed and ejection. Tomorrow he'd mount the scope, using tools from the armory. Burke leaned the rifle against the wall beside his bed, placed his compact S&W on the nightstand, and took a relaxing shower.

He heard television sounds till the game ended, and the big hacienda lay quiet. Beyond his screened window the moon was a fragile silver crescent. He watched it and listened to crickets and lizards, the faint hoot of a cactus-dwelling owl, and the mournful call of a distant coyote. Then clouds hid the moon, and Burke turned over and slept.

Because his senses were attuned to the silence and tranquility of the desert, Burke heard the plane come over. It was only a couple of thousand feet high, he thought groggily, twin props with the distinctive signature of an old C-47. He wondered if the pilot was lost in this wilderness, searching for ground lights to find his course again.

The plane seemed to be making a wide circle. As its sound diminished, Burke thought, Lotsa luck, empathizing with a fellow pilot in difficulties, and tried to summon sleep. But some atavistic instinct kept him conscious. Out of the night came soft swooshing sounds—like a brush on velvet. Or air escaping from a parachute canopy.

But that was too unlikely to consider, unless some parachute club was night-jumping and had chosen the airstrip as a landing zone. Even that possibility seemed remote; jumpers and their gear were normally retrieved by ground vehicles, but as far as Burke knew there was no usable road to the hacienda.

After a while he got out of bed and looked through both corner windows. Far away he thought he could make out a tiny orange light on or near the airstrip. Odd, he thought, unless his trainers were conducting some kind of night exercise they hadn't told him about. In darkness he found the 12-power rifle scope and trained it on the distant light. Under focus it became a single flare pot, flame wavering, almost dying in the breeze. Nothing more. Otherwise the strip was bare. Slowly he scanned the darkness, wishing for a night-vision scope as in Nam, saw motion near the supply-room barracks, and made out a figure jogging toward the entrance. One of his trainers? He watched until the figure disappeared through the open door, decided its movements lacked the fluid coordination of his instructors.

So who was it? One of the Nazi bundists returned to pilfer uniforms and military supplies? Hastily Burke pulled on running shoes, fatigue pants, and shirt. He'd ambush the intruder, get a fix on his identify, the reason for his intrusion. Practice his skills in a real-life situation.

He was reaching for the Mannlicher rifle when the floor beneath exploded in long bursts of automatic weapons fire.

Stunned by the ripping volume, Burke was frozen in flashback to the An Phuac ambush. The noise was almost deafening, Charlie was firing everything he had. His mind cleared and he gripped the rifle.

But for spotting the intruder Burke might have thought Sid, Mac, and Leroy were holding a lethal shoot-out, but when the firing ceased he heard male voices shouting in Spanish.

His skin was clammy, breathing hard and rapid.

"*¿Solo tres?*" came a voice from below.

"*Sí, Jorge, tres acabados.*"

"*Hay cuatro, chico. Busca arriba.*"

Two men pounding up the staircase. Burke grasped the S&W and lay flat facing the open door. A flash beam flickered along the hallway, doors opened and slammed shut, heavy footsteps neared.

Suddenly the beam penetrated his room, settled on the bed. Burke fired at the source—twice—and rolled over. A man screamed and fell heavily away. In Burke's nostrils gun smoke was like adrenalin. He felt the rush, crawled belly down, elbows and knees, until he lay parallel to the wall beside the door.

"*¡Carajo!*" the shot man's partner cursed. The fallen light showed his boots and legs. An angle shot. Burke pointed above the legs as muzzle flash seared his vision. A long burst raked his bed. Half-blinded, Burke squeezed off three rounds, saw the muzzle flashes train upward as the man fell back still pressing the trigger, bullets slamming into the ceiling, bringing down a shower of plaster dust and chips. The magazine emptied, and the corridor was still.

"*¿Qué pasa?*" from below.

Throat dry, Burke shouted, "*Nada. Está bien,*" and got up. Only two rounds in his pistol. He reached between the two bodies and snatched up the flashlight. If he waited too long the man below—apparently the team leader—would get suspicious, cautious. The fight had to be taken to the enemy. Burke clumped noisily toward the head of the stairs and shouted, "*¡Ven acá!*" Come here!

"*¿Tiraste el cuarto?*" Did you shoot the fourth?

"*Sí, claro que sí.*" Hell yes.

"*Voy.*" I'm coming.

Burke tiptoes into a doorway and thrust out the flashlight as the man began running up the staircase.

He came up gripping a Uzi at port arms. *"¿Dónde?"* he called. Where?

"Aquí." Burke waved the flashlight.

But something made the man suspicious. *"¿Quién habla?"* Who's talking? He asked, lowering the Uzi to firing position.

"Jorge," Burke replied, fixed the light on his body and fired once.

The nine-millimeter impact slammed the man against the wall. Reflex fired the Uzi, but it was rising, spraying bullets wildly. Burke fired his last round and saw it hit high on the chest. The receiver locked open as the man slumped down and forward, the Uzi now silent.

Three down, Burke thought as he pocketed the empty pistol. He went to his room, stepping over the first two bodies to grab his rifle. It had never been fired, he didn't know how the sights were set, what range, deflection . . . but it was what he had, and a fourth killer was loose outside and warned.

Burke paused to kick the third body, but the man was dead, eyes like agates in the flash beam. He switched off the light and pocketed the flash as he went down the stairs. No point in checking the trainers' rooms. His throat tightened.

He left the hacienda by the front door, staying low, crouching as he rounded the corner of the house. Damn, should have brought the scope. He could see the supply-room barracks now. Its lights went off. *Shit!* Burke bellied down and crawled forward. Had to see the guy to shoot him.

The plane was coming back. From its altered sound—flaps down, prop pitch increased for better bite—Burke knew it was going to land. How many men aboard? Pilot, copilot? Backup team?

He thought he saw a shadow flit out of the doorway. The first intruder? Had to down him before he could warn away the plane. The man had turned on his flashlight. He was running toward the distant strip, his light bouncing and swaying over the uneven terrain.

Stay and fight, you mother, Burke breathed, got up and began racing after him, his running shoes almost soundless on the ground.

Cactus tore at his thin trousers, spiked thighs and arms as he trailed the moving light.

He could see the plane now by its running lights, no landing lights yet from the wings. Was there an all-okay signal the pilot was waiting for? A row of flare pots?

Burke remembered walkie-talkies hooked onto the belts of the three men he'd killed. The fourth man must have one, too. *That* was how he could warn the plane. . . . He pounded on, tripping on the rim of a gopher hole, mind racing faster than his legs. Would the fourth man warn the plane? Wave off his only escape from the dark death trap?

He was closing on the light, the other man slowing, not accustomed to distance running as Burke was.

The plane passed high over the airstrip. Burke estimated altitude at a thousand feet. As he ran he watched it, saw it keep flying toward the mountains.

The ground light was stationary. Shoot now? Halting, panting, Burke raised the rifle, laid his cheek against the stock, and slid off the safety. The bastard was calling the plane. Have to chance it now. Estimated distance eighty yards, no crosswind. Body will be two to three feet to left of light. *Squeeze.*

The rifle bucked, but the light didn't waver. *Shit*, he's warned now, knows he's being hunted. The light moved. A long burst cut cactus to Burke's right. He fired at the muzzle flashes and heard a yell. The gun stopped firing.

Burke ran left, then headed toward the source of the flashes. Maybe the guy's only playing possum, waiting for me—that's what I'd do, alone in the dark, uncertain. . . . Burke slowed to a fast walk, circled closer, wanting to approach from behind, wondering what was going on in the vanished plane.

He could see the man's flashlight on the ground behind a clump of cactus. Burke moved quietly, holding the Mannlicher with both hands, ready to snap-shoot at the first sign of life. Was the man talking to the plane? Burke couldn't hear anything. He dropped low, still circling, listening. . . .

A walkie-talkie squawked near the light. The man wasn't talking back. Maybe he was down, unable to move, the walkie-talkie unreach-able amid cactus.

Twenty yards. W/T still squawking. Burke itched to get his hands on it, bring the plane in. He stopped dead and listened. Heard the snick of a bolt. The guy was waiting for him. Burke propped his flashlight in a cactus crotch, turned it on and moved quickly away.

From the ground, muzzle flashes erupted. The flashlight splintered, died as Burke fired at the flashes. Four rounds, the fourth bringing a scream of pain. No more flashes. Belly down, Burke crawled toward where he'd been firing, praying he wouldn't squeeze a sidewinder into striking.

Suddenly he was crawling on fabric, smooth as silk.

A parachute canopy.

Clouds cleared the moon, showing him a tumbled black canopy. Others nearby. One, two, three harness buckles glinting showed the fourth. Okay, *four* assault parachutists . . . unless a fifth had landed elsewhere. A distinct possibility.

Close enough now to hear stertorous breathing, a groan now and then. Moonlight reflected from the man's eyes. In prone position, Burke fired at them, saw them vanish in the muzzle blast. As the echo died away the desert was silent. No sound from the walkie-talkie. Either the pilot was spooked or the plane was too far away for reception.

Burke lay listening for movement, breathing . . . anything. Slowly he crawled forward until he could see a black-garbed figure outlined on the lighter sand. If the guy was still alive . . . too bad. Burke sighted on the chest, a down-angle shot, closed his eyes to avoid flash blindness and squeezed off the coup de grace. The body jumped like a sack of rags, lay still. Burke got up and walked to it.

His shot at the eyes had torn off half the man's head; the last shot had been redundant. Burke gripped the warm barrel and eased himself down beside the body. An Uzi lay in the sand near the right hand, the walkie-talkie a yard away, not far from the turned-off flashlight. Burke turned it on and looked around.

Three bodies in the hacienda, the fourth at his feet. He hoped only four men had come. He picked up the walkie-talkie and set it in a pocket. Then, holding flashlight and rifle, he jogged back to the big house.

Entering by the kitchen door, he turned on lights, noticed dinner dishes in the sink, and remembered the cook. Where was *mamacita?* He left the kitchen and went to his trainers' quarters. Their room lights were on; each one was dead in his bed: Mac, Sid, and Leroy, their bodies torn and bloody. Bile rose in his throat; he forced it down, left the corridor, and entered the commo room. Shot up, radio equipment destroyed. He flicked the transmit toggle to confirm it.

Christ, what motive was there? *Why had they come?* It was an organized assault. He went back to the rooms and pulled sheets over his comrades' faces, turned off their lights. Whatever its intent, the assault had ended in disaster. Seven bodies. He was the only survivor.

Without warning a chill coursed through him, and he began to shake. It had happened before in Nam, postbattle trauma. He forced his feet to carry him to the liquor cabinet, grabbed the nearest bottle, and drank deeply. As the liquor warmed his body, the shaking stopped. He wondered how to get word to Arness. Well, there was a ground-air transceiver at the airstrip shack. Maybe he could call a ham, somehow get through to his Virginia contact number. As a last resort he could walk to Artesia—wherever it lay from the hacienda— but not by night through the desert. He took another long pull from the bottle, felt his stomach rise, but kept it down.

Why had the first intruder—the last man killed—gone to the supply room? The armory seemed a more worthwhile destination. Only boots, clothing, and equipment in the supply room. Had he been confused between two identical barracks? No, the man had a light on, had been busy.

As he traversed the kitchen, Burke noticed the dirty dishes brought *mamacita* to mind again. Someone had told the assault team there were four men in the hacienda. The vanished cook had known what was coming, left the dishes, and decamped into the night. He hadn't seen the jeep; she must have taken it while all of them slept. *Damn her!*

On his way to the supply room Burke detoured to the armory for ammunition. He refilled pistol and rifle magazines, tucked a spare for the S&W in his pocket.

His gaze fell on the long table, and the rocket pistol seemed to jump into view. Take it along, he thought, could be an armored half-track out there.

He hung a loaded Uzi over one shoulder and left the armory, entering the supply room. There he turned on the overhead light and walked down the aisle between piles of footwear and clothing.

The first intruder had known what he was doing—he'd found the right building and gone to work.

At the far end the flooring was lifted into a trapdoor. Burke shined his light on what lay below and saw at least a dozen bulging body bags lying in a large pit. The zipper of the nearest one was partway down, showing clear plastic bags. He poked the bag open with the rifle sight, took a pinch and tasted. Coke.

He spat it out, but it left his tongue glowing. Each black body bag held at least two hundred pounds of refined cocaine. Say twelve bags, more than a ton of snow—already in the United States for distribution across the country.

Burke closed the trapdoor, turned off the light, and began walking toward the airstrip. The flare-pot flame was flickering. It looked lonely out there, lonely as he felt. On impulse he carried another flare pot from the edge of the clearing, set it a yard from the first one, and lighted it. If the plane came back, they'd see it, realize someone was down there, everything okay.

Weighted by weapons, Burke trudged to the radio shed where Mac had sat that first day. He looked over the transceiver with his flashlight and turned it on. After scanning frequencies he heard a ham operator transmitting. Burke called, "Breaker, breaker! Emergency. Plane down, need help. What's your handle?"

"This is Night Owl in Harlingen, Texas, where are you? Identify, clearing to give aid."

"Handle: Cardiff. Call this number and report bad situation needing full assistance."

"Gotcha, Cardiff. What number?"

Slowly Burke gave the contact number, repeated it, asked Night

Owl to confirm. When the ham had it Burke said, "Batteries low, thanks a million, signing off from somewhere in New Mexico."

He turned off the transmitter and sat back in darkness. A digital clock gave local time as 0438. Dawn was about an hour away. He stretched, bone tired, not yet feeling the pain of cactus rips and punctures because his veins were still flooded with adrenalin.

He pulled out the W-T and set it on the table. For the hell of it he held it near his lips and began transmitting: "*Avión, avión, Jorge aquí. Ven, por el amor de Dios! Todo está bien. Cargo listo. Ven, todo está bien aquí. Contesta.*"

Presently his W-T crackled: "*Avión a Jorge. Dígame—¿podemos aterrizar?*"

"*Sí, ¿cómo no?, pero rápido pa'que no queremos tardar.*"

Burke squelched and listened to the carrier hum in case the pilot had more questions.

The pilot would land at one end and taxi toward the shed. Burke left it and gazed up at the indigo sky. Between clouds he could see brilliant stars. The moon silvered the desert.

The C-47 was a narcotics carrier, sent to deal death, retrieve a long-cached fortune in cocaine. Because Burke had heard only Spanish spoken, he assumed the plane and its passengers had come up from Mexico, flying below Customs radar.

His shoulder ached from the recoil of the .375s—a hell of a cartridge, he thought—his trousers were matted with blood. And there was more to be done.

Faintly came the hum of aircraft engines; at first like the drone of a mosquito, then the buzz of a horsefly. From the east.

He limped back to the shed, recovered the W-T and hooked it in a pocket, slung the Uzi over his left shoulder, and with rifle in hand surveyed the strip and calculated firing angles.

The plane flew closer, running lights like colored stars. It was losing altitude, heading directly for the flare pots. Landing lights scythed the desert. It came in a little high for the short runway, Burke thought, then the plane nosed down, full flaps slowing, and settled on the strip. Dust spurted from the wheels each time the pilot braked, as with feathered props the plane stopped at the far end. It wheeled around and began lumbering back toward Burke. Kneeling, he sighted the rocket pistol on the cabin, holding fire until the plane was broadside, thirty yards away. It stopped then, but the fans kept turning. Burke knew the pilot wouldn't cut engines—normal precaution.

The W-T crackled. In Spanish, Burke said, "Open the cargo door for loading."

He waited until the wide doors pivoted outward and then he fired at the cabin, fired again. The projectiles exploded too high, too far to the left. He fired lower to the right, saw a cabin window disintegrate in a burst of flame, fired again. Flames lighted the cabin. Engines revved, and Burke thought: He's trying to take off. Crazy!

He could see a man trying to pull in the cargo doors, but they were too heavy and the plane was rolling bumpily. Burke fired at the open space and the projectile burst against the far side of the fuselage. Then he had only the tail and slanted wings to fire at as the plane angled away from him.

Dropping the rocket pistol, Burke hoisted the Mannlicher and began firing at the wings, hoping to puncture a fuel tank. A man dropped out of the doorway and began running from the plane. Burke sighted, followed, and moved the ramp sight past him as he squeezed the trigger. The man went sideways as though slammed by a giant fist, lay kicking on the runway. Burke continued firing at the plane until the magazine was empty.

Cabin flames spurted above the nose; the entire aircraft was haloed in a reddish glow. No way the plane was flyable. He reloaded the rifle and emptied the magazine at the wing tanks. Flames inside the fuselage were working back from the cabin. The plane slowed. A white-shirted man dropped from the door, followed by another whose shirt and clothing were flaming. He was the better target, so Burke dropped him and lost the other man in darkness.

He'd been waiting for it, but when the plane exploded it came without warning. The right wing's fuel tanks erupted, blowing the plane on its side. The fuselage broke apart. He waited until the left wing's fuel tanks completed the destruction, and then he scanned the brilliantly lighted desert. No sign of the vanished crewman. He would die in the desert, Burke thought, without water or food. If he survived to reach civilization, he would face criminal charges, and if smart would gloss over the night's events. In any case, the crewman knew nothing that could affect the security of Burke's mission. Forget him.

Burke turned his back on the inferno and trudged to the hacienda. In the kitchen he gulped down water, drank rum from a bottle, carried the bottle outside, and sat on a bench watching the night sky fade as dawn approached.

Thirteen

A BIG AIR FORCE Hercules came in a little after eight, squat and ugly as Burke remembered it from Nam. Props reversed just after touchdown, slowing and stopping the cargo aircraft short of the airstrip's end. Burke left the shack and walked to the edge of the airstrip. The plane's engines gunned, and it rolled toward him.

Before it stopped, the ramp opened and a jeep filled with black-bereted airmen rolled onto the desert floor. Each man was armed, he saw, as the jeep headed directly for him. Burke raised his arms to show that he was unarmed. Hell, they might take him for one of the baddies and shoot to kill.

The jeep braked and a captain jumped out. He strode to Burke and said, "Major Cardiff?"

"Right."

"Sir, I'm not authorized to know what took place here. Our job is to secure the area and wait for orders." His black uniform was razor-creased, black boots shining like mirrors in the morning sunlight. His gaze surveyed Burke. "Sir, I think you need medical attention. There's a medevac team aboard."

Two more jeeps separated from the Hercules and began deploying down the airstrip. "A little Mercurochrome should do it," Burke replied. "No big deal." Turning, he pointed back at the hacienda. "Six bodies there. Three ours, three opposition. One in the brush by the parachutes—" he gestured, reflexes slow, tongue thick from half a bottle of rum. "I need to contact my people."

"They're coming for you," the captain said. "We stay, you go."

"How soon?"

"Say ten minutes."

Burke nodded and pointed at the barracks. "There's about a ton of refined cocaine in that one; the other's an armory. The weapons are government property."

"They'll be guarded." The captain wore a pencil mustache, and to Burke he seemed young to be a captain. Well, the air force had a rep for promoting young. . . .

"I could use a clean uniform," he said, and pointed to where they were stored, then walked to the shed and tore off the rags he'd been wearing. Two medics came over and swabbed blood from his limbs with peroxide. One pulled out embedded *quiotes* while the other filled a syringe with antibiotics and stuck it in his rump, injected the fluid, and massaged the entry area.

The captain said, "About that stray—should we go after him?"

"You'd need dogs or a chopper—don't waste your time. A rabid coyote could get him, a sidewinder, or dehydration." Burke began getting into clean fatigues. The crisp fabric felt good against his skin.

The captain excused himself to deploy his troops. Burke heard incoming engines and saw a twin-prop plane slanting down toward the strip. He wondered who it carried.

The Hercules had moved aside, over near the smoldering C-47, to let the incomer land. Its big, heavy props stopped turning. It sat there like a grumpy bulldog, and Burke supposed the pilots wondered what in hell was going on.

The high-wing AeroCommander settled easily at the end of the airstrip, coming to a stop no farther than two-thirds of the way down the runway. It turned around and angled over to where Burke was standing. The two medics packed up their gear, one saying as an afterthought, "Any more wounded?"

"Not a one," Burke replied, and felt his throat tighten as he visualized the three bloodied bedrooms. No more fast draws and wisecracks from Leroy. No more acrobatics from Mac. No more strength tests from a Sid who was built like Jim Brown, respected his body, and loved life. All dead.

The AeroCommander's props stopped turning and the cabin door opened down into steps. A short, dark-skinned man in civilian clothing came toward Burke, who was unaware that, with Poliakoff, the man had watched him shoot out Judge Grogan's face.

Without preliminaries the man asked, "You okay, Major?"

"I'm alive."

"Leave anything behind?"

"Nothing that can't be replaced."

He looked at his watch. "If you wanna go back there—"

Burke shook his head. "It's a slaughterhouse."

"All right, let's get airborne. People wanta talk to you and quick." He took Burke's arm and started him toward the plane. After a glance at the wrecked C-47, the man said, "Pretty bad, eh?"

Burke grunted. "It wasn't a championship season—whatever your name is—it was a wipeout."

"Harry's the name—call me Harry. Watch your head, there." Burke bent down to enter the cabin. The interior was configured with lounge seats and a collapsible table. Burke noticed a radiophone recessed in a bulkhead. He buckled in and the engines started.

As soon as they were airborne, Harry made radio contact with his base—wherever it was—and reported, "Cardiff's with me, and the AF unit is taking over the ground area, sealing it off. The intruders' plane is a burned-out hulk, so surviving relatives can be told our guys died in a plane crash. He leaned over to Burke. "How many intruder bodies?"

"Six."

Harry gave the count to whomever he was talking with and said, "Yeah, we'll be in Albuquerque shortly for onward transportation. See you at Andrews." He replaced the handset and offered Burke a thermos. Burke swallowed steaming black coffee and looked down at hacienda El Quiote. As he watched, explosions ripped the big house, lifting roof sections above the walls. As the roof came down, the building collapsed inward like a funnel, settled crateriform, and flattened into rubble. Flames shooting skyward told Burke that thermite was at work. Then, just before the plane turned and blanked his view, he saw both barracks detonate in sheets of flame. Secondary explosions from ammo and dynamite shot out and enveloped the burning hacienda. His friends—Mac, Leo, and Sid—had been consigned to a funeral pyre, Valkyrian heroes, Burke thought bitterly. Ashes to desert dust.

And as he turned from the window, he knew that whatever value El Quiote once had for friend or foe, it was now utterly destroyed; nothing would remain but cement foundation slabs to show that man had ever been there.

His first reaction to the demolition was astonishment; then he quickly reasoned that obliterating the buildings—and bodies—served a twofold purpose: the government could now plausibly deny that El Quiote had been a covert training area, while keeping the assault team's sponsors ignorant of its fate. If the sponsors reconned with a low-flying plane, the pilot would report a scene of total destruction, giving the *narcotraficantes* something to ponder—with no clues to what had gone wrong and aborted the retrieval of their cached cocaine.

"How the hell did the invaders get in?" Harry asked.

"They chuted. I heard it pass over and got curious, saw one of them enter a barracks."

Harry shook his head. "How you feeling?"

"Cold. Drained. It shouldn't have happened, Harry, it was avoidable."

"Avoid . . . Don't get you." He looked away, not meeting Burke's gaze.

"When the property was confiscated, it should have been checked for a drug cache—dogs would have found it in ten minutes. That's failure one. Failure two was the total lack of perimeter security, sensors, guard dogs, whatever. Failure three was hiring unreliable help. We were wide open, Harry, and three damn good men were slaughtered in their beds."

"Any more complaints?"

Burke laughed bitterly. "Don't be a comedian, it's too early for black humor."

"All right then. Wanna talk about what happened?"

"Not to you. I'll tell General Arness, get it on tape so all you concerned assholes can listen at leisure. Any more coffee?"

Harry refilled Burke's plastic cup. He finished it as wheels touched Albuquerque Airport's east-west runway.

The AeroCommander taxied over to a beige Learjet. Harry and Burke boarded it, and when they were airborne a steward served breakfast. Burke devoured his food ravenously, and when he finished, Harry said, "Get a chance to read the briefing book—Puma?"

"Barely."

"How do you feel about—getting him?"

"Depends on local support."

"I mean—the mission's still on?"

Burke turned to him. "My brother's still in prison, isn't he?"

General Arness and Enno Poliakoff were waiting in a secure room at Andrews Air Force Base. The carpet was thick, and the room was lined with acoustic tile. After greeting Burke, Arness said, "We're keeping a lid on these unfortunate events, Tom. I imagine you'd like to sleep and so on, but we need your firsthand account while it's fresh in your mind."

Poliakoff set a tape recorder on the table and turned it on. Burke asked for coffee and began relating the events of the night. When he ended, Arness said, "It's pretty clear we screwed up on physical security. And DEA certified the place was clean, and we took their word for it." He looked at Harry and Poliakoff. "Damn! Next time we do on-site inspection ourselves." He leaned back and stretched. "Anything else, Tom?"

"Frankly, I've lost a degree of confidence in the way you operate. What else I have to say, I'll convey privately." He reached over and turned off the recorder. Harry and Enno left the table and the room. When they were alone, Burke said, "From the briefing book I rate Puma as unassailable in Culiacán. The best chance to get next to him is when he's relaxing in Guadalajara."

"I agree."

"Now, if I track Puma myself it's going to take time—considerable time—plus a high element of chance. And the longer I tail Puma, the more likely I am to be noticed. So I'll need local support, General."

"You'll get it."

"Plus commo that's somewhat more sophisticated than the Mickey Mouse set I had to use to get help."

"That was scheduled anyway. Want further training, conditioning?"

He shook his head. "I graduated around five o'clock this morning." He eyed Arness. "Unfortunately my instructors weren't able to hand me my diploma."

"I know, I know. They were the best, Tom. Replacing them'll be one mammoth task. Puts us behind schedule." He leaned forward, elbows on table. "It'll take a couple of days to lay on support arrangements. Take that time to heal and get some rest. Want to stay here at the BOQ?"

"Be more comfortable at my own place."

"I'll have you driven there."

Before leaving Andrews, Burke phoned Claire Newsome, who was ecstatic. "I'm a little scratched up, and dead tired," he told her, "but by dinnertime I should be up and around. Want to come by?"

"Hell's guardians couldn't keep me away."

"How's your father?"

Her voice sobered. "About the same, Tom. May I tell him you're back?"

"Please do, and say I look forward to seeing him."

His farmhouse was a welcome sight. Burke counted four grazing horses, and figured there were probably others down by the creek. He turned on air conditioners to freshen the air and went upstairs to his bedroom. Too tired to do more than pull off fatigues and sprawl across the bed, in less than a minute he was asleep.

When he woke it was late afternoon. His joints and muscles were stiff and the patches of antiseptic made him look like a sideshow freak. For half an hour he soaked in a hot tub, sipping a glass of brandy, pushing last night's holocaust out of his mind. He was back in civilization, and tonight he'd be with Claire. He was thankful for his blessings.

By six he had a drink tray ready and a can of peanuts set out for hors d'oeuvres. Claire's pickup bumped noisily up the road, stopped with skidding tires. She left it, walking quickly to the entrance.

Burke took her in his arms, lifted her light body and kissed her lengthily. Her arms squeezed him painfully tight; she looked at the liquor, glasses, and snacks, and said, "Uh-uh. Later, love."

He carried her upstairs and they made love with the need and urgency of lovers separated much longer than they had been. When her breathing stilled, Claire asked, "You can't just say nothing about all the scratches, dear. Out in the brier patch with Br'er Rabbit?"

"Suthin like that-all," he joked. "Night training exercise. I got lost in the woods."

"You—lost?" She shook her head. "Never. Anyway, I won't pry, told you I wouldn't." She stroked his unshaven face and trailed fingers across his bare belly. "How long will you be around? I want to make plans."

"Tonight, tomorrow . . . maybe a third day."

"Wish it were forever. Um—anticipating your return I acquired a brand-new IUD. Wasn't I foresighted?"

"And practical." He kissed her breast.

"Were you worried about—that?"

"Some," he admitted. "I'd rather not be a father until I have a wife."

"Well, not to worry, darling." She sighed. "Mother told me there'd be times like this."

His tongue touched a small, rosy nipple. "Times?"

"Episodes."

"Don't get it."

"*Involvements*, then." Her tone was exasperated. "When I'd feel in over my head."

"And that's how you feel?"

"Oh, boy, do I ever. A Roman maiden ravished by Attila, abandoned by the Appian Way." She reached between his thighs, found what she was seeking and grasped it. "Now that I have your attention, the senator insists we dine with him."

"Shit!"

Bending over she kissed what her hand was holding. "But after dinner we can come back here and you can ravish me some more."

"Sounds better—*easy* there!"

"Oh, did I hurt you? Sorry, sweet, didn't mean to. Mustn't bite the hand that feeds me—in a manner of speaking. My needs are at least the equal of thine."

Dinner with the senator was far more relaxed than on the first occasion, and Burke enjoyed it, though he would much have preferred dining with Claire à deux. While she was overseeing dessert, the senator said quietly, "Tom, I hear you overcame some unexpected difficulties."

"Unexpected is the word."

"I'm glad you survived, glad you're here. Security was slipshod, I understand."

"Wasn't any." To change the subject he said, "Has my brother forwarded a pardon application?"

Senator Newsome nodded. "He has, and I've sent it along to the pardon attorney with my endorsement. I was pleased to see him relocated to Allenwood."

Claire rejoined them and presently dessert was served—still-warm brownies topped with vanilla ice cream. They sipped coffee and liqueurs in the drawing room until the senator said, "Time for my prime-time program. You two are welcome to stay, but I imagine you'll want to be doing other things."

"Quite so, Father." Claire kissed him and took Burke's arm. "Don't wait up for me."

"That would be the height of foolishness." He smiled and shook Burke's hand. "Always good to see you, Tom. Let's hope everything works out."

In his Porsche, Burke said, "If you've got discos in mind, I'm too infirm for dancing."

"Discos? Who said anything about discos? Your place, where we can be alone."

They spent the night together, and after breakfast they went down through the meadows to give sugar and carrots to her horses. Being with her, seeing Claire in his house, on his land, seemed entirely natural now, and Burke wondered if some things were fated to be.

Although by now he was aware that he was in love with Claire, he held back a declaration. Puma was ahead of him. The first of three, and romance would have to wait.

During the day Burke watched Claire exercise her horses, and in the evening they drove to Johnson's Charcoal House in Leesburg for prime ribs. Early to bed, lovemaking, and sleep in each other's arms.

The bedside phone wakened him. Claire stirred as Burke heard Enno Poliakoff's voice coming over the receiver. Irritated, Burke said, "What the hell time is it?"

"About two. But in that city of primary interest it's only midnight. The mountain lion is on the loose with his pack, and my boss thought you'd want to take advantage of the opportunity."

"Oh."

"A car will pick you up at eight—"

"Make it nine."

"Okay, nine then. You'll be briefed for onward travel."

"And won't be coming back here?"

"Not for a while. Bring suitable clothing."

"Whatever that means."

"No tailor tags with your name sewn in."

"I buy off the rack," Burke said, "like you. Nine o'clock." He hung up and brushed stray hair from Claire's forehead, kissed her, and settled back to sleep holding her hand.

In the morning after breakfast she watched him pack a change of clothing and said, "I suppose you have no idea when you might drop around again?"

"Not really."

"Give me a hint?"

"Wish I could," he said, "but I have no idea. Honest."

"I love you, you know, and these things that may seem unimportant to you are important to me."

"I love you, too." He kissed her cheek and snapped his Samsonite suitcase shut.

"If I asked my father what you're doing, would he be likely to tell me?"

"Try if you must, but I'll be disappointed if the senator has anything to say."

She chewed the end of a thumb, as she did when deep in thought. "If I'd joined CIA, would I be able to know what you're involved in?"

"Highly unlikely," he replied. "Now leave off—please. There's a time for confidences, but this isn't it."

A horn honked in the drive.

Her arms circled his neck and she held him tightly. "Besides loving you, I admire you and I know whatever you're doing is important—so I'll be satisfied with that. Just come back, hear me? Come back."

"I will," he promised—what else could he say? And hoped it wouldn't be in a body bag.

She followed him downstairs, kissed him a last time at the doorway, and watched him walk to the waiting Ford sedan.

Burke was driven to a high-rise office building in Arlington, where the driver directed him to the sixth floor. "Environmental Improvement is the name on the door."

Burke thanked him for his trouble, and carried his suitcase to the elevator.

The hall door was open, so Burke went in, leaving his suitcase near the receptionist's empty desk. Enno Poliakoff opened an inner door and beckoned him inside.

At the conference table, nursing plastic foam coffee cups, sat General Arness and Harry lnu.

"Morning, Tom," Arness said. "Feeling fit?"

Burke nodded and took a seat at the table. Poliakoff brought him a coffee cup and set it down on a napkin, hard enough that coffee sloshed over and stained the napkin. Burke looked up to meet his hostile gaze. "Lot to cover before you leave," Arness began, "so let's get with it. First off, we got a report that Quintana arrived in Guadalajara on one of his periodic R&Rs. The DEA office is keeping track of him, but notes Quintana seldom stays more than a week, usually only a few nights. Your contact there goes by the name of Raúl López, passes as a Mexican but he's one of us." Poliakoff reached over and passed Burke a slip of paper. "Phone number," he said.

Arness asked, "What documentation do you want?"

"A birth certificate will get me into Mexico as a tourist. I'll need pocket litter, the usual sort of thing. Can you get weapons to me?"

"What's the requirement?"

"S and W compact pistol, a Brazilian plastic throwaway, and a Gyrojet rocket."

Arness glanced sideways. "You listing everything?"

"Yes, sir," Poliakoff said.

"And some expense money will be helpful—about five thousand."

As Poliakoff wrote it down, Arness said, "Travel plans?"

"One-way ticket to San Diego. Tijuana trolley across the border, fly from there to Guadalajara."

"You'll have your documentation in about two hours," Arness said. "I suggest you reserve a seat to San Diego for later today, meanwhile reading up on your target city."

"A seat in what name?"

Arness shrugged. "Pick one."

"Paul Palmer, POB: Gloversville, New York." A thought occurred to him. "That Puma briefing book was in the hacienda safe."

"It was recovered sealed, and returned to me. Don't worry about it."

Burke said, "That was a lousy show, General. Three needless deaths."

"I acknowledge that," Arness said, "but let's bear in mind that we have to expect casualties."

"Including me," Burke said thinly.

"That's right, Major, including you," Poliakoff interjected.

"Knock it off," Arness said crisply. "Get moving, Enno." Turning to Burke again, he said, "You were right about the cook, Tom—Esther Fernández. Highway patrol picked her up when she ran off the road near Albuquerque—fell asleep at the wheel. She said the *narco-traficantes* had her husband hostage, made her inform on hacienda happenings." He cleared his throat. "She's in a hospital, somewhat banged up, but I doubt she'll leave there alive."

Burke said nothing.

"There's a travel agency in the next building, Tom."

Burke left the room, took the elevator down, and consulted the travel agent. Using cash, he bought a ticket to San Diego and went back to the bare-walled briefing room. Harry was at the long conference table, maps and a tourist guide before him. "The general had to leave, but he left his regards and best wishes for mission success."

"Sweet of him," Burke said as he sat down. Ignoring Harry, he began reading the city guide and moved on to the downtown maps.

After a while Burke drew coffee at the urn and went back to the table. Gazing at Harry he said, "How do you figure in all this?"

"I do whatever the general wants me to do. Such as flying out to the hacienda on ten minutes notice. Like that."

"You hire the hacienda cook—the almost-late Esther Fernández?"

"Not me, that was Logistics's job. Apparently Security never checked her out."

"Apparently not," Burke said dryly. "One servant at the hacienda was one too many."

Elbows on the table, Harry leaned forward. "I'm damn glad you killed so many of the bastards."

"Any particular reason?"

"Name Eubank mean anything to you?"

Burke shook his head.

"Bill Eubank was one of the DEA officers Quintana flayed alive. I'm Jim Eubank, his brother."

"I see." He felt sudden sympathy for the man, understood his dedication.

"I begged to go after Luís Quintana but Arness wouldn't let me—said I was too emotionally involved." He looked away. "He was right, of course. Nor do I have your range of skills. See, I worked with Customs in L.A.—sedentary work—airports, in-bond warehouses, port inspections." His face had grown suddenly old. "Bill was my kid brother, left a wife and two children—I'm helping out." He was silent for a while. "Wish they'd killed me instead."

Burke studied his drawn face before saying, "Either I'll kill Quintana or he'll kill me. Either way, it won't be painless."

"You'll get him—the general says you're the best. Even Poliakoff says so."

"Credit from an unexpected quarter." Burke smiled tightly. "If you don't mind a word of caution—I had personal experience of Enno, and he's not the most dependable fellow in a tense situation."

"He told me about one—why didn't you have him court-martialed?"

Burke shrugged. "I was wounded, doped up for a long time. When I began thinking about it I learned Poliakoff had been wounded and sent to Letterman. By then the war was winding down. . . . I figured, what the hell, and let it go."

Jim Eubank aka Harry lnu opened the travel guide and began. "Gets cool at night in Guadalajara—the altitude. I suggest you avoid the Hyatt, Quinta, and Fiesta Americana. Find a cheap place downtown in one of the old commercial hotels where you'll be less noticeable. Food's not great in Guadalajara, but it's edible. Pay phones are practically free. Plenty of taxis, or López could get you a car."

"I'll need a getaway driver."

"Ask López. Raúl's been around the track a few times, he's reliable, but doesn't know about the hit. It's better he not know. Under investigation he might talk."

"A postmortem is something we all want to avoid."

Eubank nodded soberly. "What time's your flight?"

"Five forty-two, from Dulles."

"I'll drive you. Least I can do."

He left his true-name documentation with Eubank, exchanging it for ID and money Poliakoff delivered. Now, in the first-class compartment, Burke dined on fillet of sole amandine, endive salad, and dry Chilean wine. He declined dessert, choosing brandy and coffee instead.

It was not quite a five-hour flight to San Diego, and with the three-hour time differential, his plane touched down a few minutes after eight. In the airport he checked at the AeroMexico desk and found a Guadalajara flight leaving Tijuana around midnight.

From a pay phone he called Claire, told her he was well and not to worry, hanging up before she could get emotional. Though he missed her, he was glad to be launched on his mission.

Tomorrow in Guadalajara, Raúl López would deliver his weapons.

Fourteen

"SO HOW ARE THINGS stateside?" Raúl López asked. He was sitting across the small table from Burke in a sixth-floor room in the Hotel El Angel on Avenida Juárez, a busy street in the old downtown section of Guadalajara. The wall plaster was mottled from moisture and the air had a moldy smell. The stained carpet was worn down to the backing in trails that led from door to bed and from bed to bathroom. Rusty water had stained the tub, and the toilet tank showed verdigrised fissures on the porcelain. The single towel was thin from use and gray with age. Burke hoped for a fresh one tomorrow and planned to tip the maid to reinforce his hope. Still, he reflected, you get what you pay for, and at $9.72 per night, he was probably getting full value for his money. López had brought along a liter bottle of Don Pedro brandy to welcome "Paul Palmer." Burke supplied two glasses, and they were drinking together.

López was in his late thirties, Burke estimated, a dark-skinned, smooth-faced man with a thin mustache and curving sideburns. He wore an embroidered guayabera shirt and pointed snakeskin boots under tight-fitting cream polyester trousers.

"Things are pretty much the same in El Norte," Burke replied after a sip of the smooth Domeq brandy. "Indecisive. Unsettled." He looked at the heavily wrapped, unlabeled cardboard box López had brought in a shopping bag. "Where's Quintana likely to be found?"

"He favors a disco down on López Mateos called Big Daddy's—

123

hell, he may own the place, for all I know. Luís goes where he can spend big money and be seen doing it. At night, of course; he sleeps days."

"Like a reptile," Burke remarked.

"Right now he's at his palace in the Chapalita section. On past visits he doesn't leave there until nine, ten o'clock. Then he has dinner with his *pistoleros*—usually a couple of whores included—at an expensive restaurant. Or he'll go to a restaurant in one of the big hotels. When he wants Mexican food, he'll take a crowd to a mariachi joint on the airport road—Caballo Negro it's called. He gets really drunk there, he likes it so much. The place is a medium- to low-class joint, plenty of blue-collar stiffs eat and drink there. Roast goat, *birria*, green sauce. . . . The usual high-seasoned stuff. Chili, they think, purifies the blood."

"Got a tail on him?"

"There's fixed surveillance on his castle—for all the good it does us. We don't put a live tail on him until nightfall. He expects to be tailed, by the way, but figures he's too well protected to let it worry him." López drank more brandy. "Down here the *traficantes* go to a public official—judge, police chief, army general—and say, '¿Oro o plomo?' Gold or lead? Guess what the answer is." He stared moodily at a faded Orozco print on the wall. "The *traficantes* have money and influence—we have shit."

"What's your cover?"

"Tourist hustler, guide. A commonplace occupation that gives me contact with foreigners like yourself."

"Ever see Quintana?"

"Maybe five times over two years. Often enough to get a fix on his personality, not enough to be noticed. And I've always been with tourists, showing the sights. Just another guide."

"Got a sterile car?"

López nodded.

"After Quintana settles in a spot where he's likely to spend time, give me a call. I'll meet you in the street and you take me where he is."

"I go with you?"

"You'll wait outside in the car."

López's eyes narrowed. "Not thinking of trying to arrest him?"

"He's so notorious I thought I'd try for his autograph. I hear he can write his name."

"Hell, for signing checks an X is enough."

"Are you packing?"

"Tonight I will. All of us used to carry iron routinely, but that irritated the *traficantes*, so they paid *Gobernación* to issue an order banning DEA agents from carrying weapons. Oh, it's a lovely place to work, let me tell you."

After López left, Burke locked the door and opened the package. He took out the S&W Compact, the Gyrojet, and the Brazilian plastic throwaway, and checked the first two magazines. Fully loaded. Through the translucent grip he could count the throwaway's cartridges. He looked around the room for a cache, settling on the inside of the window air conditioner. That done, he looked down on traffic-jammed Avenida Juárez where ratty-looking buses spewed black plumes of diesel smoke from roof-high exhausts. In another couple of years, Burke thought, Guadalajara's pollution would rival Mexico City's.

He finished his drink and went down to the street, where he found an English-speaking taxi driver eager to be hired for a couple of hours' sightseeing.

At midday sidewalks were crowded with vendors selling colorful novelties, underwear, eating utensils, crucifixes inset with colored glass, machetes, sombreros, and local copies of Hermès luggage. Along the curbs were carts, whose owners offered flavored shaved ices, tacos, bottled drinks, and sections of chicken grilled over pots of glowing charcoal. The smoky scents somewhat diluted the throat-choking pall of diesel fumes. Burke coughed as he got into the taxi, thinking the city's *tapatios* were somehow accustomed to it.

He checked the hotel restaurants mentioned by López, then the disco—Big Daddy's—from the outside, and had the driver take him out the airport road to the Caballo Negro. At the bar he treated the driver to a Corona, and went to the men's room. It was dirty and smelly, the toilet bowl jammed with wadded paper and feces. Quintana might be offended by the place, but when you gotta go, you gotta go. Burke returned to the bar, finished his beer, and had the driver take him to the Plaza Tapatía, where he paid him and left the taxi, walking a few short blocks to his hotel.

The hours from two to four were siesta time in Guadalajara. Shops closed and traffic diminished. Burke lay on his bed, thinking of Claire and Terry, then forming a series of plans to kill Quintana—and get away. He found that he hadn't given nearly enough thought to the latter.

Eight hours later López called. His voice was breathy as he said, "Fifteen minutes."

"I'll be there."

Burke took the S&W from its hiding place and slid it into his pocket, got into a dark blue, loose-fitting *guayabera* that showed no suspicious bulge. His two-week growth of beard was a natural disguise.

López came by in a black Nissan that looked twenty years old, dented and rusty. "Jesus," Burke said as he got in, "will this heap get us there? It looks old enough to vote."

"It's supposed to look like a duster," López said with a smile, "but under the hood it's got eight well-tuned cylinders that Nissan never made."

"That's a comfort," Burke said. "Where's our boy?"

"Right now he's buying drinks in the Fiesta Americana lounge—a big, noisy place—you'll see." A radio receiver crackled, and as López reached for the transmitter he said, "We're not supposed to have these, either."

"But you do."

"We definitely do." He spoke in Spanish to his caller, and signed off. "Luís is still there. I'll go in with you if you want."

He shook his head. "Just want to look him over."

They came around Minerva Circle with its massive statue of the goddess, lighted fountains playing around her robed hips, and Burke wondered why Guadalajarans—Tapatíos—had chosen a figure from Greek mythology to symbolize their city. Why not an Aztec deity?

The Fiesta Americana's glass-faced bulk rose from beside a tree-lined street that traversed low commercial buildings and modest dwellings. Carbide lamps lighted carts displaying skewered shrimp and chicken; other carts were heaped with fresh-made potato chips. Taxi drivers from the hotel's rank noshed on chips drenched with Tabasco and ketchup while waiting for a fare.

López angled over to approach the front of the hotel and braked, and Burke got out. "Stay loose," he said, and walked into the lounge bar entrance.

It was a big sunken area, tables crowded with hotel guests and tourists, well-dressed young Tapatíos shaking and churning to the shrieking rhythms of a rock band.

The room's odd couple was a pair of sixtyish ladies wearing colorful turbans spiraled around their heads. A wisp of white gauze extruded from the edge of a magenta turban, telling Burke—if he hadn't already inferred it—that the ladies had come to the city for Guadalajara's famous, and cheap, cosmetic repair. Their ages showed in high-veined, wrinkled hands; "Speedy-with-the-knife González" hadn't yet worked around to their extremities.

They sipped mixed drinks and watched the gyrating younger set with wistful approval. Looking over the crowd, Burke spotted Quintana's large, central table without difficulty. Six young men around it wore Mexican cowboy clothing—darted shirts and sombreros, tight-fitting jeans and tooled leather boots, belts ornamented with silver and turquoise, massive silver buckles. No visible holsters or weapons. Burke was reminded of an old spaghetti western—bad guys living it up in a barroom with a couple of over-dressed girls, ladies of easy virtue. His ex-wife Joyce would have surveyed the scene, said, "Tacky, tacky," and flounced out, nose in the air. The only element lacking was Hoot Gibson, Tim McCoy, or Clint Eastwood sidling in to collar the black hats, but lawmen were conspicuously absent.

The table's seventh man wore a white leisure suit that fitted like a second skin. An open collar showed heavy chains hung with coins, miniature spoons, a crucifix—all gold. Six fingers wore large gold rings, some set with diamonds. Both wrists were circled with thick gold-chain bracelets. As advertised, Burke thought, Quintana was a conspicuous consumer.

Quintana's hair was bushy, untended, his mustache thicker than in the photos Burke had seen. The full beard hadn't been trimmed recently, if ever. And when the head turned Burke saw the large-nosed Indian profile, the cruel narrow eyes, and the old angled scar.

He took a small table by the doorway and ordered a bottle of Corona. In English. The waiter nodded and went away. Two of Quintana's *pistoleros* pulled women to their feet and danced, bearlike, on the crowded floor, hugging and whirling the smaller women like dolls. Sipping his beer, Burke glanced over from time to time. Quintana had his arm over the shoulder of the third female. A waiter brought him a cigar, lighted it. Quintana gave the waiter a handful of bills, and the latter bowed gratefully as he backed away. Burke remembered the poisoned cigars CIA morons had tried to foist on Fidel Castro. Try Anything had been the motto then. Nothing had worked, and Castro was more powerful than ever.

The dance set ended, the crowd dispersed until Quintana began clapping noisily. Instead of leaving the bandstand the musicians picked up their instruments and resumed playing. A *vaquero* got up and handed money to the leader, who smiled and bowed appreciatively. The noise level rose higher than before.

Burke analyzed the setting: too many innocents around Quintana's table, too hard to shoot and get away through the crowd. And just because he didn't *see* weapons on the *vaqueros* didn't mean they were traveling light. Boots held knives and pistols in easy reach.

Well, he'd seen the master at his revels, what he'd come for. He signaled the waiter for his check. The waiter bent over and said, "Nothing to pay. Señor Quintana pays for everything."

"Well, that's real nice," Burke said, "Next time I'll order champagne. Now who the hell is Mr. Quintero?"

"Quintana," the waiter corrected. "Over there, señor. In the white clothing."

Burke stood up, shaded his eyes and peered at the table. "I'm gonna thank him," he said, and began moving through the intervening tables. As he neared Quintana two *pistoleros* rose and faced him, positioning themselves protectively. Burke smiled winningly. "I wanna thank Mr. Quintana," he said. "Very generous."

One *pistolero* stepped forward and began patting Burke down. "Hey, what's this?" Burke exclaimed, stepping back. "Sorry, fellows. No offense." He merged back into the crowd, but not before seeing Quintana look up at him with his strange snake's eyes.

So, Burke thought, as he walked back to López's car, he's seen me close-up and so have his lieutenants. They've rated me harmless. Next time maybe they won't pat me down.

He got in beside López and retrieved his S&W from under the seat. "That's all for tonight, Raúl. Let's go home."

The next night Quintana was reported dining at the Camino Real, a large luxury hotel out Avenida Vallarta. In addition to the main building, with its bar and restaurants, there were room buildings beyond the patio and pool. Tennis courts, too, but the entire hotel area was surrounded by a high wall. Tonight Quintana was dining in splendor at a large candle-lit table. Same *pistoleros*, Burke noticed, but a change of women. He left the hotel and went to bed early.

In the morning Burke took a taxi to Mercado Libertad, having read about the huge city market. He wandered the stalls where produce, meat, and fish were sold—bloody beef carcasses and hogs, monster fish in varieties he'd never seen. Shawls, blankets, serapes, candy, homeopathic herbs, watch repair . . . everything under one big roof. Presently he found himself in the leather and saddlery section, passed it, and moved on into hardware. Counters displayed ugly-looking knives, from machetes to toad stabbers. He found a six-inch switch-blade to his liking and had it sharpened.

Next he stopped at a stall where a woman was hand-rolling cigars. He bought a dozen oxblood cigarillos flavored with rum.

From there Burke taxied twenty-five miles to Ajijic where, the guidebook told him, Lawrence had written *The Plumed Serpent*. It was a quaint artists-colony village on the near side of Lake Chapala. The driver pointed to a pier stained with a water line of years before, and Burke estimated that the lake had fallen twelve to fifteen feet. The driver said there used to be speedboats and water-skiers on the lake; a delicious whitefish provided employment for lakeside fishermen, but that was all over now. The lake was dead, so heavily silted that a man could walk across its five-mile width. He wrinkled his nose: The lake smelled bad. Burke agreed.

After wandering the narrow cobbled streets, Burke went into the Posada, had two beers, and ordered breaded veal cutlet, the day's special. Middle-aged and elderly people who might have been artists or writers filled luncheon tables that overlooked the lake. They seemed to be regular customers, knowing the waiters by name.

On the beach side, just beyond the dining porch, Indian women wove serapes and rebozos. As Burke left the Posada he passed a display of watercolor scenes, each one priced in dollars. The driver returned by way of Chapala, a busy town on the lake. Every other storefront seemed to offer real estate—high-priced—and Burke found the place uninviting.

On the way back he stopped at Sanborn's for a supply of English-language paperbacks. In his room he looked over his acquisitions: books by Thomas Harris, Ross Thomas, and Thomas Gifford. Was it because the name was his own? Odd, he thought. Should have varied the selections with a Len Deighton, but no Deightons were available, not even old ones. Le Carré was too fussy and old-womanish for Burke's taste. And his heroes smelled vaguely of Moral Rearmament and the Oxford Oath.

Reading, he fell asleep; he woke at dusk, and went to a nearby spaghetti joint for dinner.

When he unlocked his room door his phone was ringing.

López.

Quintana and company were at the Caballo Negro, where it appeared they intended to stay for several hours.

Burke put a razor and a small soap bar in his pocket, and wore his three pistols down to López's car. The switchblade was rubber-banded to his right wrist.

When López saw Burke slide the Gyrojet under the seat, he said, "What in hell is *that?*"

"The Empire Strikes Back," Burke told him. "Now let's haul ass."

Fifteen

EVEN BEFORE LÓPEZ cut the engine Burke could hear mariachi music blasting inside the Caballo Negro. He took the ignition key from López and tucked it under the mat. "If all goes well," he said, "you won't see this heap again. It's a write-off. We'll go in together, find a table, and order drinks. Whatever I do, stay put. Don't watch me, don't follow me."

López stared at him. "What in hell you gonna do, Palmer?"

"I don't know, so leave it at that." As he got out, Burke noted a Silver Cloud and a stretch Mercedes at the edge of the parking lot. Good. Puma and company were inside as reported.

Walking up shallow concrete steps, Burke felt a cold detachment come over him. He remembered the eve-of-battle feeling and knew his mind and reflexes were shifting to auto, like a torpedo whose coordinates have been fixed.

In the noisy, crowded room Burke peered through the haze of moving smoke for a table, not looking at Quintana's table up front near the eight-piece mariachi band.

López gave a waiter a handful of pesos, and the waiter secured them a small table near the edge of the room, not far from the *caballeros*—men's room—Burke noticed. Seated, López ordered Tecate and Burke asked for Sangrita and tequila.

Gradually Burke let his gaze drift over to Quintana's table. Nine altogether, including three women; one was large and bosomy, with

131

a prominent nose. Her hair was saffron-colored and Burke commented on it. "She ought to find herself a beauty parlor where they aren't color-blind."

López shook his head. "It's intentional. Saffron suggests Spain and with her Aztec features the lady's trying to disguise her ancestry."

When their drinks arrived Burke washed his tequila down with red Sangrita, then headed for the men's room. Inside, he slid the locking latch and looked around. The place had a toilet stall and a urinal, both smelly. There was a stained washbasin with a dripping faucet and an empty container for paper towels. Burke placed his plastic pistol inside, then closed it. Above the basin was a hinged window. Using his switchblade he sliced through lawyers of binding paint and opened it. No outside bars. On tiptoe he looked through and saw open space, a large trash-collection bin. The kitchen door was open, and he could see cooks and waiters moving around. Before leaving, Burke urinated, figuring he might not have the chance afterward.

Back at his table, he moved his chair slightly for a better view of Quintana. The drug king was wearing a cream-colored leisure suit and his standard array of jewelry. When the loud music ended, a Quintana lieutenant gave money to the leader and music resumed, even more loudly than before. Burke glanced at López and saw that his face was stiff and unhappy. "Relax." he said. "Get into the spirit of the evening. Order some food."

"I couldn't eat it," López said tautly.

"Order it anyway."

López ordered *birria* from the waiter and sat rigidly in his chair. One of Quintana's cowboy-hatted lieutenants went to the men's room and returned to the table. Quintana was kissing a dark-haired, big-breasted woman. He bit her neck and she broke away in evident pain. Quintana grinned wolfishly and grabbed the pseudo-blond on his other side. He stroked her breasts, then pinched them. Burke saw the woman's mouth open in a squeal drowned out by the music, but he felt no pity for the three whores; they were working girls paid for their time—and pain.

Birria arrived for López. "This is spicy stuff," he said with a sickly expression. "Do I *have* to eat it?"

"Pretend." Burke was concentrating. Timing was everything and everything depended on Quintana's bladder. Glancing at the saffron-haired woman, Burke was reminded of a night in Lima in the Bolívar bar, drinking Pisco sours to dull the memory of a firefight in the *cordillera* beyond Uchiza when he had lost four poorly armed villagers to the *Senderos'* two. Burke had killed both, shooting at muzzle flashes in the jungle darkness before the guerrillas withdrew from the brief battle. The blond who'd come into the Bolivar bar was tall and well dressed, and as he looked her over he decided she had come from the German Club across the plaza. After scanning the room, she took a table beside Burke's and ordered *anticuchos* and a Pisco sour, then asked Burke for a light. The match flare showed an attractive, high-cheekboned face with perfect teeth. She exhaled away from Burke and asked in English if he was American. "Hundred percent," he'd slurred and lighted another cigarillo. Her drink arrived; she lifted the goblet and said, *"Prosit!"*

"Prosit!" he'd responded. "Live here?"

"Visiting. My husband has business associates in Lima." She shrugged. "He went to Cuzco this morning, but I don't like the altitude." She frowned. "I don't like being left alone in a strange country either."

"Where are you from?"

"Berlin. West Berlin. Have you been there?"

Burke nodded. Flaming *anticuchos* arrived on bamboo slivers, and she insisted on sharing with him. They exchanged names—hers was Anna, he remembered, and somehow they'd ended up in his room for a nightcap from the bottle of Black Label he'd bought that morning at the bar. After a highball, and before they'd even kissed, Anna began disrobing. She took off each piece of clothing and folded it matter-of-factly, and asked if she should leave on her shoes. "If you like," he'd said, intrigued by her direct, Germanic approach to sex. Her build was slim and athletic without being muscular, her frizzy delta slightly redder than her shoulder-length hair. She gave him her breasts to nuzzle before drawing him to the bed. He remembered a small brown mole inside her thigh, a beauty mark really, and how because of liquor or depression he hadn't achieved erection until she took him in her mouth and brought him to full stand. To keep him that way she coated his glans with coca paste before straddling him.

"Have you any money?" she'd asked.

"Sure. How much?"

"I'm leaving my husband. I need two hundred dollars for a ticket to Miami."

A better reason than an operation for a nonexistent mother, he'd thought; he nodded and slid into her warm moistness.

Anna was a sexual athlete knowledgeable, skilled, and nearly inexhaustible. After he had taken her she revived and took him again and again in innovative positions, muttering in German, stifling climax-cries by biting her hand until finally she let him sleep.

In the morning they breakfasted together in his room. He gave her two hundred green and wished her well, and that was the only pleasant experience of the long months he fought for the peasants in Peru.

López was toying with his *birria*. "How long we gotta stay?" he asked over the blaring trumpets.

"About an hour." Burke glanced at his watch. Ten-thirteen. Quintana's bladder must be the size of a balloon. Just then Quintana shoved back his chair and got unsteadily to his feet. He shook off supporting hands of his nearest *pistolero* and weaved among tables toward the *Caballeros.*

Burke knocked back a shot of tequila and followed it with mouth-scorching Sangrita. Quintana pushed open the men's room door and went in. The door closed behind him. One of the lieutenants looked around, but didn't get up to follow as Burke thought he might; the man busied himself with the dark-haired, dark-skinned woman, and when no one at Quintana's table seemed interested in where the boss had gone, Burke stuck a cigarillo between his teeth, got up, and walked slowly and unsteadily toward the *Caballeros* door.

He didn't look back at López, but kept his eyes vacant, his lips in a slack, half-drunken smile. He was within eight feet of the doorway when a black-hatted Quintana *pistolero* scraped back his chair and came toward him. The man stopped, facing Burke, his back to the door, and waved a finger under Burke's nose. *"No,"* he said heavily. *"No. No puede entrar."*

Burke's face assumed a startled expression. "Eh?" he said, staggering backward. "Wha's matter? Don' unnastan' you."

The *pistolero's* face set in a hard grimace. "Don' go in," he grunted.

Burke stared at him confusedly. "Gotta go," he repeated. "Lemme in."

"Espere," the man said. "Wait, *gringo."*

"Can' wait," Burke declared loudly, one hand reaching for his fly zipper. He was fumbling inside his trousers when the man began patting him down. Feeling the pocketed .38, the man grunted and pulled it out. "Mine," Burke said, one hand inside his fly. He didn't reach for the S&W. Stepping aside, the *pistolero* said, "Go now. I give you after."

"Okay, okay." Burke lurched toward the door, collided with it, and turned the handle. The door opened.

Quintana was in the toilet stall. Burke closed the outer door and latched it. He zipped his fly and opened the towel container. From it he took the nine-millimeter plastic pistol, wondering if its report could be heard above the mariachi sound. Maybe not, but the guy waiting outside would sure as hell hear it.

The toilet flushed. Burke sucked in a deep breath and kicked open the stall door. Quintana was rising, trousers around his ankles. He stared at Burke as though he'd been expecting him, death in his serpent's eyes. Burke stuck the pistol muzzle against Quintana's throat and pressed a finger to his lips. In Spanish he said, "Not a sound, Luís. Killers are waiting outside. Pull up your trousers."

Quintana's eyes widened. Burke moved back a foot and Quintana hesitated, face working, wondering what to believe. "Now," Burke ordered, and Quintana bent forward, head down as he reached for his trousers. Burke chopped the unguarded neck and Quintana collapsed, forehead striking Burke's legs, then the filthy floor. Pistol in his left hand, Burke pulled out his switchblade and flicked the blade into position. Grasping Quintana's thick hair, Burke drew up the head and severed Quintana's throat in a hard, sweeping slash. Lizard boots scrabbled on the floor, the body shuddered and relaxed. Burke sliced off both ears and Quintana's nose—as Peruvian *narcotraficantes* did—and stepped back from the pooling blood. He dropped the knife in the trash barrel and climbed quickly on the washbasin. Lifting the window he wriggled through as someone began pounding against the latched door. "Luís," a voice called. *"¿Está bien? ¡Luís, contesta!"*

Burke dropped into the yard, pivoted quickly, and sprinted around the building away from the open kitchen door. Entering the parking area, he slowed and walked unconcernedly toward the superpowered Nissan, right hand touching the pocketed pistol.

He got in and fitted the key into the ignition, glad his hand wasn't trembling. The engine started, he drove out and onto the airport road. Turning south toward Hidalgo airport, he held the car at legal speed while keeping an eye on the rearview mirror. So far, no fast oncoming lights, but it would take a while to organize pursuit. With two cars they could search both directions from the Caballo Negro and both cars would be loaded with firepower.

Burke pulled the Gyrojet from under the passenger seat where he had stowed it, and held the rocket pistol between his thighs. Briefly he regretted not having let Quintana know why he was being killed, but seconds had been precious. If there was a hereafter, Quintana's soul would damn well understand as it roasted.

He had driven three miles before being slowed by a truck convoy straining up a steep, curving grade. Oncoming headlights kept him from passing the trucks, so he resigned himself to waiting it out. Downhill cars flashed past, adding to Burke's frustration. The blocking trucks slowed almost to stopping as they shifted gears, and Burke peered left enough to see if the other lane was clear. It wasn't, but in the rearview mirror he saw wide-set headlights closing on him. Fast. He tried to swing out, but an oncoming car forced him behind the truck again. Moments later the speeding car behind him took the passing lane, gambled, and overtook Burke, passing close beside him.

It was Quintana's Silver Cloud, three men in it, two holding automatic weapons. The nearest *pistolero* was the one who'd taken Burke's .38. Recognizing Burke, he started rolling down his window. Burke pointed the Gyrojet at the engine and fired two rocket projectiles, and then a third into the body.

He had never fired the pistol at night, so he wasn't prepared to see three red tracer lines just before each explosion. The Rolls's engine froze and the big car slithered away. Flames inside the car showed the driver dead, slumped over the wheel as the Silver Cloud fishtailed across the oncoming lane. Its front wheels dipped into the shoulder gully, then bucked up onto a steep earth bank. The car hung on its rear wheels, suspended for a few moments like a rearing stallion, then slid sideways and turned over. The hood blew off in a blast of flame, illuminating an oncoming car whose startled driver Burke glimpsed as he swerved past the skidding car. Then the trucks crested the hill and gained momentum on the downward slope. Now that he could see ahead, Burke swung out and accelerated past the trucks. The way to the airport was clear.

Beyond the Periférico he took the airport turnoff and settled back behind the wheel. His hands were trembling noticeably, so he gripped the wheel more tightly. Only then did he realize that the Gyrojet's firing in the car's confined space had partly deafened him. His ears were ringing and his head throbbed. All that was incidental, he told himself; the objective had been accomplished. Quintana was dead, and so were half his top echelon. A bonus for the president, he thought. Too bad I won't get credit for it.

Ten minutes later Burke steered slowly into the airport's parking lot, took a ticket from the bored attendant, and parked the Nissan near a burned-out light.

He sat there for a little while, slowing his breathing and working out his next moves of the night. Then he stuck the Gyrojet along his spine, under belt and jacket, and left the car for the airport building. Joining a flow of passengers carrying baggage, Burke entered the building, looked around, and located the men's room. There he soaped his beard and shaved it off, nicking his skin in places. He lifted the top of a toilet tank and dropped the rocket pistol in the water. Eventually an attendant would find the pistol and sell it as a novelty for a few thousand pesos. Burke kept the plastic pistol in his pocket.

Emerging from the men's room, Burke walked out of the building and got in line with passengers taking a group minibus to downtown

Guadalajara. He paid four thousand pesos to the driver, and half an hour later got off two blocks from his hotel.

In his room Burke took a long hot shower and patted after-shave lotion on his face. He drank a quantity of iced Don Pedro brandy and got into bed with a copy of Ross Thomas's *Backup Men*. He read until he fell asleep, the lights still on.

In the morning Burke had late breakfast in the hotel's small restaurant and read *El Informador* over ham and eggs. Quintana's violent death was duly reported and attributed to *narcotraficante* rivals, as indicated by the severing of *El Ciclón*'s ears and nose. The reporter opined that Quintana's murder would unleash a new wave of deadly violence as his heirs fought to seize control of the Sinaloa-Jalisco *narcotráfico*. No description of the assassin was available at press time. Burke allowed himself a faint smile, folded the paper, and paid for breakfast. He crossed Juárez to a travel agency and bought a ticket on the one o'clock flight to Houston.

In midafternoon Burke cleared U.S. Customs and Immigration, and dialed his Virginia contact number from a pay phone. When Harry's voice answered Burke said, "Cardiff reporting. Puma down."

"I know, I *know*." Emotion bubbled through Eubank's voice. "Thank you and thank God! Where are you?"

"Houston. Tell the boss I'll call in when I'm ready for the next one."

"Cardiff—wait, please . . . I need to know . . . did he suffer?"

"Believe it," Burke replied and carried his bag to the ticket area thinking that Jim Eubank would sleep better now, the ghost of his tortured brother laid to rest. That was worth the lie.

A Delta flight to Dulles International was leaving in half an hour. Burke bought a first-class ticket and boarded the plane. From the flight attendant he accepted a pretakeoff Bloody Mary and a plate of crackers and assorted cheeses. After the 727 was airborne, Burke got out the book he had begun last night, and read and dozed until the plane came down through the Virginia dusk and settled smoothly on the lighted runway.

From the nearest pay phone he called Claire, said he was on his way home, and suggested dinner together. Half-sobbing, she choked, "I'm so glad you called, I've been worried sick. But I'll pull myself together and be at your place when you get there. And"—she paused suspensefully—"I love you."

When the taxi pulled into his drive, Burke saw the inner lights on, Claire's pickup parked beside the house. She ran out to meet him as he paid the driver, and clutched him in her arms.

Then they went together into the house and made love before drinks and dinner.

Sixteen

UNDER THE SEARING summer sun the ocean was light green, lying almost flat between tides. Beyond the deep blue ocean river that was the Gulf Stream they could see the dark tracery of smoke from merchant funnels staining the cloudless horizon. Claire turned lazily on the big beach towel, and Burke applied aloe lotion to her evenly tanning skin.

They had flown to Miami and driven a rented car down the Keys to Marathon, where they found a resort inn to their liking. Senator Newsome had entered Bethesda Naval Hospital for a week of tests, and Claire agreed with Burke that it would be good to get away from Leesburg for a while. There were few summer guests at the inn, so they had their pick of accommodations, choosing a bungalow on the beach with strong air conditioning.

Yesterday they had fished the Stream bringing in wahoo, king mackeral, green-gold dolphin, jack crevalle, and barracuda. Claire had hooked and played a small white marlin that the guide released, and Burke released an undersize sailfish. It was Claire's first experience of sportfishing, and she'd learned quickly and found it exciting.

Claire had suggested Cancún or Cozumel, but Burke promised her they'd visit Mexico another time and Claire had tactfully not questioned him. So they were on Vaca Key, isolated as honeymooners, breakfasting on citrus and cereals, lunching on crisp conch fritters and beer, and feasting on lobster and stone crab in the cool evenings.

They snorkeled the clear offshore waters bringing back cowrie shells and pear whelks, moon shells and baby's teeth, small conch and thorny oysters. The collection, Claire said, would look well on his farmhouse mantel, and Burke agreed.

She was lying face down, bandeau straps untied and revealing the swell of her breasts. Burke anointed her back, letting lotion pool near her tailbone, then applied it to the beginning of her buns. Claire shivered, murmured unintelligibly, then raised her head. "Enough already, don't be a tease."

"Sorry."

"Bed's the place for sexy games, my love."

"Agreed," he said, and transferred his massaging to her shoulders. After a while she said, "Honey, I feel I've known you a very long time, but aside from Terry I know nothing of your family. How about a lesson in Burke history?"

Burke lighted a cigarillo and turned belly down on the towel. "You want history? Most of what I remember came word of mouth from my father, and it starts a hundred and fifty years ago with the Great Potato Famine. In five years between one and two million Irish emigrated west, my great-grandfather Beckett Burke among them. He didn't have enough passage money to reach New York or Boston so he was put ashore at Halifax. From there he made his way to eastern Canada where he worked as a laborer, a carpenter, ironmonger, and trapper. Beckett married a girl named Bounty Enfield who was part English, part Iroquois and taught him to read and write and figure sums. The Iroquois brought them furs to sell and they established a trading post in southern Quebec. My grandfather was born there, had six years of schooling, and set out for America. He was fourteen or so when he apprenticed himself to a well-to-do glassmaker in Canadaigua, learned glass-blowing and helped with the books. When he was twenty Enfield Burke married the boss's daughter, and took over the business when her father died. They had seven children of whom only three survived a typhoid epidemic, my father being one." He blew smoke at the horizon and watched the breeze snatch it away. "My father, Terence Burke, studied mechanical engineering at Hobart College and worked for a manufacturer of machine tools in Syracuse.

He decided not to climb that particular corporate ladder and joined a small Rochester firm manufacturing refrigeration units for motion picture houses—the beginning of air conditioning. At a church gathering Dad met an Eastman student, Patricia Coxe, and married her. He patented some improvements in cooling compressors—something I know absolutely nothing about—and accumulated enough money to set up his own consulting firm about the time I was born. I went to public schools in Rochester, and when I was fifteen Mom and Dad were drowned in a violent summer storm while sailing on Seneca Lake. Losing our parents so young was really devastating. There was no one else, so our maiden aunt Abbey took us in—Terry was only nine—and raised us as best she could. Dad hadn't left much, he'd made a lot of bad investments, and my aunt was a bookkeeper in Pittsford, so we learned the work ethic early. I had a year-round paper route and picked apples every summer. Ah, that's where I got my horny hands."

"Hands? Hadn't noticed that, just your horny mind."

"You'll pay for that." He slapped her rump and she squealed. Burke blew smoke at her golden hair. "Not much more, honey. I got through Cornell, went to war, and joined the imperialist CIA, became an adman, and met you. Story of my life."

"Hah! What I *really* want to hear are the parts you left out. When will they be revealed?"

"In the distant future." If I have one.

Turning over, Claire sat up and kissed him. "It's a wonderful story," she said, "and we're going to be a very happy couple. Everything you've done makes up for everything I haven't done. Should I go back to college?"

"If you want to."

"Two more years of scholastic drudgery?"

"No pain, no gain. But isn't that better than full-time hausfrau?"

"I don't know. I've never been a full-time hausfrau, but for you I'd gladly try."

"Hmmm. Let's not plan too far ahead, okay?"

"But I have to—it's the nest-builder in me. Or are you forever soured on marriage? I was—until I met you. But I won't get pushy.

I absolutely won't do anything to spoil this wonderful time. Now, let's snorkel a while and go to bed."

Afterward they drove to a guest lodge on Big Pine Key. There were only a few couples in the dining room, and looking toward the ocean, Burke noticed a trap setup on the seawall. After lunch the manager lent them a pair of Franchi 20-gauge trap guns, and Burke taught Claire how to hold and fire the shotgun, then demonstrated how to follow and break the moving target. They took turns pulling and shooting, but after two boxes of shells, Claire's shoulder was too sore to continue. Burke massaged it, explaining that she wasn't holding the stock firmly enough. Grumpily she said it wasn't a sport she really cared about, but she would sacrifice her shoulder and more to keep him happy.

That evening they drove down to Key West, where they dined and danced at Pier House amid a crowd of Tennessee Williams votaries.

In their room, with its standard Motel Deco furnishings, Burke watched Claire undressing, and compared her slim, boyish figure with Anna the *Alemana*'s heavier build, deciding that Claire's won hands down. Too, he liked Claire's nonprofessional approach to lovemaking; for her there were still mysteries to be explored.

Later in each other's arms, Claire murmured, "In your sleep you speak in French, do you know that?"

"No."

"Why do you talk French in your sleep, dear?"

"To keep from speaking Spanish, I suppose. Is it well-accented, colloquial French?"

"Hah! How would I know?"

Toward midnight Burke woke from a disturbing dream. Fishing, he'd hooked a muttonfish whose mouth and face eerily resembled Luís Quintana's, less the beard. Horrified, he'd cut the line and watched the Quintanafish slide back into the depths.

Now, awake, he remembered how Quintana had looked rising from the hopper, creamy trousers around his booted ankles, disheveled and ridiculous as Charlie Chaplin's Tramp, and fully as vulnerable. No fear in his serpent's eyes, just the realization of imminent death. Tecotitlán would probably raise a monument to their departed son, Burke thought, and wondered what Luana Villaverde would do. Probably find another affluent protector before the week was out.

Beside him Claire stirred in her sleep. He kissed her lips without pressure and touched her golden hair. He was fully in love with her, he admitted, but wondered what her reaction would be when she knew the truth about his devil's trade. Violence had never been part of her life, much less premeditated murder, but in time he would have to tell her and hope she would understand. Otherwise there would be an invisible barrier between them causing loss of faith and confidence, souring and destroying their love.

But he still had two targets to hit for the president, either of which could end his own life, so full disclosure to Claire could be postponed. They were together now in an idyllic setting enjoying each day and each hour, and for any man, he thought, that ought to be enough.

In the morning Claire phoned Bethesda Naval Hospital and spoke with her father. The senator was being released the following day, and much as she hated to leave the inn, she felt an obligation to go back home.

Burke reserved seats for them on an early morning flight from Miami. He hired a boat for half a day's fishing along the edge of the Stream, and where the sargassum weed was thick they raised five glistening dolphins, one a twelve-pound bull, Claire exclaiming over their loss of color as they died in the iced fish well. Then a billfish struck a small bait barracuda on Claire's line and Burke coached her until the silver blue fish was alongside, its sail meekly folded along its spine. "A good one," Burke told her as he cut the line. "Go eighty-ninety pounds if an ounce."

"Oh, I wish we'd brought a camera," she said excitedly. "Daddy'll never believe it."

"Does he know we're together?"

"Sort of, but I don't really want to emphasize it just now."

"So we'll forget your piscatorial triumph."

"It'll be our secret." She paused. "One of many." Her face tightened. "Tom, will we have many more?"

"Hope not," he said, and pointed out a school of tarpon rolling by

Seven Mile Bridge. Claire asked if they were going after the tarpon, but Burke said he was opposed to killing anything inedible, excluding sharks and moray eels, and tarpon was definitely inedible. "Still," he said, "the Silver King is a beautiful fish, especially when feeding. They favor the bay side of the Keys where the water's brackish. Any time you go after redfish in the bays you can expect to see tarpon."

"You've done a lot of sportfishing."

"Here and there. Once off Cabo Blanco, Peru, I hooked into about a thousand-pound black marlin, fought him all day, and had to break off when a storm came up. That's the loss I remember."

He noticed the lifted tail and wing tips of a manta as it idled by like a gray ghost, foraging the edge of the Stream for shrimp and bait fish. "What a magnificent animal," Claire exclaimed. "Must be six feet across."

"And very fast in the water. Rays don't bother anyone unless they're bothered. It's not a meat fish, but they're harpooned anyway. Shrimpers say they break the big purse nets."

The mate said it was time to be heading back to the marina, so they brought in the lines and lashed the outriggers and drank some iced beer and admired their catch until they were at the dock.

Burke had the mate fillet the bull dolphin, and let him sell the others for several dollars a pound. They drove back to the inn and arranged with the chef to have baked dolphin for dinner, along with fresh asparagus and fried plantain.

They snorkeled awhile, feeling the sun hot on their backs, ridding themselves of fish scales and boat smells in the warm water, collected more shells for the mantel, and set them to dry in the sun while they showered in the bungalow and made love in the cool dark room.

A little after dawn they left the inn and drove up the Keys, stopping once for gas and coffee, not talking much because the idyll was ending as they had known it must. On the Miami flight they had breakfast and dozed until Dulles International was in sight.

From Dulles they drove in his Porsche to her home, finding that the senator had not yet arrived. After the houseman took Claire's bags inside, Burke kissed and held her, saying he'd call later. Slowly, reluctantly, she walked inside the house.

He drove to the farmhouse, collected mail, and took it inside. Automatically, he played back his phone message tape and heard identical messages from Poliakoff recorded over the past three days: *"Call my office. Urgent."*

Urgent for whom? He unpacked and sorted his mail. There were credit card bills, electric and tax bills, a class plea for gifts to Cornell, real estate announcements, a salary check from Deems & Abernathy, and two letters from his brother.

Terry was well and adjusting readily to the more relaxed regimen of Allenwood, the first letter said. The second letter said Kirby had filed for divorce. Though expecting the blow, Terry found it hard to take, and hoped his brother could come soon for a visit. He had phone privileges every evening and on weekend days, so he'd be calling more frequently than he'd been able to from Lewisburg.

Burke got up and poured himself a half tumbler of Scotch and a water chaser. He knocked it back and began writing checks to cover his bills. When that was done Burke made coffee, and decided to visit Terry over the weekend. Now that his life involved Claire Newsome, he would have less time to maintain his brother's morale, but if all went well, Terry would be free by autumn.

He put dirty clothing in the washer, and while it was sloshing away Burke selected a cigarillo from the humidor box and began writing Terry.

A call from Claire interrupted him. Her voice wavered as she said her father had returned by navy ambulance. Corpsmen had helped her settle him in a first-floor bedroom to avoid his having to use stairs. "He's so pale and weak, Tom," she quavered, "and I'm not handling this very well."

"Can I help? Come over?"

"Well—he's resting now, sleeping I think. But it would do him good and help me a lot if you'd come around dinnertime. If he can't come to the table, we'll eat in his room. Would you do that for me?"

"Gladly. And since he's resting, why not come over and see your horses? They'd welcome you, and so would I."

"Should have thought of that. I'll be over in a while."

He finished the letter, thinking he'd beat it to Allenwood, and addressed it to "Jim McNally," Terry's prison alias.

That done, Burke considered Poliakoff's peremptory summons. On principle he was averse to obliging Enno, feeling that if the matter were truly urgent General Arness would phone. Instead, the next phone call was from "Harry," the alias of Jim Eubank.

"Oh," said Harry, "you're back."

"Obviously. What's on your mind?"

"I have something to show you, and if you'll be there, I can make it in half an hour. Okay?"

"Okay," Burke agreed resignedly, "but if a friend is here keep it brief, will you?"

"It's a promise."

Burke put his washed clothing in the dryer and found himself wondering how much longer Senator Newsome could last. In his bedroom Burke changed clothing, noticing that the week at Marathon had browned his skin, especially his neck and face where the Stream reflected the burning sun. He wasn't looking forward to being chez Newsome that evening, but it seemed the least he could do.

From his work phone he called Eddie Deems and asked how things were going at the office. "Surprisingly well," Eddie declared. "Being summer when a lot of offices lay off help, I was able to hire a woman who fits right in. Not that she's a threat to you, Tom, but she's doing very well."

"Good to know," Burke remarked. "I don't feel so badly about bugging out."

"No, you do what you have to, and we'll manage to keep the shop running. Ah—staying around long?"

"Probably not," he said, thinking of Harry's impending visit. "Just wanted you to know I'm alive and taking nourishment."

Through the window he saw Harry drive up in an old station wagon, and get out with a briefcase. Burke met him at the door and suggested they go down to the shooting shed.

"Worried about bugs?" Harry wiped perspiration from his face.

"Always," Burke replied, and they said nothing more until they were under the shade of the shed.

Harry unlocked his briefcase and took out a black-bound folder bearing the number 2. "Before we get into this, Tom, I have to tell you how grateful I am about Quintana. I didn't have to tell Bill's widow, she read about it and called me. Of course I pretended it was news to me, great news, the very best, and now I think she can get on with her life. At least I hope so." He swallowed. "Same for me, so I owe you a big one."

"You owe me nothing," Burke told him. "It was part of the deal." He touched the folder. "Who's the next villain?"

Harry sat on a bench and looked up at Burke. "A fellow of mixed citizenship and ancestry who does his dirty deeds between South America and the banks of Europe. Name of Hans Günther Weiskopf. Around the office he's known as Gargoyle."

Gargoyle

Seventeen

WHILE BURKE WAS READING the dossier, Harry sat at the edge of the creek tossing pebbles at the slow-flowing water. Burke heard Claire's pickup arrive, and after a while saw it proceed down through the meadow, rear end loaded with slabs of hay and sacks of oats. As horses gathered around her she stroked and fed them, and while they were feeding she nailed a large salt cylinder to the bole of a shade tree. Then she set out a wooden feed tray and filled it with grain. Much as Burke enjoyed watching her at work, the life and misdeeds of Hans Günther Weiskopf demanded his attention.

Bio data began with the arrival in Paraguay from postwar Germany of SS Major Dieter Weiskopf. Like other war criminals, Dieter had been aided in his escape by the long-established ODESSA ratline. Paraguay not being to his liking, Dieter had settled in Ecuador, where he started an import-export firm. He married the daughter of Siles Leano, who was both the sole owner of Ecuador's copper mines and a powerful senator in the legislature. Both father and daughter were full-blooded Quechua, quite a departure from the führer's doctrine of racial purity, Burke mused.

Hans Günther was born in 1947, a few months before the overthrow of President Velasco Ibarra forced the Leanos and Weiskopfs to leave Ecuador for Peru. After another coup Siles Leano returned to Ecuador, but Dieter, his wife Concepción, and their son remained in Lima, where Dieter established a trading firm that flourished as postwar international shipping returned to Lima's Pacific port, Callao.

In Lima's Catholic schools, and later at San Carlos University, Hans Günther met young Limeños who were to become his business associates and confederates. At San Carlos he studied economics, accounting, and banking, managed one of the Leano banks in Guayaquil, and learned how to conceal large deposits from government tax collectors. When he was twenty-three his father died of natural causes, the power and influence of Siles Leano having been sufficient to shield him from all extradition efforts.

At twenty-six Hans Günther married Beatriz Argensiano, the *mestiza* daughter of the family controlling much of Peru's petroleum deposits, as well as an airline. When Hans Günther met her, Beatriz was a stewardess on Papa's airline, flying to Panama, Miami, and San Diego, acquiring a taste for foreign luxuries and living, and supplementing her parental allowance by smuggling Colombian emeralds and Venezuelan pearls to jewelers in the United States.

As a wedding present, Beatriz's parents gave the couple an imposing villa near Lima's racetrack, a mansion erected by a former president of Peru whose political career was ended by coup. Having left the filth and humidity of Guayaquil, Hans Günther established his own bank in Lima and developed connections with banks in Panama, even more hermetic than those in Switzerland. The bulk of his deposits came from a few customers, men he had known at San Carlos, and commercial associates of the Argensiano family. Hans Günther conducted their business with Germanic precision, gaining a reputation for discretion and reliability. During a Swiss holiday with Beatriz, Hans Günther established commercial connections with banks in Zurich and Bern. First by courier, then through electronic transfer, Hans Günther was able to transfer large sums into the Swiss banking system where they were protected from Peru's cyclical political turmoil.

The mountain lands of the Argensianos produced both poppy and coca leaf. Papa Argensiano recruited a private army to protect his harvests from competitors, the Peruvian army, and the burgeoning *Sendero Luminoso* guerrillas. The Argensianos were producers of raw product, not processors or smugglers; that riskier business they left to others. Hans Günther, however, soon became a financial adviser to the *narcos* who were reaping incalculable profits from *narcotráfico*. His fame spread through the drug underworld, until he was laundering and investing money for the Cali Cartel and the drug kings of La Paz and Caracas.

Estimates gained through the National Security Agency's intercepts of electronic-banking transfers showed Hans Günther Weiskopf handling an average of three billion dollars annually, almost all of it drug profits.

Swiss banking authorities had declined U.S. requests to freeze Weiskopf's accounts on the specious grounds that evidence of criminality was lacking. Nor could the United States interest Peru's Ministry of Justice in arresting and extraditing Hans Günther Weiskopf to the United States; he was too well protected by family influence and massive bribery of public officials.

Hans Günther Weiskopf was known to maintain a lavish penthouse apartment in Zurich and a lakeside mansion in Geneva purchased from an heir to the shah of Iran.

The next page featured color photographs of Weiskopf. Despite blond hair and blue eyes, Weiskopf's dusky skin and prominent nose belied his Indian heritage. His wife, Beatriz, had the same café-au-lait skin, but her nose had been westernized by cosmetic surgery, and with dark eyes and hair the color of obsidian she was a beautiful, mature woman. The photo showed a necklace alternating diamonds and golden pearls worth, Burke thought, at least half a million dollars. Photographs of their two children showed the son dark as his mother, the little girl blond like her father.

Turning the page, Burke studied exterior photographs of the high-walled Lima mansion, the Zurich penthouse, and the Lake of Geneva villa. Its terraces and steps slanted down to water's edge where a long concrete pier led out to a wide boathouse. A telephoto showed Weiskopf at the wheel of a powerful speedboat, wife and children in the stern. A similar photo caught Weiskopf at the tiller of a ten-meter sailboat. An aerial photo showed the walled grounds and roof of his protected abode.

As Burke closed the dossier he saw Claire walk into the farmhouse, discreetly leaving him to his visitor.

Burke lighted a cigarillo and read about the villa's protective system. Its grounds were surrounded by a high wall topped with barbed wire. At frequent intervals video cameras swept the grounds and the house exterior. Concealed thermal and pressure sensors were activated at nightfall and avoided by patrols of armed guards with leashed Dobermans and Rottweilers. The sheet-metal main gate was manned around the clock by sentries carrying automatic weapons. Delivery trucks were escorted in and out by armed guards.

There was a green-painted helipad near the tennis court for the chopper Weiskopf kept at Genève-Cointrin airport with his Falcon jet. The chopper was used mainly to ferry Weiskopf and his family between villa and airport, eliminating traffic delays and the danger of holdups. To all appearances Weiskopf had settled in Switzerland, protected by the cantonal police and shielded inside his citadel.

Two or three times a year Weiskopf would fly to London and Paris for meetings with South American clients and cooperative European bankers. On those occasions he bought the companionship of high-priced call girls, never employing the same one twice. Aside from those lapses in matrimonial fidelity, Weiskopf appeared to be a devoted husband and father, lavishing on wife and children every luxury money could buy.

For laundering and investing *narco* wealth, Weiskopf retained twenty percent of the gross, bringing his estimated personal fortune to more than a billion dollars. Some of his more profitable investments were in German automotive and chemical plants via protective intermediaries. He invested similarly in Swiss pharmaceutical concerns, and was known to own an Alpine ski resort.

The writer of the report opined that Weiskopf's sudden disappearance from the *narco*/finance scene would cause tremendous disruption. According to a top-level Peruvian drug informant, Weiskopf was known to keep major transaction details in his head, entrusting them neither to paper nor to computer memory whence they could be recovered and used as prosecutorial evidence. The writer likened Weiskopf to a spider at the center of a web. In Weiskopf's absence his clients would be unable to retrieve deposits from the numbered accounts he maintained in their behalf.

Two years ago an emissary sent by the U.S. attorney general had offered Weiskopf immunity from prosecution if he surrendered his clients' money and informed on them. Weiskopf laughed genially and said he had no idea what the emissary was talking about.

He had his chance, Burke thought, and turned back to the photographs. One newspaper photo of Weiskopf at a Lausanne banking reception showed a rather broad, squat Indian frame. His height, Burke estimated, would be about five-seven or -eight, half a foot less than the deceased SS major who sired him. Burke reviewed the aerial photo of the villa and grounds, fixing their features in his mind, then closed the dossier and weighted it with a rifle sandbag.

He went down to the creek where Harry was watching a pair of pintails fish a shadowed pool. "I gather Gargoyle can be hit any time."

"He doesn't travel much," Harry said, rising. "Do you shoot ducks?"

"Not tame ones. What kind of ground support can I count on?"

"Same as Guadalajara. Weapons, commo—surveillance is tougher in Suisse The Swiss police don't want their millionaire guests disturbed."

Burke plucked a long blade of grass and chewed the sugar-sweet end. "I can think of a lot of ways to waste Gargoyle," he said, "but they'd endanger his family. That limits me. In Guadalajara all I had to worry about was Puma's pack of *pistoleros.* This equation is different, trickier."

Harry nodded.

"I'm thinking about documentation that would include a pilot's license good enough that I can hire a plane in Europe and keep it at Cointrin, in case I decide to get friendly with Gargoyle's pilots. How about commo?"

Harry smiled and took from one pocket a box that was slightly longer and thinner than a cigarette box. "That last NASA shuttle flight put up a satellite that'll bounce you from Suisse to Washington." He opened the box, showing Burke an instrument that looked like a pocket calculator, except that the buttons were lettered rather than numbered. "This is a messager," he said, "and we call it Paul Revere. Use it out your window or in any open space and transmit your message letter by letter. The reply comes back the same way."

"Plain text? What about interception?"

"A new frequency in the civilian band. The Russians won't be interested in personal messages, and the *narcos* haven't the technology to intercept sat traffic."

"Yet," Burke muttered.

"This comes with a clip-over shell to disguise it as a calculator." He produced the plastic shell and Burke pressed it into place.

"Batteries?"

"It comes with a nine-volt cadmium battery. The best place to test it is from your op site."

Burke nodded. "While you're getting my documentation together, get me a Ljutic recoilless rifle."

"Never heard of it."

"Custom-made, Harry, unless Treasury's BATF has one on hand." Kneeling, he drew a line on the sand, thickened it slightly at the middle, and added a short vertical stripe to one end. Between the butt and the thicker part he slanted a pistol grip. "This is the ultimate in concealable rifles," he said. "Twenty-four-inch barrel, less than four feet overall. I want it with mounts for a twelve-power scope."

Harry was making quick notes. "What caliber?"

"Three-oh-eight preferred, but I'll take thirty-aught-six if that's available. When it's delivered here I'll shoot for familiarization. The only drawback is it's single-shot."

"Ljutic, eh? Where'd you see one?"

"Baltimore gun show, priced around five thousand dollars. Of collector interest mainly, because there is only one conceivable use for the piece—distance killing."

"One way or another you'll have it. How about funding?"

Burke thought about it. "Won't be cheap and easy," he said, "so for starters I'd like fifty thousand in my name at a friendly Geneva bank. If I need more, I'll send a message by 'Paul Revere.' If I use less, your office can reclaim it."

"No problem."

They walked back to the gun shed, where Burke returned the Gargoyle dossier and asked, "How's the general keeping?"

"Out of town. But he was real pleased about Puma." Harry locked the dossier in his briefcase.

"Did López have trouble leaving the Caballo Negro?"

Harry shook his head. "In all that confusion he just melted away."

"That's a night he'll remember," Burke said with a thin smile, "and if he's smart, he'll never talk about it."

"He's been told," Harry said. "Believe me, he's been told."

They were heading for Harry's old station wagon. When they reached it, Burke said, "So—who's my case officer, Harry? You? Enno?"

Harry shrugged and looked away. "Make a difference?"

"To me it does—the difference being I have a certain amount of confidence in you and none whatever in Enno." He closed Harry's door and waved him off.

In the kitchen, Claire had made a large pitcher of iced lemonade.

"You shouldn't have," Burke said, pouring two glasses.

"And why not? If I can take care of horses, I can certainly take care of a man . . . especially if he's *my* man."

"I like the sound of that," he said. He drank deeply and brushed her cheek with wet lips. "Want to hear about my visitor?"

She looked at him steadily. "What visitor? Saw no one, nobody was here. Isn't that what I'm supposed to say?"

"Fast learner. Now, until it's time to see the senator you wanna fool around?"

"With you? I've counted on it."

So they walked hand in hand down to the creek and skinny-dipped in the pool where the pintails had been paddling. After a while they made love on the bank shaded by a tall spruce with gnarled, flood-polished roots, and for Burke there was no memory of Gargoyle or Harry or Puma or the special killing rifle or the guarded villa on the Lake of Geneva. . . . There was only her softness and sweetness and the caress of her lips and body, the whisper of breath in her throat, and he wished that it could be this way forever with no parting or sadness and just the two of them indivisible against a treacherous world.

They had dinner trays on either side of the senator's bed in a spacious high-ceilinged room whose wallpaper was of a muted floral design that suggested Colonial Williamsburg to Burke.

Senator Newsome, pale and weak, was being fed by a two-stripe navy nurse named Simpson. Lieutenant Simpson, she emphasized, and Burke supposed she didn't do windows, ironing, or bed pans. Rank has its privileges.

The dietitian had recommended tuna croquettes with garden peas, so that was the menu. Burke was eating, though Claire merely toyed with her plate. Newsome said he wasn't hungry, but the nurse lieutenant insisted on inserting spoonfuls of tuna into his mouth. In an authoritative tone she said "Sir, you have to eat if you're to gain strength. And if you don't have strength, you'll have to stay in bed."

Newsome glared at her.

"Every word I've said is true. Now, will you eat?"

"It'd go down better with some wine," he grumbled. "Any objection to that, Lieutenant, ma'am?"

"Not if it will help," she said resignedly, so Burke went to the kitchen, opened a chilled bottle of Chablis, and carried it to the bedroom. Senator Newsome brightened at the sight, and declared that it would help him digest his meal. Claire's face, Burke saw, was damp with tears she kept wiping away.

When the nurse left the room with the senator's tray, he said, "I'm greatly relieved you're back, Tom. I have an idea of what you've gone through, and I know it wasn't easy."

With a glance at Claire, Burke said, "Things fell into place, Senator. It was less difficult than I'd imagined."

"May all your challenges be similarly resolved." Newsome lifted his glass in a toast. "Now," he said, "I gather you've introduced my daughter to some of the manly sports, right?"

"That displeases you?"

"On the contrary. I was never much of a fisherman, less of a hunter. I'm glad you've filled in, Tom, and I guess the two of you enjoyed the Keys."

"Thoroughly," Claire responded; she looked away and wiped her eyes.

"So I'm well satisfied that my daughter had a strong and principled friend to help her through increasingly difficult times. . . ."

Choking back sobs, Claire fled the room. Senator Newsome sighed, "This is much harder on her than on me, you know. My end is at hand, Tom, and I'll meet it as well as I can. But I grieve for Claire. Ah—a bit more wine?"

Burke filled his glass and moved closer to the bed. After sipping, the senator said, "In view of circumstances involving us both, I'm going to be bold enough to ask if you and Claire have formed any future plans."

Burke added more wine to his glass and considered his reply. "Claire does," he said, "and we love each other, but it would hardly be fair to let her make wedding plans when I could be killed at any time." He drank from his glass. "Losing her father will devastate her, Senator, you must be aware of that. Losing me as well could undo her completely, so I'm trying to avoid a deep mutual commitment. Not that I don't feel one," he went on, "but I want her to have psychological space if the worst happens to me."

"Well, you've spoken as an honorable man," the senator said musingly, "and I appreciate your frankness." His head turned on the pillow as he looked away. "At Bethesda the doctors said I have a month to live, maybe two. I'll be on morphine soon, my mind dulled along with my body, so I'm glad we had this talk while I'm still able to summon comprehension."

Burke bent more closely to the senator's ear. "Let's suppose," he said quietly, "that I fully execute the president's commission, and my brother is freed. My next thought will be Claire."

"Go on."

"I'm troubled, Senator, because I don't know to what extent I should let her know the agreement I made with the president. If she is ever to learn that I killed to free my brother, I would want it to be from me, not the *Washington Post*. You're the only one who can counsel me, Senator. I've been frank with you, and I ask that you be equally frank with me."

For a long time Senator Newsome said nothing, face and body in repose. Finally he took what was for him a deep breath and said in a voice little above a whisper, "Tom, the question is above common-place morality and beyond the candor a husband owes his wife. Over my long years in the political arena I did things—or allowed them to be done—that I told myself my wife would be much happier not knowing about. And time proved me right. In your case a national secret is involved. Claire, whether as your wife or fiancée, is not entitled to know it. Your arrangement with the president of the United States is a secret of state. You have no right, no right what-ever, to disclose it to anyone; not your brother, not my daughter." His face turned and his gaze bored into Burke. "Should the right moment arise before I die, I will advise Claire that there are some things about you she is never to question—perhaps that will ease your dilemma."

"It will, Senator, I'm sure it will. And thank you for your under-standing." Burke managed a slight smile. "For her it will come as a voice from the mount."

"Now fill my glass again, and join my daughter. I need to rest." He gripped Burke's hand. "You *are* the son Wayne would have been, and I pray that you have a long and satisfying life—with Claire or not."

Burke found Claire at the stables. Putting his arms around her, he said softly, "Dear, your father is a unique and selfless man. His concern is not with his pain or discomfort or death, but the sorrow he's inflicting on you. So for his sake and your own, try to bear up while you're with him. What he's facing lies ahead for us all, but for your father it's come early."

She hugged him as she sobbed, then lifted tear-wet cheeks. "Is that what he told you?"

"It's what he wants."

"Then he knows . . . everything."

Nodding, Burke kissed her forehead.

After drying her face she said, "Much as I want to be with you tonight—and every night—I feel I should stay here, nearby."

"Of course—if you like I'll stay, too."

She smiled bleakly. "You'll have Wayne's room—Father will like that."

"And so will I."

*   *   *

During the night she came to him and he took her in his arms to hold and comfort her, and as he lay in the darkness beside her he remembered the night in the hacienda when he had lain alone, wakened by the distant plane. All had been calm and tranquil then, as now in the darkness of this room, but that had been a false calm before the killing and burning began.

Eighteen

AFTER BREAKFAST WITH the senator, they drove to Burke's farmhouse, where he helped Claire trailer two mounts for a show at Middleburg. Driving down Route 15 in her pickup, Burke said, "The bad news is I'll be going to Europe soon, and if you could get away for a few days, I'd love to have you with me. That's supposed to be the good news."

With a sigh she glanced at him. "You know how much I'd love to, Tom, but you know it's not possible just now. If—if my father's condition worsened or, God forbid, he died while I was off enjoying myself . . . I don't think I'd ever forgive myself." She touched his hand.

He nodded.

"We'll go another time," she said with an effort at cheerfulness. "Thanks for asking, anyway. I know you meant it."

At Gilberts Corners she swung west onto Route 50 for the final six miles to Middleburg. As they passed through Aldie, she said, "You're seeing Terry tomorrow, I know, but after that when do you leave again?"

"Not sure."

"I don't suppose you can say how long you'll be gone."

"Because I don't know. But I'll come back as soon as I can."

"More secret work," she said bitterly. "Will it ever end?"

"It will." One way or another.

From Leesburg she had worn black riding boots, white whipcord trousers and a frilled white shirt. After leading her mounts from the trailer she had Burke hold their reins while she put on a formal black coat and velvet-covered hard hat. Then she went over to the registration table and received her number for the day: 17. Burke tied it on, and saddled her horses while Claire joined a group of riders discussing the course and the rain-moist ground. Then Claire mounted Comet in a single swinging motion and began exercising him inside the ring. After a while she dismounted and took Argel around the ring while Burke cooled down Comet. She worked Argel over the bars, rode back to Burke, and said, "He's shying." Springing off, she checked each hoof in turn, and said disgustedly, "No wonder, this shoe's loose—and no farrier around. Well, I'll go with Comet."

Burke cupped his hands for her boot as she mounted Comet, then she took him over the jumps. After watering Argel, Burke tied him to the pickup's tailgate and found a bleacher seat to watch the competition. In all there were about twenty riders, from teenagers to mature men and women. Claire was median age, Burke estimated, but her equestrian skills were superior. When it came her turn she took each of the jumps without hesitation, but at the last jump Comet's rear hoof nicked the top bar and it came off, costing Claire valuable points. Her next two rounds were perfect, though, and when the event ended in midafternoon she was awarded a red ribbon.

They refreshed themselves with champagne and small sandwiches in the shade of a caterer's tent. Burke said, "If this is the life of an equestrienne's husband, it's not bad at all."

"Wait'll winter comes, dear, and everything's mucking out stables and keeping trough water from freezing."

"Ummm. Hadn't thought of that."

Back at his farm they freed the horses to the fields, showered together, and had drinks before driving near Upperville to the 1763 Inn. They enjoyed the inn's colonial atmosphere and well-prepared, unpretentious food, and decided to spend the night there—after Claire checked with Lieutenant Simpson to assure herself that the senator was resting comfortably.

They took the George Washington suite and made love in an old-fashioned, high-mattressed bed, sleeping with hands touching until well after dawn.

After saying goodbye to Claire, Burke flew to Harrisburg, rented a car, and visited his brother at Allenwood Prison Camp in an open setting of picnic tables and families with children. The day was warm, and there were no walls, fences, or guard towers to cast a pall on reunions. And it was better, Burke thought, that children not carry dark memories of their fathers' confinement. Terry looked thinner and fit from working outdoors with dairy cattle. He slept in a long brick barracks without bars, he said; the food was better than Lewisburg's, and he'd bought tennis shoes and racket from a departing inmate. A small herd of deer lived at the edge of the woods and were almost tame. With a wry smile Terry said, "I've become a nature lover, Tom. Maybe I'll never live in a city again."

"Maybe you won't have to."

"I'm thinking of settling in Alaska; still opportunities there, I hear. Some inmates are going there on release, others favor Costa Rica. I think I'd take mountains over jungle."

"Mountains are one thing Alaska has plenty of," Burke remarked. He was relieved that Terry wasn't bursting with the complaints he'd voiced at Lewisburg. So getting him to Allenwood was a major improvement. Claire had packed a picnic lunch for them—inspected by guards—and they shared cold chicken salad, brownies, and soft drinks.

"When am I going to meet this supergirl you're going with?" Terry asked.

"Her father's dying," Burke told him, "so it probably won't be until fall."

"Not like Kirby, is she?" His face fell.

"Not at all." The visiting bell rang, and families said their goodbyes and began to leave. Burke and his brother hugged each other. "I'll leave money with the cashier," Burke offered.

"Hard to spend much here, but thanks. My magazines are coming in now, and they're not stolen the way they were at the other place." As Burke turned to go, Terry said, "I count on your visits, Tom. When will you be up again?"

"Couple of weeks—I have some traveling to do."

Terry laughed tightly. "Travel—that's a banned word here, but we dream about it."

Flying back with CAVU conditions, Burke pondered his brother's character and outlook. Some of Terry's pretrial bravado was gone, but Burke had yet to detect signs of remorse. It was as though Terry had gambled everything on the turn of a card, lost, and left the gaming table confident of a future win. And after Terry's sentencing, when Burke had suggested quietly that a show of contrition might be useful, Terry had said scornfully, "Free me and they'll get all the contrition they can handle." Federal marshals had led him away.

When they were living with Aunt Abbey, Terry had broken a neighbor's windows with his pellet gun. Abbey had paid for new windows, and Terry had left it to Burke to repay her with money from his paper route. And Terry had taunted larger schoolmates into fighting him, then ran to Burke for protection. Then there was Terry's flight to Canada which he represented as morally principled, claiming his eventual presidential amnesty as total vindication.

So somewhere deep within Terry was a character flaw, a deep-seated arrogance and indifference to the feelings of others. Kirby was much the same, Burke reflected, which was perhaps why they married. But they grated against each other, hadn't smoothed each other out.

Still, Terry was his brother, his only blood kin, and perhaps prison would do more for him than all the years he had lived free.

Dusk was falling when Burke landed his Apache at Leesburg airport, where Claire was waiting in his Porsche. They drove into town and had a candle-lit dinner at the Laurel Brigade Inn. Although the setting was undeniably romantic, Burke felt that they were slipping prematurely into an almost domestic routine whereby wife greeted hubby on his return from a business trip, made things comfy for him, and gratified his physical needs. The change bothered him because he realized that Claire had come to regard him more as husband than lover, and he wasn't ready for that.

He couldn't talk about his work, and Claire was preoccupied with her father, so he was grateful when after coffee she kissed his cheek and whispered, "Your place or mine?"

"Yours," he replied, expecting a visit from Harry in the morning.

*   *   *

Toward midmorning Harry delivered the Ljutic rifle, along with Canadian documentation in the name of Roger Pierre Morillon. The International Pilots License showed him multiengine and instrument rated. On deposit at the Banque Versoix was fifty thousand dollars. Harry handed over five thousand for travel expenses, saying, "As of yesterday Gargoyle was in Geneva."

"Good. I'll leave tomorrow. Who's my contact?"

"Charles Blane—DEA. He's been alerted to give you full aid and assistance. He's not witting to your mission, Tom—what he may surmise is, well, up to him."

Burke nodded. "If Gargoyle's under surveillance, tell Blane to call it off. I don't want him getting nervous and blowing town."

"Will do."

They said good-bye, and Burke watched Harry drive away in the elderly station wagon. He was a good man, Burke thought, as he carried the rifle to the shed for sighting-in.

Its butt was a thin pad fitting into his shoulder, the trigger a pressure button with no safety. The receiver unscrewed from the barrel and took one hand-fed .308 cartridge at a time. The weapon disassembled into two pieces less than two feet long. Ideal for concealed carrying, Burke thought approvingly.

He mounted the 12X scope and with sandbag rests and Leupold scope methodically sighted-in the rifle for two hundred yards. At that setting he grouped five shots in a three-inch circle, then fired at the three-hundred-yard target, noting the clicks necessary to achieve the same pattern. He fired two boxes—a hundred rounds—of .308 soft-point lead bullets before he was satisfied with the rifle's accuracy and his marksmanship. He disassembled and reassembled the piece in total darkness, cleaned bore and chamber, and coated the metal with a light film of oil. Along with five .308 cartridges, it was ready for pouching to Geneva.

After leaving a message for Harry to collect it Burke called Swissair and reserved a seat to Geneva the following night.

That evening he dined with Claire at the senator's bedside. Burke was shocked by Newsome's appearance, the shrunken flesh on face and hands. The cancer, Claire told him later, had metastasized, and the senator refused chemotherapy and artificial means to prolong his life. The governor had decided to appoint himself to Newsome's Senate seat, and the dying man said he hoped the governor—a political ally, not a friend—would be a better senator than he was a governor. Burke couldn't help wondering silently whether Newsome's endorsement of his brother's pardon application would carry any weight after the senator's death. It wouldn't matter as long as the president carried out his part of the bargain.

That night Burke and Claire stayed at his farmhouse, and he was saddened to hear her crying in her sleep. He moved close to her and held her in his arms while the sobs subsided, and slept that way until dawn.

Over breakfast, she said," I promised Father I'd go to Charlottesville today and"—her voice broke—"make burial arrangements." Burke clasped her hands. "I can't tell you how sorry I am."

"I know . . . I know." She dried tears, managed a wan smile, and asked, "Any idea when you'll be back?"

"A week, I hope."

"And I can't know where you're going."

"Afraid not. But you'll be very much on my mind, darling."

"I want to be," she told him, "always."

Before leaving, she clung to him, covering his face with urgent kisses that left him shaken as he watched her drive away.

Burke slept comfortably crossing the Atlantic and ate breakfast just before the plane landed at Geneva's Cointrin airport, whose runways paralleled the French frontier. He passed through Swiss Customs and Immigration without hindrance. Renting an Audi, he checked into the hotel l'Aiglon on the rue Philippe Plantamour, near the public swimming pool, taking a top-floor room that overlooked the lake and the lighthouse a little to the left. Almost directly across was the Jet-d'Eau, the fountain spouting more than four hundred feet. As Paris was symbolized by the Eiffel Tower, Geneva's symbol was the towering spray. In a breeze, the high jet swayed, and illuminated by colored lights, it was spectacular by night.

From a lobby phone Burke called his contact. After a short wait he heard a man's voice. "This is Blane."

"I'm Cardiff," Burke told him. "Let's get together."

"Right. How about an hour from now. Parc Mon Repos?"

"Good, it's not far from where I'm staying."

"I'll be on the lakeside walk, green shirt, no tie."

"See you."

Burke reached the park early and glanced around for surveillance. He didn't expect any; the Swiss police had plenty of targets to cover without tailing casual tourists. After parking the Audi near a kiosk Burke bought a *Journal du Genève* and walked to a bench where he sat and scanned the paper. The day was warm; a lake breeze moved the branches of nearby aspens, and he felt an unaccustomed sense of tranquility.

A story that caught his attention was datelined Cartagena, Colombia. Jorge Ochoa Contreras, a major figure in Medellín's notorious drug cartel, had died when his yacht exploded and sank a few miles off Cartagena harbor. Two surviving crew members, blown clear of the yacht, told police they believed a bomb caused the maritime disaster. Police sources laid Ochoa's death to internecine warfare among *narcotraficantes.*

Burke wondered if the incident was one of General Arness's projects, an operation parallel to his own. Whether it was or not, the result was fortuitous. As Burke turned the page he saw a man wearing a green shirt coming slowly toward him. The man glanced at Burke, then looked away. Burke said, "I've been reading about Ochoa's yacht—Cartagena. Perhaps you heard about it."

The man sat down on the bench. "Only what the papers reported," he said. He was in his late thirties, Burke estimated, wearing Swiss-made clothing and shoes. He wore rimless glasses on a small pinched nose, and his expression told Burke that the contact was eager to please. For appearance's sake they shook hands. Charles Blane said, "I've received orders to support you in every possible way."

"Anyone else in your office see those orders?"

Blane shook his head.

"Good. I'm documented as Roger Pierre Morillon, Canadian; I have room six fifteen at l'Aiglon. Know it?"

"From the outside."

"We won't meet there, of course, so when you receive a pouched package for my attention we'll use cars. Mine is a dark blue Audi." He pointed to where it was parked.

Blane nodded. Burke continued, "I need to keep track of Hans Günther Weiskopf's movements, especially if it appears he's preparing to leave Geneva. Have you got a safe house where I can cool off for a few days if necessary?"

"I'll have one by this time tomorrow. Old Town would be best, I think."

"I trust your judgment, Charles. Do the Weiskopfs have a large circle of friends? Are they on the party circuit?"

"The general answer is no. Weiskopf has banking associates he lunches with at bankers' clubs. His wife seldom appears in public except when she goes shopping, for jewelry for herself, clothing and toys for the children. I haven't served in Latin America, but I understand Hispanic wives tend to stay in the background, focus on husband and children."

Burke nodded. "That's the custom."

"I could arrange a card to one of Weiskopf's clubs," Blane offered.

"Thanks, but I won't need personal contact with him." No more than I wanted personal contact with Charlie Cong before I killed him. To preclude more questions, Burke got to his feet. "You know how to contact me; I'll expect to hear from you."

"Yes, sir. As soon as something comes in." He left the bench and strolled down the lakeside walk until a turn blocked him from view. Burke read another page of his paper, folded it under his arm, and returned to his hotel.

After a change of clothing he drove out Autoroute 1 past Chambésy and Bellevue, paralleling the lake shore on its western side. Unlike Mexican highways, the road was smooth and well marked. The shoulders were unlittered and visible grass well trimmed. He

appreciated Swiss orderliness, cleanliness, and punctuality, rare quali-
ties in Latin America, and insufficiently honored in the United States.

Weiskopf's premises were marked by stone posterns, a high wall,
and a wide, heavily grilled gate, inside which Burke could glimpse a
guard kiosk as he drove slowly by. A mile farther along, he turned
back and neared Weiskopf's as a large silver-colored Mercedes limousine left the gate and headed south into Geneva. Burke followed the
limousine as far as the botanical gardens, where the limousine stopped
and let out two small children and their nanny. Burke continued on,
crossing at the Mont Blanc bridge, then heading up the eastern side
to the *débarcadère*. He hired a speedboat for an hour, telling the owner
he wanted to photograph some of the great mansions along the
western side of the lake.

Before the boat was off Weiskopf's pier and boathouse, Burke had
shot half a roll of color film with his thirty-five-millimeter camera. He
noticed a point of land south of the pier, photographed it, and used
the rest of the roll to capture Weiskopf's lakeside exposure from
different angles. Then he had the owner cross the lake and return by
the eastern side.

A camera shop on the *quai* promised Burke blowups by noon next
day, so he left the cassette and reloaded his camera with another.
From there he drove to the airport and hired a small French helicopter
for a tour of the lake.

He photographed the United Nations building, the Palais de Nations, that huge, luxurious monument to the world's freeloaders, he
thought contemptuously, and took views of the lakefront as the
chopper turned north along the shoreline. The pilot had provided a
map showing the marble retreats of dead and living billionaires, the
lesser châteaux of writers and dead poets, and pointed out a flotilla
of yachts racing before the afternoon's brisk wind. Without making
a point of it, Burke had the pilot fly down the lakeshore so he could
photograph Weiskopf's grounds and mansion, the long pier and
boathouse, the stubby finger of land to the south of it.

Burke left film for developing and enlarging at a shop on the rue
des Alpes, bought a bottle of Hine cognac next door to it, and
returned to his room.

Drained by jet lag, Burke soaked in a hot tub, drank brandy, and fell asleep. When he woke, the water had cooled and he had the start of a hangover. He rubbed himself warm with a big bath towel, got into bed, and slept until dark.

From aboard a night tour boat Burke observed Weiskopf's manor and lakeside grounds. Floodlights illuminated the grounds. Strings of lights outlined the pier to prevent boat collision, and the peak of the boathouse showed a light, but the grilled water entrance to the boathouse was dark. He accepted a glass of mediocre German champagne from the waiter and a chicken salad sandwich, amenities of the *croisière de luxe*, as Weiskopf's domain fell astern.

In the unlikely event that Weiskopf paid nocturnal visits to his boats, Burke could lie in wait. Or he could rig a bomb to the speedboat's ignition. . . . But he assumed Weiskopf's family enjoyed the speedboat, and destroying them would make him the moral equal of the *traficantes.* He could not live with that burden.

So as the boat plowed on through calm dark waters, Burke tossed a cigarillo butt overboard and watched it disappear. He tensed as an idea formed.

Next day he rented a small motorboat and steered it up the coastline past Weiskopf's place. Pretending engine trouble, he let the boat drift a while, the wind pushing it toward Weiskopf's boathouse.

The water side of the boathouse was closed by a metal grille with wide-set bars, intended to safeguard the boats, not to prevent a person from slipping inside.

As he labored on the boat's engine he saw Weiskopf strolling out on the pier, two large Rottweilers playing around his legs. The man who moved three billion a year for distant *narcotraficantes* was wearing yellow trousers, blue espadrilles, blue blazer, yellow shirt, blue cravat, and a Greek-style yachting cap. He disappeared inside the boathouse, and soon the heavy grille gates swung open, revealing Weiskopf in the cockpit of his speedboat. A woman in white jeans hurried out to the pier, waving at Weiskopf who waited with a look of impatience and he didn't bother to help her board. As soon as she was seated, he backed into the lake with a powerful engine roar, spun the wheel, and accelerated until the stern lowered and the bow lifted clear of the lake. A white rooster tail soared behind the speedboat as it headed east across the lake, hiding boat and passengers from Burke's view. From his rented boat he photographed the open boathouse, and turned back to the *débarcadère*.

From there he drove out to the airport and entered the Civil Aviation office. He bought coffee and looked through the runwayside window at the private tie-downs and service hangars. A clerk told him *M'sieu* Weiskopf's Falcon jet was undergoing routine maintenance, but his Bell helicopter was out on the tarmac. Burke scanned it over the rim of his coffee cup, noting the chopper's painted numbers, finished his coffee, and left Cointrin. On the way back he collected his enlargements and studied them in his room.

Before bed that night he set his wrist alarm for one o'clock, Swiss time, and when it wakened him, Burke got out the messager and opened the window. He pushed the red TRANSMIT button, and pointing it skyward, at the invisible geostatic satellite, punched out the following message:

> OUT OF THE NIGHT BLACK AS A BITCH AND
> INTO THE DIN AND THE SMOKE . . .

He canceled TRANSMIT and set the device on RECEIVE. He held it in the same position for a while, then alerted by a brief buzz, saw digital letters spell out:

> . . . CAME A DIRTY OLD MINER FRESH FROM THE CREEK
> WITH A RUSTY LOAD IN HIS POKE. END MSG

Burke smiled. Paul Revere worked, and all that was lacking was the rifle. Tomorrow it should be in his hands.

Nineteen

THE NEXT MORNING Burke drove twenty-five miles to Lausanne and found a scuba shop where he purchased French-made diving equipment: black wet suit and buoyancy compensator, air tank and regulator, wrist compass, fins, and mask with snorkel tube. On the way back along the lake he turned onto a tree-hidden promontory he'd noted from the boat, where he parked the Audi and got into diving gear.

For about ten yards the lake bottom sloped gradually downward, then dropped off. Burke inflated the BC for neutral buoyancy, checked tank pressure, and swam underwater until his bare wrists and ankles absorbed the glacier-fed water's chill. Ten feet down he could see no more than a dozen feet ahead, despite bright sunshine. He checked the glowing dial of his wrist compass and found it sufficiently accurate for his purpose. Ore deposits under the lake bed were bound to cause minor deviations.

He swam toward shore, surfaced in shallow water, and saw a uniformed policeman staring down at him. *"Bonjour,"* Burke said, unslinging his tank.

"Bonjour, m'sieu. You enjoy the diving sport, it seems?"

"Ardently," Burke replied. "And you, officer?"

"I am not an enthusiast, but I must inquire: you were not fishing, were you?"

"By no means."

"Bon. Such fishing—without hook and line—is forbidden."

"I assumed as much." Burke flopped awkwardly toward the gendarme in his flippers, and mustered a genial smile. "I would never abuse the hospitality of your hospitable nation."

The policeman smiled. "Surely you are a diplomat on vacation, *m'sieu*. Permit me to warn you of the dangers of diving alone. Here is this isolated place you could suffer a disabling cramp and die unnoticed."

Burke sat down and pulled off his flippers, leaving on his rubber headpiece, the mask half-covering his eyes. "You've got a darn good point," he agreed. "I just couldn't wait to try out this fancy new equipment. Next time I'll bring my wife, okay?"

Still, the policeman lingered. "The water is cold, *non?* Though *genevois*, I have never bathed in the lake for that reason. I and my family, we prefer the *piscine publique*."

Burke shrugged agreeably. "Still, we Canadians are accustomed to cold. Some crackpots called Polar Bears even dive under winter ice, but I call that excessive."

The policeman nodded thoughtfully. "Quite excessive—and perilous. So you are Canadian, *m'sieu?* By chance are your papers in your car?"

Burke shook his head apologetically. "They are in safekeeping of the hotel concierge."

"A wise precaution indeed. And which hotel, if I may inquire?"

"The Hilton."

"Ah, then you are with one of the international bodies that favor Geneva with their presence? OPEC, perhaps?"

"No," Burke sighed, "a mere tourist. However, my name and passport number are to be found on the rental papers in my car's glove compartment, if you care to examine them."

The officer shook his head. "I will not trouble you more, *m'sieu le Canadien*. You appear an honest person, if a bit reckless." He touched a finger to his cap. "Have a good day, and remember not to dive alone."

"I shall," Burke promised. He watched the officer return to his Renault and drive away.

Burke peeled off his wet suit and warmed under the sun. Then he stowed his gear in the Audi's trunk, got into street clothing, and drove back to Lausanne. At the scuba shop he bought an underwater light, a leg knife, and a waterproof zipper bag about thirty inches long. Big enough for the Ljutic and its scope.

At the hotel there were no messages, so Burke lunched at a nearby Möwenpick grill and drove to the airport. His International Pilot's License permitted access to enter the Civil Aviation section, and he walked down the row of private aircraft until he was at the repair hangar.

Weiskopf's Falcon was there, two mechanics working on the landing gear. A white-shirted flight engineer was watching them as Burke circled the plane slowly and admiringly. When he rounded the wingtip he asked, "This yours?"

"No, and I wish it was," complained, the engineer, "because if these mechs don't finish pretty soon, I'll be out of a job." He gave them a disgusted glance. "They were supposed to finish yesterday, but they got pulled off to an Arab job." He gestured at a Boeing 727 with Arabic markings. "Money talks, eh?"

"Always has," Burke commiserated.

"Not that my boss hasn't plenty. But the whole city bows and scrapes for these oil Arabs."

One of the mechanics gave him a baleful glance, but he said nothing.

"So," said Burke, "you put in a lot of flight time?"

"Not so much—but when the boss wants to go he expects everything ready. Can't blame him. And after this system's fixed it has to be checked and recertified. You're a pilot, right? You know the drill."

"Yeah," Burke said. "What's the Falcon's cruising speed?"

"Five-twenty-five knots at twenty K. Make London in under two hours." He looked down at the mechanics. "If these guys ever finish. At this rate, there's no way we can fly tomorrow." He shook his head. "And there aren't enough Swiss inspectors, so it's wait for mechanics then wait for inspectors when we could be airborne."

Burke looked inside the cabin and found it configured with lounges and a pull-down bed, a wet bar in the galley. "Real comfort," he said. admiringly. "You guys travel first class."

"All the way," the flight engineer said proudly. "You jet qualified?"

"Just fans," Burke admitted with a touch of regret, "but I get around. Good talking to you." He left the Falcon and looked over a Learjet and a Mitsubishi before strolling out of the hangar.

The plan he'd formed was far from perfect, but given the sudden time constraint, he had no option. From a pay phone Burke called Charles Blane, who was holding a package for him. "Good," Burke said, relieved. "How about half an hour at the Palais de Nations esplanade?"

"I'm driving a silver blue Peugeot."

"Brush contact only," Burke hung up, looking at his watch.

There were tour buses, private and official vehicles crowding the broad paved area that faced the United Nations building. Burke didn't seek a parking place but drove slowly back and forth as though waiting for a UN employee, and finally saw a silver blue Peugeot heading for him. Blane barely paused to thrust an athletic bag through Burke's open window.

Burke opened the bag in his room. Packed in heavy cardboard, the disassembled rifle was surrounded by foam rubber, five soft-nosed .308 cartridges packed in a plastic container. The scope was protected by a foam cylinder, and as far as Burke could tell, it had survived the diplomatic pouch undamaged.

He assembled the rifle and checked bolt and receiver, chambered a round and ejected it smoothly. Then he set the scope in its mounts and sighted out the window at a weather vane about two hundred yards away. The reticles crossed on the vane. Burke chambered a ready round, removed the barrel, and nested the scope weapon in his waterproof bag, blanketing it with foam rubber. He zippered the bag shut, praying it was as watertight as advertised. Contained air would give it a certain amount of buoyancy, he figured, which would be offset by the rifle's eight-pound weight.

Only the hard part lay ahead.

Burke poured a drink and lighted a Cuban cigarillo, sat in a chair, and hooked his heels on the window sill. Gargoyle was proving a much harder target than Puma. He hadn't yet figured how to hit him, much less how to get away with his own life. If the first try failed, he mused, he could stall Weiskopf by sabotaging his plane, but the money man would be warned. So it had to go perfectly.

He studied the enlarged photographs again, realizing that by night the landmarks would be different. The wooded point of land south of Weiskopf's pier was about two hundred yards from the boathouse. But an estimate wasn't good enough. After putting away the photos, Burke went down to a camera store and bought a Zeiss optical range finder. A pharmacy sold him a box of mothballs, and from a pay phone he called Charles Blane and levied a special requirement: a thermite bomb with time-delay fuse.

Burke waited until Blane replied. "Not available locally. I'll have to get it from Wiesbaden."

"I need it now. Today."

"You'll have it."

With that assurance Burke drove his Audi to the point of land and got a range-finder reading of two hundred and twenty-two meters to the boathouse. Burke put away the range finder and calculated yardage.

A meter was about forty inches. Times two twenty-two was eight thousand eighty inches. Divided by thirty-six? Two hundred and forty-six yards. Longer than his estimate by twenty percent.

Bad guess, he reproached himself, then remembered that cross-water distances were deceptive. No way now to sight-in the additional range. He could hold higher on the target or get fifty yards closer—and the only way to accomplish that was through water.

Well, he thought, why not? In Nam he'd accepted risk of exposure without question. If Blane and Wiesbaden came through, it was on for tonight.

At the Banque Versoix, Burke withdrew forty of the fifty thousand dollars deposited to the account of Roger Pierre Morillon. Liquidating the entire sum would have raised eyebrows at the bank. Besides, what he could not accomplish with forty thousand dollars could not be done with fifty.

He took half in green dollars, half in Swiss francs, walked to the men's store recommended by the bank's *sous-directeur* and chose a waterproof plastic money belt, zipper-closed and Velcro-fastened. His next step was a camera shop where he purchased a lightweight aluminum tripod stand with telescoping legs that extended to five feet. The finish was mat black, for bird-watchers, Burke presumed. He also bought a roll of ASA 1200 film. Back in his room, he loaded his camera with the superfast film in case of a question about what he was doing around the lake at night with a camera.

He loaded his money belt with the cash, his false passport, and Paul Revere. He screwed the camera onto the tripod's base plate and put the assembled unit in the athletic bag Blane had used to deliver the special rifle. His diving gear was in a large rubberized carrying bag in the trunk of his Audi. Only the bomb was missing.

His watch showed three o'clock, and he realized he had eaten nothing since an early breakfast. He ate at a modest grill on the rue Gevray near the hotel: rump steak, noodles, and brussels sprouts, with a half-liter of red Alsatian wine, and returned to his room. There he stretched out on his bed and reviewed the sequence of actions that would commence at nightfall. Had he forgotten anything? He glanced at his bags and mentally inventoried their contents.

One thing he must *not* do was fail to pay his hotel bill. This nation of innkeepers pursued deadbeats ferociously. And the Audi must be returned; he had no desire to do time in a Swiss prison as a car thief, nor to draw attention to himself.

The phone woke him. Burke heard Blane's voice: "Your merchandise is ready, sir. How would you like delivery?"

Burke shook himself awake. "Any suggestions?"

"Well, I'm at the airport. I thought I'd come back by way of the *gare*, the central railway station, and meet you at the snack bar for coffee."

"Sounds good," Burke agreed. "Say, half an hour?"

"I'll be there."

Burke paid the hotel cashier, informing him he would be leaving in the early evening, then strolled the five blocks to the Gare de Cornavin, where he bought a Montreal newspaper, took a small table, and ordered coffee and a sweet roll.

The large main area had vaulted ceilings that echoed the sounds of train announcements from unseen speakers. Fewer than a hundred people were going to and from trains; baggage porters pushed laden carts in both directions. The fin de siècle decor was restrained, Burke thought, in keeping with Swiss frugality. The only policeman he saw was lounging beside one of the departure gates.

Over the edge of his paper Burke saw Blane enter the waiting room and walk casually to his table, setting an Adidas shoe bag at Burke's feet. "How's the coffee?"

"Try a cup." Burke signaled the elderly waiter. Leaning forward, Blane said, "You never know about this military stuff, so I ordered two items."

"Good thinking. As of now, I want surveillance pulled off him, with this exception—I have to know if he leaves his place. Can do?"

Blane thought it over. "That big stretch Mercedes he uses has tinted windows, so unless you're up real close, there's no telling who's inside—especially after dark." He paused. "We're talking after dark, aren't we?"

"We are."

"Well, the chauffeur won't be taking out the limo for groceries, the children will be in bed, and the woman hardly ever goes out after dark. So the odds are high that if the Mercedes leaves, he'll be in it."

The waiter placed cup, saucer, and spoon before Blane, then a small creamer. "So let's leave it at this." Burke said thoughtfully. "If I don't hear from you in my room by nine o'clock, I'll assume the man is at home." He took a bite of strudel. "We won't be meeting again, so let me thank you for your help. If the army had worked this efficiently, we wouldn't have lost Vietnam."

Blane colored and muttered appreciation. "One final thing, Blane," Burke went on. "You're out of it now. You never heard of me, whatever happens."

"Understood. I took a safe house for you over by the university. Address and key are in the bag. It's an apartment on the rue St. Léger. No doorman, no nosy neighbors."

"Hope I won't need it," Burke said, "Thanks."

"I'll be at the usual number until midnight, if that's long enough."

"Should be." They shook hands and the DEA agent left the station.

The bag held a resealable container of heavy dark plastic. Burke took out two cylindrical thermite bombs and their time fuses. The bombs were taped together, making a single unit. The timers could be set for delays of fifteen minutes to six hours. He resealed the container and added it to the camera bag.

He emptied the bathroom cabinet of shaving gear and put the items in his suitcase, which held only a change of clothing, then carried the suitcase down to the trunk of his car.

The sun was already down behind the western mountains; darkness spread over the lake. Lights twinkled along the shoreline. Street lamps came silently to life. Night had begun.

Burke waited.

Twenty

AN HOUR PASSED, and no abort call from Blane. Burke imagined the Weiskopfs dining on silver plates, drinking fine wine, enjoying their secure affluence. Weiskopf was not a boastful brigand like Luís Quintana; he worked quietly with the cover of respectability. Yet his impact was deadlier.

The sky was quite dark now above the lighted city's glow. The jet rising from the lake appeared as strands of colored glass. Burke heard church bells toll nine.

He glanced at the silent telephone. For a brief moment he was tempted to call Blane. No, he had to take Weiskopf's presence on faith.

After a final check on his room, Burke carried his two bags down to the parking lot, then drove the Audi over the rue du Léman to the *quai* and turned left onto the route that led north along the lake. He drove slowly, with no sense of particular urgency. Against his face the wind was bracing. There were a few lights out on the lake, fishing boats with carbide lanterns. The gaily lighted cruise launch was crossing toward the eastern side; time for complimentary sandwiches and champagne.

Faster cars passed him as Burke slowed to look for the turn-in. Spotting it, he drove carefully into the woods and turned off the car's lights.

For a few moments he sat in darkness, adjusting to silence and pitch black. Then he got out, stripped, and drew on his wet suit, working methodically to shoulder his air tank, strap on leg knife and wrist compass, tie the lamp lanyard to his waist. Before putting on the mask he removed the snorkel tube. Carrying fins, camera bag, and gun bag, Burke entered the water; the fins slipped on more smoothly over wet skin.

Standing knee deep, he opened the camera bag and got out the bag of mothballs; he opened his wet suit and placed it against his chest, then closed the zipper. He removed camera and tripod, extended the three legs, and moved further into the water. He could see Weiskopf's lighted pier now, the boathouse at the far end. After pacing off fifty yards he set down the tripod in four feet of water, pressing its spiked ends into the sandy silt. He removed the bomb container from the bag and hooked it to his belt. Then he submerged the gun bag under the tripod, letting out enough air for it to sink.

The compass gave a reading on the boathouse of 011 degrees. He let air out of the regulator, checking the flow before clenching the mouthpiece between his teeth, then pulled down his face mask and quietly submerged. The sealed lamp illuminated the uneven, rocky bottom until, as he angled farther from shore, the bottom dropped out of sight.

When he had swum a hundred yards Burke surfaced just long enough to sight on the boathouse and alter to a direction offering maximum concealment. Submerged again, he kicked smoothly and rhythmically, letting the big fins thrust him powerfully forward. His depth gauge showed seven meters, a depth at which he knew he was entirely invisible to anything but the strongest, deepest-penetrating searchlight, and there was no reason to think the boathouse was so equipped.

In another five minutes he drifted to the surface, saw that he was nearly off the boathouse entrance, and went down again. The next time he surfaced, the outline of the boathouse and its closed grille gate, was in clear view. He sank down to ten feet and swam under the grille, flashing the lamp briefly to avoid it, then surfaced between the hulls of the sailboat and the power launch.

Removing the mouthpiece, Burke breathed night air and rested. He had breached the fortress, but it was not time for self-congratulation. His watch showed ten-fifteen when he climbed up a wooden ladder to the foot walk that ran inside the boathouse.

Enough light leaked into the boathouse from pier lighting to reveal coils of rope and sun cushions, a stand for fishing rods, a sail locker, and a string of colored pennants. He leaned over the speedboat's transom and unscrewed the gas tank cap, emptied the pouch of mothballs into the tank, and replaced the top. There was enough gasoline in the fuel lines to back the boat into open water, after which the naphthalene-gasoline mix would foul the carburetor and stop the engine. It was the first sabotage trick he had ever learned.

Now he opened the bomb container and carried the mated bombs to the point inside the boathouse that was farthest from the speedboat. Shielding the lamp, he set each timer for forty minutes and activated them. Their spring mechanism gave off a muted ticking. Burke piled cushions on the bombs to silence them, and climbed back into the dark water.

He swam back under the grille and took a reciprocal compass bearing of 191 degrees. After twelve minutes he saw the bottom begin sloping upward; he checked course again and surfaced to orient himself. Through the dripping faceplate he saw waterborne light, made out a boat with two men fishing. Their boat was drifting shoreward; in a few minutes they would be close to the camera stand.

He could hear their voices over the water; not words, just the uneven rhythm of casual conversation. That would change when their lantern cast its light on the camera atop its stand. He had to act fast.

Submerging, Burke swam directly to the camera, found the tripod with his lamp, put down his feet, and rose behind it. Silently he shed his tank and buoyancy vest, shoved up the mask to clear his eyes, and tilted the camera skyward. As he peered through the viewfinder at the heavens, he thought of the ticking bomb fuse. He had only a few minutes to get the fishermen away. Filling his lungs, Burke shouted in French, "*Allo!* Mind moving away?"

Startled, both men turned to stare. "What's that? What are you doing out here?"

"Trying to photograph Arcturus," Burke said irritably.

"Why don't you do it from shore?" the other man called.

"City lights ruin the starlight," Burke replied, in a reasonable tone. "Just as your lantern does. So please move away."

"Well—all right," the man called. "Don't want to interfere with science, do we?" Both men laughed. Burke heard oarlocks creak as they unshipped their oars. "Many thanks," Burke said. "Until just now there's been cloud cover. There—it's clearing." He clicked the shutter. Oars dipped in water. One of the men said, "No fish here, anyway. May you have better luck than we've been having." Burke clicked the shutter again, watched them row away until their light was lost behind a bend of land.

For a while he listened, then ducked down and brought up the gun bag and took out the scoped Ljutic. He screwed the barrel to the loaded receiver and rested the forend atop the camera. Through the scope he could see the lighted peak of the boathouse; beyond the reticles the magnified light bulb seemed as big as a balloon. His feet and ankles ached from long immersion in cold water, his knee began to throb dully. He didn't look at his watch—that would only lengthen his waiting time.

First-floor lights went out in the villa and Burke wondered if Weiskopf might not have left while he was working in the boathouse. No, he'd heard no car engine.

But what if the explosion didn't bring him down the pier? What if he decided to let his boats burn? *If, if, if!* What if the fishermen came back for a closer look? What if another boat appeared? He hadn't factored in those unpredictables—no one could, he told himself.

He saw flames shoot out of the near corner of the boathouse before he heard the detonation. The corner vanished and flames climbed toward the roof. Burke turned the scope on the villa.

Within moments a man burst out of a terrace door and began running toward the pier. Guard, servant, or—?

The short, pajamaed figure ran in a loping gait, and as it entered the floodlit zone Burke could see whitish hair. Weiskopf.

Following him came a guard with a leashed Doberman. Boathouse flames reddened their figures as Weiskopf raced toward the boat-house. Burke saw Weiskopf disappear inside the boathouse, and in a few moments the grille gates began swinging outward. Through the crackling flames came the heavy barking roar of the engine starting. Burke tensed and laid his finger on the trigger button. His body was cold and rigid, his mind totally concentrated on the boat as it began backing into open water. The engine coughed, caught again, and died. The boat coasted backward, losing momentum. Weiskopf left the wheel and jerked open the engine housing. Bent over he made a poor target. Burke licked dry lips. The boat was now dead in the water. Weiskopf stood up and began shouting at guards on the pier. Flames illuminated him as Burke fixed the cross hairs on the target's upper chest. The target was motionless when Burke fired. The report's sharp crack reverberated across the water. Burke saw Weiskopf slammed back against the far gunwale, one hand jerking to his chest. Quickly Burke ejected the shell and reloaded. Weiskopf's body was barely visible, but it was not moving. His white hair was reddened by the spreading flames as breeze or current slowly turned the boat. Burke felt he had time for a second shot. The first might have been heard by Weiskopf's retainers, but they wouldn't have seen the distant muzzle flash. As he sighted he saw Weiskopf's body slide out of sight.

The stern was swinging toward him. Burke sighted where he knew the gas tank to be, and fired.

To Burke's ears the second shot sounded louder than the first. Then flame shot a hundred feet in the air, spewing debris over the water. Burke swung the scope toward the pier. Half a dozen people stood paralyzed by the hellish sight of the burning boat. Through the scope Burke recognized Weiskopf's wife, Beatriz. She was behind a wheelchair she had been pushing, and in the chair sat a blanketed man. His hair was white, features lined but Nordic, and Burke exhaled in surprise. The old man had to be onetime SS major Hans Dieter Weiskopf, cared for by his son—a son who could no longer hide him. Burke could now expose him, and in Germany there was no statute of limitations for war crimes.

He eased the rifle into the water, picked up the camera stand, and began walking toward shore. On the rocky beach he pulled off his swim fins and carried them toward where he had left the Audi.

He saw a glimmer of light that at first he identified as reflected moonlight. But after a few more steps he saw his car's inside lights were on, and a man was pawing through Burke's clothing.

Later Burke realized he had reacted unintelligently, impulsively. Instead of approaching unheard and taking the thief, Burke yelled, " '*Allo*—get away from there!"

Turning fast, the man jerked a revolver from his belt and fired.

Twenty-one

PAIN, HOT PAIN seared Burke's left thigh. He dropped, rolled over, and saw the man come toward him, revolver waving.

The man's eyes, accustomed to the car's light, couldn't quite make out Burke's black-clad body, but Burke could see clearly a young, hard face. Burke drew the heavy diving knife—one edge serrated, the other razor-sharp—from its leg sheath, and held it by the pointed tip. As the man neared, Burke flung the knife. End over end the knife whistled like a boomerang, struck the man's thorax and entered.

With a shriek, the man staggered backward clutching the knife handle. His revolver dropped, and Burke lunged. He butted him over and drove in the knife to its hilt. The man gasped and blood bubbled from his mouth. His struggling weakened, and the glaze of death dulled his eyes. Burke pressed his neck and felt no carotid pulse. He rolled off and turned the lamp on his thigh.

Blood welled from the bullet-torn rubber. His fingers widened the gash, revealing a three-inch wound. He reached over and pulled the knife from the dead man's chest, then sawed off the leg rubber. From it he sliced a long strip and tied a tourniquet above the wound. Then he got up and pulled off the rest of his wet suit, leaving everything in a pile beside the body, which he now saw was in a dark gray uniform. Who else could he be, Burke asked himself, but one of Weiskopf's guards?

The rifle's second muzzle flash had been spotted, and the guard had come to investigate, while the others were busy at the fire. Bad luck for me, Burke thought, worse luck for him. But if he hadn't shot me, I wouldn't have killed him. *Shit!*

He limped to the Audi, turned off its lights, and got into shirt and shorts, for his body was chilling from cool air and blood loss. He used his pocket handkerchief to form a compress over the wound, held it in place with the tourniquet. He stripped off the money belt and tossed it on the front seat. Then he pulled on his trousers and got into shoes.

Voices came across the water. The boathouse roof had collapsed and the sailboat was burning. A dinghy neared the almost sunken speedboat; only its foredeck was above water, the prow angling steeply skyward. Weiskopf's body might float free, Burke thought, but it would be mangled.

He got into his coat jacket and turned on the dimmers. Leaning against a tree was a Honda motorcycle—the guard's. The tableau was one the police would puzzle over before reaching any conclusion. He remembered the dive knife, got out and inserted it in the chest wound, wiping his prints from the handle. The police would find a fired revolver, a stabbed corpse, and diving gear. There was no reason to drag the offshore water, but if they did, they would find the rifle and its carry bag. They might conclude that the motorcycle's owner had shot Weiskopf and in turn been slain by unknown parties. Or more accurately, that the guard had encountered Weiskopf's killer and in turn been slain.

The press, well aware of Weiskopf's drug connections, would theorize that he had been liquidated on orders of a dissatisfied client. So much for the investigation.

Tonight, Burke reflected, he had become a widow maker. Weiskopf's children would continue to be reared in luxury, given every advantage. It would be up to their mother whether they became criminals like their father, but in his absence the children now had a chance to become decent citizens.

Burke drove out of the trees, turned off the dimmers, and waited until the highway was clear before driving onto it. He turned south toward Geneva, his leg throbbing. He could lay up in the safe house, but in the morning his leg might be too stiff for walking. So he had to keep going.

Leaving the lakeside highway, he turned inland on the route des Romelles past the bois de Vengeron, continuing southward as airport lights came into view. He pulled over to roadside long enough to loosen the tourniquet around his leg and fill his wallet with money from the waterproof belt. He tucked the messager in his breast pocket and laid his passport on the seat atop the car's rental papers. After tightening the tourniquet again he continued on until the highway looped around and descended into the tunnel that crossed under the airport runways. When he emerged from the tunnel he was on French soil, in front of the Customs and Immigration station.

After the inspector courteously examined his passport and car papers, he asked, "And what will you do in France, m'sieu?"

"Spend an hour or two at Divonne, the casino tables."

"Then you had best make haste. The casino will close in an hour." He returned Burke's papers and stepped back.

Driving at legal speed took Burke twenty minutes to reach Divonne. At the night-duty pharmacy he bought gauze bandages, tape, and antibiotic powder, then checked into a room at the casino's hotel. He cut his blood-soaked handkerchief from the wound and rebandaged it. After swallowing four aspirin tablets he got out Paul Revere—the messager—and pointed it at the sky, transmitting only two words: GARGOYLE DOWN.

Then he got into bed and despite dull pain in his thigh fell quickly asleep.

In the morning his leg was stiff, so he had breakfast in the room rather than hobble around the dining room. Mild exercise helped, and after leaving the hotel he drove an hour and a half through the clear morning to Lyons airport where he turned in his Audi at the rental agency and took the next flight to Paris.

While waiting at Charles de Gaulle airport for an afternoon Pan American flight to JFK, Burke browsed the shops and bought perfume and lingerie for Claire, and an attractive emerald-cut topaz birthstone ring. For himself he bought Hine cognac and Black Label Scotch, then drank a split of champagne in PanAm's first-class departure lounge.

After takeoff Burke asked the flight attendant for aspirin and a double cognac, saying he didn't want to be disturbed for the meal. She showed him the engraved menu with its choice of sautéed trout, prime ribs, or rack of lamb, but Burke waved her off.

She woke him to buckle his seat belt, and through the window Burke watched the spires of Manhattan come into view.

After clearing Immigration and Customs, Burke phoned his Virginia contact number and heard Enno Poliakoff answer.

"I'm at JFK," he said, "and I'll be taking the Delta shuttle to Washington National. I need a bit of medical attention when I get there."

"Hospital?"

"Just a bullet graze."

"I'll give you a name."

After a few moments Poliakoff said a Dr. Philip Tarkington would take care of him. The doctor's office was at Eighteenth and K in the District. "Need help getting there?"

"No." Burke hung up. Not a word from Enno about Gargoyle. Well, maybe his two-word message hadn't been received.

He bought a *Daily News* and found the story on an inside page. Reputed drug financier Hans Günther Weiskopf had been killed when his boat exploded near his Lake of Geneva home. Foul play was indicated by Swiss authorities, who called Weiskopf's death a contract killing. The body of a man they termed the actual assassin had been found not far from Weiskopf's estate, and police investigators theorized he had been silenced by his sponsor. Geneva's chief of police warned international drug dealers to keep their quarrels out of Switzerland. "They may enjoy a certain immunity in their own countries," the chief said at a hastily called press conference, "but in Switzerland we will prosecute narcotics trafficking and murder to the full extent of the law."

Bravo for Switzerland was Burke's first reaction. Then he reflected that the Swiss had had years to prosecute or extradite Weiskopf.

He rode the shuttle bus to La Guardia and boarded a departing shuttle for Washington. Half an hour after landing he was lying on Dr. Tarkington's table, gritting his teeth as the physician closed his thigh wound with five stitches. The doctor was a short, wiry man, whose thin face was adorned with a pencil-thin black mustache. He worked quickly and skillfully, with no comforting words. After bandaging he injected antibiotics in Burke's left cheek and gave him a prescription for mild pain pills. "There's a drugstore on the street floor," he said, and pulled off his surgical gloves. "Pay the receptionist."

Burke eased onto the floor and pulled up his trousers. "I thought this might be on the house."

"I'm discreet, but I don't work for free. See me in a week and I'll remove the stitches." He dropped the bloody gloves in a container and Burke left the treatment room.

As he paid with a hundred-dollar bill, Burke noticed that one wall of the reception room held a large, recessed aquarium containing tropical fish, waving fronds, and a miniature diver that burped air from time to time. The scene reminded Burke of his recent underwater work, and he looked away.

During the taxi ride to Leesburg, Burke felt drowsy from the pain pills. As the taxi pulled into his drive he saw Claire's pickup parked under the shade of a tree.

She was not in the house, but from the back porch he saw her cantering bareback through the meadow. His shout brought her racing to him, and when she was in his arms, sobbing with happiness, he kissed her and told her he was truly glad and grateful to be home.

Twenty-two

WHEN CLAIRE SHOWED Burke into her father's room, that evening he was appalled. Under the sheet the senator's body was shrunken, and skin clung to his skull like loosely applied putty. Morphine kept Newsome comatose most of the time and his periods of lucidity were infrequent. Still, a bedroom television set was on, without volume, in case the senator woke and wanted to watch. "I'll tell him you came," she said, as they left the room, "and that will cheer him."

"You're very brave," Burke said and kissed her cheek, "and I'm sure your father knows it."

"When you're not around I feel absolutely helpless. If I didn't have my horses to care for, I'd go crazy."

At the front door he said, "I'm sorry about this meeting, but it shouldn't take long. Maybe a couple of hours."

"Will it be all right if I stay at the farmhouse?"

"Perfect."

He drove to the Arlington high rise and entered the Environmental Improvement office on the sixth floor. To Burke's disappointment, General Arness was not at the conference table, just Poliakoff and Jim Eubank—Harry. Burke took a seat near Harry and stretched out his left leg to ease discomfort. "General avoiding me?" he asked.

Poliakoff shrugged. "You're not his only specialist, you know; he has others to see to."

"I hope so," Burke said easily. "I can't eliminate all the villains on the list."

Poliakoff said, "That was a nice touch in Geneva, turning suspicion on the guard."

"I thought so," Burke replied. He took a roll of money from his pocket and handed it to Harry. "Here's what's left from Geneva, plus ten large at the Banque Versoix. Charles Blane did a first-class job supporting me."

Harry handed over a sealed envelope with Burke's personal ID, and Burke returned the Morillon documentation.

"So," Poliakoff said, "how about a report, Major?"

Burke looked at him. "I did the job, Enno, that's my report."

"Yeah, but the details?"

"The press had details."

Poliakoff shrugged. "If that's how you want it."

"That's how I want it." He smiled thinly. "Trade secrets."

Harry broke the tension. "How's your leg, Tom?"

"Healing. Stitches out in a week. I'll want that long to rest up."

"Just as well," Poliakoff said, "because your next target is traveling and it'll be a while before we get a location fix."

Burke nodded. "Well, let me know."

The garage was dark now, and he remembered waiting as night fell over Geneva, how he'd swum through dark waters. Doubtless the fishermen had reported photographer's presence to the police, ending speculation concerning Weiskopf's killer.

As he drove back to Leesburg the wire recording made at Camp David came to mind. It was much safer in Peter Ward's office vault than in the farmhouse, which had been entered and searched even before he left for Mexico.

Terry was as well off at Allenwood as could be expected in prison circumstances, and his brother was making resettlement plans, something he'd been unable to do at Lewisburg. Burke anticipated seeing him freed before autumn.

His farmhouse was lighted, Claire in the kitchen. He grabbed and lifted her from the floor, kissed her until she scrabbled for breath. "God, but I'm glad you're here, honey! You're the only stable part of my life," he told her, and kissed her lips again.

"Oh, darling, I'll always be here for you—don't you know that by now?"

"I've hoped," he said and lowered her gently, watched her continue preparing dinner. Then he drew her into the living room, and while fillets were broiling and potatoes baking, Burke got out the presents he'd brought for her. She loved the Guerlain scent, and mischievously asked if he'd bought it for prior amours. "Absolutely not. Thought we'd start fresh," he said, and was rewarded with a kiss. The Hermès lingerie, she declared, was a perfect fit. "Next time you're in a lingerie-buying mood, I'd love black lace."

"I thought it was a little . . . outré for a senator's daughter."

"Oh, I'd never buy it for myself, but I'd love it if you would."

"Aha! I've been waiting for that kinky strain to surface—now we know."

"Kinky, slinky, what's the diff?"

"Depends who's wearing what."

"Oh, Tom, you're a cross-dresser? And I thought you were so straight."

"Thought or hoped?"

Her head turned sharply. "Do I smell meat burning?"

"You do. Hurry."

Broiling-pan grease had caught fire, but their steaks were un-scathed. While Claire served, Burke opened a bottle of Louis Jadot burgundy, sampled it, and filled their glasses.

As before, Burke was impressed by how natural it felt to sit across the dining table from her. It was habit-forming, a habit he didn't want to break..

After dinner Burke opened a chilled bottle of Heidsieck, and Claire toasted his return. "I've got some free time now," he said, "so why don't we open up your Bethany Beach place? Why wait for Labor Day?"

"I'd say yes in a minute, but you know Father's on oxygen and God knows what else. When we went to the Keys, his condition wasn't critical."

He took her hand. "Suggestion withdrawn. We'll point for Labor Day."

"I don't care where I am, Tom, just so I'm with you." She sipped champagne. "How much free time?"

"Probably stretch it to ten days, maybe more."

"And after that?"

"When I get back it'll be forever."

They took the Heidsieck to the bedroom, and while Claire was showering Burke undressed quickly and got into bed. But as she stroked his body her hand found the bandage, and she pulled away the covers and stared for a moment. "Is it bad?"

"No."

"Hurt?"

"Hardly at all."

Tears welled in her eyes. "I want to know how it happened, but of course I can't ask. Father told me there were things about you I shouldn't question. I suppose he had something like this in mind."

"Possibly. Now let's put it out of our minds." He drew her closely against him and kissed her nipples.

"Ah, Tom," she murmured, "you're such a wonderful lover, and I love you so desperately much. You love me, too, I'm sure of it."

"I do," he admitted, "of course I do."

"But you won't consider marriage."

"I consider it all the time, darling, but it's not for now—you knew that when we met."

"All right, I'll quiet down, I've made my point," she said submissively. "All I wanted to establish is that you have no objection in principle to marrying me."

"C'mon honey, you know better than that!"

She kissed the side of his face, licked and nibbled his ear. "I know, but I need to hear you confess it now and then." Her body turned slightly. "Is that better for you?"

"Better."

"Less painful?"

"Nothing," he said hoarsely, "is going to keep us apart."

"Tom—oh, Tom. Soon . . . please, soon . . . I'm so wet. . . ."

His life flowed into her receiving warmth; she shuddered, sighed, and lay with him utterly relaxed.

That night while they were sleeping in each other's arms, Senator Newsome woke briefly, pulled off his oxygen mask, and died quietly in the darkness of his room.

The late senator's sister, Barbara, came from La Jolla, his brother, Raymond, from Grosse Pointe. For two days the senator lay in state under the Capitol rotunda while colleagues, friends, and constituents filed past his catafalque. In the National Cathedral the dean conducted final services attended by senators, congressmen, the president of the United States and five members of his cabinet. Burke glimpsed General Arness seated unobtrusively in a pew at the rear of the great cathedral.

During the eulogy Burke found his gaze slipping to the president, seated to their right, and when the eulogy ended and the presidential party rose, at the president's side stood the aide who had received Burke at Camp David. Tor Daggit Burke recalled. Burke looked at Daggitt, who blinked, then looked *through* him as though they'd never met. Burke had hardly expected congratulations; after all, for Daggitt the relationship had to be disavowable.

White House helicopters airlifted the senator's casket and the Newsome family, with Burke at Claire's side, to Charlottesville, where he was interred in the family plot near the university he had attended as a youth and loved as a man. Afterward they were flown back to Leesburg, where Burke left Claire with the relatives who were staying in the big house, and a circle of school and equestrian friends.

Claire had managed well under the circumstances, difficult circumstances at best. Burke poured himself a stiff drink and wandered around the house wondering what help he could be to Claire. She should get away from home and all its memories, before grappling with the condolence letters, estate lawyers, and the multitude of details that survivors inevitably face. Neither he nor Claire had gotten much rest, and her dependence on him was as obvious as it was touching. If anything were to happen to him, Claire would be devastated.

The implication was that he should handle himself more cautiously, expose himself less to danger. But he knew from combat experience that those who tried to avoid risk often found themselves in harm's way.

And his commitment had to be honored, Otherwise, the risks he'd run to terminate Puma and Gargoyle would be for naught and Terry would stay in prison for God knew how many years. Much as he ached for a life at Claire's side, Burke knew he must follow the course he had chosen.

Burke composed a letter on his word processor and had it printed out in three copies:

Gentlemen:

It has come to my attention that former SS major Hans Dieter Weiskopf has been living in seclusion at the Lake of Geneva villa of his son, the late Hans Günther Weiskopf.

When recently observed, Hans Dieter Weiskopf was in a wheelchair. Owing to the death of his son, a decision may have been reached to move him to a more secure location, for which reason I urge that prompt action be taken to bring this war criminal to justice.

A concerned citizen

He addressed plain envelopes to the Washington embassies of Israel and the Federal Republic of Germany, a third to the Vienna Documentation Center, Attention: Dr. Simon Weisenthal.

Burke reviewed his Faustian bargain with the president. Only extreme frustration could have brought the nation's chief executive to condone a covert conspiracy of worldwide murder. Last week the umpteenth Colombian justice minister had resigned, bowing to threats against his and his family's lives, and only yesterday a Medellín judge had dismissed charges against two notorious Colombian cocaine barons, men high on the U.S. wanted list—"extraditables" they called themselves. Had the judge been influenced by fear or by money? ¿Oro o plomo?

As in Vietnam, the narcotics war was not his personal quarrel; a sense of duty motivated him. But reprisal for the murders of his friends at hacienda El Quiote—that part would be personal.

From his humidor he took out a cigarillo and lighted his first in days, drawing in the coal smoke appreciatively. Then he went out and carried oats to the feed tray, slabs of hay to a spot near the salt lick. As Claire's horses gathered for their evening feeding, Burke found his thoughts returning to the war against drugs. The deaths of even a dozen major *narcos.* represented only a temporary setback to the growers and refiners and distributors, the money managers. Replacements would spring up like dragon's teeth, the lure of huge profits simply too great to be ignored by those who, like Luís Quintana, had been born into abject poverty.

Burke knew that a few senators had quietly suggested legalizing narcotics in the United States, and felt it made sense. In practical terms, banning narcotics was as ineffective as outlawing sex. Bootleggers and gangsters had *wanted* Prohibition, which had made them wealthy. If drugs were legal, demand would lessen, and though there would always be addicts, just as there were alcoholics, the public benefits would outweigh the cost of addiction treatment, and billions of tax dollars could be turned from drug interdiction to pay for housing and environmental improvement. That was Burke's personal opinion, and for all he knew the president might share it. Still, he recognized its political unlikelihood, and so the losing battle would go endlessly on.

He went back to the house and was sweeping the kitchen when the phone rang. He heard General Arness's voice: "Be there a while?"

"All evening."

"Good. I'm on my way to Dulles and thought I'd stop by, it's been a while since we talked." In less than ten minutes a car pulled into the drive and Burke opened the door for Arness. They shook hands and the general accepted Burke's offer of Black Label. "Straight up, please."

Drink in hand, Arness gestured Burke outside. As they strolled toward the barn Arness said, "I was glad to see you at Claude's services; didn't realize you and his daughter were so tight."

Burke shrugged. "Anything special on your mind?"

"Congratulations on taking out Gargoyle so neatly. But I hear you were wounded. How are you?"

"Mending nicely, thanks. Which way are you heading?"

"El Paso—EPIC."

"EPIC?"

"El Paso Intelligence Center at Fort Biggs. Where all narcotics info feeds in for analysis and distribution."

"Never heard of it."

"DEA likes it that way."

Burke sipped from his glass. "So how's the project going?"

"You may have read about Ochoa—Cartagena?"

Burke nodded. "I wasn't trying for a copycat kill, it just came out that way."

"So we're reducing the list—slowly. Too damn slowly, Tom. I just spent a couple of hours with the AG, the president's so-called drug czar, and Tor Daggitt. I came away with a disheartening statistic. The DEA estimates that this year Ecuador, Colombia, Bolivia, and Peru will produce a quarter of a million tons of coca. In its refined forms, most of the leaf will head for the United States. Our enforcement agencies are overwhelmed. I suggested defoliant spraying to kill the bushes whether the growing countries like it or not, but no one even listened." He paused. "I take that back. The AG pointed out that it's illegal in the U.S. to spray marijuana fields. How can we force spraying on other countries?"

Burke grunted. "Like trying to export democracy to countries that aren't interested. If you're depressed, I don't blame you."

"It's reaching the point," Arness said, "where the final option is using our army and air force to destroy those coca crops, but that'll never happen because the administration is worried about being charged with intervention—which of course it would be."

"So what was the meeting—a bull session? Or was something accomplished?"

"What it accomplished," Arness said, "was getting me to realize the very guys who pressured the president to take unprecedented action are getting very dispirited. Politically they can't go back to the president and say, 'We were wrong, we underestimated the immensity of the problem.' That's not done in Washington." Irritably, he shook out a cigarette and lighted it. "Not doable anywhere, I guess, Tom. Hell, twenty years ago I was telling Westy the war was unwinnable, at the same time he was telling Washington and the world he saw 'light at the end of the tunnel.' Remember that?"

"Only too clearly."

"I was right, but my timing was rotten. So I've decided not to add my dime's worth this time. When I'm told to break camp, I'll do it, like the good soldier I've always been."

"So it's all going down the chute," Burke remarked tonelessly. "Not a big morale booster, General, when I've still got a body to bag." He paused. "That's still scheduled?"

Arness nodded. "Once we locate the target. And if you're worrying about that pardon, I'll see the agreement is honored. Do the job, take care of yourself, and things will work out for you and Terry." He looked away at the silhouettes of horses grazing by the pond in a setting of pastoral tranquility. "The White House calls this a war, but as far as I can see it's barely a small-arms skirmish." He gave Burke a bleak smile. "But as we have cause to know, wars aren't always won on the battlefield."

"Or lost there," Burke supplied.

They walked back past the farmhouse toward where Arness's car and driver waited. As they shook hands Arness said, "Tor Daggitt is the ultimate political animal, Tom. Apparently you rubbed him the wrong way at Camp David. Did you?"

"He tried to pass himself off as the president, but I held out for the real thing." Burke smiled. "Always supposing the president *is* real."

"Real enough, and hungry for reelection. Good luck, Tom." Burke watched his taillights recede down the drive and reflected on Arness's depression. The uncertain trumpet again. Well, as in Nam, he'd go on with the job he had to do, get it over with as soon as possible, leave the rest to the politicians. He gulped down his drink and went off to bed.

Late in the night the phone rang. Groggily Burke answered and heard Claire's tremulous voice. "I feel lost without you, terribly alone. I want to be with you, but I can't without offending . . . proprieties."

"I understand," he said soothingly. "You'll feel better after a good night's rest. Get to sleep, darling."

"I will . . . I must. I *have* to. Because in the morning I'm going to La Jolla with my aunt. I'll call as soon as I get there."

"I'll be waiting for your call," he murmured sleepily. "I love you. Good night." He tried getting back to sleep, but something gnawed at his subconscious. Finally he got up and went downstairs to arm the security system. No use having it if it went unused.

Walking back through the living room, he glanced at his gun cabinet and remembered the Ljutic he had left on the bottom of Lake of Geneva. By now, he supposed, it had been found, and he hoped that the special rifle was sterile as it was supposed to be. That had been Harry's responsibility. Otherwise there was a possibility the Ljutic—a rarity—could be traced. Well, he had enough to worry about.

In the morning Burke went down to the fields to see to the horses and plunged into the pool where he had dipped with Claire. Then he made a big breakfast for himself and watched morning TV news.

In the pool his thigh bandage had loosened and when he removed it he saw that the wound was healing well. Rather than visit Dr. Parkington again, Burke snipped the five stitches, knowing the subdermal thread would dissolve in time.

When Claire's pickup pulled into the drive and braked near the barn, Burke went out hopefully, but only the groom got out. Burke hailed the young man, whose name was Twombley, and walked up to him. Twombley wore a frayed straw hat and work-worn denims. His face and arms were deeply tanned, and his hands callused from stable work. "Mr. Burke," he said, "I'll be coming around while Miss Claire's gone."

"How long is that likely to be?"

"At least a week, maybe two, but I'll see to 'em however long she's gone."

Hearing the telephone, Burke went back in and recognized Harry's voice.

"I can get there in an hour, okay?"

"Okay." Burke hung up. Harry would be bringing a dossier: Target Three.

Burke shaved and changed into street clothes, wondering how long he would have to get to wherever he was going. He made coffee and set out two mugs, and after a while Harry's station wagon, dustier than ever, rolled down the drive.

He handed Burke a locked briefcase, and they carried their mugs to the rear porch. From where they sat they could see Twombley unloading feed bags and carrying them into the barn.

"How do you feel, Tom?" Harry asked.

"Fit. Ready to go. Who's villain number three, and what's his code name?"

Harry smiled uneasily. "Centaur," he said, "and this may go down a little hard, but this time it's not a he, Tom. It's a woman."

Centaur

Twenty-three

"A WOMAN!" Burke stared at him in disbelief. "Never heard of a major female trafficker. Mules, sure, women who smuggle powder in their panties and hidey-holes, but that's small-time. You're not kidding?"

Harry shook his head. "You know the saying about the female of the species being more deadly than the male? Well, Centaur fills that bill and then some." He tapped the briefcase. "Code names aren't supposed to reveal anything about the subject, but whoever stuck her with Centaur got it right. She's half human, half animal—and she's bi, keeps her own harem, gorgeous broads, too." He shook his head. "All that talent wasted." He unlocked the briefcase. I've got some grocery shopping to do, so I'll come back later, okay?"

"Okay." Burke watched Harry return to his car, then carried the briefcase to his work area. The Centaur folder was classified SENSITIVE/ LIMDIS/NOFORN, as expected.

Names used over the years included Faiza, Samar, Mona, Sara, Nadia, and Zaida. Last names: Zahid, Sadek, Awad, and Zakari. For purposes of this sketch, the compiler wrote, Subject will be referred to as Mona Zakari. She was born in Lebanon of a Syrian-Azerbaijani father, Yusaf Zakari, and a French woman, Marie Dessus, a dancer-prostitute of the category referred to in the Middle East as *artiste*, who used the cabaret name "Monique."

Following a bitter quarrel with Yusaf, Monique moved to Los Angeles, California, with her small daughter and resumed her dual profession, becoming popular in Arab and Middle Eastern circles. When Mona was eleven, mother and child were deported back to Lebanon, the proceedings citing Monique as a prostitute and illegal immigrant.

A year later her mother either gave or sold her to a wealthy Turkish merchant, Karim Khaled, who had extensive land holdings near Balikesir, Turkey, and in the Dhali region of Cyprus, devoted almost exclusively to the cultivation of opium poppy. Khaled was active in the Greek-Turkish struggle for domination of Cyprus. Reputed to be impotent as a result of heroin addiction, Khaled took voyeuristic pleasure from female orgies that included his young wife, Mona. At seventeen she was widowed when Khaled was killed on Cyprus by Cypriot guerrillas, and she inherited his considerable wealth.

Apparently realizing that she needed a protector and counselor, Mona elevated her husband's chief accountant to the role of consort, married him, and after several years, dispensed with his services entirely. Rumors current at the time had Mona poisoning her husband; other rumors had him killed by bandits in an Algiers *suk*. By this time Mona had taken firm control of her husband's opium business, and developed ties with French heroin refiners based in and around Marseilles. Her next marriage was to a Beirut banker of French extraction, Pierre Auguste al-Hosni, who laundered and invested her opium profits. This marriage lasted two years and ended in his death, attributed to street fighting in Beirut. However, banking sources in Beirut indicated that al-Hosni was attempting to take over his wife's opium business.

Of part-Syrian ancestry, Mona readily established commercial relations with the Syrian occupiers of Lebanon's Bekaa Valley, long a leading source of Middle Eastern opium. Her payments for Syrian gum opium included protected transportation to such Mediterranean ports as Tripoli, Latakia, and Famagusta (Cyprus), whence it was shipped to heroin refineries in Turkey and southern France.

In the last three years Mona Zakari had become the principal Middle Eastern harvester and exporter of gum opium, selling an estimated fourteen tons annually, with annual net profit estimated at between six and eight hundred million dollars. This supported homes or apartments in Nice, Monaco, Paris, Damascus, Cairo, Tehran, and Algiers. Zakari traveled extensively via personal aircraft and her two-hundred-foot yacht, *Kismet,* which she kept at Monaco. She employed a corps of bodyguards, and traveled in company of numerous show-girl types, who served as her lovers. Mona changed residences frequently and unpredictably. In the Arab cities her physical security was evaluated as impregnable, less so in Europe.

She frequented the Monaco Casino, winning or losing large sums with apparent indifference. Nominally Muslim, she drank alcohol and ignored the restrictions of *Sharia.* She was known to use cocaine and marijuana, though not heroin.

The next pages contained photographs of Mona's residences in the seven named cities, captioned with their addresses. Burke copied the Paris, Nice, and Monaco addresses and turned to a color photograph of a large yacht at anchor in Monaco harbor; a portion of its afterdeck was marked as a helipad. The yacht was painted white with green-and-black trim. A green stern flag was embroidered with the Arab crescent.

He was unprepared for the next pages.

The first photograph was of a slim Arab girl around eleven years of age. Her gauzy dress was modest in comparison to the belly-dancer costume of her mother beside her. The mother's curly red hair and pale sensual face contrasted with the girl's straight hair and unformed features. The mother's right hand rested casually on her daughter's shoulder.

The next photograph was of a teenage Mona, hair chestnut now, and shoulder length. Her face resembled her mother's but with an Arab cast, nose somewhat prominent. The third photograph showed Mona dancing in a café. Her figure was now voluptuous, her hair was redder and much longer. The photographer had caught her in a spin that flared her hair and showed her sensual mouth and eyes registering exaltation.

A passport photograph dated last year showed a beautiful young woman staring somewhat arrogantly at the camera. To one side her physical characteristics were given as Height: 5'10", Weight: 152 lbs.

Burke looked back at the dance photo and decided her figure could only be described as zaftig. Her partner, he now saw, was a diminutive, fined-boned oriental girl.

At the bottom of the page was a note: the videotape was made clandestinely in Nice last March. There was nothing else in the dossier.

Videotape? Burke reached inside the briefcase and brought out an unlabeled VHS tape.

As he walked to his VCR he realized he'd visualized an ugly old crone, a Gypsy fortune-teller stereotype. How off the mark he'd been.

Burke sat back to watch.

The camera had been shooting through one window into another some twenty or thirty feet away. Though only part of the target room was visible, it was obviously furnished lavishly in the Arab style, with tassled cushions around the perimeter, a lush carpet, and heavy scarlet drapes at the far side. Three nearly nude women lay on cushions. The oriental girl was one; another was European and larger; the third, pale and skinny, had undeveloped breasts with almost invisible nipples. He became aware of a steady, rhythmic beat, the harsh, grating dissonance of a synthesizer, as from the right there appeared a long-tressed blonde wearing a wide-brimmed white fedora, a black G-string, a black band around her breasts, and black spiked shoes. She turned slowly to the rhythm, provocatively displaying her bare rear, body partly bent forward, knees flexed, smiling naughtily as the three watchers applauded. She danced back then forward to greet a woman who suddenly appeared from the left.

It was Mona Zakari, dressed in a sequined green lamé cheongsam that clung to her from ankles to throat. It held her legs together so that she moved sinuously as a cobra, bending and twisting to the rhythmic beat in open, erotic invitation. Her eyelids, Burke now saw, were heavily made up, darkened with kohl. Her lips were a blood red slash, giving her pale face a barbaric cast.

Dropping her head, she flung it back abruptly, her thick red mane flaring, then her blond partner was moving around her, not touching but inviting her touch, while Mona writhed and undulated in a sensuous world of her own.

Now the blond unhooked her top and tossed it at the lounging women. Lewdly she rubbed her breasts against Mona's breasts and belly, but Mona danced on. Then as the beat became more insistent, Mona began undoing her dress, starting at the high collar, peeling it down below her large, mature breasts. She touched and played with them until the blonde pressed them with hers again and they swayed together, arms trailing, their movements perfectly coordinated, as if they had so danced a thousand times before.

Kneeling before Mona, the blond drew down the cheongsam, exposing her mistress's nakedness, kissing her thighs until Mona stepped clear of the dress and shot her arms high over her head in feral ecstasy. The blond tossed away her fedora and undid her G-string. She pulled Mona's thighs apart and pushed her face into Mona's crotch. Mona clutched the blond hair and licked her lips lustfully as the blond's mouth excited her.

The blond's hands cupped and massaged Mona's breasts until Mona sank to her knees and kissed her partner's mouth. Rapturously they lay on their sides until Mona pressed her partner on her back and began slow possessive thrusting, as though a man and woman were making love.

Burke watched a few moments more, then extracted the videotape, wondering why it had been made. Blackmail was the first idea that came to mind. Some entrepreneur had photographed Mona Zakari at her most relaxed, and planned to profit from it. That had to be the motive behind the clandestine photography, since Burke could not imagine an agency of the U.S. government sponsoring a pornographic film—and that was what it was. A blue movie.

Well, he had seen Mona now in all her naked, perverse glory, and he would recognize her instantly, anywhere. And the four women who served as her playmates, they too he would recognize.

He wondered if Mona knew the film had been made, if she had been sent a copy with a price tag. He lighted another cigarillo and decided that Mona would be indifferent to the film itself, but outraged by the arrogant intrusion of the photographer. Mona's recreation room was in easy pistol range. But if Mona had seen the film she would know it, too, and by now changes would have been made.

Burke wondered what had happened to the photographer.

As he smoked he decided the tape could not have been made without inside information—probably from one of the four women involved. Mona's harem, Harry had called them. It had required acquiring the apartment opposite, arranging to have *her* window open at the right time. . . . The kind of preparation he would need to order to kill her.

Kill her? He felt the normal male aversion to injuring a woman—any woman. And now that he had seen her, could he do it? He had to remind himself that she was corrupt, not because of her choice of pleasures but because of her poppy fields. Her business acumen, her ruthlessness in rising to the top of a violent trade dominated elsewhere by males was admirable. Like Puma, she had come from nothing and achieved everything, without the sustained violence that characterized Luís Quintana's life, but not without murdering along the way. She must be forty, yet her flawless, unlined skin and muscle tone made her appear ten years younger. That alone proved she was not a heroin user.

Mona Zakari would use her sexuality as lure and sword against males, had probably learned the technique from her mother, the Middle Eastern *artiste*. What had happened to Monique? Burke wondered. Dead, probably, since the dossier had no recent mention of her. Well, she was not a factor in his mission. Only Mona Zakari—Centaur—counted, not *maman*. And as Harry had remarked, killing a woman was a proposition that was going down hard. Questions needed to be answered.

After a while Burke heard Harry drive in and park his station wagon. He went out to meet him, and handed back the briefcase.

"Well," Harry said with a lascivious grin, "what'd you think of the movie?"

"Moving," Burke replied, "but I could have done without it. What the dossier didn't say was why eliminating Centaur is so essential."

They strolled toward the porch. After a few moments Harry said, "Because she rules an empire made up of competing interests. Without her, it will all come apart. She's the only one with the right Syrian contacts—in Damascus and Algiers they treat her like a queen and never try to cheat her."

"Why not?"

He shrugged. The Arabs are proud an Arab woman can rule a man's trade. And they need the revenue to buy arms from China and Czechoslovakia, pay their soldiers."

"Why can't they take the gum direct to the refiners, eliminate her entirely?"

"I suppose they're satisfied with their arrangement. She saves them the trouble of dealing with the refiners, negotiating prices. The Syrians deliver to Centaur and get paid on delivery. Besides, if Centaur is caught, they can disavow their dealings with her."

"Is she on our extradition list?"

"She hasn't been in the U.S. for twenty years, where's the jurisdiction?"

"How about France? Monaco?"

"She's been meticulous not to break French or Monegasque law. And of course in the Arab world she's a heroine." He grimaced. "A heroin heroine."

"Easy," Burke cautioned, "don't get into bad habits." He watched two horses drinking from the pond. "How about fiscal infractions? Banking?"

"Her banking is in Liechtenstein—Vaduz—deposits and withdrawals done electronically. We know that from NSA intercepts and informants. In Vaduz she's a valued client; hell, she keeps that little principality fiscally sound."

"Does she go there?"

Harry shook his head. "Never, as far as we know. But on several occasions bank officers have gone to her yacht to transact business. Perfectly legal. No, she can't be extradited because she's never been indicted anywhere. Aside from having been deported as an illegal alien when she was a kid, there's no rap sheet on her." Stopping, he looked at Burke. "You don't like the mission, do you?"

"That doesn't mean I won't do it. Where is she now?"

"Monaco, aboard her yacht. We lost track of her in Algiers, picked her up in Cairo, and lost her again. She only surfaced yesterday. How long she'll stay in Monaco is anyone's guess."

"What support arrangements are laid on?"

"A man from Marseilles, name of Michael Birely. He's current on Mona's doings, or should be."

"I'll want another plastic handgun and the plastic-fiberglass knife I saw at the hacienda. Anything else in that line I figure on getting in Marseilles." He shook his head and smiled slightly. "That lawless town."

"Papers?"

"I'll have to think about that. As for funds, I'll take along fifty thousand FF, maybe a thou in Swiss francs for tipping money."

Harry was writing hurriedly in his notebook. "Paul Revere?" he asked.

"Absolutely. To do my sums on when I'm not cavorting with the harem crowd."

Harry made the notation.

Burke rocked back and forth on toes and heels, finally saying, "I'll go as a Peruvian national. That'll give me a scent of the drug métier if anyone's interested in what I'm doing along the Côte d'Azur."

"Sounds good." Harry looked at his watch. "I'd better get going. And I don't envy you, Tom, having to waste a beautiful broad like Mona."

"I've worked it out," Burke said, "rationalized it. Just before I blow her brains out I'll tell her it's nothing personal."

"Yeah," Harry said wryly, "I'm sure she'll understand."

Cardiff II

Twenty-four

I WAS FLYING to Europe. Not Air France to Nice as I'd told Harry, but Sabena to Brussels, back-tracking to Paris on the TEE, the Trans-European Express.

From Paris I took the bullet train overnight to Nice and checked into a three-star hotel two blocks from the *plage*. At high season all the four- and five-star hotels were solidly booked, but a two-hundred-franc *pourboire* to the desk clerk got me a fourth-floor corner room that provided a ten-degree glimpse of the Mediterranean, the glistening gold beach, and its colorful changing-cabanas and umbrellas.

I had placed a call to Michael Birely from inside the train station, and he'd agreed to start the hundred-mile drive from his post in Marseilles. I reminded him that the coastal route was a tourist's dream, taking him through La Ciotat, Hyères, Saint-Tro', Cannes, and Antibes, and promised him a worthwhile lunch on the Promenade des Anglais. He was taking full advantage of it, slurping up snails drowned in garlic butter, quaffing an '87 Montrachet, and not caring that the fringe of his blond mustache was acquiring samples of both.

The open-air restaurant featured umbrellaed tables and a lot of bathers enjoying the cuisine. A smaller number of patrons were clothed in light summer wear like ourselves.

Birely was a man of thirty-four or so, with sandy hair, pale blue eyes, and chalk white teeth. He'd gone to Ohio State and emerged with an ROTC commission and a degree in French literature. When he grumbled about having missed Nam, I told him to thank his gods that he had, and to hang on to his reserve commission for the next one.

I was enjoying my lobster mayonnaise nested in endive too much for immediate shoptalk. The wine was excellent, and the sun reflected off the water with an unrelenting glare. Also, we were enjoying the uninhibited display of nubile young creatures in G-strings and *rien en plus*. On that beach it was easy to tell the girls from the boys. I said so and Birely agreed. Then he interested himself in the menu and ordered frilled lamb chops and new peas from Grasse. Eating tender pink-white bits of lobster, I reflected aloud that the French—so incompetent in so many things—ate well in war or peace. Birely nodded and squinted at the water. "How are you papered?" he asked in offhand tones.

"Peruvian, name of Ricardo Hubler Gómez. Been to Peru?"

He shook his head.

"I put in some time there, and decided I'd have a better chance passing if I could talk knowledgeably about the country of my presumed birth. I picked Hubler because it's a fairly common name and there are plenty of WW-Two leftover Germans in Peru, some sought over here, others forgotten."

"So Gómez is your mother's name."

"Right. In Latin America the choices are limited to the given name."

"Hell, in France names have to be taken from the Academy-approved register." He shook his head. "Crazy."

"Well, it instills a certain amount of order among the populace—and simplifies police archives."

The wine arrived before his chops, but we tucked into it anyway, and Birely remarked that there were certain advantages to pulling duty in France.

"Married?" I asked.

"Uh-uh, and that's a closed chapter of my life. Bell, book, and candle."

"A witch, eh?"

"Yeah. But it's one thing to date in college and then find out what the lady's really like after the vows. Once burned, twice shy."

"Say, that's a nifty saying," I kidded. "I'll remember to use it."

"Lay off, Ricardo," he said gloomily. "You look like a man with a lady in his past."

"She's a lawyer now," I said, "so I don't know if she qualifies as a lady. Anyway, speaking of ladies, is Madame Zakari still around Monaco?"

"As of this morning she was."

"Does she still use her pad here?"

"Not for, oh, four months."

That would be about when the videotape had been made, but I didn't say so, not knowing if Birely knew about the photographic intrusion on her privacy. "So," I said, "she hangs out on the *Kismet* most of the time?"

"Daytimes. Hits the casino pretty heavy at night, with her body-guard and a girlfriend or two. You want close-in coverage?"

"I don't need to know what she eats or her casino score, just whether she takes off. If she does, I want to know where she's headed, boat or plane."

"Her plane's at the Aéroport du Plage. We'll know when the crew starts making preflight checks. Before *Kismet* sails, it always takes on stores, so there'll be a couple hours notice either way."

"And where does she go?"

"There's one general clue," he replied, moving back to allow the waiter to serve him. "If she's headed for an Arab city, she wears Arab garb right up to the veil. If she's heading for Paris, say, she wears western dress." He nodded thanks to the waiter and addressed his meal. After a few mouthfuls of rare lamb he said, "Great meal," shoveling in the peas, "and worth the drive from base. Need wheels, by the way?"

"Hope not," I said, "but I'll rent if necessary. The local speedsters think every day is Grand Prix day and drive accordingly."

"Yeah, but I drive plenty defensively. I don't want to die in a heap of smoking metal. My aim is to expire in the arms of, say, yon sly fox."

I glanced at his target and recognized an oriental girl with coal black bangs, tapered legs, a red G-string, and a gauzy bra as one of Mona's girls. "Yeah, that'd be something."

"Hi," he said, as she strolled past. She gave him a blast-freeze glance.

"Die, Yankee sojer," I hissed, "you time have come—and gone." I couldn't help admiring the rear view. Small, well-muscled, active buttocks. Birely was watching, too. Disconsolately he said, "I say it's spinach and the hell with it."

I turned to him with fresh appreciation. "So George Price has fans in the younger generation."

"He do. And as for that Bangkok binzel, I was thinking of someone *like* her, but friendly. The way most natives are." He sighed regretfully and savaged the rest of his meal. Plate empty, Birely asked if I wanted him to stay around Nice for a while. I said no, that wouldn't be necessary; he could return to the grime and stench of Marseilles and earn his pay, I'd call him if needed.

We shook hands; he thanked me again for the class-A cuisine and went off to the parking lot behind the hotel. I ordered coffee and lighted a Cuban-rolled cigarillo, having decided to survey the scene as any macho South American would. The Oriental was on the loose, maybe along with the other team players. And where they were, Mona Zakari was likely to be.

I spent an hour girl-watching, recognizing only the undernourished girl who'd watched Mona dance. In flimsy lavender shorts with matching bra and high-heeled shoes, she was trolling all right, but for which sex I couldn't guess. Attractively dressed, she might have made a connection, but every prominent rib suggested a starved refugee.

I shifted in my chair because the knife next to my spine was getting uncomfortable. Made in Finland of a steel-hard fiberglass-plastic compound, it was nine inches long and an eighth of an inch thick at the haft. The double-edged blade was razor sharp, but the knife was not one for heavy duty. Leroy had suggested a number of uses. Nonmetallic, it was undetectable in airport screenings and pat-downs.

I was dressed in that season's de rig Riviera wear—baggy cotton trousers tight around the ankles, knotted scarf for a belt; V-cut pink shirt with loose sleeves, whose overhang easily concealed the plastic

Brazilian-made pistol at my waist. Espadrilles on my feet and a bored expression on my face made me one of the crowd.

On the beach and along the promenade a lot of money and a great deal of sexual hunger were visible among the varied sexes soaking up rays. When the breeze changed I could sniff marijuana, and I'd noticed a good many coke spoons dangling from gold necklaces. In this hedonistic, pleasure-seeking society, I was an alien. Claire should see it once for shock effect and be content ever after to live quietly with me in Leesburg.

It was midafternoon when I got back to my hotel. My room was high-ceilinged and airy, walls flocked in blue patterns that were meaningless to my tired eyes. The closet was walk-in size, and the ample bathroom featured a large tub with shower and a gleaming white bidet. After turning on the ceiling fan, I stripped and lay on the bed, tired from plane-train travel, contemplating an evening at the casino. Not knowing the *Société*'s current dress rules I'd purchased a tuxedo, shirt, tie, and patent-leather shoes, and stowed them in the closet.

Le Soleil de Nice, purchased on the promenade, carried a brief story about the arrest in Geneva of Hans Dieter Weiskopf, formerly an SS major. Weiskopf was being held in the cantonal prison hospital pending extradition formalities requested by the German government. Looking up at the slowly rotating fan blades, I felt satisfied. Bringing the old man to justice had been an extra dividend of the Gargoyle mission, and I wondered if Centaur would produce anything of comparable worth.

After four hours' sleep, I got up, showered, shaved, and dressed for the evening. The Finnish knife lay comfortably along my spine, the plastic pistol under my belt, concealed by my dinner jacket. A taxi took me over the few miles of serpentine road to Monaco and let me off at Monte Carlo Casino, once Onassis's domain. From the broad staircase I could look out over the glistening slope of the Condamine and down to the boat-crammed harbor, and wondered which of the many large yachts belonged to Mona Zakari.

Tuxedoed door guards let me through with barely a glance— Monegasques were not admitted to the gaming tables—and I made my way over marbled floors to the dining room. But for the tables it could have been a ballroom. The decor was Empire in gold and blue, and the pendant chandeliers scintillated with thousands of tiny lights that were reflected by the gleaming table silver. Each of the fifty-odd tables was draped with crisp white napery, and set with floral adornments and candles in silver holders. The maître showed me to a side table from which I could glimpse roulette action just getting underway. If Mona Zakari was coming to the casino, she'd probably dine aboard *Kismet* and arrive later making a grand entrance with her entourage. I planned on staying until she left in order to check out her departure transportation. Killing her aboard her yacht would mean being trapped there, and the thought of a firefight with a dozen bodyguards was unappealing.

The waiter recommended a shrimp cocktail, Channel sole, and *haricots verts*. I nodded agreement and asked the sommelier for his selection: a white Bordeaux, *premier cru* Haut-Brion of recent vintage. During dinner the gaming crowd multiplied. Most of the men wore dinner jackets, the women were elegantly gowned, and everyone seemed to have a tulip of champagne in hand, except for the robed Arabs, of course, who sipped Evian as they gambled.

After a demitasse I paid, tipped the sommelier, and strolled into the gaming hall. For starters I bought a thousand francs worth of roulette chips, placed half on black, and presently watched the croupier rake them in. From a passing cigarette girl I acquired four Havana cigarillos, lighted one, and watched the play before betting again. This time I laid two hundred and fifty on red and recouped my previous loss. Players around me were almost equally divided by sex, though few appeared under forty. I heard a babel of tongues—Italian, English, Arabic—with French predominant among the gamesters.

For a while I watched chemin de fer, a game popular with the Arab contingent, who gambled recklessly and seemed indifferent to losing. To them, money, like oil, seemed a renewable resource. Their aides had large sacks of money hanging from their waists and made frequent trips to the cage to purchase more chips. The next time I filled the Porsche's tank I was going to remember where the profits ended up.

After finishing my champagne I played blackjack for half an hour, impressed by the dealer's dexterity, and won two hands out of five, leaving behind chips worth six hundred francs.

The time was now nine-thirty. I positioned myself at the far end of the room, from where I could watch the entrance, took another glass of champagne, and began wondering if Centaur would appear.

Precisely at ten o'clock I noticed a stir by the doorway and saw Mona come in. Her flaming red hair was drawn back by a silver band that matched the costume she wore: silver blouse cut to show her bosom to advantage; black cord around her waist, accentuating her full hips; and silver harem pants. Accompanying her were two obvious bodyguards—mustached, dark-skinned men, the Oriental girl, and the lush-bodied brunette who had been another of the dance watchers.

Mona went directly to the roulette wheel. A bodyguard handed her a large stack of chips that she placed unhesitatingly on the board. Both girls wandered off to the bar for champagne, while the bodyguards stood on either side of Mona, not watching the play, but glancing around like Secret Service men. I found standing space away from the right-hand bodyguard, and watched Mona play. Unlike the Arab males, she placed her chips according to a system of her own. It seemed to consist of doubling after a loss, shifting to a sequential number, and betting only a set amount after a win. Her silver-clad arms sparkled as she shoved chips forward and, more rarely, hauled winnings in. Within half an hour she was wiped out and a bodyguard went off to the cage for more chips. The remaining bodyguard lighted her cigarette in a long silver holder. Until her chips arrived she chatted amiably in French and English with players on her right and left. Her girlfriends drifted back, the brunette bringing Mona a glass of champagne, the Oriental eyeing me as though she'd seen me before but couldn't remember where. Well, no problem there; it would be Birely's crass behavior she recalled.

As her stacks dwindled, Mona grew snappish with the croupier, imperious with her gofer girls, and snotty with her bodyguards, who were doing a lot of footwork bringing chips from the cage. So far she'd dropped at least fifty thousand dollars, enough to be an irritant.

Her mother had to work and whore to put food on their table, so Mona understood the value of a dollar.

As time passed I noticed that not a single male tried hitting on her, though there were plenty around the gaming room. Unattached females, too, for that matter, but none in Mona's league. Gigolos roamed the casino, alert for a lonely, well-heeled female, age unimportant. I saw several connect, then head for the gaming tables where their sponsors bankrolled them. The old song "Just a Gigolo" seemed to tell all anyone needed to know.

By midnight I'd had six glasses of champagne and despite an excellent dinner was feeling a little light-headed. I saw Mona shove her last pile onto red, and the ivory ball dropped on black. The croupier raked her chips away.

With an exclamation of disgust—in a language I took to be Arabic—Mona noisily backed her chair, and without a word strode from the table. The bodyguards quickly got into stride, followed by the two fluttering girls, while a lot of heads turned to watch them leave.

Then play resumed.

I waited a few moments before walking to the broad, columned entrance, where Mona stood tapping her silver-shod foot in irritation. Presently a gold stretch Mercedes swung up to the staircase, a bodyguard opened the rear door, and Mona got quickly in, followed by her retinue, bodyguards on either side. The limo's rubber screeched as the driver accelerated and turned hard at the same time. Before taillights vanished I motioned the doorman for a taxi, tipped him, and got into a little Renault.

"Follow that car," I instructed in my best Philip Marlowe voice, "I think it's going down to the harbor, but follow it."

"Easy," the driver said, shifting ahead. "How many gold limousines can there be?"

"In Monaco," I replied, settling back, "one never knows."

The Mercedes drove rapidly down the Boulevard Albert I to the harbor, and stopped beside a long green-white launch idling at the pier. I paid my driver, moved back into shadows, and watched the party step down into the launch. It made a ninety-degree turn from shore, and accelerated out among the close-tethered boats—irresponsibly fast, I thought; but if Mona liked speed, she could afford the costs.

I wished I'd brought binoculars, but in a few moments I saw a gangway light up at the side of a large green-white yacht half a mile away.

The only vulnerability I'd detected had been in those few moments when Mona left the limo and walked to the waiting launch. She was first over the gunwale, unscreened by bodyguards or girls, and her silver costume made her a first-class target. And as I squinted at the yacht, I saw silver glinting as she went up the gangway. Again she was first, again unshielded. Suppose, I were in a steady boat, fifty or a hundred yards from *Kismet*. A gimbal rest would steady the rifle while a night scope zeroed in. Not bad for a preliminary idea, but it needed refinement and I had limited time. If Mona got in a snit over her gambling losses, she might head for Damascus or Algiers.

I headed for the taxi rank when a deep brown Lincoln braked just ahead of me. A door opened and two men got out, both in street clothes. As they turned toward me, one said, "Evening, Major. Hoped we'd catch up with you sooner. Couldn't enter the casino, not being properly dressed."

The streetlight was behind them, so I couldn't see their faces, but the voice was vaguely familiar. "Well," I said, "you caught up with me. What's on your mind?"

"Message for you," the other man said. He was slightly smaller than the first man and had a splayfooted walk. Ten feet away I recognized them: Meaching and Kiley, grunts from Vietnam days and Poliakoff's shabby circle.

"What's the message?"

"Step into the car," Kiley said. "Top secret—sensitive. Your eyes only."

Maybe the Centaur mission was off and I could leave Mona Zakari to her profits and pleasures. Hopeful, I got in after Kiley, Meaching behind me. A pistol barrel bored into my ribs and I glimpsed the sudden glint of metal. Before I could dodge, the cosh struck, darkness exploded into unbearable light, and as consciousness faded I heard a voice growling, *"That's the message, Major. Get dead."*

Twenty-five

IT WAS UTTERLY dark now, and my breathing was labored as I swam deep in the waters of the lake. Whether to or from Weiskopf's place I couldn't remember because I'd lost my bearings. I was tired, my head throbbed, and my air tank must be giving out. Too dark to read my compass, too inky to see the pressure gauge.

Distantly I made out a glimmer of light and thrust toward it. The light came from the surface where there would be air to breathe. I came up in a rush, saw lantern light from a boat, a man poised with an oar. As he struck at me I saw his face—Judge Grogan. The oar slashed water beside my head. I ducked down, came up at the other side and pulled down the gunwale with all my strength. Grogan pitched backward and the boat drifted away. Grogan was coughing, crying for help, yelling that he couldn't swim. I gulped air and submerged, leaving him somewhere in the dark.

Drown, you merciless bastard, I thought, and then my mind blanked—anoxia? I was in a room, a dimly lit room, hearing the pounding of a drum that became my temple pulse. I was lying on my back, too exhausted from swimming to move. Claire materialized from the background, spoke, but I couldn't hear her over the throbbing drumbeats. She grasped my hand and tried to draw me up, but I was too heavy and she too weak, so I lay there and watched her vanish like smoke into nothingness.

I wept.

Tears wet my cheeks. I felt a tongue licking away my tears. An animal? I saw copper hair, a forehead, the face of Mona, tongue extruding from scarlet lips as she lapped my cheeks.

I tried to touch her face but couldn't move. Naked, she sat up, gave me her breast to suckle. Beside her the titless girl appeared, took the other nipple in her mouth. Strength flowed into me. Their hands warmed my chilled flesh. Mona spoke softly in Arabic, but I understood: You can do it if you try, she was saying.

I wondered how she knew.

The Oriental and the tall brunette were dancing together, the Oriental's mouth brushed the taller girl's breasts as they moved and pressed together. What was a male doing in this sapphic scene? They didn't want whatever small service I might be able to perform, but to exhibit themselves to the enemy.

Together, Mona and her friend tried to draw me to my feet, failed. I realized I was tied to the floor, no wonder they couldn't manage. Poor Claire, she'd tried, too.

Dark fog like the heavy exhaust of Guadalajara buses flowed into the room, surrounding the women, who gradually faded from view. I tried reaching for them, but my arms wouldn't move. My pulse throbbed with mallet blows. Again there was only darkness.

My eyes opened and I saw moonlight through a window. I was lying on my side, hands bound behind me, ankles bound, too.

I began remembering. Suckered by two pals of Enno's. Their message: *Get dead.*

Well, that was being up-front, right? They hadn't even had to trail me to Brussels and Paris, they'd known my destination. Birely would have made a routine contact report. Innocently. Now knowing there were men on my trail. Not Arabs, not even nasty Latinos. Amerikanskis hired for a job. Mercenaries.

I wondered how much they were paid. Five large? Ten? For them that would be a fortune. As grunts they were always begging and borrowing, Poliakoff staked them from time to time. My master sergeant, the miserable, treacherous prick.

The moon was setting. Maybe three hours to dawn. Where my plastic pistol had been there was nothing. I remembered the Finnish knife, rolled on my back and pressed down. Hardness. They'd have found it if they'd strip-searched me. Career incompetents. Could I free it?

Footsteps. I rolled on my back again. A door opened, light flared into my eyes. "How you doin', Major?" Kiley's voice.

"Alive," I said, "and that's a hard way to cancel a mission."

"Shit, you were always a hardass, know that? Rules, orders, never any slack."

"Slack's for slackers," I said, and got a kick in the ribs. "Whose idea?" I gasped.

"Guess."

"Has to be Enno—you were always his gofers."

Kiley laughed unpleasantly. "I ain't sayin', but someone back there don't like you."

I thought it over, said, "This is a presidential mission I'm on—know that?"

"I'm real impressed. But the prez is gonna be disappointed in you, Major, real disappointed. As of now the mission's aborted. Couldn't bring yourself to waste the broad. Sentimental."

I squinted up at him, no gun in his hand. "Where's Meaching?"

He smirked. "Callin' home."

"Then what?"

"Depends what he's told."

So that was why I hadn't been shot and dumped; they needed final word. "Worst case?"

"You'll take a ride. A boat ride. One way."

"I'm afraid of water."

"Got reason to be. Lost your ass at the casino, drowned yourself. Poor Major Burke."

"And you figure you'll get away with it?"

"A thousand percent sure. Fail-safe."

I grunted. "That's what they always say. But the smart ones look for an alternative that's risk-free and profitable. Know what I mean?"

"How profitable?"

"Get Meaching and we'll discuss it."

"I don't need him."

"I do," I said.

"Why?"

"Mutual confidence. Three-way."

His mouth twisted as he thought it over. As a young grunt Kiley had a mean face. Fifteen years hadn't improved it. "Talk money," he said.

"I make a deal with you, Meaching doesn't like it, I'm screwed."

"Worsen' that," he sniggered, "you're dead."

"So, get Meaching."

He knelt down, checked my bonds for tautness, got up and left the room. It was a dark and dusty place: shabby, gut-sprung sofa, two worn chairs, a battle-scarred table, threadbare carpet, and grimy window glass. The kind of place where dopesters and fugitives holed up; penultimate stop before prison or the morgue.

On street level there would be a telephone. Or Meaching had broken into another apartment to make his call and verify my fate; rat-faced Kiley had already revealed what it would be.

Through the door I could hear a few sounds, enough to tell me it was an apartment house. Turning toward the window I saw the moon impaled on TV antennae. That put me on the third or fourth floor. Too high for a jump, much too high.

What I needed was time. By daylight it was harder to kill a man, less safe.

My hands were numb from restricted circulation, skull felt squeezed in a vise. Physically I was in no shape to try anything that required strength or fast action. But I could talk.

Shuffling steps from down the hall and Meaching came in, followed by Kiley. My plastic pistol was in Meaching's belt. He stopped beside me. "What's your offer, Major?"

I gazed up at him, wet my lips. "It goes like this. You walk away, report me dead, and I stay out of sight until you have time to collect from . . . whoever."

"And for that you pay—what?"

"A hundred large," I told them. "Francs or dollars."

Kiley stepped toward me. "You got that much lyin' aroun'?"

"If you know anything about my mission, you know I get what I ask for. No, I don't have a hundred thou at hand. But I can get it in about, oh, six hours. After a phone call to Marseilles."

They looked at each other. Meaching rubbed his receding chin. To lubricate his thinking I said, "That's a big take for doing nothing."

Kiley said, "Suppose we go for it, what's your move?"

"My mission's terminated. Obviously I don't enjoy the confidence of my employers, so let's look down the line and suppose I start yelling about two hit men sent after me. First question is what was I doing in the south of France? Second question, any witnesses to the alleged conspiracy?" I looked from one face to another. "Where's the satisfaction?"

Meaching gave a scant nod. "See what you mean."

"Besides, the money's nothing to me—but I can get it."

Kiley looked at his partner. "What's another day or two?" he urged.

Meaching chuckled unpleasantly. "Against a hundred thou— *nada.*"

"My thought, too. Okay, Major, we'll talk details and get back to you." He started to leave.

"Meanwhile," I said, "unless you loosen my wrists my hands will drop off—and I'd as soon be dead as go around with a pair of steel hooks for paws. And a mouthful of water will go down like wine."

"Jesus," Kiley said, "you want everything your way, doncha?"

"When I'm paying," I said, "seems only fair."

Meaching got down beside me and gave me a finger's worth of slack. It wasn't much, but I could feel blood rushing through those veins. I stretched fingers and clenched them, working stiff joints until Kiley brought a stained coffee cup half full of water and held it so I could drink. It tasted moldy.

Then I was alone.

The door was closed, the moon almost down, but I no longer needed light. They hadn't used wire or nylon line around my wrists like the Viet Cong, but finger-thick hemp whose rough uneven fibers itched my wrists. On my side I worked up the back of my dinner jacket and pulled out my shirt an inch at a time. My fingers felt the knife's smooth blade, and I began to work it clear of the belt until my fingers closed around the haft.

Very carefully I drew it out, and with a short hold began nicking into the rope. There was sweat on my face and blood pumping through my head, and I was afraid of fainting. But I clenched my teeth until the knife cut through the rope, and I pulled my wrists apart.

I massaged my aching shoulders and elbows, then cut away the ankle rope. Holding the knife to my lips, I kissed it as though it were a crucifix, and thought about what to do next.

If I tried to walk out, a floor creak might give me away—and they had handguns. If I made it to the street, they'd come after me, so it had to be here and now. Sitting up despite skull pain, I replaced the ankle cords to look as though they were undisturbed, but didn't bother with the wrist rope.

Standing, I did knee bends to increase circulation, then sat down facing the door. Whoever entered couldn't see my hands, and the right one was gripping the Finnish knife.

Sweat was drying on my face, my flesh was chilling as body and mind meshed in single-purpose synthesis. If only one of them entered, that was my prayer. But if both came back . . .

My senses were critically sharp; I heard water running in a distant part of the building. My wristwatch showed ten to five. By now the moon was invisible behind the nearby buildings. I wondered if I were still in Monaco and if not, where?

Footsteps again. Who?

Meaching came in and opened his mouth to speak, but I whispered, *"Shhh.* C'mere."

"Huh?"

"I've got a better proposition for you. Can Kiley hear us?"

His voice lowered. "Not if we talk like this." He came closer. "What's the deal?"

"Closer," I muttered, "can't take a chance on being heard."

He bent over, face a foot from mine, expectant. "What is it?"

"There isn't any reason . . . " I began, as my left hand hooked over his neck and my right hand slashed his throat. Gurgling, he tried to pull away, but my left hand held him down while my right plunged the blade into the cervical plexus, severing the spinal cord. He was dead before he fell across my thighs. I kneed him away and pulled the plastic pistol from his belt. There was a splash of blood where I'd cut his throat, but the heart wasn't pumping out more. Listening for Kiley's tread, I went through Meaching's coat pockets, got out his wallet and passport, stuck them into my jacket as I got to my feet.

There was a light switch beside the door. I clicked it off, stood in darkness beside it, and held the throwaway pistol in my left hand.

Minutes passed. I glanced at my watch from time to time, wondering where Kiley was. Maybe he'd sent Meaching back to finish me and was waiting below in the Lincoln. Crouching, I went through Meaching's pockets, groping for car keys. Kiley must have them, I reasoned.

Footsteps.

I pressed back against the wall, but when Kiley saw the room was dark he held back. "*Meach!* Where the hell are ya?"

He stopped in the entrance and reached around for the switch. I grabbed the hand and struck upward with my knife. It entered his glottis, penetrating flesh and gristle to the haft, and Kiley staggered into the room. I tripped him and he fell across his partner's body. I shut the door and switched on the light.

Kiley was rolling on the floor, hands tugging at the knife, blood spilling everywhere. His mouth kept opening, but only rasping sounds came out with bubbles of blood. He tried to get up, but I kicked him back. He had the knife out and that increased the flow of blood. I thought of a pistol shot to end his agony, but an unsilenced report would bring neighbors—and police.

I pried his bloody fingers off the knife, held down his head, and parted his cervical vertebrae the way a torero kills a bull, the way I'd killed Meaching.

His head lay across Meaching's legs, and as I watched, his eyes became dull. The muscles relaxed and his entire body went limp as a wet towel. Well, Sparky, I thought, no more shit from you. Ever.

I walked through the scantily furnished apartment to the bathroom, where I cleansed my knife and washed hands and face, used a damp washcloth to remove the bloodstains on my dinner jacket.

Still dark outside. I opened the window and looked down, counting four stories to the alley. The big Lincoln was parked there, so I searched Kiley's pockets until I found the keys; I took his holstered .38 snub-nosed Bodyguard and stuck it in my belt.

There'd been a bottle of imitation bourbon on the kitchen table. I sniffed it before taking a long pull, hoping it wasn't poisoned. The raw liquor burned my throat like Drāno, but it made my heart pound faster and dulled head pain. I wiped prints from the bottle and poked my head from the window. No one in sight, alley empty. I hauled Kiley's body to the window and levered it over the sill, heard it squash below. Did the same with Meaching.

Then I turned off the light, closed the door, and took the back stairs. I opened the door cautiously and looked left and right. Nothing. Nobody. I hauled both bodies onto the front seat of the Lincoln and propped them against each other. Wasn't easy, because the fall had smashed their bodies to jelly and their released waste stank worse than a stable.

There were cleaning rags in the trunk. I grabbed out a handful and uncapped the gas tank, then lowered the makeshift wick until it hit gasoline, left it there.

Next I opened the hood and wrenched the copper fuel line from the carburetor. The stench of gasoline filled the air. Closing the hood I looked around.

A truck passed the far end of the alley, sweeping street gutters. From my pocket I took a beat-up cigarillo, lighted it, and leaned against the building until the truck was a block away. Then I lighted the tank rag and walked rapidly to the near end of the alley, turned the corner, and slowed to normal stride. I was almost at a brightly lighted intersection when the Lincoln blew with the force of a half-ton bomb.

I never looked back.

Twenty-six

FROM VILLEFRANCHE——that's where I'd been sequestered——I hitched a two-mile ride to Nice in a flower camion, sharing the seat with a plump middle-aged woman who had a silky mustache and a teenage son on his way to work. To explain my disheveled appearance I told them I'd tried to keep a thief from stealing my car; he'd knocked me out and the car was gone. I'd reported the theft to the police.

They expressed sympathy and let me off a block from my hotel, and when I tried to pay, she said I could buy a flower. So I chose a fresh-cut yellow rose and handed her fifty francs. Too much, she protested, but I pointed out that a taxi would have cost me twice as much.

Before entering the hotel lobby I stuck the rosebud in my lapel, collected my room key at the desk, and went up to my room.

I hadn't looked in the mirror since the previous night, and what I saw told me the evening attire would never serve again. Cognac was a considerable improvement over Drāno-flavored bourbon, and I sipped a double shot while waiting for the tub to fill. It had been a long, rough night and my nerves were taut as piano wires. Intuition told me Poliakoff had sent the killer team, but I had to be certain. Arness had been depressed, ready to throw in the towel. Could it have been the result of having issued orders for my demise? But that was crazy. Arness had recruited me, set up the Camp David meeting, confirmed I had only Centaur to kill . . .

I sank in tub water to my chin. Warmed inside by brandy, externally by steaming water, I felt myself gradually relax. An ice pack on my head would help, but more than that I needed sleep.

Mike Birely wouldn't be at his desk in Marseilles for at least two hours. Should I have him meet me in Nice, or go to Marseilles? Overnight, Birely might have received official word regarding the Centaur mission. If so, I wanted to know what it was, and judge whether I was on the termination list. For critical things like that, Birely would be out of the loop. But as Kiley had snickered, someone back there didn't like me, so until I could take counteraction my life was on the line.

The comedy team would have had time to report my capture to their principal(s) and perhaps to file a further report on my freedom proposal. What they had *not* done was send a termination notice, so "someone back there" was still waiting for news.

I hadn't found a Paul Revere on either body, but I hadn't been looking for the compact communicator, and if they had one, it could be in their hotel luggage or the now-destroyed Lincoln.

I blotted my body with a warm towel, pulled down window blinds, and got between cool sheets. My last conscious thought was that I was going to have to leave Nice expeditiously, but where to go?

Despite window blinds, the room was uncomfortably warm when I woke at ten twenty-two. I left the bed stiffly and turned on the overhead fan, upped the blinds enough to admit some air, and treated myself to a needed shave.

After dressing in street clothes, I consigned my wrinkled evening attire to the corridor trash chute and packed my suitcase including the S&W Bodyguard. Next, I stuck the plastic pistol in my waist, the Finnish knife that had proved so useful along my spine. After paying my bill I took a taxi to the airport and used a public phone to call Mike Birely in Marseilles.

"I was getting ready to phone your hotel," he began without preliminaries. "A little while ago the lady of interest flew off to Paris."

"I know," I lied, "and so I'm calling you. How much cash can you let me have?"

"How much do you need?"

"A hundred thousand green or franc equivalent. More if available."

"Can do," he said. "It's going on noon, so I'll hit the bank right away. Where do we meet?"

"I'm at the airport." I glanced around the lobby. "There's a boutique called Quelque Chose, beach wear. I'll be lurking nearby in, what . . . two hours?"

"Do my best."

So Mona Zakari had decided to forget her casino disappointments in the City of Light, giving me a plausible reason for going there.

I bought an Air France ticket to Paris on the 3:12 flight, went into the restaurant, and had a long, slow meal. I bought *Le Soleil de Nice* and read it over Irish coffee, and replenished my supply of Havana cigarillos. For years the U.S. Treasury had been attempting to bring Fidel Castro to his knees by banning the importation of Cuban tobaccos. At last notice, Fidel was still in charge of Cuba and American aficionados of Cuban leaf had to smuggle it in or enjoy it abroad. I was one of the latter.

After prechecking my suitcase to Orly, I went into the men's room and got out Meaching's passport and billfold, examined them in the privacy of a stall. It held less than a thousand FF, thirty-two U.S. dollars, and a driver's license giving the hometown of Jason Y. Meaching as Oxon Hill, Maryland. Four identical business cards offered his services as a private investigator: NO JOB TOO SMALL, NO JOB TOO LARGE, the teaser read; to which could be added: All offers considered.

There was a Diners Club card that I laid on the floor near the commode. Some petty thief could end up with a lot of questions to answer. According to the recently issued passport, Meaching had been forty-one at the time of his death; close to my own age, but I wasn't planning on using it, though in Paris I might be able to trade it for another. In the barbershop I treated myself to a trim, mud pack, massage, and manicure. Noting my skull bruise, the barber offered to cover it with a small bandage. I preferred a touch of alcohol, and when he applied a saturated pad, the antiseptic burned like a brand. The manicurist, who looked as though she'd stayed up too late too many nights in too many strange beds, nevertheless did a professional job on my nails, suggested polish that I declined, and buffed them instead.

As I lay back in the chair, enjoying the astringent witch-hazel pack, I reflected on my lack of remorse over Meaching and Kiley. The latter was the more deserving of death; at Da Nang he'd battered a young prostitute mercilessly until MPs, drawn by the *mama-san's* shrieks, dragged him away. For what I considered attempted murder, Kiley received only thirty days detention, reduction in rate, and a fine that covered the battered kid's hospital costs. I remembered Kiley at the NCO club, boasting about the episode, and standing drinks all around. Well, the army wasn't selective in those days.

Toward two o'clock I went window-shopping, passing Quelque Chose twice before spotting Mike Birely. Carrying a blue nylon sports bag, he followed me to a bar.

"I'm thirsty," he said. "What should I drink?"

"Lemonade, but I recommend *fine café.*" I looked him over carefully, but I saw no weapon bulges, and his manner was relaxed. After the waiter brought our order, Birely got down to business.

"The bag holds a hundred thousand in FF and fifty thousand dollars. Hope it's enough, because it's all I could collect on short notice."

"Want me to sign a chit?"

"I'd appreciate it." He shoved a typed half-sheet across the table and I receipted for the funds as Ricardo Hubler Gómez. He put away the receipt, which I thought might be useful if or when he was interrogated by people like Poliakoff. "Did a couple of fellows find you?" he asked.

"What fellows?"

"Two showed up yesterday afternoon. I had no official word about them, so I stalled. They wanted to know where you were staying, stuff like that."

"What did you tell them?"

"Said you might be around the Monte Carlo tables."

"Keep your mouth shut, will you, Mike?" I said testily.

He swallowed. "Sorry I said anything . . . Ricardo. You going to Paris?"

"I'm scared to tell you anything, but I'll say enough to justify the funds. I'm going to try for a technical installation on her apartment. With conversations between Mona and her Riviera refiners on tape, maybe we can get the French to indict her."

"Maybe," he said, "but not unless you grease the gears of justice."

"For the present I don't want your Paris colleagues in my way. And Washington doesn't need to know my whereabouts. People who shouldn't talk at all talk too damn much." I sipped my cognac-laced coffee. "If those two show up again, call the cops. I'd like to know who they are and why they're looking for me." I smiled. "My American Express check is in the mail."

"They asked for Hubler," he repeated defensively.

"Let the flics deal with them, okay?"

"Okay." He finished his coffee and got up. "If I don't see you again, take care."

"My watchword." I watched him drift away.

So thanks to Birely's loose lip I'd been scooped up without warning. I'd wondered how Kiley and Meaching knew where to find me last night and now I knew. Thanks a bunch, Mike, I thought bitterly, though I appreciated his unquestioning response to my request for capital.

After finishing my coffee I waited in the departure lounge until flight time.

I had close to two hundred thousand dollars worth of executive branch money, and I intended to use as much as necessary to find out who had marked me for termination, and why. If there was a narcotics informer in his unit, General Arness ought to know about it. The sickening hacienda massacre came into mind, but I hadn't been the specific target.

I reproached myself for killing both Meaching and Kiley; I should have tortured one until he spat out the name of his sponsor.

The flight was called, I found my seat on the Boeing 737, and held the money bag on my lap all the way to Paris.

Because of the *grandes vacances*, the *fermeture annuelle*, the city was partly depopulated, the better hotels and restaurants operating with skeletal staffs but staying open. The smaller mom-and-pop places were shuttered as I'd learned during my summer language course at the University of Paris.

I found a hotel on the rue de l'Arcade a block from the church of the Madeleine, near a hand laundry and three passable-looking restaurants. The room wasn't much—lumpy bed, rust-stained tub, and grimy windows—but it wasn't for long. I'd taken a chance showing Meaching's passport to the desk clerk, but I figured it wouldn't get on the Interpol watch list for another couple of days.

Or maybe never, I mused, if the team's sponsor wanted to play things really tight. Still, I couldn't risk using it; I had work to do, but not necessarily what Arness's group had ordained.

I stashed all but five hundred francs in the hotel's lockbox and went down the street to the nearest restaurant, Tante Marie, for an aperitif and a look at the menu. I was too tired to poke around Paris for Michelin's perfect restaurant, so I settled for pepper steak flambeau, blanched *asperges*, and a small, crisp salad. Chairs and banquettes were covered in red velvet that blended with the walls' dark pink. The far end had a small service bar where a young man and an older woman were toasting each other, and aside from them no other customers. It was a family-style restaurant in a quiet neighborhood of small shops and old apartment buildings rent-controlled since the end of World War II.

The maître—who was also the proprietor—recommended the house wine, so I tried a demicarafe of red and found it unobjectionable. He confided that the wine came from his wife's family's vineyards in the Auvergne and if château-labeled it would bring a fancy price. I said I was a partisan of vin ordinaire and his was splendid. That exchange established enough rapport between us that he catered to my every whim, such as having the peppercorns well pounded into the tender beef and using Courvoisier in the sauce. As I was finishing dinner, white napkin tucked well up under my chin, he said it was a privilege to execute the orders of so discriminating a patron. I invited him to take a Calvados at my table, and sitting across from me, hair and mustache dyed black, hair plastered across his skull, he reminded me of Finney playing Hercule Poirot. I toasted his good health.

Entente having been established, I apologized for posing a probably improper question. But would he by chance he know of a person able to correct the deficient documentation of an affluent foreigner? Not myself, I assured him, and not a criminal, exposing Meaching's passport briefly to his gaze, but my *petite-amie,* whose husband had dispatched a veritable army of spies to find and harass us.

He stroked his mustache tips, and nodded sympathetically, finally admitting that his chef, an immigrant from Sri Lanka, had faced a similar situation only a few months ago. Happily, an individual of the métier had arranged everything so meticulously that the authorities were satisfied and no longer bothered the chef with tedious and sometimes menacing interrogations.

He excused himself, entered the kitchen, and returned with a scrap of paper penciled with a name and address. "I should mention Sarik Singh as a reference. For these things are accomplished best by word of mouth in confidence, *n'est-ce pas?*" he whispered conspiratorially.

I agreed that was entirely so, complimented the proprietor on his excellent cuisine, and paid a bill inflated to include the cost of consultation. I'd taken the first step to going underground, and saved myself considerable time canvassing the Left Bank. Besides, the meal itself had been worth every franc. Despite the mattress, I slept the sleep of the drugged, waking when strong sunlight pried my eyelids apart.

I took the metro to the Montmartre station, and found the recommended studio behind the bourse on the rue Saint Marc. Its sign offered artistic framing and restoration of oil paintings, documents, and photographs. Behind the scarred wooden counter a wisp of an Annamese man with thick spectacles was attending to two customers. His white hair and long white beard gave him the appearance of Ho Chi Minh, an unsavory resemblance I tried to ignore.

His eyelids narrowed at the mention of Sarik Singh and he left me to make a lengthy phone call. Returning, he beckoned me through the curtained doorway into his work area. Seated at a drafting table with a high-intensity light was a woman around the proprietor's age, surrounded by inks of various hues, nib pens, quill pens, solvents, and delicate rigging brushes, infrared and ultraviolet lamps. This was where the forger's work was done.

The man gestured me to a seat, sat facing me, and made an A-frame of his hands. "So," he said in a voice just above a whisper, "how may I serve you?"

I handed him Meaching's passport. He looked at the photo. "Not you," he said.

"Nor the name. I need something usable."

"What do you have in mind?"

"What have you got?"

"French, Mexican, Panamanian, Italian, Norwegian . . ."

"New or used?"

"Some new, some used." He reached around to the desk, pulled out a drawer, and set it across his lap. The Panamanian and Italian passports were pristine. Because I didn't speak Italian I selected the Panamanian, and he put the others away. "What name?" he asked.

"Carlos Ventura Bustamante." We hadn't talked price, but that was coming up next. "Three thousand francs," he intoned, "and the American passport." He flexed it back and forth in his fingers.

"On condition you don't circulate it for six weeks. Also, I need the new documentation now. Today."

He glanced over at the woman and spoke to her in an unfamiliar tongue that resembled Vietnamese. Without looking up she replied, and he turned to me. "At five," he said. "Now I will take your photograph."

After leaving Meaching's passport and a two-thousand-franc deposit, I left the atelier and took the metro to the Champs-Elysées station. From there I walked up the avenue Wagram to the apartment building cited in Mona's dossier. Like the adjoining buildings it was of gray stone, six stories tall, and graced by a mansard roof. A wide porte cochere was closed, and a uniformed gendarme lounged beside the pillared entrance. Parked before it was a stretch Mercedes with CD plates and small flags on each front fender. The flags showed horizontal bands of red, white, and black, two green stars on the white center band. Black for oil, red for blood.

Syria.

Someone from the Syrian embassy—possibly the ambassador—was calling on a resident of the building. Well, why not? Mona did business with Syria, and Paris was a convenient place to conduct it.

I strolled past, half-hoping to see a sign advertising an apartment for rent, but of course I saw nothing of the kind. Parisians who could afford a Wagram apartment used unobtrusive rental agents. On the other hand, the best-informed people in Paris were the concierges who managed the buildings. The police used them as in-house informants when inquiries were made.

I walked as far as the avenue des Ternes before doubling back. Now a second limousine was parked, sporting CD plates and fender flags of the Islamic Republic of Iran. Apparently a heavy sit-down was taking place, comparable to a Vegas conclave of *capi di tutti capi*. Dividing turf and calculating profits. Mona's role, I speculated, was that of negotiator or arbiter. She provided location and refreshments and looked after her own interests. So high-level a role lent more merit to her assassination.

On impulse I rang the concierge's bell, and waited while the nearby gendarme eyed me suspiciously. After a while the door opened and a fat, gray-haired woman asked what I wanted.

"If I could step in . . . ," I said. She glanced at the gendarme and moved aside so I could enter the cobbled courtyard. She closed the door and I followed into her glass-paned office. A desk was cluttered with papers, one corner held an old kerosene heater, and the wall behind her was hung with a board containing keys. To one side a door connected with her living quarters and from it issued the heavy odor of cooking cabbage. I told her I was visiting for several weeks and asked whether an apartment was available for short-term use.

As she considered, I laid five hundred francs on the table. "I expect to pay key money. Perhaps occupants have left for the *grandes vacances* and their habitations are vacant?"

She put on spectacles and examined a calendar. "You could stay no more than three weeks—is that sufficient?"

I nodded. "And the rent?"

"Eight thousand francs."

"That's agreeable, madame," I said, knowing that the owners would never see it. A high price, but after all, it was the choicest section of Paris.

As she took charge of the "key money," I counted out eight thousand francs and shoved them across her desk.

"Your name, *m'sieu?*"

"Ventura," I told her. "Carlos Ventura," and noticed that she didn't inquire the spelling or write it in her ledger book.

"Inasmuch," she said, "as I am occupied here, I will ask you to enter the apartment unaccompanied." She gave me a key from the board and I stood up.

"Those limousines in front . . . " I said, ". . . do diplomats live here?"

She shook her head. "One floor is occupied from time to time by a wealthy Arab woman and her . . . ah, retainers." Her face registered distaste. "When she entertains, there is much music and noise, but you will have to put up with it."

"I'm prepared to," I said, "and thank you, madame. Please notify the gendarme that I am entitled to come and go."

Nodding, she stuffed my francs into a desk drawer and locked it.

Key in hand, I entered the lobby and took the elevator to the sixth floor, stepped out, and was braced by two men I recognized as Mona's bodyguards. One said, "What floor do you want?"

"Fourth."

"This is the sixth. You made a mistake."

I glanced at my key, shrugged, and said, "So I did," stepped back into the elevator and got off two floors below.

My new lodgings were attractively decorated. Persian rugs and Louis Quinze furnishings; pedestals held plaster heads of Montesquieu, Apollinaire, Dumas *fils*, and Voltaire. Glassed cabinets shielded oriental and South Seas bric-a-brac; an antique desk held ledgers and bundled correspondence. A TV and VCR were positioned on a nearby stand. Continuing my survey, I found three bedrooms with made-up beds, a servant's room, and a small, tile-countered kitchen. There was drying food in the refrigerator. I lifted the wall phone and heard a dial tone. Excellent. I walked to the window and drew aside curtains to look down at the street. The diplomatic cars were gone.

With a noiseless hydraulic drill and a probe mike the diameter of a knitting needle, I could have tapped into Mona's living room and recorded future meetings. But I lacked the equipment, and in any case, CIA or DEA might already have installed listening devices, making mine not only redundant but a threat to theirs if mine were discovered. Besides, previous experience with floor mikes had taught me that I was likely to get a lot of foot noise and not much by way of conversation unless all participants were seated near the mike. So I laid in bottled drinking water, liquor, bread, cold cuts, and cheese, and decided to get a reading on Arness's plans for Mona Zakari.

The kitchen window offered an unobstructed air space. I extended the messager and punched out:

DON'T SEND MY BOY TO HARVARD
THE DYING MOTHER SAID.

Hoping the satellite would pick it up.

While waiting for acknowledgement I poured Black Label over ice and added a splash of Evian. While I was sipping the day's first drink, the Paul Revere sounded and I watched the reply move across the miniature screen:

DON'T SEND MY BOY TO DARTMOUTH
I'D RATHER SEE HIM DEAD. ADVISE LOCATION.

Ignoring the query, I sent one of my own:

ADVISE CENTAUR STATUS.

The reply was:

CENTAUR ON HOLD, COME HOME.

To that I transmitted:

NEED ALTERNATE TARGET SELECTION. ADVISE SOONEST.

NEED YOUR LOCATION FOR CONTACT

was the response.

I thought the situation over, well aware that some serious cat and mouse was going on, and I didn't like it any better than I liked Meaching and Kiley's unexpected visitation. Who was transmitting to me? Poliakoff? General Arness? Did it make a difference? I decided to spread around some hope, so I messaged:

TRAVELING YOURWARDS NEXT AVAILABLE FLIGHT.

That should take pressure off me in Europe and give me time to case Mona's pad should she become my target again.

I finished my drink and at four-thirty I left the apartment.

My Panamanian passport was ready. I signed it and paid the thousand-franc balance. Ostensibly I was now a citizen of Noriegaland named Carlos Ventura Bustamante. Before leaving the atelier, I used the slicing board to cut up my Peruvian passport, eliminating that part of my recent past. Back in the apartment, I wrote a letter to Peter Ward, Esq., telling him I'd fallen out of favor with my sponsors and asking him to verify my brother's location and condition.

Composing a note to Claire was much harder. I started twice, tore up the sheets, and settled for saying I would have to stay longer because of unexpected complications; I loved her and would see her as soon as I could. By now the post office was closed for the day, so I put the letters in the mail chute for pickup in the morning.

I turned on the TV set and was watching world news when I heard the doorbell ring. Thinking it was the concierge, I opened the door and saw one of Mona's bodyguards standing beside her Oriental girl. To her he said, "Is this the man?"

Without hesitation she pointed a finger at me and hissed, "He is the one!"

Before I could move I was looking into the barrel of a gun.

Twenty-seven

AS THE BODYGUARD shoved me into the elevator, I didn't resist. He had a gun, I was unarmed, and as the elevator rose I appraised him. He was shorter than I was, wore a close-trimmed beard, and had gold in his mouth and on his fingers. His gray, western-style suit was tight on his welterweight frame. Dark eyes, Semitic nose, and olive skin completed the picture of an Arab hired gun. On the sixth floor the Oriental girl, opened the apartment's heavy door, her face sulky, and I wondered why she was mad at me.

The other bodyguard was inside the vestibule. He gave me a thorough body search, finding nothing except my newly issued Panama passport. He held it while opening the inner door, and as I entered I saw a setting out of the Arabian Nights.

The room was entirely surrounded with translucent white silk drapes, carpeted in white, and strewn with white leather ottomans decorated with semiprecious stones in damascene designs. At the center of the room, a low table of white marble bearing a brass coffee service; at the far end, a raised dais with more ottomans and four Arab hookahs. As I stood there between the bodyguards the Oriental girl glided toward the dais, vanished behind curtains. In Spanish I said, "Impressive—but why am I here?"

The bodyguard shrugged, said in French, "I don't understand."

I shrugged back and waited.

Presently I saw a figure beyond the dais. Under baggy, almost transparent, harem pants she wore a gold girdle that covered her crotch, a gold bra shimmered under a short, open vest. Gold necklace, gold wristlets, gold anklets, and gold sandals glinted as she parted the curtain to mount the dais. Mona Zakari's hair was drawn back from her forehead by a golden clasp. I gazed at her with open admiration. She seated herself cross-legged and spoke in Arabic to the body-guards, who bowed and stepped aside, one bringing her my passport. Her gaze left me long enough to scan the passport. In Spanish I asked indignantly, "What's this all about? Why was I brought here?"

In French she said, "I do not speak Spanish. Do you speak French?"

"Some."

"Then let us speak in French." She glanced at the passport again. "Perhaps you speak English, too."

"I do."

"Come." She pointed to an ottoman a few feet from her own. It sank under my weight and I arranged myself before her, lower than the mistress of the house.

"Why did your man force me here at gunpoint?"

"Because it was said that you have been following me."

"Who said it?"

"Vu Tien, the girl who pointed you out. You were on the prome-nade at Nice, watching her. She and Hakim say you were at the tables that same night. Now you are here in my building."

"Much of that is true," I acknowledged, "but along the promenade there were scores of young women. If Vu Tien was there, she was one of many who passed while I was having lunch. As for the tables, I was indeed gambling at Monte Carlo; so were two or three hundred others. Yes, I watched you play, trying to figure your system."

Her smile barely turned the corners of her painted mouth. "And did you analyze my system?"

"I abandoned the effort—you were losing."

"Luck was against me. But how do you explain your presence in Paris?" Her tone was tolerant with a hint of amused interest.

"I have business here."

"But—in this building?" Her eyebrows raised.

"The concierge can best answer that, madame. I wanted an apartment in this area and applied at several buildings for a vacancy. The concierge rented me the fourth-floor flat for three weeks—the occupants are elsewhere. Considering the price of good hotel rooms, I thought it a bargain."

Her expression showed she wasn't convinced, and I hadn't expected her to be. Frowning slightly, she said, "I place little faith in coincidence, *m'sieu.*"

I leaned forward. "Did I seek you out? No. Hakim brought me here—I don't even know your name. Why would I be interested in the sixth-floor occupant?"

She shook her head and her hair brushed her shoulders lightly. "I think only you can answer that." She hesitated. "Are you a CIA agent?"

"No."

"Of the DEA?"

"Certainly not."

"Hakim says you must be. It would account for everything."

"Hakim lies."

That brought a burst of Arabic from the bodyguard. Mona responded calmly and turned to me. "He says he will fight you to the death. That will prove who is the liar."

"A rather antique concept," I said, "trial by ordeal. No thank you, madame. Your man is armed."

Angry words from Hakim. I didn't look at him. I said, "If this is a police matter, I am amenable to seeing the police. That seems a civilized way of settling it."

Her gaze turned to Hakim, but she said nothing. "In any case, why should I fight a man with whom I have no quarrel?" I continued. "I am a banker, investor, a broker, not a professional strongman like your bodyguard."

Hakim pulled off his coat, exposing two shoulder-holstered pistols. He laid them in their harness on an ottoman, drew an undershirt over his head, faced Mona, and began speaking in short, angry sentences. When he stopped, Mona turned to me. "He demands to fight you without weapons, man to man."

"Why?"

"Because you have insulted him. Arabs do not take insults lightly."

I studied the powerful pectorals covered with curly black hair, bulging biceps and deltoids, flat thorax and stomach. Built like a Turkish wrestler. In a fair fight Hakim could probably beat me, but I didn't think he was planning to fight fair; performing before Mona against an infidel, he would want an edge to ensure victory. He drew back in a half crouch, poised like a boxer, fists clenched.

I sucked in a deep breath, sighed, and looked at Mona. "Sure you want this?"

Her eyes glittered with anticipation. "It is necessary."

I started pulling off my coat. "He's big and strong," I muttered, "probably kill me." I dropped my coat on an ottoman, undid my tie, and got out of my shirt. "But if I happen to win, I want a reward."

Her smile became laughter. "What kind of reward?"

"Have dinner with me."

"*Din*—? Hakim, you hear that? You will not force me to break bread with this impudent infidel?"

"No, madame," he said hoarsely; he feinted with his left hand and kicked at my throat. Dodging, I grabbed his ankle and twisted the way Mac had shown me, the way we'd practiced countless times on the mat. I yanked his other leg off the floor and he fell heavily on his back. Before he could roll away I jammed my shoe in his crotch and kept pressing down. Hakim's yells filled the room as his hands clawed at the foot crushing his testicles.

Mona clapped delightedly. Lessening the pressure, I ordered, "Tell her whether I am CIA, DEA. Yes? No?"

"*Ey-ey*," he yelled until I stepped harder on his crotch. "*La'ah*," he moaned. "*La'ah, la'ah* . . ."

"Voilà, madame. My accuser recants."

Her smile was broad, excited. "Point made. Let him go."

"Please."

"*Please* let him go."

To Hakim I said in French, "Swear by the Prophet you have done with me, will never try to harm me in the future. Swear it!"

"I . . . ," he gasped, beads of perspiration on his forehead, "I swear by the Prophet."

I stepped back, freeing him. For a moment he lay prone, then turned over and from his knees shied a side kick at my leg. I kicked the small of his back, just below his neck. He collapsed on the white carpet. I picked up his holstered guns, pulled out a nine-millimeter Beretta, and turned to the other bodyguard. "Got a problem with me?"

His gaze darted to Mona. She said, "There is no need for bloodshed. Hakim's quarrel is not Abdullah's. Be satisfied, Carlos Ventura."

"I haven't heard from Abdullah."

He shrugged. "Madame speaks for me. I am her servant."

I laid down Hakim's weapons and got into my shirt. While knotting my tie I said, "Where would you like to dine? Maxim's? Tour d'Argent?"

"My chef," she said, uncoiling herself as she rose, "is from the St. George in Beirut. It will please me to dine with you here."

Hakim moaned. He got up on hands and knees, unsteady as a badly beaten dog. I tossed him his shirt and jacket, and Mona spat a string of angry words at him. He crawled away, followed by Abdullah. Almost my height, Mona faced me. "I am called Mona Zakari," she said huskily. "Will you dine with me?"

"With pleasure."

One hand stroked my arm; her scent was musky, heavy, her eyes sea green. "Are you who you say you are?"

"I am."

"Nevertheless, I believe you followed me here. Why?"

"Oldest reason in the world. In Monte Carlo I realized you were the most beautiful, most attractive woman I'd ever seen."

"And you mean me no harm?"

"None." After all, the mission was off.

Taking my hand, she led me to the dais, seated me across a low table from her, and clapped her hands. In a few moments the undernourished blond appeared, wearing a mock maid's costume in black. The crotch was divided, her bra a band across her upper chest. She stood submissively while Mona turned to me. "Drinks?"

"Scotch on the rocks, Evian."

"Vodka on the rocks for me, Babette."

The blond nodded and went away. "I know little of Panama. My yacht has transited the canal twice. Of Panama that was all I cared to see, Carlos."

"A small country," I said, "with large problems." Turning, I waved my hand. "All this is yours—or your husband's?"

Her laughter twinkled. "Mine. I have no husband. So I live as I choose, do that which pleases me."

"You live very well. Do you—I mean—have you business interests?"

She nodded. "I am, let us say, a broker. In the Middle East it can be very profitable."

"And you have found it so."

"Precisely." She drew in a deep breath and her breasts swelled against the flimsy fabric until I could see the dark nipples. "I find it flattering that you pursued me, Carlos. Is that your practice?"

"No," I said truthfully. "The urge was irresistible."

That, too, pleased her. The provocatively clad blond arrived with two drinks on a silver tray. Mona took hers, I took mine, and Babette set aside the tray. Kneeling, she crumbled greenish gray material into the hookah bowl, lighted it, and drew on the pipe until it was going. She handed the tube to Mona who drew in deeply, exhaled, and passed the pipe stem to me. Before I sucked in the water-cooled smoke, I scented hashish, heavy, cloying. I drew smoke into my lungs, felt the hit, and exhaled, Mona watching me. Her pupils were dilating.

Throat dry, I said, "Good stuff."

"From Iran. The ayatollahs forbid it, but the law is widely disobeyed."

"Persian hash," I murmured, starting to feel a little giddy. "My first."

She inhaled again and gave me the mouthpiece wet with her lips. "There is a Koranic saying that when a man and a woman are together the third person is Satan."

"In this case a hookah."

She reached over, touched my forehead, my hair. The hash was getting to her. Hell, it was hitting me. I took her hand, kissed each finger in turn. It seemed to take a long time. She shivered, drew deeply on the water pipe while she let me play with her hand. As the fumes invaded my brain I replayed her dance with the white-fedoraed girl, just a kaleidoscopic glimpse; visualizing her copper red hair, the wantonness of her lovemaking . . . I realized I'd wanted her, desired her ever since that moment. I reached behind her neck, undid the bra clasp, and let it fall across her lap. I touched one breast, the other, reliving the fantasy. Mona murmured, pressed my hand to her breast so I could feel the erect nipple. She murmured, "Do you have a family?"

"No."

"And you are not wealthy."

"No."

She drew on the hookah and held the smoke before letting it drift from mouth and nostrils. "But you would like to be."

"Who wouldn't?" I took a short pull from the pipe and laid it on her thigh. "Why? What's on your mind?"

"Perhaps you could be useful to me."

I grunted. "As Hakim's replacement? Forget it."

"No. During dinner I will think about it."

Dinner? I'd forgotten dinner. I sipped my drink, barely able to taste the liquor; sipped again to moisten my smoke-dry throat. I hoped she liked men as well as women. I drew again on the hookah, leaned over, and kissed her nipples. She shivered again, said huskily, "I like that."

"So do I."

She sipped vodka, made a face. "I don't really like liquor. The Koran forbids it."

"The Koran forbids many pleasures."

"So I don't follow Islamic rules." She drew on the mouthpiece and inserted it between my lips. I drew in lightly and gave the pipe back to her. I wasn't used to the drug, not having smoked any since Nam, but to her it was an old friend. She was undoing her filmy trousers. As she rose they dropped away, leaving only the gold girdle around her hips and crotch. Like Salome, who must have been an ancestor, she began to dance. There was no music, no rhythmic drums, but they weren't needed. Anklets and bracelets clacked like castanets, the gold necklace brushed her nipples as she spun and dipped, writhing erotically, invitingly.

She pulled the clasp from her hair, letting it swirl, around her shoulders, hands pushing up her breasts, fingers twirling her nipples, then her arms were above her head as she whirled in place. As in the videotape, she seemed deep in a world of her own, unaware of her surroundings. I looked around for watchers, saw none in the immense room. We were alone, except for Satan.

With her dance this Scheherazade was telling me a tale as ancient as mankind, a revelation of desire. I felt like Süleyman watching a favorite slave girl perform for his pleasure. The scene was hypnotic. Another pull on the hookah wouldn't hurt, I told myself, and drew in deeply. Momentarily I saw two Monas, synchronized twins, then they fused and I saw the golden girdle drop away.

Except for gold adornments, she was naked before me, her copper-red muff her only concealment. Her hands pressed into the curls, lifted and wove fantasies in the air. A light film of moisture covered her body. I held out the pipe stem and she bent over to take it between her lips, breasts swaying before me. I lifted them in my palms and she kissed my forehead, tongue licking downward until it was circling my lips lasciviously. The tip parted my lips, thrust inward like a warm velvet probe while her hands pulled down my jacket, undid my tie, unbuttoned my shirt, unbuckled my belt. Presently I was naked, too, and with hands on either side of her head, I drew her undulating body down. Her face vanished between my loins as she took me into her mouth. My hands caressed her moist body. I didn't care whether she was saint or devil; I wanted to possess this gorgeous bitch completely, if it cost my life and my eternal soul. If she resisted, I was prepared to rape her, brutalize her into total submission.

Instead, she rose to her knees, edged forward, and fitted us together, and with a shuddering sigh began possessing me. As in my fantasy she gave me her breasts while we thrust together, her hips urgent as a man's, rotating and thrusting until we climaxed. Her torso dropped forward on mine, cushioning her lush breasts against my chest. Our open mouths pressed together, hers a fiery volcano. Shivers coursed her body as her climax faded. Her lips trembled, tears wet my cheeks. I held her tightly in my arms until her spasms eased and ended.

It could have been the hash, but our sex was the most intense I'd ever known. So what if it wasn't *love*making; at the very least it was world-class fucking, and I reveled in it by whatever name.

Closing my eyes, I lost track of time, and after a while she rose from me and took my hand. Groggily I got up and let her lead me behind the dais, through silk curtains, and into a tiled room with a sunken Jacuzzi. Together we entered warm, perfumed water.

She sat me on a submerged step, circled my hips with her legs, and kissed me.

Inevitably I rose to the occasion, hugged her body tightly as her hips undulated. "You are a most satisfactory lover, Carlos," she murmured.

"You're terrific," I said, thinking her philosophy was fuck first, friendship follows. "You must have many lovers."

"No," she said, "oh, no. If I let an Arab man make love to me, he would think he owned me, take advantage of me, so—" She didn't finish the thought as with fluttering eyelids she climaxed. Peripherally I could see a nearly naked Vu Tien bringing a hookah to poolside. The Oriental girl knelt and crumbled hash in her small fist, filled the pipe bowl, and lighted it. When it was going she passed me the stem and I inhaled. Mona's eyes were closed, so Vu Tien took a deep drag and smiled at me, a savvy little sinner. I caught her hand and drew her down into the water where she undid her silver girdle and knelt behind her mistress.

Vu Tien's hands replaced mine as she began stroking and kneading Mona's back. I felt her hands come between us to hold and smoothly compress Mona's breasts. It was rapidly becoming a three-way scene, something I hadn't been part of since two Bennington roommates, Flopsy and Cottontail, took me to bed one spring break in Fort Lauderdale. I reached around and clasped my hands behind Vu Tien's back, drawing her against Mona's. Like a kitten, the Oriental girl rubbed her body against Mona, who turned her head and gave Vu Tien her mouth to kiss. Throatily she moaned, and I slipped the hookah stem between her lips long enough for her to fill her lungs with smoke. Her pupils were so large that I could hardly distinguish the green irises. She kissed me lengthily, then took Vu Tien's tongue between her lips. The drug was disorienting me, distorting my senses so that I barely realized who was doing what to whom. Nor did I care.

Mona eased off my thighs into Vu Tien's arms. Face to face they embraced in the hip-deep water, droplets like liquid diamonds running down their skin. As I watched they rubbed nipples together, finally breaking their embrace to take me between them. I had to bend over to kiss Vu Tien's lips, tasting the softness of her tongue while her hand found my crotch and caressed me.

With feline ease the Oriental mounted my hips with her legs and I saw her slick black pelt lower until we were joined. Mona was licking her mouth and nipples, making Vu Tien's smooth vagina contract, milking me. I wondered if my recent accuser was doing penance on my penis, and I heard a brief laugh issue from my throat. As Vu Tien worked herself up and down, I saw Babette appear, dragging two upholstered mats to poolside. With three of us getting it on, there wasn't room for her, so she sat on the edge of the Jacuzzi, feet in the water, and watched us enviously.

After Vu Tien came, Mona drew us onto the joined mats where Babette dried our bodies with warm towels. In my ear Mona whispered, "You don't mind about Vu Tien?"

"Hardly," I said and kissed her lips. "This is one place where three's company."

I could see Babette parting Mona's thighs, then the bobbing of her blond head. Vu Tien joined them and presently the three girls were in it together, all mouths and muffs occupied. I drew on the hookah stem until Mona was on her knees and I took her from behind. Babette's lips were pressed to Mona's while Vu Tien caressed the blonde's barbered delta. My drugged body couldn't climax when Mona did, and despite the excitement of the scene I found myself yawning. All good things come to an end, and presently we uncoupled and lay in each other's arms. My eyelids were leaden. I tried to say something, couldn't, and gave up. Slept.

When I woke, only Mona was beside me. "Hello," I said.

"How are you? You slept a long time. Are you hungry?"

"Ravenous."

"Then we'll eat."

My eyes felt pressed together by unkind hands and for a while it wasn't easy to focus. Mona's hair was dry, I noticed, again held back from her forehead by the golden clasp. She took my hands and helped me to my feet, led me to the dais where Babette and Vu Tien served us artichoke soup and roast lamb stuffed with dates and spices, iced wine from a crystal decanter, and mint tea. The girls were lightly attired, where Mona and I were still naked. I wondered where Hakim and Abdullah were, hoped they weren't peeking from behind the arras.

The two girls were in their servant mode, no longer avid sexual partners; silent, subdued, altered like chameleons. When dishes were cleared away from the low table, Babette poured syrupy Turkish coffee from a tall, curved brass ewer, and it cleared my head of residual symptoms. Vu Tien brought us silk caftans, and when we were alone again Mona asked, "Have you thought about it?"

"I'll never forget it."

"I mean working for me."

I'd forgotten her offer. "Doing what?" I asked.

"Dealing with Latins for one thing. Counseling me, being my companion."

I kissed her ear. "You've done so well alone, why take on a helper?"

"Because I'm tired of business. I'm rich, I want to enjoy life, travel." She touched my loins. "Make love with you."

She had a point, but I stuck to business. "What kind of work?"

"Does it matter? You said you were a broker, an investor. I need a broker I can trust. Invest your time with me and you will be richer than you could imagine." She took my hand. "Close out your business, learn mine. I'll pay you, say, half a million dollars a year, more if you want."

"A generous offer," I admitted, "but why should you trust me, Mona?"

She shrugged. "Instinct."

"Your instinct has served you well, has it not? But was it ever wrong?"

"At times," she sighed, "and logic tells me not to trust you now. If you were me . . . ?"

"I'd go with logic."

She clapped her hands delightedly. "That proves my instinct was right. If you were not to be trusted, you would have said instinct—am I correct?"

"Guess so," I said grudgingly, unwilling to probe the intricacies of female reasoning.

"Besides," she said breathily, "no other man has followed me as you did, fought for me, desired me as you have, Carlos. That more than anything makes me want to trust you."

Lacking a ready response, I looked around and asked, "Is this your office?"

"My yacht is my office. Does that appeal to you?"

"Very much. But I'd like to know what it is you buy and sell."

She regarded me for a long time before saying, "The juice that comes from poppies. It's no secret that I'm a grower, one of the biggest in the world. You're Panamanian, you must have contacts there, government contacts, that can be useful in my trade."

"Panama is largely a transit point," I said. "There could be labs in Panama I don't know about, but probably small scale. Even with Norieaga gone."

"Still, I should like to know details. Go there, wind up your business, and make inquiries for me." She squeezed my hand. "Come back with your information and we will make decisions."

"You're amazing. Make love with a stranger, then make him a partner."

"My judgment is seldom wrong."

"Except at roulette."

She smiled. "But the enjoyment of gambling is well worth whatever I lose—and I win more often than I lose." She turned on her side to face me. "*Tiens*, Carlos, what do you say?"

"How can I refuse?" I kissed her, thinking there was no way I could turn down her offer. To do so would reinforce Hakim's suspicions. Then a little poison in my coffee and . . .

Her hand caressed the outline of my face. "Of course," she said in harder tones, "should you betray me, you would be made to suffer horribly—before death. Do you understand?"

"I understand."

Twisting away, she said, "Let's be more comfortable," and led me to a large bedroom whose low bed was easily big enough for four. As we shed our caftans I whispered, "The girls were a novelty, but I don't need them, Mona. Just you."

She undid the clasp, and hair feathered her shoulders. "But from time to time . . . ?"

"As desired," I agreed, closed her mouth with mine, and felt the richness of her body pressing against mine.

When she was asleep beside me, I pulled a silken sheet over us, thinking how strangely everything was turning out. From a termination target Mona Zakari had evolved into lover and employer. I wondered how I could handle both roles—and for how long.

Twenty-eight

BABETTE SERVED OUR breakfast in bed: hot breads with aromatic honey and head-clearing Sumatran Mandheling coffee. When I went into the big marbled bathroom, I found shaving gear laid out for me. Mona came in and sat on the bidet, watching as I shaved. "It's been so long since a man has been with me," she said, "that I'd almost forgotten what it's like."

"And now that you're remembering . . . ?"

"It's wonderful, Carlos," she said, and her face glowed. "While you're gone I'll miss you terribly. Don't linger in Panama."

"You'll have the girls for company."

She made a moue. "Hardly the same, *chéri*. They're just . . . useful. . . . And safe."

Carefully shaving my upper lip, I said, "Of the two, only Babette is lesbian, right?"

She nodded.

"And Vu Tien goes either way."

She rose from the bidet, loins dripping, and walked into a shower stall that could accommodate six and a picnic table. Before turning on the spray, she said, "Again, they can be useful."

I joined her in the cubicle under spray that came from every direction. We soaped each other's bodies, and rinsed in water cold enough to make me gasp. My thigh scar and the older leg wound's outline turned blue, and she dried them tenderly but asked no questions.

In the bedroom we dressed, my bag having been brought up from my apartment, and I saw that the S&W .38 was lying on what had been my overnight pillow. Mona said, "I don't suppose you would have that if you didn't need it."

"Panama is a lawless country," I said, "like some parts of Europe. I'm accustomed to the gun. Mind?"

"It could be useful, Carlos, protecting me."

"Ah—you have enemies?"

"Everyone with wealth has enemies. The men I do business with, for instance, would like to sell the poppies themselves."

"And who are these men?"

"French, Iranian, and Syrian. You will meet them in time."

No names, just nationalities. Fine. Getting out of this tender trap was all I could handle for now.

Babette came in and helped complete Mona's toilet, flaring the skirt of her green dress, bringing shoes and handbags for Mona's selection, brushing and fluffing out her hair, and slyly kissing the nape of her mistress's neck. The spontaneous affection showed dedication and loyalty.

From a round jewel box Mona drew out an emerald necklace that matched her dress and asked me to set the clasp. "You're going somewhere?" I asked.

"*We* are going somewhere," she corrected. "You'll escort me to the Louvre, we'll have luncheon in the Bois, visit Van Cleef's, and take high tea at the Ritz." She turned to me. "Things I've always wanted to do." She noticed my puzzled expression, kissed my lips lightly, and said, "I never had a man to take me. Now I do."

"With or without your bodyguards?"

"Without, of course."

That wasn't quite the case. Abdullah drove the Rolls Silver Cloud, Hakim beside him. A privacy panel separated us from them as we held hands and nuzzled down the Champs-Elysées to the Louvre. It was a gray day and slightly misty, not enough for pedestrian umbrellas nor for the black slickers traffic cops kept neatly rolled by their feet.

Mona and I went in by Pei's pyramidal glass entrance after she'd instructed Abdullah to wait outside.

As we came into the rotunda, Mona halted, awestruck below the Victory of Samothrace. I left her while I bought a guidebook, then led her to the Mona Lisa. Another long pause while she admired the famed portrait along with a crowd of Japanese tourists. Then on to the Apollo Gallery and the crown jewels exhibit. As Mona viewed the Regent diamond and the Bretagne ruby, her expression grew covetous, as though she were mentally pricing that which was priceless.

Tintoretto's *Suzanna Bathing* impressed her, but Veronese, Giotto, Fragonard, and Watteau left her cold. "It all looks so *old*," she complained. So we walked into the Tuileries gardens and strolled the half-mile graveled path with flower beds and greenery on either side to the Musée du Jeu de Paume, our hair and clothing damp from the mist. Just inside, a placard on an artist's easel advised patrons that the Impressionists collection was soon to be moved to the Orsay Museum just across the Seine, adjoining the Palais de la Légion d'Honneur. Fewer tourists were in attendance, probably because of the inclement weather, so there was no jostling for viewing space as I showed Mona the French Impressionists: the Monets, Pissarro, Cézanne, and Degas. Toulouse-Lautrec's painting of Jane Avril interested Mona, but much less than Gauguin's *Women of Tahiti*, which I suspected she wanted to buy. Or steal.

After an hour with the Impressionists we were picked up by Abdullah across from the Hôtel de Talleyrand. He drove us over the Seine at the Grenelle bridge and past the Auteuil racecourse into the Bois's greenery. At Longchamp Hippodrome, Abdullah turned right and let us out by the Grande Cascade, a pleasant waterfall, where we enjoyed an open-air lunch of pâté sandwiches, cheese, and chilled wine, the skies having cleared. When our glasses touched, Mona said, "I haven't felt this free since I was a child."

"And where were you then?"

"Los Angeles for a time," she said wistfully, "then Beirut."

I pointed at the barely visible crown of the Eiffel Tower. "If you haven't been there before, you should see the view of Paris by night."

"Tonight?"

"Why not? And Notre-Dame."

Small yellow butterflies fluttered over the grass; larger ones, copper-colored and spotted with black, hovered by a stand of wildflowers, monitoring a bee taking nectar in the sunlight.

"It's such a perfect day," Mona murmured, "I want it to go on forever." She drank from her glass and I replenished it. It was almost impossible to believe that she was the queen of Middle Eastern heroin, so tranquil and lovely was her face. Whoever compiled the character profile in her dossier had been way off base, as Washington estimates often were. But no informant source had known Mona as intimately as I was getting to know her, and very probably none ever would. Since meeting her, I reflected, my life had moved to fast forward, episodes crowding together with dizzying speed. For a moment I thought guiltily of Claire, justified this as part of the job I'd undertaken for the president, for my brother. But the truth was somewhat different; I was falling under Mona's spell. I wanted to be with her, make love with her, show her worlds she'd never seen before. In that moment Washington and Leesburg were very far away. My thoughts were interrupted by her saying, "You're so silent, *chéri* . . . What's occupying your mind?"

"Oh," I replied, dragging my mind back to the present, "I can't help wondering what I'll be doing for you, what my role will be."

"But I've explained that, haven't I? Let's just work it out as we go along. If the money isn't enough . . ."

"More than ample," I said. "It's just that I don't want you ever to regret choosing me as your aide."

"I trust my judgment." She touched my wineglass with hers. "So you must trust me."

God, I thought, that's exactly what I'm beginning to do. Watch it, Burke, don't get sucked into the vortex and find you can't get out.

After lunch we were driven to the place Vendôme, where Mona knew the fashionable shops and their extortionate prices, the Hôtel Ritz and, of course, Van Cleef & Arpels. As we entered that glittering establishment Mona paused and pointed at the tall bronze column dominating the open square. "What can you tell me about it?"

"Just that the statue is Napoléon and the bronze comes from cannon captured at Austerlitz."

She took my arm. "I *knew* you'd know about it," she said happily, and drew me into the showroom. She was waited on with deference and respect. From trays of jewelry she selected a diamond-platinum bracelet and an emerald brooch. Green was definitely her color. The salesman brought out a tray of watches. To me, Mona said, "I want to buy one for a friend. Which would you choose?"

"They're all sensational," I said, examined a thin platinum-cased Piaget, a Vaucheron-Constantine, and a Girard-Perrigaux whose dial numbers were brilliant diamonds. "Just a personal preference," I said, "but I don't like diamonds on men. Give him this Piaget."

Nodding, she told the salesman she'd take it, and when he returned with the wrapped box she handed it to me. "A souvenir of this wonderful day," she said as I gulped in surprise. "It's much more than a souvenir," I said, reluctantly taking the gift. "It will always bring back memories."

"Exactly."

When the bill arrived for her signature, Mona signed without even glancing at the total, which I estimated at fifty or sixty thousand dollars. Just a little impulse buying, I reflected as I tucked my new watch into a breast pocket. Mona dropped the jewelry into her handbag and we went out into the square where the Rolls waited.

All this conspicuous consumption, I told myself, was heady stuff for a scholarship boy from Cornell, but then everything that had happened since yesterday was surreal. Reality had better set in, and fast.

The Rolls took us to the Place du Parvis, a section of which was being excavated to uncover Roman ruins. While we stood and silently gazed at the facade of Notre-Dame, tourists around us were busily snapping photographs of the ancient cathedral with its gargoyles, Kings' Gallery, and great Rose Window high above.

Entering the Portal of the Last Judgment, we followed a guided tour through the nave and transept, leaving through the cloisters. There in the flower-scented walks we strolled quietly isolated from the buzzing hum of traffic and I suddenly felt we were being watched.

I hadn't *seen* a watcher nor even heard footsteps. I wondered if Mona sensed anything amiss, but her expression was relaxed. Could it be a watcher in her employ, a protective presence? I drew her close and whispered, "Keep walking, I'll catch up in a moment."

"But why?"

"Don't ask, do it." I knelt and fumbled with a shoelace while Mona walked on. I turned my head and glimpsed a figure moving quickly behind a tall shrub. I dodged off the walk and came around behind a stockily built man in a plain gray suit, wearing worn black shoes. I stuck my index finger against his spine and said, "Lost your way? Perhaps I can help."

His body tensed, but he said angrily, "Don't be a fool, I am of the police."

"Prove it."

Slowly his right hand reached into the nearest pocket and came out with a leather *carnet*-holder. The same hand opened it and held it up for inspection. PREFECTURE OF POLICE was imprinted on the credential, which gave the man's name as Philippe Roger Gorain. His face matched the *carnet* photo. "Sorry," I grunted, and drew back my finger. "Why the special attention?"

Turning, he replaced his *carnet*. "The company you keep. May I see your identification?"

I produced the Panamanian passport, and after leafing through it he returned it to me with a shrug. By now Mona was coming slowly toward us, a perplexed expression on her face. "What you do in Panama and elsewhere is your affair, *m'sieu*. But be very careful what you do in France. Have I made myself clear?"

"Perfectly clear. For your information, Madame and I are taking a lovers' tour of Paris."

"Keep it at that," he said curtly, turned, and walked rapidly away. I rejoined Mona and explained the incident. With a short laugh she said, "I am accustomed to surveillance. I'm glad the man was of the police."

"And if not?"

"Then you were here to protect me. And you were very alert, Carlos. My mind was on other things." But the flic's intrusion had spoiled the cloisters for us, so we walked the outside length of the cathedral and connected with the Rolls.

The time was too early for the Ritz so I had Abdullah drive up the Champs-Elysées to the Arc de Triomphe. Its roof offered an excellent, unobstructed view of Paris, the traffic feeding in from all six Grandes Avenues, of which Wagram was one. Mona pointed out her residence to the north, and we headed home.

As I undressed I got out my passport with a sense of relief that it had passed Gorain's casual inspection. Probably he hadn't seen many Panamanian passports and didn't know what to look for. Still, the purchase money was well spent, for if I hadn't been able to produce ID, the flic would have been within his rights to hold me.

Mona joined me in the shower, where we began making love. Afterward we slept for an hour, got dressed, and were driven back to the place Vendôme and the Ritz. I was careful to wear my new platinum watch.

Although I would have preferred liquor, I settled for tea and pastry with Mona. She loved sweets, she said, and as far as I could determine she had no calorie problem. At a corner table four Arab males were eating and talking animatedly. When Mona saw them her expression hardened and she turned away. "Two of them are my competitors," she said in a low voice. "*Our* competitors, actually. Hassan is the one with the scar, Amir wears the beard. Remember them."

I nodded and poured more tea.

"I think you should leave soon for Panama. When you return, I'll be on *Kismet,* so join me there."

"As soon as possible," I promised.

At dusk we rode the elevators to the top of the Eiffel Tower and watched darkness cover Paris. Descending to the restaurant, we had cocktails at a window table, watching the glittering lights of the great city below as we talked and drank. Heavily on my mind was the realization that when I left Mona I would never see her again, half a million dollars a year notwithstanding.

We ordered dinner from the maître—lamb pilaf for Mona, filet mignon *à point* for me—and when our table was ready the maître showed us to it. "Not quite la Tour d'Argent," I remarked, "but we'll go there another time."

Sipping Evian, she asked, "How long do you think you'll be away?"

"Ten days, two weeks."

"I could send you in my plane." I shook my head. "That would attract questions. No, I'll fly commercial as I always do, get rid of business, and fly back to Nice."

"Rather than do without you, I'll gladly buy your business interests." She twirled the glass stem between her fingers and eyed me speculatively.

"Well, that's a friendly offer," I acknowledged, "but I'd have to be there in person to sign papers, Panamanian law being what it is."

"So be it. But afterward you won't have to worry about laws. Anywhere."

"Good. But hasn't the narcotics business ever bothered you? I mean the addicts all over the world?"

She shrugged. "Why should it? I don't make opium or supply needles. I cultivate and harvest flowers that grow wild everywhere in the world. I didn't create the demand, Carlos, and if people are foolish enough to become addicts and destroy themselves it's their problem, not mine." She paused, "I happen to believe in free choice . . . don't you?"

I thought it over. "I do," I replied reluctantly, then the arrival of our dinners detoured that line of discussion.

After dinner—ten o'clock by my new Piaget—we rode to the top of the tower again and looked down on Paris alight with all its nighttime brilliance.

"Those lights," Mona murmured, "like countless jewels, Carlos. Algiers, Cairo, Damascus—nothing can compare with this."

"Unique," I agreed, in some ways her enthusiasm was almost childlike. That unexpected naïveté was one of the things that made Mona's personality so complex and challenging. And although she owned everything money could buy, she was a misfit in any society.

Over the next two days we went out to Fontainebleau and Versailles, where the king's and queen's opulent suites gave Mona new decor ideas that I suspected she planned to incorporate into her own residences. So while we were touring Malmaison I talked about comparative religions until she lost interest in everything except the marriage, coronation, and fates of Josephine and Napoléon Bonaparte.

By now, I knew, Washington was wondering what had happened to me. I hadn't reported in as my final message promised, so where the hell was Cardiff? That night, I informed Mona, would be our last for a while; I had to get down to Panama and wind up my affairs so our collaboration could begin in earnest. "Besides," I told her, as we dined on a Bateau Mouche gliding along the Seine, "I hate being watched and followed wherever we go. Most of the time the surveillance is discreet and the watchers keep their distance, but even here"—I gestured at a couple three tables away—"we're spied on. So I want to leave Paris and join you on the yacht."

She eyed the pair I'd indicated. "Those two? And I thought we were free." She sighed, "Oh, Carlos, it's an annoyance, but nothing compared to the pleasure of going out with you, doing so many things I've never done before. I've loved every moment, but yes, it's time for a change of scene."

The waiter poured more champagne as the boat took us by the Ile de la Cité. Illuminated, cleansed of centuries of grime, Notre-Dame had the luster of old gold.

"I haven't seen the girls around lately," I remarked.

"Oh, I sent them on ahead. We don't really need them, do we?"

"Not if you don't."

"Only as companions, loyal friends." She clasped my hand. "They were substitutes for the real thing."

"I've wondered the extent of their loyalty, Mona."

"Babette is committed to me through love. Vu Tien—" she spread her hands—"says she loves me, but it may be only the pay, the gifts, the travel. . . ." She looked away, gazing at the gracefully arched buttresses of the cathedral. "I like to be made over, flattered, cared for."

"What woman doesn't?" I kissed the back of her hand, and when the boat turned for the homeward leg I paid the bill and we finished the last of the champagne.

Abdullah was drowsing behind the wheel, but Hakim was alert and jumped to open our door. We drove along the Champs-Elysées and halfway around the Arc to avenue Wagram, thence to Mona's building. The usual gendarme was absent, and I wondered why.

The Rolls was left in the courtyard while the bodyguards accompanied us in the elevator to Mona's floor. Abdullah posted himself outside the entrance door, Hakim locking the door behind us and taking a chair just inside.

We went to the sleeping quarters, Mona discarding clothing on the way so that she was naked by the time we reached our bed. "Shower together?" she asked.

"Love to." I pulled off my jacket, undid my shoulder holster, and slid the .38 under my pillow.

"Why that, Carlos?" Mona frowned.

"The gendarme's missing—piss call, maybe, but you've got enemies."

"Abdullah and Hakim are here to protect us."

"Then three guns are better than two." I kissed her lips, stripped rapidly, and joined her in the shower. After we dried each other's bodies, Mona scented mine, then hers, with a provocative, musky cologne. I turned off lights and drew her to the bed. Through silken drapes the lights of Paris entered in a diffused, misty glow. I kissed her breasts, possessed her nipples, and presently her thighs parted to take me in. We made love languorously as though we had all the time in the world. Finally she moaned out her climax and I thrust quickly to bring on mine.

She was the first to fall asleep, lips slightly parted, her glorious hair fanned out on the pillow beside me. Gauzy curtains moved in the night breeze; I kissed her lips lightly and joined her in sleep.

I was awakened by an alien sound, realized it was the door opening. Groggily I wondered who was violating our sanctuary. The girls? No, they were on the yacht. I lay still, eyelids half-parted, and stared at the door.

Very slowly it opened inward until I could see the figure of a man. I didn't think of the gun under my pillow until I saw the one in his hand.

Twenty-nine

I WAS REACHING for the .38 when the intruder raised his gun and fired. Both bullets hit Mona's body, jolting it and bringing a brief cry from her throat. I saw the gun swing until it pointed at me. I saw the muzzle flash, heard the sharp report, but by then I was off the bed and leveling the .38 at the gunman. Half-blinded by muzzle flash, I squeezed off three rounds, heard a hoarse yell, and rolled away.

Hidden by the bed, I crawled over the carpet until I could look around toward the convulsive sounds. The man was down, rolling from side to side, gasping for breath, pistol fallen free.

I got up, toed the pistol farther away, and looked down at Hakim. Through his dying agony he gasped, "You . . . disgraced me . . . and she . . . let . . . it . . . happen." A final shudder shook his body. I placed the arch of my foot over his throat, pushed down to make sure. I turned to the bed, sure she was dead. There were entrance wounds in her breast and throat. Whatever else Hakim had been, he was a marksman. I pressed Mona's wrist for pulse, found none, and felt tears well in my eyes. But this was not a time for emotion.

Where was Abdullah? Was he part of a murder conspiracy? If not, he'd think I killed them both. I had to make sure of him.

Naked, I went through the apartment to the front entrance, called "Abdullah" in a low voice, but heard nothing. Then I noticed shoes, legs on the floor beside me. Turning on the overhead light, I saw the rest of him. Face blue and swollen, tongue extruding like an obscene slug. A thin cord ligature circled his neck almost invisibly, so deeply had it bitten into the flesh.

I retraced my steps to the bedroom, and tried to keep my eyes from the bed as I dressed. I began putting on the shoulder holster, stopped, and tossed it into my open suitcase. After wiping my prints from the .38, I clasped Mona's cooling hand around it, then nudged the revolver a few inches from her fingers.

Touching her flesh made my throat swell until it was hard to breathe. I cleared my shaving gear from the bathroom, closed my suitcase, then turned to look at Mona Zakari one final time.

In death she was still as beautiful as in life, the voluptuous perfection of her figure unforgettable. I bent over and kissed her parted lips, knowing that her tongue would never again touch mine. Tears fell on her cheeks and forehead. I wiped my eyes, hoisted the suitcase, and walked through the apartment.

I could spend the rest of the night in my apartment, make plans in the morning, except that now I was pulsing with adrenalin that wouldn't let me sleep. Nor would memories of Mona. Besides, police would question every building occupant, and when that took place I had to be far away.

After closing the entrance door, I entered the waiting elevator. At street level I followed the hall to the doorway, past the concierge's dark quarters. I cracked the street door and looked around. No gendarme visible, no pedestrians on the walk. The fashionable avenue was still. Had Hakim bribed the gendarme? Killed him as he'd killed Abdullah? I would never know.

My watch showed three-fifteen; murderer's hour, I thought, as I began walking toward the Arc de Triomphe. I saw a taxi rank, got into the first cab, and told the driver to take me to Charles de Gaulle Airport. He named a price and I accepted it, not wanting to bargain and become more memorable. My own mind was a kaleidoscope of the horror I'd left behind. Had I loved her? What difference did it make now? I couldn't prevent tears flooding my eyes.

As we crossed Paris to the northeast, I thought of how much of Paris I hadn't had time to show her. From the port de la Chapelle the driver took autoroute A-1 for the thirteen miles to the airport, and for a while I tried closing my eyes only to find my mind replaying frames of my days and nights with Mona. So I stared through the window at buses, trucks, and cars, forcing my mind elsewhere. The effort wasn't entirely successful, and I found myself wondering if Hakim's dying words were true. His explanation was credible, given the Arab macho temperament, but the presence at the Ritz of Mona's two competitors opened the possibility that Hakim had been paid to eliminate Mona—and me. But no one would ever know, I told myself, and the three killings would be laid to narcotics trafficking.

Unless, of course, Babette and Vu Tien told a story—that implicated me.

At the Pan American counter I paid for a tourist-class ticket with a bundle of francs from my bag. I had almost everything Birely had given me and it would keep me going long enough to settle with my employers and see that Terry was freed.

The flight to New York left at 06:15. Plenty of empty seats, so after the big 757 reached altitude I raised seat arms and stretched out. When drinks were offered I bought a double Scotch although I'd had several in Le Bistrot, the airport's all-night bar. I craved unconsciousness to dull the raw pain of memory, but the liquor had no more effect than a sip of Evian, and I was only able to doze over the Atlantic.

I came through U.S. Customs and Immigration at an early hour, taxied to La Guardia, and took the next shuttle to Washington National.

In midmorning I registered at the four-star Madison as Robert Maguire of Syracuse, and after I was settled in my room I went down to a pay phone and dialed the Virginia contact number. I left a message on the answering recorder that Cardiff was back and wanted debriefing by the general. Then I went into the dining room and ordered breakfast, the first food I'd eaten since the night before on the Bateau Mouche.

The memory tore at me. I went back to my room, showered, shaved, and got into the last of my clean clothing. I had more at the farmhouse, but I wasn't ready to go there, not until I had answers about the Meaching-Kiley mission. For all I knew, successors had been pointed at me. Harry—Jim Eubank—might know, but would he tell me? He owed me one, but he was a weak reed.

By now, I thought, Peter Ward would have received my letter from Paris, have had time to look into Terry's status. Should I start there?

Claire would be worrying, I was sure, and the fact that I thought of her made me realize I was coming out of shock. I had to get Mona and our Paris idyll out of my mind, concentrate on immediate moves.

There was no one in Arness's operation I could trust completely. The realization chilled me. What had I come home to?

Last night I hadn't been able to think clearly. My prime thought had been to get out of Paris, away from the death scene, and Washington seemed the most secure and logical destination. Now I was less sure.

I phoned Ward's office, but his secretary said Mr. Ward was in court and wouldn't be in until afternoon. I left my true name and said I'd call later. The Piaget read 10:52, so I went down to the lobby and dialed the number again. To an unfamiliar voice I said, "Cardiff again. The general around?"

"Don't think so, but I'll check." The line hummed and I was grateful for the absence of Muzak. In a couple of minutes I heard Harry say, "Welcome back; we'd begun to think we'd lost you. Where are you?"

"Philadelphia. Where's the general?"

For a few moments the line was silent, then Harry said, "All I can tell you is he's not available."

"You're allowed to tell me only that he's not available, or don't you know his whereabouts?"

"Don't give me a hard time, Cardiff," he said weakly.

"*Me*—hard time? Harry, this is the real world. People are dead all over the place and I need to report. But only to our boss, *capisce?*"

"Enno's in his place."

"That's not comforting news," I said, "so I'll call in now and then, until the general schedules a meet. No satisfactory response your end and I'll debrief elsewhere."

"Jesus, Cardiff, don't—" I hung up and left the booth, feeling hollow and betrayed.

If the general had vanished or been disappeared, Tor Daggitt would do.

Passing the news stand, I bought the morning paper. The president's war on drugs was making progress, a lead story said, citing new cooperation from Mexico, Colombia, and Peru. High fucking time, and it had taken the *Sendero* guerrilla bombings and assassinations to make the Peruvian government face reality. Well, better late than never. I dropped the paper in the nearest trash can and entered the park at Thomas Circle.

Sitting on a bench, I decided I ought to get to the farmhouse before a reception committee was organized. Poliakoff and Company might believe I was in Philadelphia, but not for long. Whoever sent Meaching and Kiley to intercept me on the Riviera could easily dispatch men to nearby Leesburg.

But how to get there? To rent a car I needed credit cards I didn't have, and to call Claire might put her in harm's way. A taxi would attract too much attention in the countryside. So I left the park for a drugstore and called Deems & Abernathy.

Disguising my voice, I asked for Mr. Deems, gave a false name, and heard Eddie's familiar voice. "Eddie," I said, "don't mention my name."

"Okay, okay," he said in an alarmed voice, "anything you say. What's new?"

"I need your wheels for a couple of hours. Can do?"

"Sure. I—I guess so."

"Job related," I said to make him feel better, "and I'll be forever grateful. I'll wait in front of the Jefferson. How long?"

"Fifteen minutes okay?"

"Terrific." I walked it in ten. Eddie pulled into the hotel drive two minutes later. His car was a dark blue Audi, a serious yuppie car. After we shook hands I got behind the wheel. "I'll have it back here by five, keys with the doorman." He closed the door but didn't back off. I added, "If anyone should ask, you haven't seen or heard from me, okay?"

"If that's how you want it," he said uncertainly.

"You were always a good guy, Eddie, now I know you're reliable."

"Yeah, thanks, but—wait a minute, Tom. What the hell have you been up to?"

"You wouldn't believe," I said as I pulled away.

Before turning in at the farmhouse drive, I passed it twice, looking for hidden cars, surveillants, Claire. The place looked deserted, so I drove in and parked in shade behind the barn.

Two horses were grazing in the meadow, another wading and drinking in the pond. A bucolic scene, and reassuring. After disarming the alarm system, I entered the house and smelled the mustiness of disuse. That Claire hadn't been in and out recently gave me cause to think she was still in La Jolla—and out of danger. Or had the last weeks made me paranoid?

No, hell no. Danger was far from imaginary.

I changed clothing in my bedroom, packed an overnight bag with more, and went downstairs to where I'd cached a spare plastic nine-millimeter pistol among the pots and pans. I was placing it in my bag when I heard the sound of an incoming vehicle. I saw Claire's pickup raising a dusty trail toward the barn. Twombley, I thought. But the figure emerging from swirling dust wasn't the groom's, it was Claire's. Wearing jeans, boots, and a Madras shirt.

In moments she'd see Eddie's car, so I had to do something. Stepping onto the back porch, I called, "Hi!" as cheerfully as I could.

The sound of my voice stopped her. She turned, peered at me, and began running. I met her halfway and folded her into my arms. As we clung together she felt wonderfully soft, and her hair held the magical freshness of youth. I needed her, wanted her with me, was forever grateful for her love. These thoughts and emotions coursed through my brain as I pressed her to me, and Claire sobbed with happiness, tears rolling down her cheeks. I dried them as I walked her to the house, but the flow seemed endless. For a while we said nothing, just stood in the kitchen holding each other until her spasms ended. She dried her eyes, blew her nose, and looked up at me with a fey smile. "I got your letter only yesterday, so I'd resigned myself to a long wait. But suddenly you're here! When did you get in?"

"About ten minutes ago, hadn't had a chance to call. Anyway, I wasn't sure you'd be home."

"You should have called from the airport," she said reproachfully, "and let me come for you."

I shrugged. "Jet lag disorients me. I thought of that too late."

She hugged me tightly. "So, now you're back—permanently."

"Wish that were so, but this is just a pit stop. I have to leave again."

"Oh, no! Where, and how long?" she wailed.

"Let's go visit the horses." I opened the porch door. For a few moments she hesitated, then strode past me into sunlight. Taking her hand, I walked her past the barn and when we were near the pond I said, "I hoped I'd never have to, but now I have to level with you."

"The truth? What—?"

I kissed her and said, "I love you very much. That's truth number one. Truth number two is that the work I've been doing was at the president's direction. Your father was aware of it and approved. What I did was to free my brother, but somehow the deal's soured, come apart. I'm here secretly—clandestinely—and for a while I have to stay out of sight."

"How—how long?" she faltered.

"Until I'm out of danger. Until I'm satisfied there's no danger to you."

"To *me*? But—why? I—I don't understand."

"The hostiles can't be sure how much you were told by your father—"

"Nothing!"

"Or how much I've confided in you." I swallowed. This was rocky going and I could see only incredulity in her face. "In Europe a hit team was sent to kill me," I said finally. "Others may be lined up behind them. If they can't erase me, I'm pretty sure they'll try for you. So—"

Sobbing, she clung to me. "I'm not afraid. I just want to be with you, share whatever danger there is."

"Darling, sweetheart, listen to me," I pleaded. "I have to work this out alone—it's not something we can do together—understand? And I have to know that you're safe." Throat tight, I continued. "You have to go away from here, honey, some place. . . . Your uncle . . . can you stay with your uncle in Detroit?"

"Grosse Pointe," she said dully. "Yes, I can—if you force me." She stepped back, framed my face with her hands. "Tom, what's happening to you, to us? This is all so wild, I wouldn't believe it if you weren't telling me." Her eyes narrowed. "What *were* you doing for the president?"

"I won't tell you," I said, "because I have to shield you. It's the least I can do, the best I can do, darling." I glanced at my watch. "My lawyer is Peter Ward. When you're safely away, let him know where you are and I'll do the same. He'll be our letter drop."

"Peter Ward," she repeated flatly.

"I have to go now. See to your horses, go home, pack, and leave. If anything happened to you because of me, I could never forgive myself. So, please, *please* do as I say." I held her in a tight embrace, we kissed, and I got into Eddie's car, stopping only long enough to get my bag from the kitchen. Looking back, I saw her staring after me, face rigid. I could only hope she'd do as I asked.

After leaving Deems's car and keys at the Jefferson, I taxied to my hotel and left my bag in the room. Another taxi took me to Peter Ward's office, where I gave my name to the receptionist, who asked me to wait. Five minutes later Ward opened the door. "Please come in." He closed the door behind us and studied me, face gravely serious. "I've been expecting you."

I sat down in a leather-upholstered chair. "You have?"

"Your brother, Terence, has disappeared."

Thirty

I STARED AT WARD while he seated himself behind his desk. "You mean Terry escaped from Allenwood? Took a walk?"

He shook his head. "It wasn't an escape, Tom. He's lost in the prison system, on purpose, I tend to believe."

"Lost himself, or was lost by others?" Shocked, I wasn't understanding clearly.

"I think he's been put on ice, hostage to your good behavior. But let's go back to your Paris letter. I called Allenwood, representing myself as your brother's attorney. The superintendent's office said they had no record of any 'Jim McNally'—his protection name, right?"

"Right."

"So I called the Bureau of Prisons here, went over for a talk with the regional director; that was yesterday. Same answer. No record of 'McNally' in their files. I knew that was the old police runaround, but I didn't feel I could ask for Terence by his true name." He paused and gazed at me. "Or am I repeating things you already know?"

Slowly I shook my head. "No idea," I replied tightly and met his gaze. "Is what I left with you still safe?"

"Secure until you want it."

"That could be soon," I said, "considering all that's been happening."

"Then maybe you'd better give me more background, so I'm not punching in the dark."

"I am," I said with a bitter laugh, "so join me."

I told Ward the whole story, named the Washington players, the overseas targets, Kiley and Meaching, related what I knew of the presidential decision to create Arness's organization, cited Senator Newsome's approval, and mentioned my concern for Claire.

"Will she follow your advice?" Ward asked.

"I think so."

"It's good advice," he said, "and I hope she won't be endangered. Now from what you've told me, I don't see you involved in an ongoing crime or conspiracy—"

"I'm through with it, out of it."

"—and so the information is shielded by lawyer-client confidentiality." He got a yellow legal pad and pencil. "Let's have some of those names again."

After jotting them down, he said, "It's possible that hostile elements will seek a grand jury indictment and issue a warrant for your arrest. Until I'm served such a warrant, I have no obligation to produce you."

"I understand that, but I can't imagine them taking the legal route, pushing me to testify."

"Unless they hope to flush you into the open—where something can happen that silences you forever." He looked down at his notes. "Tom, I can't know where you're hiding or any alias you may be using. Does Claire know?"

I shook my head.

"Good. You've kept her as clean as possible under the circumstances. Now your third target, the Zakari woman—you weren't instructed not to eliminate her."

"The message said she was on hold."

"And you didn't kill her."

"No." I remembered the opening door, the two muzzle flashes, the bullets jolting the body beside me, the little cry. . . . "I couldn't have," I admitted emotionally, "there was a bond between us."

He nodded sympathetically. "Any idea why her name was removed from your target list?"

"The only possible explanation I've come up with—however far out—is that by keeping me from completing my side of the bargain, the president wouldn't have to pardon my brother. While in the inner circles Mona remained a target to be eliminated by someone other than myself."

"As happened."

"As happened," I repeated, "though I don't think Hakim did it for Arness. Either he did it to regain face, or at the instigation of Arabs who wanted her removed from the scene. He's dead, and at this point his motivation doesn't matter."

"Nevertheless, the French may be looking for you."

"Probably. And the flic who followed us at Notre-Dame got a look at me and my passport." I looked away from him. "The bedroom scene I left behind won't fool them for long. Mona didn't fire the revolver, so there's no powder trace on her hand." I touched mine. "I killed Hakim while he was after me."

"Perhaps," Ward suggested, "the French, for their own purposes, will accept the mise-en-scène at its face value and leave you out of it."

"Perhaps." I pulled a wad of currency from my pocket and handed it to my attorney. "Retainer. A hundred and twenty-five thousand francs, worth twenty thousand dollars."

"I'll prepare a receipt, keep it for you."

"And I need a large envelope."

He produced one from a drawer, then stood near the window while I stuffed it with the bulk of my cash. That left about six thousand dollars in my wallet. I sealed the envelope and wrote my name across it. "Keep this for me," I said.

"Having no knowledge of its contents, I'll hold it for you pending further instructions," the attorney assured me. He resumed his seat behind the desk. "And now?"

"I don't see much point in your continuing to try to locate my brother. They've made him a nonperson. My prayer is they haven't had him killed."

"Mine, too."

"So I'll work the dark side of the street, see what I can come up with."

He nodded. "Any ideas about Bill Arness?"

"Three. He's part of this conspiracy to silence me and is hiding out. He's innocent and has been sent off to some remote part of the world where I can't reach him. Or he's legitimately 'unavailable,' as Eubank said."

"But you don't believe that."

"I think he's being shielded from me. By Poliakoff."

"Who you see as your principal enemy."

"As *an* enemy. The principal, I think, is someone else."

"A reasonable operational premise," Ward agreed with a wry smile, "subject to further investigation."

"I'll claim that recorder now."

He left the office for his vault and returned with an envelope. I put it in my pocket and got up from the chair. "I'll be in touch," I said, "mainly for messages from Claire."

Ward stood and extended his hand. "I won't wish you luck, since in our former profession we learned you make your own luck. So whatever you do, I hope it will be successful."

We shook hands and I left the office feeling that Peter was more than an attorney; he'd become a needed friend.

I remembered having sent audio tapes from Deems & Abernathy for replicating at an electronics store on K Street. It wasn't far away, so I walked there and made two cassette copies of the wire recording. I replaced the recorder in Ward's envelope, and returned to his office, where I entrusted it to his secretary. With the duplicate cassette in my pocket I taxied back to the Madison, where I rented the public stenographer's typewriter and composed a letter:

> After listening to the enclosed recording I think you will
> agree the time has come to issue a Presidential Pardon to
> Terence Burke. The three assigned targets are dead,
> completing my side of the bargain.

If within two days the Pardon has not been granted and
Terence Burke produced, a copy of this tape and related
information will go the *New York Times* and the *Washington
Post.*

Cardiff

I enclosed the letter and one cassette in a stamped envelope addressed to: The Hon. Tor Daggitt, The White House, 1600 Pennsylvania Avenue, Washington 2500, D.C.

I mailed the envelope in a corner box for five o'clock pick-up. The
tape should reach Daggitt the next day, and I could imagine with
what distaste its contents would be received.

At a drugstore phone I dialed the Virginia contact number and
heard Harry's voice answer. "Cardiff again," I said. "Any signs of the
general?"

"No, that situation is the same. But Enno is anxious to see you."

"That'll be the day when I report to my sergeant," I snorted, "but
I'll agree to meet him for a chat. Let's lay it on now."

"Good idea," Poliakoff cut in from an extension. "I'll meet you in
Philadelphia or you can come here."

"Well," I said, "since my home and interests are down your way,
I'll make the trip. Metroliner does it in, what, three hours?"

"About that. The office will be closed so we have to meet elsewhere. How about your house?"

"Okay with me." My wristwatch recalled Mona. "Let's say eleven
P.M."

"I'll be there."

"Alone, Enno. Make sure you're alone." I hung up and strolled back
to the Madison. Around eight I got into a dark suit and tucked the
plastic pistol into my belt. From the hotel I took an airlines van to
Dulles airport, then taxied to my house, arriving there at nine-fifteen.

I opened my gun cabinet and got out my Weatherby rifle, still
scoped from the day I'd shot out Judge Grogan's face. That day
remained vivid because it was when everything with Arness began.
Where the hell was he, now that I needed him?

After loading the rifle I turned out house lights, had a Scotch on the rocks, and felt some of my tension fade. In the dark I reviewed all that had happened, and wondered how to handle Poliakoff. So far he'd had things his own way, but without any clear idea of his motivation, I couldn't judge his actions.

After a while I walked through the country night to the barn and unlocked it, leaving the door slightly ajar. My Porche was inside, a little dusty but otherwise the same as I'd left it. I sat on a fender, unlimbered my rifle, and sighted through the door opening. Crickets rustled in the hay, an owl hooted in the distance.

Waited.

At ten o'clock headlights flashed in from the highway, and I watched a car follow my road until it veered off into border shrubbery and disappeared. Car lights went off and I recognized Poliakoff's burly silhouette emerge by the roadside fifty feet away from me. For a few moments he stood in the moonlight staring at the dark house. Then he turned, said something I couldn't hear, and two men came out of the shrubbery. All three wore dark clothing. Through the night's stillness I could hear Poliakoff say, "Burke's drug-dirty, switched sides, but he's no fool, so he could come early to the meet." He looked toward the pike. "If a taxi brings him, wait till it goes away. If he drives himself, let him get out of the car." He faced the house, back to me. "Ted, find a spot on the front porch. Sid, take the roadside over there where he's likely to stop, keep back in the bushes. Got it?"

Murmurs of assent before one spoke up. "Sure this caper is authorized?"

"Questioning my authority?" Poliakoff snarled.

"Well, no, but I want to make sure everything's kosher."

"Like Temple Emmanuel," Poliakoff retorted. "I'll wait by the front steps there."

My cross hairs steadied on the ground at their feet. Before they could disperse I fired, keeping the barrel inside the barn to hide muzzle flash. I thought the shot would freeze them, but the man called Ted spun around and fired wildly at the barn, so I shot him through the thigh. He grabbed his leg, his pistol dropped, and he hit the ground.

Over his screams I called, "Party's over, boys. Jackets off, toss the iron away."

Slowly Poliakoff pulled off his coat and dropped it, revealing a holstered handgun. Sid did it faster and tossed his weapon toward the barn. Poliakoff drew out his gun and dropped it nearby. "Sid," I called, "you better drive your partner to a hospital. That cool with you, Enno?"

He shrugged. "You're calling the shots, Major."

"Like old times," I said, "and that's how it'll stay. Sid, get the car and move off, then disappear. As Enno will tell you, services no longer needed. Right, Enno?"

"Right."

"And, Sid," I continued, "you were lied to—Enno can't authorize anything. Keep your mouth shut and cover your ass. Get moving."

Sid scuttled away, and presently the car backed out of its hiding place. As it turned around, its headlights played across Enno standing, and Ted writhing on the ground. Sid hoisted Ted into the backseat, slammed the door, and drove out toward the highway. "Enno," I called, "walk toward the barn." When he didn't move I fired a bullet between his feet. He moved then, slowly, surlily, until I told him to halt ten feet away. Hoarsely he said, "Gonna kill me?"

"Why not? You sent the comedy team after me."

He shrugged. Tacit admission.

"They tried, give them that." I wanted to kill him, but I wanted more from him. "Where's the general?"

"I don't know."

"Bullshit." I fired again between his feet. "Next one's the kneecap, pal. Where's Arness?"

"Fort Holabird. Locked up pending court-martial."

"For what?"

"Misuse of funds."

"A phony charge if I ever heard one. So with the general out of the way, you're in charge, that it?"

"Something like that."

"Don't be evasive, Enno," I warned. "This is the time for truth and your life's hanging by a thread." I slid more cartridges into the magazine, knowing the metallic clicks resonated in the still night air.

He stiffened. "I was only carrying out orders."

"And you liked it. Congenial work. Whose orders?"

"White House," he said, a little too quickly.

"Don't tell me the president has time to deal with li'l ol' Enno Poliakoff. So who was it?"

"Daggitt." The name squeezed from his throat like a chunk of ice. "Why?"

"He never liked the project, felt the risk of exposure was too high. He wanted to protect the president. For that you had to be silenced."

"Sounds plausible," I said, "but I have another theory. You were bought off, Enno. Paid to screw up the project by drug lords who wanted protection. When they saw Puma and Gargoyle go down, they pressured you to have me terminated. How's that for an operational theory?"

"Stinks."

"Prove otherwise."

"Daggitt'll never talk."

"Everyone talks," I said heavily. "But to protect himself Daggitt will swear he never gave you orders, doesn't even know you. Meaching and Kiley won't be around to testify, but Ted and Sidney will. They'll vomit it out, Enno, to save their own skins."

Fiercely he snarled, "If I go down, Burke, you go with me."

"Where's any evidence I violated U.S. law? If Arness tried pinning anything on me, he implicates himself, so you're all alone, Enno. You take the fall by yourself."

I shoved the door open and walked toward him, rifle crooked in my arm. "Lie down," I ordered. "You're beaten but dangerous. Belly down, Enno."

He dropped to his knees, eased forward on his hands, lay flat. "Where's my brother?"

"Don't know. Anything happens to me Daggitt'll have him killed."

"I doubt that," I said, "because Daggitt will have to deal with me."

For a time neither of us said anything. I could hear his heavy breathing. Finally he said, "They have the senator's daughter."

"You're lying," I snarled, feeling a chill grip my spine.

He looked up at me, a sneer on his colorless face. "She was picked up driving to the airport. She's been watched while we waited for you to surface. You stir up trouble and she's dead as her dad."

I wanted to jam the rifle muzzle in his ear and blast his skull apart. He said, "Go ahead, try calling her. Like I say, she's gone."

It must be true, I thought, because a lie was too easy to disprove with one phone call. I felt bile rise in my throat. The opposition now had two hostages to my good conduct. I was responsible for their lives.

"All right," I said, "your pals may have Miss Newsome, but I have you, and we're going to get some law on the scene. Sooner you're behind bars, the faster you get used to it. A long term, Enno, and you won't like it at all. Get up slowly. We're going into the house, where I call the FBI."

"You're crazy—they'll never believe you."

"Maybe not, but it's a good story. On your feet." I stepped back in case he tried a desperate lunge at me. But he'd spotted Sid's gun in the grass. From his knees Poliakoff went for it, came up with it, and fired.

The bullet hit my rifle stock, nearly tearing it from my hand. He fired again, but Poliakoff was never a good close-in fighter and he'd hesitated, letting me dodge aside. I had no time to aim, so I threw the rifle at him, striking him across the face. He yelped and fired wildly, and the bullet whistled above me as I tackled him. He went backward under me, and we fought for the pistol in his hand. He was taller, but I was stronger, and gradually I bent his wrist downward, my toes digging in the soil for purchase. Below the colorless hair I saw the whites of his eyes as he strained, gasping, to control the gun. Suddenly its explosion deafened me. Muzzle flash reddened his face for an instant and then his body went limp. For a few moments I could see nothing; when vision cleared I saw blood spreading across his chest. His mouth was open in the slackness of death. Like Meaching and Kiley, he was gone.

I staggered to my feet and went into the house, found my bottle in the dark kitchen, and downed a long slug. It warmed my body, cold but for the sweat on my face and forehead. I looked at the telephone. Useless to call the FBI. I had nothing to deliver.

The court might call it justifiable manslaughter, but that was a big if. So I had a disposal problem. My ears were still ringing from the shot, my pulse racing from the struggle.

I thought of burying his body far down in the meadow, but sooner or later it could be found. How about the Newsome acreage? No, the groom slept by the stables, the houseman inside the house; they'd hear me drive up.

The wall clock's numerals glowed in the dark. Ten-forty. I had to reach a decision in case Sid and Ted sent the law or other colleagues here. If they were smart, they wouldn't, but I figured they had only body-temperature intelligence to have been convinced by Poliakoff's lies. Whatever the case, I couldn't risk being found with Enno's body. Days of interrogation would follow, and I had Claire and Terry to free.

Into my mind drifted a scene I'd once enjoyed. I'd found the remote sand-and-shale beach along the Potomac near White's Ferry when I'd been looking for a place to fish for bass and carp.

I left the kitchen and went outside, returning with my rifle and its bullet-holed stock. After setting it in the gun cabinet, I secured the house and armed the system. Then I went to the barn and guided my Porsche to Poliakoff's body. It was heavy, but I managed to heave it onto the passenger seat after a few tries, and carefully stuck his pistol in his pocket. The butt end encountered something and I brought out a small, cheap address book. I stuffed it in my pocket and buttoned Poliakoff's jacket over his bloody shirtfront.

From behind the wheel I slanted his torso over against the closed door to make it appear that my passenger was sleeping, head on the doorsill. I didn't turn on the headlights until I was driving west on the highway, heading for Enno's place of interim repose.

Thirty-one

AT LEAST, I thought, as I drove through the night, I was away from the old homestead even if I had a corpse riding beside me.

Traffic was sparse, no cops on the road, but I stayed well under the speed limit, turning off just east of White's Ferry.

Nearing the fishing spot jogged my memory, and I steered the Porsche as far from the road as scrub growth allowed. I dragged the body from my car and carried it into the heavy foliage, getting hands and wrists scratched as I lumbered along. In a small clearing I lowered the stiffening body and placed the revolver in his hand. The paraffin test would confirm that he'd fired it, and I hoped the coroner's verdict would be suicide of an unhappy individual, a depressed Vietnam veteran, Nam being the catchword that ensured plausibility.

For a few moments I surveyed the scene, decided footprints in the sandy soil would be charged to Poliakoff, glanced a final time at my old enemy, and got back into my car.

I'd disposed of the corpse, but I was tired from exertion, nerves frayed from the stress I'd just lived through. Before I could confront tomorrow's problems I had to rest. So I drove back to the farmhouse, and from the pike I peered along my road for signs of life. Nothing. The place was as dark as I'd left it.

I drove on a ways, then turned back, reasoning that if Sid had squawked about the fracas, the law would be all over the place: lights, K-9s, and general confusion. Still, sleeping in the farmhouse was a needless risk, so I drove warily into the barn and barred the door. I folded one of Claire's horse blankets into a pillow, covered a pile of straw with another, and lay down. The summer night was warm, and as I lay there and tried to relax I thought of Claire, terrified and intimidated, and regretted implicating her. But it was that or lose her trust and love. Her father, I mused bitterly, would not have considered it my finest moment.

Eventually, sleep came.

The sound of a vehicle awakened me. The sun was up and I rose stiffly to peer through cracks in the barred door. I gripped my plastic pistol, until I saw Claire's pickup, young Twombley at the wheel. I dusted off my clothing and unlocked the barn door as he braked nearby. "Morning," I hailed him.

"Oh, Mr. Burke." The young fellow was startled. "You've been away. Miss Claire left yesterday, which is why I came."

"Glad you did. Any word from Miss Claire?"

"Not yet, but she was supposed to call last night." He shrugged. "Probably too tired."

"I'd say. Look, my Porsche isn't working. How's to give me a ride to the city?"

"Sure—just let me look after the horses, okay?"

I disarmed the alarm system, showered, shaved, changed, and joined Twombley in the pickup. On the way into the District I didn't need to talk much, since Twombley had opinions on the money made by vets and farriers, reasons for the poor corn crop, the unreliability of well pumps, and the chances of Leesburg High's fall football team winning the state championship. I listened, guided him to Scott Circle, and gave him ten dollars for his trouble. It was a short walk to the Madison, where I had a large breakfast before going up to my room. Nine-thirty, my Piaget told me. Twelve hours ago I'd been waiting for Poliakoff to arrive. Well, I thought, he'd come, and gone, moving Daggitt to the top of my list.

I wasn't familiar with White House mail distribution, but I figured Daggitt wouldn't receive my letter for another two or three hours, after the Executive Protection Service had checked the envelope for a letter bomb.

I perused the paper for possible news of Poliakoff, but it was early. I needed more time to work things out—if they were workable—and my biggest risks lay just ahead.

To rent a vehicle I'd have to produce driver's license and credit cards I didn't have, and I hadn't hot-wired a car since college days. What I did have was cash, and with several thousand dollars in my pocket I went looking.

I rode a bus up Thirteenth Street as far as Meridian Hill Park where I got off and walked. Not a great section to visit after dark, but in sunlight it looked harmless, even hospitable. Black children played stickball in the street, and a spirited game of basketball was going on behind a playground fence. Wheelless cars rested on blocks in front yards or narrow driveways. I walked four blocks before spotting the black-and-yellow cab parked against the curb. Its owner, a gray-haired black with nicotine-stained teeth, was behind the wheel, head back, jaws open, eyes closed. From the curb I reached through the open window and touched his shoulder.

"Wha—wha—?" He came groggily awake, peered up at me with narrowed eyelids, licked his lips. A smell of sweet wine hung around him like cheap perfume. "Working today?" I asked.

"Some." He picked up his chauffeur's cap and fitted it on at a rakish angle. "Where you wanna go?"

"What's your name, sir?"

"Amos—Amos Jeffers. Why you wanna know?"

"Because I'm going to offer you a holiday, Amos, all expenses paid. Like the idea?"

"Love it," he said. "Wha's the catch?"

"You know the saying 'money talks and bullshit walks'?"

"Sho' do." He was sitting straighter now, receptive.

"Well, the situation is this—I've got money, but I'm walking."

"How much money?"

"A thousand here and now for the use of this elegant car until tomorrow. How's that strike you?"

"A *thousand?*" He peered at me suspiciously. "Mickey Mouse dough?"

"Hardly." I peeled off three hundred-dollar bills to whet his appetite, let him eye them, fondle them in his hand. "You gonna pull a bank job?" he asked. "No, I don' wanna know."

"I've got half the money in town, Amos, so banks aren't involved. It has to do with my line of work. I'm a P.I. on a divorce case, at least the husband who hired me thinks it'll turn into that. My own heap's been spotted by the wife, so I need something different to tail in." I dropped a fourth bill into his hand. "Are we talking?"

"You sho' ain't walking'." He grinned, opened the door and got out.

I lifted the cap from his head and put it on mine. "License, too, Amos. For our protection."

He fished into his billfold and dug out a worn, dog-eared D.C. license whose expiration date was three years ago. The license was so old it carried no driver photograph—an obvious plus.

"Lissen," he said, rolling his tongue over his teeth, "any damage, you pay, okay?"

"Okay."

"Leave the heap anywheres around here, I'll find it. Hell, man, she ain't wuth no thousand as she stands."

"Will it start?"

"Jus' turn the key."

I got behind the wheel and started the engine. The car shook until more cylinders fired, then vibration eased.

"Hey"—he stuck his hand in the window—"the rest what you owe me."

I counted out six more bills—money that had traveled from Marseilles—and laid them across his palm. His grin was moon-wide as he stuffed them into a trouser pocket. "Name's Amos Jeffers," he said happily, "so's you don' forget it."

"How could I?" I asked, "when you're the only friend I've found all day?" I slid the clutch into gear and bucked off from the curb. In the rearview mirror I saw him wave good-bye. I'd left him enough to throw a block party, so I hoped he wouldn't spend it all on Gallo, or get mugged.

Where seat fabric wasn't worn to the threads, it didn't exist. A much-fondled rabbit's foot dangled from the mirror by a string. The interior of the taxi smelled of sweat, dust, oil, gasoline, and old beer. As Amos acknowledged, the heap wasn't worth much, but I was grateful to have it.

I turned south and drove down New Hampshire Avenue to Dupont Circle, then cut back on Massachusetts to Scott Circle where I left cab and cap in an all-night parking garage. Now I could go wherever the hell I wanted. Pleased, I selected a pay phone at random to place my White House call.

The switchboard operator transferred me to Daggitt's office. I said I was Enno and Mr. Daggitt was expecting my call.

"Sorry, sir, but Mr. Daggitt is with the president. I expect he'll be available in an hour or so."

"Fine. Please tell him I called and will call back. Thank you, ma'am."

I hadn't expected to reach Daggitt first try, but Enno's name would rattle him.

Until that moment I'd forgotten the address book, so I went to a sidewalk bench and opened it. "G. Arn." was the first entry, with home and office phone in Poliakoff's cramped hand. Jim Eubank's name was there—as "Harry"—with his home telephone number. Daggitt's name wasn't written out, but I finally extracted it from the T page as "T.D." Following the initials were a private White House extension, then "T.D.'s" home telephone, which could be useful.

On impulse I went back to the pay phone and dialed the office contact number. When Eubank answered I said, "Harry, I'm tired of games. Where the hell's Enno?"

"Enno? You mean you didn't see him?"

"Hell, I waited two hours, gave up, and got drunk. I repeat: Where the hell is he?"

"Cardiff, listen, he hasn't been in today. I called his apartment earlier but no answer. Maybe he's . . ." His voice trailed off.

"Met with an accident? That's possible, all these crazy drivers. Better check hospitals, county police, okay?"

"Yeah, sure, I'll get on it. And listen, thanks for calling."

"Any time. General still not around?"

"Afraid not."

"I'll call later, Harry. If Enno shows, have him stand by. I've wasted enough time on this."

"Right—I'd be mad, too." His voice lowered. "You nailed Centaur, didn't you?"

"What makes you think that?"

"A flash from EPIC."

"In the papers yet?"

"Will be."

"I'll discuss details with the general," I said, "and you can tell him so." I hung up.

Major General William Arness, USA (Ret.) confined at Fort Holabird to block the White House channel.

So Daggitt thought.

In my hotel room I watched an early TV soap, got bored, and switched to CNN. I wasn't going to call Daggitt for a while. Let him sweat. And having seen his TV performances I knew he wasn't a man who divulged information easily. He was ten times smarter than the late Enno Poliakoff, probably smarter than the president he served. And enormously dangerous to me.

I turned off the television and stretched out on the bed. My thoughts drifted back to Mona and I wondered under what circumstances her body had been found. Well, I'd never know; all that mattered was whether I was wanted for her murder. I doubted I'd be the first to know.

After a while I dozed off, and when I woke it was dusk. Headlights of homeward-bound traffic reflected off the ceiling, and pedestrians crowded the walks. I could see the Capitol's lighted dome, golden in the late sunset, and thought of the country I'd fought for, the bizarre crew running it. Could they ever be removed?

I thought of Poliakoff's body, a bloated thing now, in the concealing shrubbery. A bad soldier makes a bad civilian, the saying went, and Enno had been one of the worst. No way I could summon pity or regret.

I didn't let myself think about Claire.

Instead, I stuck the plastic pistol in my belt, and went down to the dining room for a prime rib dinner. It could be my last, so I indulged myself, ordered wine, and found everything served with style.

When I left the hotel, the street lights were on. I walked to the drugstore and dialed Daggitt's private number. Two rings and he answered; the White House never sleeps. "Enno?"

"Enno won't be calling. Been reading your mail?"

"You bastard!" he snarled. "You'll never get away with blackmailing the president!"

"Who's talking blackmail? I completed my half of the bargain. It's pardon time."

"Listen to me," he said in a hard voice, "you can forget the pardon. You turn that recording over to me or no one will ever see your brother again."

"And Claire Newsome?"

"She'll be released when I get that recording, not before."

"So many threats, reveal a position of weakness," I pointed out calmly. "You know it, Daggitt, and so do I. You'd be better advised to draw up those pardon papers and get them signed. Meanwhile, free Miss Newsome."

"You'll go down, too."

"I'm ready for that because taking you with me will be a downright pleasure—and the president won't dare to intervene."

Silence, except for line hum. Finally he grated, "I've underestimated you all along. Now you've become a threat to the presidency itself. I'll have you hunted down like the criminal killer you are."

"But not before I've told my tale, Daggitt, so factor that in. You've become an embarrassment to the presidency and you'll be cut loose without a handshake or a smile, like others before you." I paused to let him think about it. "Then you'll do time, hard time, the kind my brother was doing. Can you imagine hearing me tell how I killed for the White House, under a grant of immunity? One phone call hands you over, Daggitt, and here's something you haven't considered: How did I get your private number?"

Silence lengthened. Finally he said, "Where's Enno?"

"I can kidnap as well as you can, so consider all the stories he can tell."

A nervous cough cleared his throat. "I think we ought to talk things over face to face, set aside emotion, and get to the crux of the situation. How soon can we meet?"

"How long to get the pardon signed? One hour? Two?"

"Two at least."

"Good. You bring the pardon and I'll bring the recording. It'll take me a while to reach your area. I can be there by eleven."

"Come directly to the White House, I'll—"

"Still playing me for a fool. We'll meet where sharpshooters can't pick me off. What car do you drive?"

"Lincoln sedan. Silver." Meaching's Lincoln had been dark brown, I remembered. These people liked Lincolns.

"You'll drive it," I told him, "with Miss Newsome. She'll tell you how to reach my farmhouse. When I see her *and* the pardon, you get the tape."

"I agree," he said—a little too quickly.

"Just you, me, and Miss Newsome. Any outriders and you'll be tomorrow's headlines. Understood?"

"Understood," he said, defeat in his voice. "And after the exchange?"

"First we settle the present. Oh, did I forget to mention General Arness? He goes free, too. Clean plate, Daggitt, no leftovers. Phone Holabird now."

"Sure you don't want Bill to join the party?" he sneered.

"He's got his own problems. Eleven o'clock."

Hanging up, I wiped moisture from my face, tense from the exchange. If Daggitt recorded the conversation, I didn't care; he'd never want anyone listening to the tape.

I walked to the all-night garage, paid the parking fee, and drove across Key Bridge to Virginia. The homeward rush was over and traffic agreeably light. I had to figure all the angles, find an edge against one of the more intelligent men in America. He'd been a corporation lawyer, one of the best, but he'd never done military service, seen combat as I had. Admittedly a slender advantage, but I hoped our meeting wouldn't turn into a combat situation, because of Claire.

On his side Daggitt could invoke the protective resources of the federal government: the FBI, Secret Service, D.C. SWAT teams, the air force, army, and marines. The advantage to him was overwhelming—except for one thing. Daggitt valued his life more than I valued mine, and I didn't think he'd want to risk it over a pardon and the freedom of one young woman.

As I drove toward my farm I thought of the night when a not dissimilar meeting had been arranged. I'd expected Poliakoff to bring gunmen, and he had. Whether Daggitt tried the same ploy remained to be seen. But as before I had the advantage of familiar turf, and darkness enhanced my odds.

Half a mile from my drive I switched off the old cab's one operational headlight, braked suddenly for a deer bounding across the road, took a deep breath, and drove on. Turning into my drive, I steered Amos Jeffer's creaking cab down behind the barn where I'd left Eddie's car the day before. Seemed like a week ago, a month even.

I entered the house and got the Weatherby from my gun cabinet, picked up a box of .300-caliber, 180-grain ammunition, and pocketed it beside the second cassette I'd copied from the wire original. That one was my life preserver; my life and Claire's. Nine o'clock. Two hours to go. I made coffee and drank it black, selected a Winchester .30-06 from the cabinet, loaded it, and carried it up to the bedroom whose windows overlooked drive and barn. I opened both windows and stood the Winchester, a fallback, between them. After a second coffee I carried the Weatherby to the taxi and laid it across the front seat, rolled down the windows, and returned to the dark kitchen. Daggitt wouldn't need Claire's directions to dispatch killers to my house. I took a utility flashlight from the broom closet and tested the light. Batteries okay, they'd hardly ever been used.

I didn't think Daggitt would have much trouble getting the president to sign Terry's pardon; presidents usually signed whatever a close adviser recommended, and Daggitt could attribute the urgency to national security. Even if the president was at Camp David, a White House chopper could speed Daggitt there and back in ample time.

Anyway, that was Daggitt's concern. At stake were his career and the presidency itself. Tonight his single-minded goal was to protect both. I didn't trust his intentions, but I hoped his intelligence would restrain him from some impulsive, irreversible move. Still, his pride was wounded and he feared me, making him a more formidable adversary than ever before.

Nine-thirty.

I went up to the bedroom and sighted my Winchester through the window, sweeping a hundred and eighty degrees. Good coverage, but over only half of my land. Were I planning to assault an isolated farmhouse, I'd airlift a team and deploy them half a mile away, have them approach low and from the rear, advance scouts to the far side as spotters equipped with walkie-talkies.

But this had been laid on as a peaceful meeting. I leaned the rifle against the wall and went back to the kitchen thinking about Claire. Inescapably I loved her, wanted her as a wife. If I wasn't infatuated, as I'd been with Mona, my love was going to prove durable; I'd make it so. After the exchange, after regaining her, we'd have to go away. Mexico could be our temporary haven, a place to buy new identities, then move down through Central America until we found a country where we could live securely. After a year or so I'd have Peter Ward assess the situation and we'd decide whether to return. Becoming an expatriate had never appealed, but it beat being dead. I remembered Daggitt's threat to hunt me down.

I shined the flashlight on my watch—nearly ten o'clock. I didn't expect Daggitt for another hour, but scouts would come earlier. Taking the flashlight to my road, I left it centered there, then drove Amos Jeffers's taxi to the highway. I turned toward Washington, drove a quarter mile and made a *U*-turn onto the far shoulder, switched off lights. From there I could make out my dark farmhouse. The rearview mirror would alert me to approaching vehicles.

A cattle truck passed, then a red late-model Jaguar, then a period of darkness during which only an opossum sauntered across the road. A metallic green Corvette streaked by, reminding me of the green lamé dress Mona had worn when I'd first seen her dance. Who had that video cassette? Out of respect for the dead, it should be destroyed, lest it become a porno flick for some office crowd.

Close to eleven, a pair of wide-set headlights brightened my rearview mirror. I scrunched down in the seat and saw a long silver Lincoln sedan flash past. I started my engine and ground off the shoulder onto the highway.

I'd glimpsed Daggitt's face, thin lips clamped in concentration, Claire beside him.

Accelerating, I was only fifty yards behind the Lincoln when Daggitt turned into my drive. I made the turn on two wheels and in a moment swung hard left as I braked. My taxi came to rest across the road behind the Lincoln, blocking exit.

Pocketing the keys, I leveled my rifle across the doorsill and called, "Daggitt—get out and walk as far as the flashlight. Claire, stay where you are." The driver's door swung open and I saw Daggitt get out, holding a large brown envelope. He trod five paces to the flashlight and halted. Carrying the rifle, I went over to Claire's door. "Whatever happens," I told her, "don't leave the car." The pallor of Claire's face knotted my stomach. I walked beyond the Lincoln and pointed the rifle at Daggitt.

"That's not necessary, Burke," he said tightly, and I was glad he was as tense as I. "Here's the pardon. There's Miss Newsome. Now I'll take the tape recording."

"Where's my brother?"

"Petersburg prison."

"He'd better be in good condition," I said, "or you'll suffer."

Daggitt nodded. In his labyrinthine world, reprisal was just part of doing business. "You'll find him in good shape."

"And General Arness?"

"I ordered his release. By now he should be home." He glanced away from the headlights, squinting into darkness.

"A final question," I said. "Before I left Europe, I was told to forget target number three. . . ."

"But you killed her anyway," he interjected.

"A bodyguard did that. So tell me, why was her life to be spared?"

He looked down at the ground. "In the Arab world she was well regarded, considered a fair-minded mediator. We were planning to use her to gain the release of western hostages in Syria, Iran, and Lebanon. She'd agreed to try."

Yes, I thought, that would be like her. "So why was she target-listed?"

"An interagency foul-up. CIA and DEA listed the woman without telling State. When the secretary learned of it he came to me, blew his stack. I canceled the kill." He spread his hands. "We're trying to find a replacement, but her access was unique."

I nodded agreement and pulled the tape cassette from my pocket. "Here it is."

"The original?"

"Yes," I lied.

"How can I be sure of that?"

"You can't. I might have cached a spare somewhere to be produced in the event of any sort of accident—so lay off."

He shrugged. "There will be no follow-up. Now, one last item: I want Enno Poliakoff."

"Understandably. But his betrayals are over. He's dead, by his own hand."

His eyes widened in surprise. "Where's his body?"

"In another day or so it'll be found."

"You killed him, Burke," he said angrily.

"I wanted him alive, able to testify if needed. My loss."

"But suicide? Why—?"

"Couldn't stand the thought of a future without you."

Daggitt glared at me. "The tape."

"Open the envelope."

Wordlessly he drew out a sheet of White House stationery, slanted it toward the headlights. I saw the bold-print word *Pardon*, and in the text my brother's name. The document bore the president's signature. Taking it, I said, "It better not be revoked," and gave him the cassette.

"So it's a wash. You're quite an operator, Burke, but I can't wish you well." He began walking toward the Lincoln.

"Didn't expect it," I said. "Claire, get out now."

White-faced, she left the car as Daggitt opened the driver's door.

Before she reached me I said, "He may have a gun, go to the house."

"Oh, Tom," she said tremulously, and began walking away. Daggitt called, "Burke, move that car!"

As I stepped toward it, I heard the flutter of helicopter rotors. Through the trees its spotlights blazed as the chopper roared toward me. For a moment I was frozen, then the area was brilliantly lighted and bullets pocked the ground near my feet. I could see two men firing from the gunship's door. A ladder hung below them, and Daggitt was running toward it as the chopper steadied above.

I ran to the Lincoln, lifted my rifle. Daggitt grabbed the ladder. The chopper lifted and banked around, muzzle flashes spitting from the doorway. The firing platform was too unsteady for accurate shooting, and bullets smashed into the Lincoln as the chopper maneuvered.

I shot at the flashes, saw a man fall backward. The chopper turned, trailing the ladder and Daggitt, who was climbing upward a rung at a time. I began firing at the rotor shaft and gearbox, saw sparks where my bullets hit. The chopper turned, and while I was reloading, the other gunman resumed firing at me. I could move faster than the hovering gunship, so I was behind the Lincoln when bullets hit where I had been. Crouched, I could see Claire cowering on the front porch. The lone gunman stopped firing to change a magazine, and I fired at the gearbox again.

Daggitt had nearly reached the doorway when I saw smoke coming from the gearbox. The chopper jerked upward, rotated, and gained altitude as it banked away. I glimpsed Daggitt gesturing in my direction, then he was hidden by trees. The rotors made harsh straining sounds as the chopper fought to gain altitude. I got up and jogged to the porch, took Claire in my arms.

She was shivering, face streaked with tears. I kissed her, then turned to watch the chopper's distant lights. Suddenly there was no more rotor sound. I knew what that meant and put my arms tightly around her shoulders.

An orange-red fireball rose above the treeline and one boom of detonation echoed across the meadow.

"Oh, God," she gasped, "we've got to help them!"

"There's nothing to help." I stroked her hair. "I know from Nam. Believe me."

"Oh, Tom. Tom, Tom, Tom . . ." Her voice rose, nearing hysteria until I shook her.

"Stop it! We have ourselves to think about."

Roughly, I drew her into the house, turned on lights and found the Scotch. "Drink," I ordered. "Don't think about it. Drink!"

Her hand trembled as she lifted the bottle. Presently she set it down. "They tried to kill you," she said dully.

"I thought there'd be an attempt, but I didn't figure on a chopper." I kissed her forehead. "Are you all right?"

"I wasn't mistreated, just kept in a room."

"I'm sorry," I said. "You can't know how sorry I am."

Her body slumped in my arms and I lowered her into a chair. "Can you drive?"

"I—I think so. Why?"

"Have to get Daggitt's car to Washington." I took her hands. The trembling had stopped. "I'll be all right now," she said quietly. "Where do you want me to drive?"

"Meridian Hill."

Thirty-two

CLAIRE FOLLOWED ME at a steady fifty miles per hour until we crossed Chain Bridge into the District. Followed at thirty up Thirteenth Street until I pulled over at Florida Avenue and got out. "Far enough," I said as I opened her door. "Leave the keys and come with me."

When she was beside me in the taxi, I made a *U*-turn and drove south. "Why did we leave Daggitt's car there?" she asked.

"Because it's a likely place for theft or stripping. And very far from Leesburg."

"Are we going there now?"

"I have a room downtown."

I turned into the hotel garage, got my key from the desk clerk, and led her to my room.

After locking the door, I said, "Ain't much, but it's shelter for the night."

"Wonderful! I don't think I can stand any more excitement."

I kissed her tenderly. "I made a devil's bargain, but it's finished now. We're both free."

"And your brother?"

"Tomorrow. Hell, it's nearly three o'clock."

"And I'm exhausted."

For a while she lay rigidly beside me in the aftershock of violence and death. I reached the first stage of sleep before I felt her body, warm and smooth, move against mine. We kissed then, held each other, and soon were making love. For me it was an affirmation of life, of a future to be lived. A repudiation of Death that had brushed us and been denied. I loved her more than I'd ever loved anyone.

After room-service eggs and bacon I phoned Peter Ward and asked him to bring my bulky envelope to my room. He arrived half an hour later and I introduced him to Claire, took all my cash, and gave him Terry's pardon. Ward studied it and nodded. "Outside usual channels," he said, "but I'll arrange your brother's release today. Where will you be?"

"Not sure. I think we ought to stay away for a while."

"That may be wise," he said soberly. "Morning news reported Tor Daggitt's death in a chopper crash. Two Secret Service men, pilot and copilot. No survivors."

Claire turned away, went to the window, and looked down.

"I guess the president will have to get himself a new counselor," I said.

"The line's already forming," he said. *"Plus ça change . . ."*

After he left us we packed, and I went to the parking garage and slid Amos Jeffers's license and twenty dollars under a windshield wiper, with a note asking that the taxi be returned to him. We took a taxi to Leesburg airport and flew to Hot Springs in my plane. We spent two days at the Homestead, then flew down to Sea Island, Georgia, where we stayed at the Cloister, a large and famous ocean-side resort, and were married by a Glynn County justice of the peace.

After Terry was released, the White House press secretary declined to answer questions concerning the presidential pardon, saying the president was observing official mourning over the tragic death of his friend and adviser, Tor Daggitt. In any case, the press secretary added, executive pardons were granted at presidential discretion and were not subject to question.

I didn't want to answer questions either, so I refrained from phoning Terry, though I sent him thirty thousand via Peter Ward.

After two weeks Ward told us he thought it was safe to return. A new presidential counselor had been named, and his staff was gearing up for the coming reelection campaign.

So we returned to Leesburg, where I put my farm on the market, and moved into Claire's larger home.

For a while I kept a rifle beside our bed in case of uninvited night visitors, but none ever came, and after the president was defeated in November, we began to live a normal life. Terry visited us before leaving for a Wildlife Federation job in Juneau, and told me I was a very lucky man. I knew I was, and, for more reasons than he could imagine. Terry's parting words were: "You kept your word, Tom. Don't know how you did it, but you set me free. How can I ever repay you?"

I thought about the recent past, and managed a crooked smile. "Stay out of jail," I told my kid brother, and gave him a good-bye hug.

General Arness and his wife left Washington for a retirement village near San Antonio, and I never saw him again.

Two weeks after his death Enno Poliakoff's body was discovered and identified through personal documents and dental work.

Tor Daggitt's Lincoln was never found.

Epilog

ALL THAT WAS last year.

In the spring our daughter, named Claudia after her late grandfather, was born, a sweet, pink-faced child, gurgling and adorable. After work I take over feeding and diapering while Claire prepares dinner.

We don't go out much, socialize mainly with her circle of equestrian friends, finding in our small family all we need.

But sometimes at night I leave the bed and stand by the window, looking out over the dark and silent fields. Then I remember how it was that night when we stood atop the Eiffel Tower and watched the lights of Paris below. In those vulnerable moments I can almost feel the touch of the strange, exotic woman still haunting my life, who so easily gave me her love and trust. I try to banish memories, to put her ghost to rest.

But I doubt I ever will.